I0728197

# A BOND OF TRUST

## SHIFTER CITY FATED MATES
### BOOK 4

## JAYMIN EVE

# CONTENT WARNING

Your mental health is important to me! If you need any specific information about what might be included, please contact me at jaymineve@gmail.com

Triggers include:

- Death of a parent
- Evidence of torture
- Dead bodies as a result of torture
- Abuse by a parent
- Discussion of suicide
- Past trauma/flashbacks
- Panic attacks
- Scenes of sexual nature with dominant alpha males.
- Pierced body parts
- Violence
- Stalking
- Kidnapping
- Graphic death
- Blood and Gore
- Therapy and healing in unconventional ways
- Torture
- Betrayal by friends

# STAY UP TO DATE

You can keep up to date with my releases by following me on Instagram, joining my Facebook group The Nerd Herd, or subscribing to my newsletter.

This is where you'll get all updates and information about my worlds and publishing schedule.

# CATCH UP ON THE WORLD

## A CURSE OF FATE

Emmeline is a wolf shifter in a world where all packs live in cities, with multiple alphas, betas, deltas, and rarer: omegas. These designations form quintets, packs of five, and are governed by alpha councils. Emme is an omega, just like her mom, who was killed by a pack of alphas when Emme was fourteen. This was the catalyst for her to run from the cities and the alphas who controlled them. She swore she would never end up like her mom.

Fast forward over a decade and Emme has been moving between human cities, avoiding the five major pack cities at all costs, and keeping her head down. An unfortunate series of events finds her in the path of an alpha with tracking capabilities. She runs again, but he tracks her and drags her to Golden Claw, the largest of the five pack cities.

Here, she faces the Alpha Council, charged with being a rogue—a shifter without a pack city affiliation. But when they discover she's an omega, they are less inclined to give her the usual sentence of death.

When one of the most powerful alphas scents Emme as his true mate, it's Emme's worst nightmare, as she believes that if she bonds with an alpha she'll be killed the same way her mom was. Her mom's pack was a scent match too, and they still murdered her.

When she finds out that this alpha is one of four alphas in her scent match, she believes her life is over. Quintets are usually made up of one alpha and a mix of delta and betas. Her pack, though, consists of four alpha males, making it strong, and *dangerous*, especially for an omega.

Just like her mom's.

Emme has no choice but to reject the alphas, which receives mixed reactions from the four.

Hunter, the entitled alpha, doesn't give up when he sets his mind to something, and he's determined to win her into the pack by whatever means necessary. He convinces her to move into their pack house for a while, save up some money, and not worry. He also promises not to bond her without her explicitly begging for it. Hunter is an obsessive and possessive alpha stalker, with a goal of keeping his pack safe, and as strong as it can be. Also... hand tattoo. That is all.

Kellan, the golden retriever alpha, comes in with his sweet and kind soul (though don't underestimate his ability to rip another shifter's head from his shoulders if he looks the wrong way at Emme). Kellan would follow her through this life and into the next no hesitation. Emme, who has been alone her whole life, is won over by Kellan's sweet and unconditional obsession with her.

Slade is a scary dragon shifter. Cold and clinical, he has an observational interest in Emme. She certainly intrigues him. He keeps an eye on her through security cameras, and is as intense a stalker as Hunter, just in a less forceful way. For now.

Finley, a bear shifter, doesn't take her rejection well. It triggers his childhood trauma where he was rejected and hurt by his family. He decides she is toxic to them all, and he's determined not to have her in their lives.

Once she's in the pack house, bonds start to form between Emme, Kellan, and Hunter, despite her best efforts to reject them. As an omega, who can stand outside of normal pack dominance, she is desired amongst alphas, and her pack is determined to keep her safe. During one attempted kidnapping by a guard on the Reeves pack security team, she fights back long enough for Hunter and Kellan to arrive and destroy the shifter, which seals another portion of their relationship. Emme grows even closer to those two.

While investigating the attempted kidnapping to find the source—the guard was a hired hit— the end of *A Curse of Fate* finds Emme and Slade on motorcycles, heading to an interrogation. On the way, they're blown up by a rocket, and an injured Emme is thrown into the back of a van before she blacks out. When she wakes again, she's in a basement cell, bars blocking her exit. Slade is across from her, in another cell, restrained by magical bands.

When her kidnapper steps into the room, she freaks out because it's the entitled alpha of her mom's old pack. They've been searching for her, and when she showed up on the pack register for Golden City, they took their opportunity to track her down.
This is where *A Twist of Luck* begins.

# CATCH UP ON THE WORLD

## A TWIST OF LUCK

Book two starts with Emme and Slade as prisoners in Silver City, where they were taken and held by Blaine and his alpha pack. The Rogers pack (Blaine's pack) uses magic to keep them contained. Meanwhile, back in Golden Claw, the Reeves pack (Emme's pack) are hunting down anyone involved with Rogers pack for information to find out where their kidnapped pack members are. They get a lead that Rogers pack is in Silver City, and jump on their plane to head straight there.

In Silver City, the kidnappers underestimate Slade's power, and he busts through his cell to comfort Emme during a panic attack, which is triggered by being held captive again by Blaine and his pack, as they destroyed her mother and tormented her growing up.

After Slade scares away everyone in the house, they head upstairs to discover the house is magically locked down, and it'll take the dragon shifter hours to smash them out. Thankfully, by the time he breaks through, the rest of the Reeves pack have shown up with their own witch in their ranks. To fight magic, you need magic.

They decide to regroup and head back to Golden Claw, since Blaine and his pack have vanished, but on the way to their plane they're ambushed by a witch. She tries to hit Emme with a knockout spell, but Kellan gets in between them. He's taken down by a spell that can only be lifted by the witch who cast it, and unfortunately, she's dead via Sladdy—I mean Slade—the dragon baddie.

They rush an unconscious and possibly dying Kellan back to Golden Claw and demand their ally witch (Jewels) figure out how to save him. With time running out, they do everything they can to keep Kellan's energy flowing strongly, including *almost* naked pack huddles.

Eventually, Jewels and her coven come up with a solution, but they're afraid Kellan is too weak to fight, even with the counterspell. With no other option, they give him the spell, and in the end he's so weak that he can't survive, and Emme makes the choice to bond with him in the hopes she might be able to share some of her energy.

Which works!

She gives him the strength to fight the spell. This is one of her greatest fears in bonding to alphas, as she feels this is what destroyed her mother, but she notices no changes with Kellan, and he doesn't try to take any more of her wolf essence.

After this, everything is going fine as they deal with the Alpha Council, and what the future plans for Blaine and his pack are. Silver City puts up roadblocks toward hunting the Rogers pack. Red tape and paperwork get in the way.

Toward the end of the book, Emme bonds with Hunter (her entitled alpha) in a lovely *Hunter and Prey* scenario, through the forests of Golden Claw. She makes this decision because she loves him and trusts him completely. He's done nothing but support and care for her almost since the first moment he dragged her into their lives.

Bonding is still an experiment at this stage, as Emme still doesn't know what will happen if she bonds all four alphas, but she's willing to try. Her life was empty without them, and they've shown time and time again that they're nothing like her mom's pack.

She also grows closer to Slade (dragon shifter, aka scary motherfucker) as he attempts to teach her how to defend herself, which leads to a prank war. During one of these pranks, where Emme turns off the cameras momentarily, she gets herself into a bit of trouble.

She opens a book in her room about omegas and packs—a book brought to her by Chelsea from the Thenguard pack; a book she hasn't touched since that attack at the guard house in book 1, but which she hoped might give her answers to her designation as an omega in a pack of alphas.

The book is spelled, and has been waiting there all this time for her to open it. As soon as she flips the page, the spell is enacted and she falls under Chelsea's control. It binds the two omegas together, and she has to follow Chelsea's actions.

Chelsea takes her far from Golden Claw and deposits her in an old house, right into the clutches of the very alpha who's been trying to kidnap her all along. It's not the alpha she expected. Blaine is still there of course, but he has a boss (or father, more accurately) running the show.

Who also happens to be Hunter's father.

He is the big bad alpha behind everything. He has been kidnapping omegas and experimenting on them for years. It was Fletcher who orchestrated Blaine and his pack into her mother's life, and got them to drain her mother until she chose to end her life.

Now he wants Emme.

Hunter's father calls a familiar-looking shifter into the old house. If it weren't for the scar on his face and shorter hair, the shifter stalking toward her would exactly resemble Slade Riverson.

This darker, scarier version of her dragon bites and forcibly claims her under his alpha's command, and with the last of Chelsea's control still flooding her system, she's forced to bite him back and seal the bond forever.

This is where *A Claim of Fortune* begins.

# CATCH UP ON THE WORLD

## A CLAIM OF FORTUNE

This book starts with Emmeline captured and forcibly bonded. A week after the kidnapping, she's moved to a strange place with her newly bonded dragon shifter. He looks exactly like Slade but is quieter and has a scar on his face, and shorter hair. He's also high on her shit list for forcing a bond on her and removing her free will.

She soon learns that this shifter is a weapon of Fletcher, Hunter's father, and doesn't even have a name. She names him Talon, giving him his first slice of humanity. She's also fairly sure he's a scent match for her, and she can't figure out how that's possible when she already has four mates (to form the perfect quintet).

The rest of her pack, including Entitled Alpha Hunter (wolf shifter), Slade (dragon shifter), Finley (bear shifter), and Kellan (wolf shifter) are out searching for her. Finley has turned into a bear and has been tracking her in his beast form the whole time.

He ends up being the first to find her in Texas, and breaks into the underground bunker. He tries to fight Talon to get her back, but he is no match for a dragon shifter. They still get away thanks to Talon losing control and shifting inside.

Emme soon figures out that Finley can't shift back, as his bear protects him in highly emotional situations. Eventually, her presence helps him return to his human form, and of course, he opens his big fat mouth and says something asshole. That's the moment Emme decides she's had enough. He's dead to her. Finley realizes he screwed up badly.

They're still trying to escape though, with Talon and Fletcher on their asses, and thankfully the rest of their pack shows up to help. Slade and Talon battle in the air (dragon fight!) while Hunter and the others reach Emme. Eventually, they manage to incapacitate Talon and get away before Fletcher arrives.

Back in Golden Claw, Talon is locked away in a chamber in their basement while they try to figure out what to do with him. Since he's newly bonded to Emme, she can't be too far away from him.

For the next while, they search for Fletcher and the witch he is using to try to take over the shifter cities. They find out he wants to be ultimate alpha and return all packs to the old way of life—no more quintets. He's in hiding though, so they try to get the Alpha Council on board with helping.

Finley starts therapy and healing for Emme, knowing that much of the reason he treated her badly was for fear of losing her. And that if he doesn't change and step up, he really will lose her. For good.

Emme grows closer to all the alphas—except for Slade—who draws back in guilt and fear over his doppelganger forcing the bond on her. He spends a lot of time with Talon, trying to get information, but Talon will only talk when Emme is there.

Emme also starts martial arts and endurance training, strengthening herself as much as she can so she'll stop being the vulnerable link in the whole quintet.

Talon eventually reveals that Slade and he were twin souls, born in the same egg; Fletcher tore them apart at birth. This is why both of their dragons are uneasy and restless, and they have never felt in control. This also explains how Talon is a scent match for Emme, and the quintet energy remains intact, despite there being six in the group now. Slade and Talon are two sides of the same essence coin, and stand as one part of the quintet.

Emme slowly warms to Talon, who she realizes in many ways was just as much a victim of Fletcher as she was. She also warms to Finley when she is brought into his life more, and he shows her that he's a really gooey grouchy bear under his gruff exterior.

Toward the end of the book, when they're heading for their first real family barbeque, Emme feels a disturbance in the street with her bonded pack members. She had been ice skating with Finley, and they rush home to find the street filled with magic, though there are no witches present.

Sorenson, Hunter's best friend and the entitled alpha of Chelsea (the omega who betrayed Emme in book 2), comes for Emme and Talon, saying that if he brings them back to Fletcher, he will release his pack. He arrived with specifically designed spells that locked down the street and the alphas. He just didn't expect Emme and Finley would be away when he arrived.

Finley manages to knock Sorenson down before he's hit by the same spell, and his bear bulk pins the alpha to the ground. That gives Slade the time he needs to break free from the spell and tear Sorenson's head off. As the rest of the street starts to push through the magic, a familiar witch appears, dragging with her some leverage.

Leverage in the form of Emme's best girlfriend, Cora.

The witch who was behind this shit all along was Jewels, who they thought was their ally. She was working with Fletcher too, and she arrives to finish what Sorenson started—returning Emme and Talon to the evil alpha. At this point, Emme believes Talon is growing as a person, and will no longer blindly believe in Fletcher's plan, so she calls him out to help them.

Slade fights Jewels, and Cora is thrown free—injured but not critically. Jewels reveals that she kept their essence (from book 2) that was supposed to help Kellan. She was never helping him, and she used that essence to power her spells so she'd be stronger against the Reeves pack.

When Talon arrives, a weird energy fills the street, and then Slade and Talon *Mighty Morphin Power Ranger* themselves into Slalon, a combined dragon beast that's massive, with two heads. Twin soul dragons were the warriors for their clans, and they are near magic-proof, while being super huge and strong.

Jewels panics as she realizes she can't best them alone and disappears to get backup. Enforcers start arriving just after she's gone, which is in time for dozens or more of witches to appear in the sky above, along with Jewels carrying Fletcher.

A fight ensues, but with Slalon they have a huge advantage. Fletcher believes he can still control Talon, and banks on that, but when most of the witches are taken out, and Jewels dumps Fletcher in the street to fend for himself, he realizes how wrong he was.

Talon knows a real bond with Emme now, and when Fletcher hurts his mate, all loyalty is gone to his former alpha. Slade, Talon, and Hunter destroy the only father they've ever known, and with most of the witches dead, and Jewels vanished once more, it feels like victory is in their hands.

Emme bonds with Finley, having finally forgiven him, and trusting that he's changed for the better to make their relationship work. The next morning, there's a loud, magical knock on the front door, and an alpha is standing there, one who is familiar, only through photos, as he was one Slade tried to track down.

He is Emme's long-lost father, and he is there to warn them about Jewels.

What looked like retreat was all part of her plan. She needed them to kill Fletcher (she couldn't due to the alliance she held with him). If any who were blood, or as good as blood, killed Fletcher, she could use that energy to power a massive curse.

One that would give her complete control over the beasts of all shifters.

They have until the next full moon to stop her or lose their ability to shift, and their autonomy forever.

This is where *A Bond of Trust* begins.

*This is for those who've always fought alone.*

*You deserve an alpha to dote on you.*

*Or a pack of them.*

# CHAPTER 1

TALON

The wheel was foreign under my hands. It felt breakable, like if I squeezed just a little too hard, it would crack and shatter into carbon and Alcantara pieces. I'd recently learned what the G-Wagen's steering wheel was made of, courtesy of my mate, Emme.

Not that she'd said much else about the vehicle itself, other than asking if I wanted to have my first driving lesson.

We'd just come from trying to visit the Annandale pack's house but hadn't even made it to the end of their street. Warrick met us on the road, and while he took the baked goods and apologies from Emme, he hadn't let her any closer.

They weren't ready.

But if I had to hear my mate's silent sobs for one more second, I was going to crush and burn this fucking car. And maybe also this world that kept on hurting her.

"Okay, I'm fine now," she said, sniffling, and I wondered if she could sense how I fought my demons in the face of her sadness. Sadness I couldn't fix. "Let's get this lesson moving. We don't have a lot of time before our ceremony."

Her existence had been torn to pieces yesterday, but I'd learned there was never enough time to deal or heal when magic was involved. To fight Jewels, we had to complete our quintet bond and strengthen our pack. Still... "Are you sure you're up to the ceremony today?"

I didn't care what it cost us, if she needed another day I'd stand in everyone's way to ensure she got it.

Turning fully in my seat, I took in her unnaturally drawn features, even as the blue of her dress reflected the golden sheen of her skin. My mate was stunning. I didn't deserve to be in the presence of such beauty but fuck the goddess if she thought I'd ever give Emme up.

"Yes," she cleared her throat and forced a smile. "I'm absolutely up for it. I want us to be as powerful as possible. But first… let's teach you to drive."

Before I could respond, a motorcycle engine revved. Hunter and Slade were with us, the entitled alpha on his Honda, and my twin on his Ducati. Now that we'd embraced the twin soul connection, I could feel Slade in my essence, almost as strongly as I felt Emme.

Then there was the rest of my pack.

*Pack.*

For a shifter who'd never really had anyone, it was a huge responsibility to now have many to keep safe under my dragon wing. Thank the goddess my wingspan was large and capable.

Emme turned to meet my gaze, and honestly… I was once again fighting the urge to shift into my beast, steal my mate away, burn the car to the ground, and fly her out of this fucked-up place. If only that wouldn't damn all shifters, including Emme, to a curse that would steal our ability to shift by the next full moon.

Slade revved his engine again, as a reminder we were on a deadline, and I bit back my snarl. Everyone in this pack enjoyed cars, bikes, engines, and speed. I only enjoyed one of those, but maybe I'd change my mind when I learned how to control these unnatural pieces of metal.

Hence why I was here today, killing time before the ceremony.

With the only shifter I'd ever tolerate a lesson from.

Frankly, Emme could teach me the ancient art of knitting and I'd hang on every damn word. If anyone else tried though, I'd use those same knitting sticks to ensure they wore their intestines as a scarf.

"It's not critical for me to learn how to drive," I reminded her, my voice rougher than I intended. "Firstly, I can fly much faster than any car. Secondly, there's no shortage of shifters in our pack who can drift around a fucking corner."

Emme's lips twitched, and my beast calmed when a brief peal of laughter escaped her. After all of her sadness, that light, delicate sound had me desperate to hear more. My life wasn't one for light, and she was a miracle I never expected. I'd kill my former alpha, Fletcher, a million times over if that meant having Emme laugh just once.

"One day, when you race on the track with us all, you'll understand why we love to drive. Not only is it fun, we're competitive as fuck. Kellan always wins, but there will come a time when someone knocks him off his pedestal."

"I could kick his ass without even trying," I decided.

Confidence went hand in hand with being a dragon, and if I wanted to beat him, I would.

Emme patted my arm and every part of my body stood to attention, eager for more. "Of that, I have no doubt. But don't underestimate our Golden. He drives like a shifter with a death wish, and Slade hasn't bested him yet."

Kellan, the other *light one* in our pack. I'd never met an alpha like him before. My dragon was torn between enjoying his banter and wanting to punch him in the teeth.

Still, he was pack, which made him ours.

"Okay, show me what to do," I said, facing forward, feeling the stare of the entitled alpha and my twin. Outside of the engine revs, both showed surprising patience, but we could only push them so far.

Emme leaned toward me as she pointed out the parts of the car, including the start button, wipers, hazards, and how we signaled to turn. Her scent washed over me as she flicked her hair back, and it took every ounce of my hard-fought-for focus to not drag her into my lap.

"Are you listening, Tal?" she asked with a smirk, and since I never lied to her…

"You're a huge distraction in the best way," I murmured.

The lightest hue of pink tinted her cheeks, and the chocolate and honey tones deepened. "I'm going to be a much bigger distraction soon," she replied, voice raspy.

I liked that sound. I liked everything about this shifter. Enough to be worried that I might take over my twin with obsession and stalking.

"I haven't thought of anything else since we decided last night," I told her, and that blush darkened, spanning down to the tops of her breasts, visible in the cut of her dress.

With a shake of my head, I forced myself to look out the front window, which was dull and uninspiring compared to Emme. "Let's focus on the lesson so I don't ravish you here and now."

Another scent spike, but she sucked in a fortifying breath and ran through drive, reverse, park, and other features like the low range for off-roading. "You shouldn't ever need that for regular driving," she added, "since this one is always in four-wheel drive mode and can handle a fair amount of rugged terrain."

This car had nothing on my beast. "If I get stuck, I'll just tear the roof off and fly away."

Another burst of laughter from her, and my cock jerked in my pants. To have my body react so strongly was a new experience, and I found myself curious about what the rest of the day would bring. There were no real nerves, as I knew instinct would guide me in claiming my mate.

But the anticipation might kill me before that moment.

"The doors will still work," Emme said around her laughter, "but sure, tearing off the roof is always an option."

I barely heard her over the roar of my beast.

Scent matches were intense, and I drowned in the animalistic needs coursing through me.

"Okay, well, let's try moving," Emme said, and she moved away to sink into her seat. "Foot on the brake before pressing the start button."

Following her instructions helped my focus, and it seemed straightforward and simple. The car moved as soon as I lifted my boot from the brake, and I enjoyed the little jolt forward when I hit the gas. It was smooth, the wheel responding to the smallest adjustment, which kept us on the straight road. It did take me a second to maneuver my boots on the pedals, as everything in here was too fucking small, but eventually I got the hang of it.

After ten minutes I felt confident in controlling the machine, and another ten minutes had me ready for more speed. I pressed my foot harder, and on either side of us the bikes kept pace easily. "I want to try one of those next," I said, eyeing Slade.

*Top speed, brother,* I said through our bond. *Show me how fast it is.*

Emme must have caught some of my curiosity through our connection, as she turned to examine Slade. When he took off in a roar, her breath quickened, and I didn't need a mental connection to know she wanted to be out there on her Panigale.

Slade's motorcycle moved like the wind, sleek and black and lethally fast. "Yep, I definitely need one of those," I decided when he disappeared from sight. I was finally beginning to understand.

"This is one of my happy places," Emme murmured, watching the world go by out her window, her long legs sprawled out in front of her. "Cars, my mates, and no one trying to kill us." A sad bark of laughter left her. "At least not right this second. I can't believe my alleged father is in the house, and he's half fucking witch and half shifter, just blowing all my conceptions of our races out of the water. How did this even happen?"

"Fletcher would have known more," I grumbled, flexing the weak wheel again. "His death needed to happen, but it clearly set in motion a chain of events that might be even worse."

Emme swung in her chair toward me, eyes narrowed. "Don't you dare feel guilty for the choice you made, Talon Riverson. We had no idea what that bitch-witch had set in motion, and the world will always be better without that monster in it. We'll just deal with the next challenge, as we always do." She paused, and took a few breaths, visibly calming. "I do think you should take us to his compound, if Jewels hasn't figured out how to burn it all to the ground already. There might be clues there."

"I will take you," I promised her. "I don't know what remains of it, but it makes sense to search it in our quest to track the witch. I was never allowed into the underground rooms, but I could smell the darkness from my cage."

Even when I'd been on board with Fletcher's plan to take over the cities and return shifters to their former glory, he'd never fully trusted me. I knew the reason why now: Slade. He tried to beat it out of us, but the twin-soul bond trumped all except my bond to Emme.

"Will you show me Golden Claw?" I asked, wanting my last niggling doubts over the way the cities were run put to rest. "I know it's the largest of the cities, and the closest to mimic how the human world functions."

She nodded, and I was drawn to the row of straight white teeth working over her plush bottom lip. "Yeah, it's the largest and most similar to a big *human* city. I just..." She swallowed roughly. "I'm worried that you won't like the advancements and start rallying for us to bring the old ways back."

The thought had crossed my mind, but even if I never fully

shunned Fletcher's vision, I loved Emme more. *I would change for her.* I would adjust and adapt until she was permanently in her happy place. "I choose you, Sweet Honey," I said softly. "In a city, in the desert, in the middle of the ocean. Whatever it looks like, I choose you. You have nothing to worry about."

Her lip popped free, and I was caught in her fucking glorious smile. "Tal! You like me, you really like me." There was a teasing lilt to her voice, and I recognized that this was her way of joking with me. Such a novel concept, and *goddess*, I was completely and totally gone over my omega.

"I love you," I said suddenly, returning my eyes to the road in time for Slade to race back into view. "I really fucking love you."

I'd never said those words to anyone before, and I expected them to burn in a way that even a dragon was unfamiliar with. But they flowed like water filled with contentment.

Emme was silent for a few seconds, and I slowed the vehicle to give her my full attention. She stared wide-eyed and unblinking, her smile long gone. My heart clenched hard, and the fires raged in my gut as moisture once again clouded her icy-blue gaze.

"Are you okay?" I growled, hitting the brakes, slamming the car in park, and reaching for her. "What's wrong?"

When she squeezed her eyes closed, I had to force my dragon down. Neither of us liked when she cut herself off from us. "Mate." My rumble filled the cab. "Tell me what's wrong so I can fix it."

She shook her head, a hint of a smile finally on her lips. "Some days it's hard for me to believe we ended up here. When you forced the bond, I couldn't imagine liking, let alone loving you. Yet here we are." With that, she opened her eyes, and I was locked in her brilliant blue gaze which calmed the inferno in my gut. "I love you too, Talon Riverson. *I love you.*"

This was also the first time I'd ever heard those words said to me, and if anything in the world was going to take me out, it was this moment. *Fuck.* My chest ached like it was caving in but also exploding at the same time.

My voice was a whisper. "Say it again. *Please.*" Who knew that the day a dragon begged would be this one. *Not fucking me.*

Emme leaned over and pressed a kiss against my cheek, before moving down to my lips. Featherlight kisses, and between each one, she whispered her love.

With a growl, I reached out and yanked her over the center console and into my lap, trying to fit my limbs and mate all in the stupidly small metal box. "I would kill and die for you without thought, Sweet Honey," I rumbled, hoping she heard the absolute truth in that. "Destroy cities, raze alphas to the ground, and crawl on my fucking hands and knees to reach you. You're it for me, Emmeline Anders. You're my one and only, and if that's not love, I don't know what is."

She leaned back so our gazes could connect, and when the moment extended for four long, tension-filled seconds, she lurched into me. Her fingers attempted to grip the short strands of my hair, and I held her face, forcing myself to be gentle. She was so fragile, and I had to temper my strength to ensure she remained in perfect condition.

I understood why my brother chose not to spar with her most of the time. It was terrifying to think that one slip of control… *Never*.

She groaned against my lips, and I demanded entry, my tongue brushing hers as I chased her sweet taste. Her wolf rose up to frolic with my beast, and he treated her with the sort of reverence he'd shown no other. This was what I'd searched for during my empty life: love, a mate, a pack.

I finally had something to fight for, and I would not let that witch steal it all away.

# CHAPTER 2

EMME

*Talon fucking Riverson.*

He'd never needed a name to be powerful and enticing, but now that he had two—adopting the same family name as Slade—he felt even more magnetic.

*I love you.* Those words were on repeat in my head as he kissed the sanity out of me. Like, this man could freaking kiss, and considering I was the one and only shifter he'd ever touched this way, it was *all* instinct.

He'd told me he loved me. He. Loved. Me.

And I loved him.

I'd expected with our horrible beginning, those words would be hard to say, but they'd burst from me like I'd been holding them back for years. My feelings for Talon were strong and complex, and I already knew I couldn't live without him. I couldn't live without any of my mates.

When I pulled back from the toe-curling kiss, my breaths were ragged and heavy, and I tried to ignore the pulsing in my core. We had a bond that was ninety percent complete, and there was only one step left, which both of our beasts pushed us toward.

After a morning swept up in grief for Cora, Warrick, and their pack, it was nice to have a brief moment of normalcy.

"Damn," I huffed. "That was perfect, Tal."

His chest rumbled, and the dark planes of his gorgeous face briefly lit up as he smiled. "I could kiss you all day, sweetness." His voice lowered. "And all night."

I resisted the urge to rub up against his dark cargo pants, as the scent of my arousal spilled through the cab. Talon's nostrils flared, and I cleared my throat while I scrambled back over to my side of the car, fixing my dress as I went. "Enough of that, mate. We have an appointment to keep, and since you are more than competent driving on a straight road, how would you like to try heading into the city?"

Talon never asked a lot of questions, as he generally trusted what I asked of him. No doubt that had a lot to do with the way he'd been trained to follow commands and never think for himself. "If you lead, I will follow," he said, as if to reiterate my thoughts.

I shook my head. "That's not how this pack works. If you're not comfortable driving in the city, or if you'd like to observe the shifters in their natural environment, then I can drive us there."

His big hands flexed against the poor steering wheel again; it was a miracle it hadn't shattered yet under his hold. "Actually, I would like to observe. I have chosen my path in life, and it is you, but I still find myself curious of the reasons Fletcher wanted to destabilize everything."

The death of Fletcher Davenport, *aka evil asshole*, hadn't miraculously resulted in Talon completely abandoning the dead alpha's philosophy. He still believed, to some extent, that falling back under a single alpha rule was the way for our species to prosper. A part of him would always worry that we were diminishing our animal instincts by domesticating into cities.

It might be good for him to immerse himself in the way we lived now—not that he had time to do much more than glance out the window today. We were busy trying to stop Jewels from destroying our world. She was worse than Fletcher, wanting to bring all shifters under *her* control, our beasts no longer ours to command.

A future I'd rather die than let happen.

Hence why, outside of this brief interlude for a driving lesson on our way to the ceremony, we were on the clock and counting down to the next full moon.

The deadline helped me compartmentalize the sudden appearance of my *father* and the truth he'd brought with him. A truth that changed everything. I was not only shifter.

*Witch-shifter.*

My darker thoughts were disturbed by a tap on my window. Hunter leaned against his bike, his charcoal suit jacket open and displaying the expanse of his wide shoulders. He wouldn't normally dress this way on a motorcycle, but we were all in our *ceremony outfits*. When he crouched down toward me, he stared straight into my damn soul.

The stormy gray of his eyes were light, as if the dumpster fire of a world burning around us didn't bother him. "You okay, baby?" he asked, voice muffled through the door of the armored vehicle.

I was tempted to haul myself onto the back of his bike and lose myself in my entitled alpha and the speed of his motorcycle. Backpacking for Hunter was one of my top-tier fantasies. I'd never allowed myself to even think about it with Slade, the other dragon shifter in our pack. Mostly because he had a strong touch aversion, and I wouldn't want him to feel uncomfortable with me plastered to his back.

But Hunter… Hunter liked touch. Very, *very, much.*

I hit the button to roll the window down. "We're good," I said, sensing Talon lean closer behind me. His smoky maple scent was strong and steady. *Calming.* Just like Hunter's mocha. "We're ready to head for town now."

Hunter's visor was flipped up to show the small crinkle beside his eyes as he smiled. "Okay, little mate. We'll follow as your guard."

Talon rumbled. "She doesn't need any guards beside me."

Hunter's shrug said he didn't completely disagree, but we'd also learned the hard way that there was magic not even a dragon could withstand. "We'll see you in there," he said, dropping his visor and kicking his long leg back over the bike.

Slade, the silent giant clad all in black, remained comfortably perched on his bike. This dragon shifter was the only one of my pack I didn't wear a claiming bite from, and had always been the hardest alpha to get close to. Even after everything that had happened, we hadn't talked about our relationship outside of confirming that we would bond today.

It bothered me that it might be out of necessity and not choice, but circumstances dictated the timeline, and I had to roll with it.

At least he had confirmed that he'd found peace in his dragon bond and no longer believed he could destroy me. So there was that. I just wasn't sure it was enough.

We had to go into this final battle as strong as possible, and Constantine, the shifter *claiming* to be my father, didn't believe I could access true magic until my shifter soul was complete. He had a lot of *claims*.

I had no idea how I felt about any of them, or even if I believed a single word from his mouth.

But we'd learn soon enough if he was right.

When I went to open my door, Talon leaned over and captured my arm. "Wait," he ordered, unintentionally dropping dominance into that command, even though it wouldn't work on me.

What did work on me was the mate bond, and I remained in an aching, flustered heap as he raced around the car to open my door. No one raised him to be an alpha of honor, but the instinct was deeply ingrained. He'd shown that from the first moment he brushed my hair and soothed my beast.

When he helped me out of the Benz, he leaned down to drop a kiss on my cheek and escorted me to the driver's side. I felt the burn of Slade's gaze, even unable to see his expression through the dark tint of his helmet. That dragon took tall, silent, and deadly to a whole new level.

The urge to prank the cold bastard again was a niggling need, but it would take a hell of a lot more planning with the way he monitored me via the approximately eleven billion security cameras he had installed everywhere.

After helping me into the driver's side, Talon clicked my seatbelt in, before he jumped into the passenger seat. Wasting no time, I swung the car around and got us on the road to town. Talon had barely even needed a driving lesson, having mastered the basics already. Even though flying would always be his first choice, it was good to know that he could drive if required.

Which meant it was time to head to the sacred space we'd reserved for our pack bonding.

This morning's ceremony wasn't the kind that involved sex and bites. It was an energy sharing between the alphas that would strengthen our quintet. Hunter, Kellan, Finley and Slade had already had this ceremony before, but Talon needed to be brought into the fold.

After that, the sex and biting would happen with the twins and me.

I was the heart of our group, and the only one who would fully claim the alphas. They would be brothers in essence, and together we'd form the strongest bond of our kind.

A bond I no longer feared would spell my death.

"You want to be part of our pack in this way, right?" My need to give Talon an equal voice, as he'd always been dismissed by his alpha, had me double checking. "Not just with me."

There was no hesitation in his reply. "Yes. They already feel like my brothers, and I guess I can handle sharing you with them."

After today he'd be a full pack member, registered with the Alpha Council and everything. They'd taken the news of a second dragon surprisingly well, but they were trying to mend bridges with the Reeves pack, after dismissing our concerns over Fletcher.

Which ended with a massive battle in our street.

Talon and I didn't talk again until we reached the built-up areas of Golden Claw. He was the sort of alpha I could exist in comfortable silence with; the warmth remained without any need for conversation.

In the city, he pulled his enigmatic gaze from my face to observe the shifters around us. His dragon focus locked in on the various alphas, betas, and deltas hurrying about their daily lives with work, school, and college. We had sports teams, we had office buildings, and we had many cafes and restaurants, quite a few owned by the very pack he'd found himself part of—not that money meant anything to Talon.

Our pack might own Reeves Industries, a billion-dollar company, but it wasn't even in the top one hundred of the best parts of them. I'd live in a hovel, with a fucking pair of roller skates as my transport, if it meant I got to wake up every day with these possessive, dominant, gorgeous alphas. You couldn't buy what truly made life worth living, though I would admit that after driving supercars, the benefits were *very* nice.

"They just don't feel like shifters," Talon noted, his flat expression visible in the reflection of the window. "Dressed in so many clothes, with buildings closing in around them. It's constricting."

I nodded, taking in our surroundings with an open mind. "I'm not going to argue that we do sacrifice a sense of freedom and wildness for this life. But our ancestors weren't out there naked or in their beast forms sleeping on the ground either. We literally haven't done that since the first of our kind. This is our evolution, and what you might notice if you look past the veneer of civility is that they're happy now too."

It might not be the same as the past, but it also wasn't worse. Just different.

Talon acknowledged my words with a few nods. The shifters on the streets would freak out if they knew a dragon had them in his gaze, even if he meant no harm.

When we stopped at a set of lights, Hunter and Slade pulled in on either side of us, and we all got more than a few stares. Everyone knew the Reeves pack—we were impossible to miss.

It was a pack that everyone adored and feared in equal measures, and I still found it hard to believe I was part of their world. After a lifetime of never being wanted, I now had so much love and care in my life that it was oftentimes overwhelming. This was the part that made this pack so special, never the money.

At the next corner, Hunter pulled out in front and I followed him along unfamiliar streets. We moved from the dense urban landscape into nature: shrines to our goddess, parklands, and small huts. I trailed the bike all the way to a parking lot and pulled into a spot beside a familiar Bugatti. Kellan had parked his baby away from the main lot so no one would accidentally scratch it. Not that anyone would dare unless they had a death wish.

The bites on my neck tingled as I closed in on my mates, two of whom stood at the entrance of the sacred land dedicated to the moon goddess. Kellan and Finley were in suits as well, leaving Slade and Talon the only two dressed like they were SWAT officers. Which was their fanciest attire, so it worked out.

My gaze lingered on Golden Boy first. His tan suit was a near perfect match to his wolf pelt. Then I moved on to Grouchy Bear, in a navy number with no tie. Most of the alphas hated ties or any real restrictions on their beasts. Finley and I had a rocky start to our pack life, but we were healing in the most wholesome of ways. We'd sealed our bond two nights ago, and I would forever cherish that brief moment of pure bliss with him before my world fell apart the next morning. With the arrival of Constantine and his unwelcome news.

When I turned off the engine, Kellan had my door open and seatbelt undone in a flash. When he lifted me out into his arms, he spun me around until the pretty blue dress I wore with tights and brown leather boots flared around me. My feet hit the ground in time for a scorching kiss on my lips, and I loved his caramel scent and warm embrace.

*Golden.* My sweetest alpha. Who could also turn deadly when his pack was threatened. "Shortcake," he groaned. "I fucking missed you, and I love this matchy-matchy blue dress with your eyes. A shifter could forget what we're here for with you looking like that."

It had been less than two hours since we all ate breakfast together, but for Kellan Jackson, two hours apart was an eternity.

His second kiss was more demanding than the first, and by the time he handed me over to Finley, I'd forgotten my name, the day of the week, and the *new* end-of-world issue we faced.

"Hey, darlin'," the bear drawled, and all of my insides turned molten at that sinfully sexy rumble. "I missed you too. You look stunning… a perfect gift from the goddess."

The thick dark lashes surrounding his whiskey-colored irises dragged me under, and all I could think about was how he'd fallen asleep last night still buried inside me. Finley was insatiable when it came to touch and remaining close, and honestly, the big alpha had me addicted.

Except for Talon, after each of my bondings I'd had a night or two alone with that alpha, letting our essences really settle. And there were two more to go.

"I missed you both too," I said with a sniffle, popping up on my toes to press my lips to Finley's. As always, the bear kissed me until my lungs ached from a lack of breathing.

And I wouldn't have it any other way.

# CHAPTER 3

EMME

"Did you speak to the council about the logistics of incorporating a sixth into our quintet?" Kellan asked Hunter as we approached one of the largest huts in the sacred park.

"Yeah, they don't care," Hunter scoffed. "Those useless fucks are so far up my ass at the moment I wouldn't be surprised to find them in the hut today. It wouldn't have mattered anyway. I'll never again seek permission from them to protect and strengthen my own damn pack."

Slade nodded, expression grim. "This is not their business, and I've calculated our odds against the Termaine witch and her allies. We have a much better chance of survival with a completed and fully strengthened quintet. Talon and I are one essence, twin souls, and this should work."

*Completed and fully strengthened.*

Slade's gaze slammed into mine, the biting green of his eyes darker than usual. A spaceship could have landed on my foot and I wouldn't have been able to look away from him. The knowledge that there was only one way to complete a quintet like ours flowed in the air between us, and Slade wouldn't have used those words mistakenly.

He was ready for the full bond, and I was hyperventilating at the very thought of finally, *finally* getting my hands on that god of a shifter.

Would I survive the experience? *Probably.*

Would I be forever changed by the experience? *Absolutely.*

"Agreed," Hunter said abruptly. "So, let's get moving so we can face this next battle at full strength."

His hand landed on the back of my neck, and I shivered at the possessive grip. He slowly dragged me into his side, until I was encased in heat and the scent of coffee and chocolate. His hold remained solid as we entered the hut, which was octagonal in shape with light, wood paneled walls and low ceilings. The alphas had to duck through the doorway, and then once we were inside, the space shrank around their huge bodies.

"Cozy," I murmured, taking it all in.

Kellan smirked lazily. "There's a reason for that."

Anticipation had me quivering in Hunter's hold, and when the alphas started to move in a circle around me, my pulse raced. Hunter was the last to step back, leaving me in their center.

"You don't technically need to be here for this," the entitled alpha murmured, his voice low and deep. It echoed around the room, and my beast howled in response. "As you're the central, and we bite you to seal our bonds. But we want you here today."

"It will add strength," Slade confirmed.

Talon, Finley, and Kellan remained quiet, but all three of them kept their focus on me, and there was a sense of family, love, and acceptance in this sacred space.

A sense of finally finding my place in the world.

"I want to be here," I whispered, my gaze moving between all five. "I want to feel you bring Talon in as the final piece of our pack."

Intense violet, green, black, grey, and amber stares met mine, and I was suddenly breathless. Hunter broke the moment to light the five candles already set out on small stands around the room. As they burned, an earthy scent filled the hut, holding hints of lavender and pine.

With the final wick alight, a weighty pressure fell over us, and Hunter returned to his place in the circle. "Bond magic is as ancient as our kind," he started, "born from the first shifters, who were cursed by the witches themselves. We stand here today, brothers by choice, with our beasts connected in essence."

The five alphas closed in until their shoulders touched, and I ended up facing Slade and Hunter. The dragon showed no sign of discomfort as he pressed against Hunter and Finley.

As their scents mixed with the burning candles, my head turned light and floaty. Hunter started to chant, and I had no idea what language he spoke in, but it wasn't English. It sounded like a spell, but there was no residual sulfur to accompany it. All five alphas joined in on the second round, but this time it was in English. *"Beast of my beast. Heart of my heart. Bond of our soul. Essence never to be torn apart."*

They switched to the other language, and this time I was sure magic coated these words. I might hate witches, but our two races were intrinsically tied together, whether we wanted to be or not.

Through the bonds I held to most of the alphas, I felt their essences pulsating, and I found myself reaching out to stroke the one that felt like Finley. The bear's eyes turned molten as he attempted to step toward me, only to be stopped by Hunter's growl.

"Don't break the circle yet," our entitled alpha said with a shake of his head. "The ritual isn't complete."

Finley huffed, his restless gaze on me, and I very much enjoyed his flushed cheeks and blown pupils… My bear was aroused.

My gaze slid down to find his blue suit was useless at hiding an erection. Though, it wasn't really the suit's fault, since the bear was big *all* over.

"Ice," he warned, his voice a rasp. "Baby. I only have so much control."

Pressing my lips together, I worked as hard as I could not to smile, but fuck… the power at my fingertips was next-level.

"What did she do?" Kellan piped up, looking between the two of us, his expression filled with curiosity. "Come on, pretty mate. Show the class."

*Okay then, Golden.* I stroked his connection, without even having to lift my hand or touch the bite. Kellan's affability instantly morphed into a groan; he too tried to break the circle, and got stopped by the others.

"Snow," Slade warned. "No more until we finish our bonding."

A pout formed on my lips, which brought a dark smile from him. "Brats get punished," he murmured, and there was so much promise in that statement that I had to press my thighs together once more.

All of the alphas released pained sounds this time, and it was absolutely thanks to my scent exploding through the room. "Your faults," I muttered, trying to think unsexy thoughts.

Which was next to impossible when surrounded by literal perfection of the male form.

Thankfully, the ritual ended not too long after, as the candles burned out, and the pressure faded.

Talon breathed deeply. "I can feel you all in a different way now," he noted, running a hand over his face. "I felt you all through Slade and Emme before, but now it's a real bond between brothers."

There was a change inside me too as I absorbed the strong flow of their essences. "You're powerful together," I whispered, overwhelmed and emotional in a way that had me fighting back tears.

"We are powerful," Hunter acknowledged with his satisfied smile. "The sixth was accepted, just as we anticipated."

That distracted me from my burning eyes. "Wait, what would have happened if Talon wasn't accepted?"

"Nothing," Hunter assured me. "The magic would have snuffed out much faster, and we wouldn't sense him in our quintet essence."

"He feels like Slade," Finley said, wiggling his shoulders, as if to work out tense muscles. "But I can also tell them apart. It's a weird yet interesting dynamic."

I didn't have a claiming bite from Slade yet, but to test a theory I stroked along my bond to Talon. When his smoky maple scent spiked, Slade reacted too, the pair of them on either side of me in a heartbeat.

"Naughty, naughty, Emmeline," Slade murmured, while Talon just released a huff of smoke-laced air. "You shouldn't play with the bonds like that."

"They're definitely connected," I said breathlessly. "*Very* connected."

My head spun as they full-bodily pressed against me, especially Slade, who used to avoid prolonged physical contact. There was not a flicker of retreat in his gaze today, and I wasn't sure if I regretted my actions, or… if I was going to stroke the bond again.

*Brats get punished.* Yes, please.

"Not the time," Hunter drawled, eyeballing the three of us like he was figuring out how to smack all of our heads together.

Slade and Talon didn't release me; my knees were weakening under the dual assault of commanding presences. Before the literal puddle in my panties took me out, Talon's arms wrapped around me and I was hauled over his shoulder. Like a bag of fucking potatoes.

"Wait!" I snapped, pushing through the clouds of my arousal. "Put me down, you giant asshat."

That had the dragon pausing, and he lifted me up and away from his body like I was a fucking child. How did anyone hold a grown, not particularly small woman, out like that and show no strain? It wasn't natural or fair and *I was definitely not complaining.*

"Asshat?" he queried, tilting his head in that animalistic way of a dragon.

*Do my words make more sense when you tilt your head, sexy beast?*

Keeping my mental talk to myself for once, I shrugged as best I could in this position. "It's not a literal observation," I said, annoyed by the way he continued to hold me up under my armpits. "Now put me down. Where the hell were you even taking me?"

His smile was as slow and dark as the shadows in his eyes. "To my bed."

*Fuck.*

"Our bed," Slade drawled, standing side by side with his *i-fucking-dentical twin.*

*Double fuck.*

"Our world is ending," Hunter muttered on a ragged sigh. "I don't have time for this shit."

Twin rumbles emerged from the dragons, but our entitled alpha didn't give a fuck. "Enough," he snapped. "Put our mate down and take a damn walk."

Hunter stepped closer to me. "And, Emmeline, no more touching the bonds or whatever you've now discovered you can do—"

I stroked his bond.

*Whoops.*

# CHAPTER 4

EMME

Hunter had clearly anticipated that move from me, and in return I got the darkening of his eyes and a deep, wolfy rumble from his chest. There was a promise in his gaze though, that he would be addressing my tiny acts of rebellion later.

*Oh no, I'm so scared right now.*

"You three go for a walk," Hunter ordered the dragons and me. "Show Talon some of the city. Breathe some fucking air. Talk to each other and make sure you're all okay with the next steps in the bonding process."

Slade turned his head side to side, as if stretching tension from his neck. "We'll head for the apartment."

That had me pausing. "Apartment?"

I knew they owned multiple buildings, but he'd said *apartment* as if it was more than just their usual rental or investment property.

Hunter let a rough laugh escape him. "It was once Slade's escape, where he could watch over the city he controlled. He hasn't used it since you came into our lives."

For once, I decided not to overthink it and trust in my pack. We had to complete the bonding to fight in this war we didn't sign up for, but more than that, I wanted to complete the bond.

I'd go wherever they led.

Finley stepped closer, oozing protectiveness as his bear rose up. "You're ready to bond with both Talon and Slade, right? You don't have to rush. I don't care if the world is ending."

The dragons in question remained silent at my side, showing no anger or unease over his question. "I'm ready." There was no hesitation in my response, and the alphas relaxed around me.

My wolf howled, so excited to finally complete her pack.

"Come on, Snow," Slade said, holding his hand out to me. When I placed my palm in his, he threaded our fingers together and my heart almost stopped. When Talon did the same on the other side, it took everything I had to just walk and breathe.

Kellan released a groan, which thankfully broke some of my panicked tension. "I swear to the shifter goddess," he said, exaggeratedly fanning his face, "we need to see this bonding. Their fucking chemistry is already destroying me, and they're only holding hands."

He tilted his head back to howl to the sky, but Hunter slapped a hand over his mouth as he dragged him from the hut. We followed into the icy winter air, which cleared the haze in my mind enough that I could function once more. The fire of my dragons encased me, keeping me warm.

"Now, annoying pup," Hunter said in his most patient tone, "you will not sneak over to the apartment. Let them have their moment to fuck and bond. We all had ours."

Heat rushed to my cheeks at the casual discussion of me getting railed by two massive shifters. Two massive *dragon* shifters, who were currently holding my hands, and engulfing me in the burn of their energy.

Hunter's expression morphed into a smirk as he stepped over to me. "Her skin pinks up so pretty," he murmured, cupping my face. "Our perfect little omega."

If the heat flooding me was any indication, I was pink all over. Slade's chest rumbled but he didn't stop Hunter from pressing his lips gently to mine. "Thank you, baby girl," our entitled alpha whispered. "You're the only piece of this puzzle that is irreplaceable."

Fear struck me like a blade to the chest. "Not for me," I replied with a panicked huff. "I can't live without any of you. It's fucking ridiculous how obsessed I am with all five of you possessive assholes."

Kellan snorted. "Told you that we'd grow on you."

"Like a fungus," Finley added cheerily. Well, it was cheery for him.

Talon and Slade squeezed my hands, at the exact same time, as if they'd coordinated it. Which was possible with the way they could mentally communicate.

"The obsession goes both ways," Hunter reminded me, stepping back, his expression reluctant. "Now go. Before I steal you away and keep you naked and sated in my bed for the next week."

"Fuck the witches," Kellan growled. "I'm so sick of their stupid shit."

That made six of us.

Finley and Kellan dropped kisses on my lips after Hunter.

Finley's was firm, his fingers threading through my hair as he held me close. Kellan pressed light caresses over my face and freckles, until he cupped my chin, and swept his tongue across mine. When they walked away with Hunter, I forced myself to ignore the wrench in my chest at being parted from them.

"Come on, Snow," Slade said, but didn't pull me along. He gave me the time I needed to start moving.

"We're here for you, Sweet Honey," Talon added.

As I stared between two faces that were unearthly in their beauty, an urgency to claim them swept through me. I started to walk, and they caught up in a single stride. We had quite a few blocks to reach the city, and at first we were alone in our little bubble.

When we reached downtown the sound of chatter and vehicles was joined by the scent of city living. It wasn't a bad scent—a mix of gasoline, food and shifters—but it also wasn't the more natural scents of the outer regions. Talon's hands grew tense around mine, and I wondered how his first immersive experience in the cities would go. Almost instantly his beast started to rumble, and that drew the attention of those around us, who immediately backed away.

"You two are the biggest predators they've ever had in their orbit," I reminded him. "It's not a weakness for them to back away... it's smart. Survival instincts and all that. The city living didn't remove that."

Talon's lips settled into flat lines; his eyes were almost as flat. He was so calm and gentle with me that it was easy to forget the lethal, dangerous assassin he'd been for almost two decades.

"I don't care about their weaknesses. I just don't like the way they're looking at you," he said, not bothering to keep his tone down.

I tugged him to a stop, and Slade paused with us, wearing an expression that lingered between amusement and annoyance.

"They're just curious," I said, and Talon focused on me long enough to stop terrifying the locals with his dark glare. "We're a powerful pack, and I've been mostly kept hidden. I'm sure rumors have been raging around since the attack on the compound too."

Shifters had died during that attack.

Marcus had died. He was a shifter I cared about, and my heart ached at what Cora, Warrick, Richard and Sierra were going through.

It hurt this morning when they turned me away, but I knew they were grieving. I'd keep showing up, in whatever way they allowed me.

Talon's expression softened; I doubted he'd missed my pulse of grief. "Okay, mate," he murmured. "I trust your judgement here. They're not weak, they're wary. And they're not trying to steal what's mine, they're curious about our power."

Slade huffed, and I had no idea how he made one noise sound so satisfied. "They know better than to even get close to me."

I nodded. "That's also why they're looking—Slade doesn't touch. Anyone. Ever. And here we are, just casually holding hands."

Slade dragged me closer, leaning down as he said, "Mine. My fucking mate. *Mine.*"

The smile that ripped across my face felt unhinged. "Yes, caveshifter. I am yours. As I am Talon's. You're all good boys, sharing as well as you do."

Slade's lips twitched, though his jaw remained rigid. "There's only one good boy in this fucking pack, and it's not either of us. You have no idea what you're stepping into with us, Snow. But it's too late to back out now."

This wasn't the first warning he'd issued me, and just like with all the others, whatever flicker of concern I should feel was crushed under my excitement. "I was born to handle you," I said with a shrug. "Literally, according to fate. And more than happy to take the job."

He mumbled something that sounded a lot like *"We'll see,"* but he got us moving again before I could ask him to repeat himself.

Lots of shifters bowed as we crossed their path, with even more fearfully side-eyeing Talon. He continued to stare at them like they were bugs and he was the exterminator sent to delete them from this world. It was amusing to see them turn other alphas into stumbling, fearful messes.

More annoying were the females who didn't appear to care how scary my dragons were. Alpha, beta, and delta ladies turned *drooling over them* into a competitive sport, and then it was my turn to rumble and glare. Which unfortunately did not have the same effect as the dragons.

When a leggy blonde got a little too close to Talon's side, his teeth clanked together with a snap and she scurried away. My beast and I preened in satisfaction, thankful that none of my pack ever made me question their feelings. They were as obsessed with me as I was with them, and if that wasn't your quintet, you needed to send them back.

Once Talon was done taking in the shifter city, he returned to watching me, the burn of his gaze scorching. He lifted my hand, and when he pressed his lips to the top of my knuckle, I felt that touch in the deepest recesses of myself.

"You are glorious," he said, still not bothering to keep his voice down. "There's not a shifter alive who could compare to you. I always knew it, but today has only reiterated the point. You, Emmeline Anders, are incomparable."

*Goddess.* My lower lip trembled but I kept it together. "I feel the same about you," I managed to say, wanting him to feel as loved as I did. Neither of us grew up with love, so it was a much bigger deal for us. "I feel it for all of my alphas."

Talon tugged me close enough to kiss, and Slade blocked us with his wide shoulders, so others couldn't be part of the moment. "Let's go," I whispered against Talon's lips. "I'm ready to seal this bond. *Please.*"

It was the *please* that had their energy igniting. They moved much faster through the streets, all but carrying me between them. Shifters scurried out of our way, but I barely saw them as I anticipated what would come next.

The final strands of our quintet were about to be sealed. I would finally claim all of my alphas.

I'd never been more ready.

# CHAPTER 5

## SLADE

My dragon was restless, but not in the way he'd been for most of my life. This was a restlessness built of needing to finally claim his mate and pack.

In all other ways, the discord between us was settled, the distance that had kept us on opposite sides of our essence closed. We had a new connection that both thrived and brimmed with power. Before bonding with my twin, I hadn't realized how weak I'd been, at odds with myself and fearful of the beast within. All along, that disconnect had been the missing part of my soul. Or parts, really with my twin, Talon, and my mate, Emme.

Emmeline Anders was the reason I breathed. The reason I killed. The reason I existed.

Now that I was secure in my beast, and had made the decision to bond our souls in the way designed by the goddess, she would be eternally mine.

My mate was about to find out the true depth of a dragon protecting and hoarding his treasure.

Emmeline would be owned, claimed, and fucked until she couldn't breathe or stand, and while there was nothing gentle in my soul, for her, I'd temper the fire.

The worst symptoms of my touch aversion had faded with the healing of the rift, until it was almost nonexistent within my bonded group. But I would still need to be the one in control. Hunter had told me that our mate was fairly submissive during sex, which wasn't a surprise. Her strength came in other ways.

I had no idea how this would all play out today, but every part of me was ready to take this step—denying myself for so long had been both painful and exhausting.

Emme's scent deepened when the large, ornate elevator opened to reveal the top-floor apartment. It was a private entrance for my penthouse, though we also owned the whole building. Which, outside of occasionally hosting friends and family on the lower levels, remained empty.

"Oh my," Emme breathed, pausing to gawk at the interior. "This is impressive, and very much how I imagined billionaires would live."

It was plain and cold compared to our home, but filled with luxuries. "This has never been more than an escape for me. A way for my dragon to sit up here, above the world, watching over our domain."

Emme nodded as if she understood. My little Snow was always so understanding.

As she stepped closer, her scent engulfed me and my cock throbbed. I'd been hard for hours in anticipation of what today would bring, and while I might not have experience with my mate yet, instinct was already guiding me.

I brushed against her, needing to feel her soft skin.

Her breath hitched, and she tilted her head back to meet my stare. Emme could meet my gaze in a way that few managed, and when my beast flashed into my eyes, she did the opposite of most. She stepped closer.

I brushed my fingertips down her soft, perfect skin, tracing freckles until I dipped down to gently grasp the dragon necklace she wore. She hadn't taken it off since her birthday, and fuck if the sight of it didn't send another wave of possessive need through me.

"My pretty little brat," I rasped, the beast joining in my tone.

Emme's lips parted as she swallowed roughly, her throat moving under my touch. "What are you thinking about, Scary Shifter?" she asked, her eyes so blue and wide.

My prey caught in her trap.

"I'm going to claim you very soon, Snow," I promised, tasting her on my tongue though I hadn't kissed her yet. "And taste that perfect cunt."

Her scent flared; her cheeks pinkened with both need and surprise. "Fucking hell, Slade. You need to warn a girl before you descend into dirty talk. I'm not sure I'm equipped to handle that without combusting."

Releasing the dragon pendant, I slid my hand behind her head to grip the back of her neck. When I slowly dragged her forward, she tilted her face up, not even remotely fighting my hold. She handed over control without a peep from her plump lips.

Leaning down, I scented along her throat, picking up the sweeter, deeper notes of arousal and... *more*. "You're fertile," I noted, inhaling stronger, needing more. "You want dragon babies, little mate? You want us to breed you?"

Her entire body shuddered, and she was panting in her reply. "I took the birth control potion, since my period is due any day."

My dragon roared loudly, and Emme jerked back as if she'd heard that internal sound. Talon stepped in on the other side, trapping her between us. "Our beasts don't like the magic blocking your fertility from us," he murmured, voicing my internal rage.

Emme couldn't meet his gaze as I held her chin captive, keeping her focus on me. "You're not ready for young yet," I said in my deepest tone. "Which we understand. But I don't like the taint of that spell in your arousal. We want you filled with our younglings. We want to breed you."

Her breaths came out faster and faster. "Would..." She huffed. "Would I have eggs?"

Oddly, she didn't sound disgusted by that possibility. "Your curiosity makes sense," I noted, forcing myself to fall back into logic and reasoning. I was spiraling out of control, and she was far too breakable. "While the *egg* is more like an external amniotic sac, we honestly have no idea what would result in dragons born from a wolf shifter. There's no precedence for it. It's been a long time since there was any of our kind to know, and we were both born from two dragons."

A bitter tinge edged out the sweetness of her scent. "You don't even know if I can carry a dragon baby, do you?"

A truth I couldn't deny, but it didn't matter. "If dragons die out with us, then that was fate's design," I reminded her. "It will be a life well lived."

Conversation faded as I leaned down, knowing that if I didn't *finally* taste her, I would spew enough fire to burn the city around us. Emme gasped once more, and the sound was absorbed by my lips pressing against her. My first kiss.

Our first kiss.

My dragon heat filled the apartment and Talon's surged as well, even as he backed up a step to give me this moment with Emme. When her lips parted under mine, her sweet taste filled my mouth, and with a roar of need I wrapped an arm around her waist to bring her closer to my height.

Hunger was an avalanche. I'd never been swept away by anything before.

But today my need crushed me.

As my tongue tangled with hers, I wanted to be closer. I needed more.

I wanted to *fucking devour* her.

I pressed her into the wall, her dress hiked up over her tights, and she gave herself into the kiss as she arched against me. Her scent and those small mewling sounds she made drove my beast insane.

Very quickly, I learned what she liked as I kissed her, what pressure of my lips had her scent spiking, and the way I could use my tongue to bring about a tremble in her limbs.

She was soaking through my pants as she rubbed against me, and I wasn't sure I'd ever be able to stop touching and tasting her. How I'd lived without Emme was beyond my understanding. Not even death could steal this bond.

"Slade," she cried, really arching into me. My dick throbbed in my pants, and all I could think about was slamming into her, claiming and possessing. "I thought you said you hadn't done that before."

"I haven't," I said, licking up her throat, my jaw aching as I fought the urge to bite her.

*Not yet.*

Her pulse beat hard and fast under my touch, reminding me how delicate and soft she was.

Anyone who wanted to hurt her would have to go through me. I'd tear them into so many pieces that not even DNA would identify them.

Dropping her head back, she breathed out a reverent sound. "If this is you without experience, I might not survive experienced Slade."

It was all instinct. "Experience isn't important when my soul knows you better than I know myself."

Her sob was ragged as I dragged my tongue and teeth across her jaw. "Slade, please," she begged, and the rush of fucking power I felt wasn't safe when dragons craved that above all else.

"Patience, Snow. Not even if the witches were standing outside our fucking door would I rush this moment."

Her eyes rolled back in her head; small cries and moans spilled from her lips. She moved with wild abandon in my embrace, chasing her pleasure, and I had to admit that she was more than strong enough to survive this bonding. She'd been strong enough all along.

I would finally claim my mate.

By the time I set her on her feet, her pupils were blown out, and her legs buckled under her. I kept hold of her until she pulled herself together.

"That was..." She shook her head. "Honestly, I don't have words to describe it, but high fucking five on a perfect first kiss."

The flushed pink in her cheeks slowly dripped down her throat and under the neckline of her dress. "Take it off," I ordered, my gaze dragging along her body. "I want to see my mate. *Mine*." The last word was guttural and all dragon.

Emme's eyes widened, but she didn't argue, slowly lifting the blue dress to reveal a black bra beneath. "Good girl," I murmured, and was rewarded with more pink tinting the exposed skin on her arms and chest.

As her body shuddered, she closed her eyes. "You're going to control everything that happens here today, aren't you."

It wasn't a question. *She knew me.*

Despite the brief time we'd truly been in each other's lives, Emme had seen the real essence of who I was, and she was well aware of the beast and our needs.

"Will you fight my control, little one?" I asked. "You should be well aware that you're the sole reason for my existence. I will deny you nothing. But my beast is all instinct in this claiming."

The blue of her eyes was piercing, and she didn't flinch away from my gaze. "No," she said, her expression filled with a dozen emotions, but none of them fear. "I will not fight you, Slade Riverson. I want your control, because I know it won't be for your gain. It will be for mine."

Ah, my clever omega. "Always, sweetheart. *Your* pleasure. *Your* needs. *Your* release. Your desires are what makes me happy, and even more, knowing I'm the one to fulfill them."

"And me," Talon added, a hint of amusement in his dry tone. "My dragon likes control too, but thankfully not as strongly as Slade's. Otherwise, we'd be in trouble here."

Emme looked between the both of us. "Should we— is it better to do this apart? I don't want…" She broke off again, as if searching for the right words. "I don't want to take away from this moment with either of you by doing this together to save time."

Until I met my twin, there would be none I'd have shared this moment with. Not even Hunter.

It wasn't in my nature.

I was too dominant, and would be a danger to any who touched my mate during my time to claim her. But Talon was different. He was the other half to my soul, and our beasts knew we needed to do this together.

"Together," Talon confirmed, the word echoing through our mental bond.

A smile split Emme's face, and with it a sprinkle of nerves, but she didn't back away.

"We will do this together, and it has nothing to do with the witches," I told her, needing to set her mind at ease. She hadn't said anything, but I knew the way she thought. "I would be claiming you today, curse or no curse, Snow."

She choked back a happy sob, and I wrapped her up in my arms once more.

My dragon needed his mate, and so did I.

Emmeline would be ours today in all ways, and nothing would fucking stop us.

# CHAPTER 6

EMME

With its acres of black and white marble, huge living and kitchen, and floor-to-ceiling windows that showcased half of Golden Claw, Slade's apartment was the epitome of money and class. But the awe I'd felt stepping through that entrance had nothing on the moment he finally kissed me.

*Our first kiss.* I'd waited a long time to have him lose control and devour me with the same desperate need I felt for him, and it was well worth the wait.

The dragon shifter was huge everywhere.

His scent and energy poured through me until the tethers of my existence rearranged to connect with him. There was no evidence of his touch aversion, and absolutely no evidence that he'd never kissed anyone before.

On slightly wobbly knees, my panties and tights soaked from *one fucking kiss*, I let him lead me deeper into the apartment. A space already laced in the scents of chocolate, honey, marshmallow, and maple.

The heat of their internal fires warmed the rooms, despite the clear evidence of no one being here for a long time. A layer of dust permeated the air and furniture, but as Slade passed through each area, he swept up every speck. Goosebumps covered my skin as his power caressed me, and I knew I'd just experienced the closest thing to magic a regular shifter would get.

"That's why no one cleans your room," I said, blinking at the now spotless surfaces.

Slade shot a slow, amused smile over his shoulder. "Exactly, mate. I don't need anyone in our space."

Our. Space.

"I—" I was a damn stuttering mess around this shifter. "I don't understand."

I mean, I did understand what that meant, but I desperately needed him to explain.

His hand landed on the back of my neck again, in a firm, possessive hold, and I almost melted under his commanding presence. "My territory is open for you and Talon only. The rest of our pack knows to wait for permission, but neither of you need to ever ask. It's my nest, and since you're the other parts of my soul, it's also yours."

Talon's dragon let out a rather impressive growl, which Slade returned so rapidly that it had to be instinct. Just seeing the two of them together healed cracks in my heart that I hadn't even known were there.

This entire day was going to be healing. Talon had already bonded us through the bite, but we would reconfirm that today without any magical influence behind it. And Slade, the last holdout from my pack, would finally be mine.

It was overwhelming to know that our quintet would soon be completed.

There was also a slight sense of awkwardness, as I hadn't really planned my other bondings. They'd been more spontaneous.

"Let's start with a bath," Slade suggested, and I wondered if he could feel my tension.

It would explain why he chose one of my happy places to kick this all off.

He strode down a white-tiled hall, and I found myself wrapped in Talon's arms as we followed. My wolf whined, and I almost laughed at how badly we wanted to claim our final two mates, even if we were nervous as fuck.

We passed multiple bedrooms until we reached one so large it had to be the main. Unlike Slade's room in our house, there was no computer equipment in here. All it held was a bed large enough to be two kings pushed together, decked out in black satin bedding.

The bank of windows were unadorned by curtains, showcasing the world below. We were high enough that no one else could see us up here, which gave the illusion that no one else existed.

Slade didn't pause at the view, continuing into the ensuite bathroom. The bedroom carpet was plush under my boots, and the fact that I was only half-dressed hadn't really registered until I noticed my shoes. These alphas frazzled me in a way I had no experience with, and no skills to overcome. Maybe I never would learn how to function around them, but there were worse things than being frazzled by the beauty, power, and strength of your mates.

Talon's combat boots clanked on the tiles, but none of us left any dirt in our wake, as the dragons continued to clean as they moved. The lighting adjusted under their command, and they wisely chose just enough illumination for ambience without being overly bright.

Slade's bathroom was a designer's dream of black marble, with lightning strikes of grey, white, and gold through the veins. It was half the size of the bedroom and had what looked like a small wading pool at one end. If that was the bath, it would take a week just to fill it.

Slade hit a button and adjusted the temperature as water fell from two large faucets and the ceiling. *Okay, maybe not a week after all.*

When he was finished with the bath, he gave me his full focus, and I swallowed roughly as intensity pulsed in the air. Talon pressed into my spine, his arms wrapped around me in a firm but not overpowering hold. The dragons were always careful with their strength around me, even as I felt the barely leashed power behind their grip.

I'd also seen Slade crush a skull with his bare hands.

The same hands which were about to touch me in a completely different way. He reached out and brushed his fingers across my shoulders, slipping the bra straps down until the full swell of my breasts came into view.

Talon's hand caressed my stomach, his lips lowering to press against my bare shoulder. Slade dropped his head as well to taste my skin, getting low enough to scrape the edge of my nipple, which shot tingles down to my core. "You taste sweet, Snow," he groaned, the rumble in his voice vibrating over my sensitive nerve endings.

"Like fucking heaven and damnation wrapped up in one pretty package," Talon breathed, lapping at the side of my throat.

My core throbbed with enough force to almost knock me down. There was no relief, not even when I squeezed my thighs tightly. I'd never felt this unhinged and desperate, as I fought my desire to claw their clothes off.

When a whimpering plea sprang from my lips, Slade chuckled, the sound one of dark satisfaction. "Patience, Omega. The journey is as important as the destination."

I couldn't argue, but this girl needed snacks for her journey.

Two huge snacks to be accurate.

My limbs were heavy, and felt beyond my control as the twins slowly, piece by piece, stripped the rest of my clothes from me. Talon might be letting Slade dictate the pace, but he was just as dominant in his own way.

They were hungry beasts too. Their teeth and tongues traced every piece of skin they exposed. I'd never been stripped so slowly and thoroughly in my life. By the time I stood naked before them, I was panting and my body thrummed and ached. The low lights in here highlighted the gleaming paths they'd traced over my skin, and none of us could miss the arousal slipping down my thighs.

Neither of them had touched me anywhere too intimate yet, but they were getting closer to my core, and I was a hot, needy, dripping mess.

"This is the type of torture that I crave and despise," I cried, my legs shaking under me. I dug my nails into my palms until I drew blood, but it didn't remotely squash the roaring need. "I'm dying here."

Slade's growl was a loud snap with bathroom acoustics. "You're not dying today or any day. Everyone else in the world will be dead first."

"Agreed," Talon bit out. "We should just kill them all first to ensure her safety."

Ah, my psychopathic dragon shifters. Their version of love was terrifying and *exhilarating*.

Murder plans were put on hold when Slade pulled off his shirt, and then when Talon joined him I was a goner, mesmerized and obsessed. The need to touch them just about floored me.

My gaze took in their massive, bronze chests, and the only differences were the piercings and the tattoos on Slade—

"Wait," I whispered, stepping closer. "You added to your tattoo?"

Between the two raging beasts, where only darkness had existed, was now a glowing white wolf. *My wolf?*

I reached out to touch it, before jerking my hand away as a force of habit. Slade captured my fingers though, slamming our joined palms against his hard, burning chest. Right on the wolf.

"I didn't add to it. You appeared after my first joining in the twin bond."

*Me. Between my mates.*

"This is goddess blessed," I choked out, feeling elated and off-kilter all at the same time.

Slade gaze was filled with green flames. "Yes, Snow. You were always the third piece of us. The rest of our pack is a bonus, but the three of us were meant to be as one.

That statement felt right in a way that very little in my life ever had. Since my hand was already on his chest, I moved it tentatively, unsure if he'd allow me to explore him. "This is okay, right?" I asked, wanting to give him the choice.

"More than okay," he replied, in that same deep rasp. "You never have to ask permission to touch me, mate."

That burn was back behind my eyes, my heart filled with as much heat, but I managed to keep it together as I explored the dragons depicted on his body. With each touch, a shudder rocked through Slade, followed by a low groan when I caressed the tiny white wolf that lit up the darkness between brothers.

My own beast preened inside me, proud to be represented on her mate's skin. To be the light between the shadowy twin dragons, was intense and overwhelming.

When I moved on, I grazed the silver piercings in his nipples and was reminded that he enjoyed pain with his pleasure. My touch turned firmer, and I pulled against the bars, cataloguing every flare of his nostrils and spike in his scent. All the while those otherworldly green eyes bored into me.

Not wanting to leave Talon out, I shifted my stance and placed a hand on each of them, greedily lapping up their full attention. Even locked-in predatory gazes didn't deter me, and I only grew more confident with each touch.

Slade canted his head to take me in, and as his focus draped over my bare skin, I was reminded that they'd already stripped me completely naked, while they still wore pants and boots.

Which felt decidedly unfair.

Sliding my palms lower, I managed to get the button on Slade's pants undone easily—he was on my right and dominant hand side. Talon took a little longer, but neither of them hurried me. Eventually his button popped too, and with each fork of the zipper lowering, I felt a reciprocating pulse in my core.

*Fuck. Me.*

The goddess had outdone herself in the creation of these two. All of the alphas in my pack really.

The heavy lengths of their cocks emerged from their pants like weapons of destruction finally freed to play. When I wrapped my palm around each shaft, I had a very real moment when I wondered if maybe I was in over my head.

They were long and straight, with not a single curve along their length, and when I attempted to close my fingers around the girth, I wasn't even close. "Snow," Slade breathed, his eyes slitted as he watched me.

It wasn't a question or a warning, just a sigh of my name, so I continued to explore.

They were so hard their skin appeared stretched almost beyond capacity, the thick heads a deeper red than the rest, and they were both leaking pearlescent beads of pre-cum.

The need to taste them was intense, but I wasn't quite finished exploring. This had been a long time coming for me, and I wouldn't rush the moment.

The underside of Slade's cock was pierced, and while I'd guesstimated the number of bars the first time I caught a glance, today I could count them one by one.

*Seven.* Spanning from tip to root.

The metal was hot to touch, and I shivered at the thought of not only taking his intimidating length and width, but all of those piercings too. It felt impossible, but I was willing to give it a red hot try. Emphasis on the hot.

"Can I taste you?" I asked, glancing up from under my lashes, both hands overflowing with them. "Please, Alphas."

I rarely used that title with my pack, but I already knew Slade craved my submission. Similar to Hunter, but also in his own, dominant ways.

Talon enjoyed it too, even with his more tempered strength. "Yes. Fuck yes, Sweet Honey."

Slade was slower to respond, as he reached out and grasped my chin, tilting my head back until I was helplessly held in his thrall. "Make sure you use teeth," he ordered, and as he freed me, air rushed back into my lungs with force.

A whimper escaped me, and I managed to dial it back before I fully embarrassed myself. But… *holy shit…*

# CHAPTER 7

EMME

As I stared between the twins, instinct told me it would be a mistake to start with Talon.

Slade's nostrils flared as he watched me watch his brother.

"You're more dominant than Talon," I noted, still stroking my hands along the velvet steel of both alphas.

Slade grunted, and *holy alpha response* that was hot. "Yes, I was the first pulled from the egg. I'm the oldest by our laws."

Talon groaned and dropped his head back until all I could see was the thick, powerful muscles moving in his throat. "Slade is the only one I will concede dominance to. Hunter gets it by proxy, which I accept as I don't want the political role."

Just like his brother.

Slade and Talon fell silent, and neither of them pushed me, seemingly content with my slow exploration. The bath continued to fill behind us, and I was suddenly very happy at how huge it was. We needed this time.

Leaning down, I ran my tongue over the moisture beading at the end of Slade's length, groaning as his sweet and smoky flavor coated my tongue. My wolf howled as I started to claim the final of our quintet.

We were filled with instinct built of our race, and I was lost to the sensations as I stroked Talon with one hand, while tasting Slade.

Relaxing my jaw, I attempted to take as much of him as I could, which turned out to not be much at all. Okay, new training was needed on jaw dexterity *stat*.

All this time I'd thought running would be the exercise to take me out, but it looked more likely it was going to be dragon dick. *Oh, how terrible.*

"I know Hunter has already spoken to you about this." Slade's half-lidded stare scorched into me. "But *red* is your safe word if you want us to stop. Don't forget to use it, Snow. I might not have experience, but I know my need for control and dominance can be overwhelming. I want you to know you're safe with me."

*Red.* I doubted I'd ever use it, but it was a good reminder.

"Nod for me," Slade bit out, his jaw tensing as I took him deeper. "Show me that you heard and understand your safe word."

I was nodding enthusiastically before he even finished, which got a grunt of satisfaction from them both. Relaxing, I shifted my angle and slid my tongue along the first two piercings, groaning at the smooth, heated texture in my mouth. Slade's hands fisted in my hair as he thrust deeper, taking control, until I was gasping for air between each push. Saliva spilled from the corners of my lips and my eyes watered, but I fucking loved every second of it.

A satisfied smile filled the dragon's face. "Such a pretty omega," he crooned. "Mouth full of my cock, while your hand strokes my twin. But I think you can take more of us, Snow."

There was legitimately no way that was true, but in the spirit of insanity I gave it my all.

When my grip firmed up, a deep rasp echoed from Talon, filling the tiled room. At the same time, I let my teeth scrape over the underside of Slade's shaft, metal clanking with each movement. The odds of chipping a tooth were high, but there was a higher chance I'd choke to death first.

Slade's chest rumbled as I pressed my teeth into him, and with each thrust, pre-cum and spit ran down my chin. His eyes were glowing orbs of green, and my fingers stilled against Talon, nails digging in as I held on for life. He didn't pull away, so he was either panicking or into it.

Either way, I was being mouth-fucked by a monster cock and trying not to choke to death on it.

My core throbbed as Slade thrust until stars danced along the sides of my vision. My thighs trembled like I was about to orgasm just from the taste and force of the dragon, and when he slowed, I eagerly slid my tongue over the tip.

I released Talon in time for Slade to lift me into his arms, his mouth crashing against mine in another one of those dominant kisses. "I will never have enough of you," he growled in a deep bass. "Never e-fucking-nough of you. My obsession grows daily, with no limit in sight."

*Have mercy on me.* All the times I'd fantasized about Slade losing control and sealing our bond had nothing on the moment itself.

With one last kiss, Slade handed me to his twin, who took his turn to taste my lips as well. Talon's touch was slightly softer, but no less dominant or consuming. As he pressed kiss after kiss to my lips, our tongues tangling together in desperate need, he carried me over to the bath.

Slade turned off the taps, leaving only the waterfall shower falling softly to the steaming surface. When he shucked off his pants and boots, standing in all of his naked glory, thick, muscled thighs visible beneath his jutting cock, I inhaled audibly.

Talon chuckled as I gawked like this was my first day seeing a naked male. "We will never get sick of you looking at us like that."

He set me on my feet, and in seconds he was naked too, and I was *so screwed.*

They both pressed into me until I was the filling in a dragon shifter sandwich. In sync, they grasped my biceps and waist, lifting me into the bath. The water wasn't as hot as the dragons themselves, and I sighed at the soothing sensation of it wrapping around my calves and thighs.

When I sank into the smooth seat carved into the side, the water lapped at my chin, and the twins followed me in, muscles flexing and holding my focus until they disappeared under the water.

Was there a possibility that dragon shifters had extra muscles compared to regular shifters?

As they took the seats on either side of me, their long limbs fitted with ease, and the sheer size of this bath made much more sense.

"Relax," Slade ordered, and like I was born to obey him, I found myself sinking deeper into the heat.

He reached for a scrub cloth that he then liberally doused with a sweet and smoky bodywash. The scent reminded me of both dragons.

"I don't want to lose her scent," Talon complained, reaching out as if to stop his brother.

Slade ignored his outstretched hand as he stroked the cloth over my chest. "You won't," he assured him. "Her scent will only grow stronger when mixed with ours."

I'd been through this before with the alphas and knew he was right.

Talon decided not to argue as he leaned down and breathed against my throat. "I love scenting you on me. On us."

"What—?" I breathed deeply to get myself under control, which was an impossible task with an alpha washing my skin, his hands slowly tracing over the scar on my back. None of my pack appeared to care that I wasn't perfect like most shifters, instead treating my flaw like a warrior's trophy. It made me think of it in a similar way.

I'd survived. More that survived, I'd found true happiness.

Or more accurately, it had found me.

Talon dipped my head back before he started to wash my hair, and when his strong fingers massaged my scalp, I was groaning again. "What do you think... think will happen once we complete the quintet?" Words were hard around these two.

Talon's chuckle was deep and rumbly, adding to the orgasmic sensations tingling through my body. "This is my new favorite version of you, mate. Raw, needy, and overwhelmed by us."

Slade released a grunt of agreement, his hands moving beneath the water as he washed my tits, my nipples aching with each caress. "Once we're bonded, I believe the full potential of our power and beasts will be unleashed. A stronger connection, increased power and strength, closeness between our beasts, and... possibly the ability to mentally communicate."

"You've thought about this a lot," I noted, breathing embarrassingly heavy as he stroked the cloth lower. Talon pulled me back against his chest as he rinsed out my hair using the water falling from the showerhead. "I wonder if the magical side of my essence will add another dimension."

Slade answered so quickly, I knew he'd already considered all possibilities of magical interference. "Yes, there's no doubt it will. Everything that would normally happen will most likely be amplified with magic. This is a first-of-its-kind bonding when you take into account that there's six in our quintet, it's an all alpha pack with an omega, and then we have magic. There's no way to accurately guess at the results."

His words were important, but at the same time the cloth hit my thighs and his fingers brushed over my clit. I lurched as white noise filled my head, every cell in my body turned on. I would hazard a guess that if one of my alphas even breathed on me in the right way, I'd orgasm into next week.

When my hair and body were thoroughly washed, I was moved fully under the rainfall showerhead once more, and they both held me as I closed my eyes and let the stream coat us.

Ever since I'd been dragged kicking and screaming into this world, the Reeves pack had cared for me. Thoroughly. Unconditionally. Without any expectations in return.

It was so much more than I deserved, but I was too greedy to ever share it.

Slade kissed the side of my throat, disrupting the tears threatening to fall. "Clean and relaxed," he murmured between kisses. "And now it's time for us to get you worked up and dirty."

*Yes. Please.*

My lower half clenched on nothing, and the ache of emptiness nearly drove me insane. Thank the goddess I was only minutes away from being filled and sated. There was no way these two, even as virgins, weren't about to fuck me within an inch of my life.

I might not be able to predict what our full bond would result in, but I could predict the path that would get us there.

# CHAPTER 8

EMME

The bed in this apartment was bordering on obscene, from the size, to the comfort, to the feel of expensive sheets. Bedding fit for the last two dragon shifters in existence.

After the bath, I'd been thoroughly dried with the sort of tender care and attention to detail that I associate only with *my* alphas. The nerves had been mostly kept at bay by the throbbing need driving me crazy, but now that I was sprawled across the bed, with two sexy and naked males staring down at me, a shot of tension had me clutching the black sheets on either side of me.

Slade's expression was shadowed and unreadable, but the rumble rocking his huge chest remained familiar. "You want us, but you're not quite ready."

"I'm ready," I protested. "I want you both. Today."

Not even Slade could pick up hesitation in that statement. Still, he watched me in a way that indicated he saw the few nerves. "It's normal to feel nervous the first time you sleep with someone."

Talon rasped out a noise that sounded like agreement, and Slade gave a single bob of his head. "If you care about someone, you should be afraid to touch them the first time," he said, as if the thought just occurred to him.

I blinked, pushing myself up with my elbows so I wasn't completely flat on my back. "What do you mean?"

Slade placed one knee on the bed and my stomach jumped like I'd been thrown off a cliff. He was just so big everywhere, and the intimidating length between his thighs hadn't softened even a fraction. I'd heard the phrase *dick drunk* before, and I finally understood what the authors were talking about—I could not look away, think straight, or function in any way around my naked mates.

I barely comprehended his next words. "You fear screwing it up, and touch is so intimate." When he reached me, Slade hovered his hand just over the top of my skin. "My touch aversion stole a lot from me," he said, giving me the animalistic tilt to his head as he studied me.

"You wish you pushed yourself to touch more before me?" I asked, and yeah, I was being *that* chick. But it was so new having his attention in this way, and I wanted the reassurance.

I wanted everything from him.

His snarl ripped through the room. "Only with you, Emmeline. No other will ever feel the press of my touch. No other will ever know me as you do. There's been none before you, and none after. *Just you.*"

As hypocritical as it made me, since I hadn't come to Slade a virgin, I was innately pleased by that statement. "I wish I waited for you, but from the moment I stepped foot in this city, there's been no one for me other than our pack."

Talon slid in on my other side, his hands tracing through the damp strands of my hair. "We would kill any who even tried," he said simply.

When he tilted my head back, his kiss was deep and slow. My fingers relaxed against the bed, and I moaned into him as Slade's hot mouth closed over my nipple. This was torturous and delicious.

Both of them released almost identical sounds of rumbling need. When I attempted to lift my arms, wanting to anchor myself to the twins, my wrists were secured above my head in Talon's grip. He wasn't hurting me, but I could feel the unyielding strength of his hold, and knew it wouldn't be easy to break free.

"Slade needs to be in control," he breathed against my lips, sliding his tongue deeper as his thumb brushed over my wrist.

As I writhed, my mind consumed with the sensations flooding me, it took a beat to remember they could mentally communicate. "I never said you two could gang up on me," I choked out, my hips arching as Slade pressed kisses along my stomach, his tongue tasting me on the way.

Talon's laugh was a deep, delicious sound that only added to the stimulation wreaking havoc on my body. When Slade slipped between my thighs and inhaled deeply, Talon shifted down to glide my right nipple into his mouth, still holding my hands captive.

Slade slid his tongue slowly through my core, before he groaned and buried his face, devouring, as contented rumbles filled the room. He took his time exploring, and I knew he was cataloguing every time I reacted to what he did, learning and adapting. *Fuck.* This alpha was a quick study, and he had me quivering in his hold so fast it was like fantasy come to life.

When he pressed a finger inside me, stretching me just with that one touch, I cried out, and his growled response sent vibrations into my clit. An orgasm ripped through me, and I near bowed off the bed at the force of it, my choked cry splitting the room.

My reaction appeared to even shock the alphas as they stilled. "Holy goddess," I gasped, my body throbbing and oversensitive. "Sorry, that kind of came out of nowhere."

"Never apologize for your pleasure," Slade said, and could dragons purr? Because he sounded pleased as fuck. "You just squirted all over me, and I'm only annoyed that I couldn't keep all of that delicious release in my mouth." He dropped his head and ran his tongue over me, before plunging it inside, over and over, until I was about to scream again.

Rocking against him once more, I was breathless. "There'll be plenty more where that came from. If... if my past experience is any indication, there's—oh fuck... there's no shortage of orgasms to go around..."

"We will win," Slade said, his confidence filling the massive room. "I love my brothers, but they have nothing on dragons. We will destroy your concept of how many orgasms your body can sustain and still want more."

I was going to die. The most perfect, wonderful death.

He slid his finger from my clit to my ass, and I could *hear* how soaked I was. Slade's face was a picture of satisfaction as he lifted that hand toward me. "Taste yourself, Snow."

Hunter had me well versed in enjoying my own release. I was never surprised those two were raised together. Opening my mouth, I savored the mix of Slade and me.

Talon growled. "I want to taste her too."

Slade shifted back just enough for Talon to slide the hand not holding me captive between my thighs. The scrape of his fingers elicited more moans from me. His hand glistened as lifted it to his mouth, his tongue darting out to catch my release before it fell. "Fucking delicious," he groaned. "I could live on your cunt, Sweet Honey. I wouldn't need anything else."

My breaths turned rapid and uneven, and I was about to demand he prove that statement, when Slade lowered his head again. His tongue moved faster this time; he thrust two fingers inside me, hurtling me into two more screaming orgasms before he conceded his spot to Talon.

Slade captured my hands while Talon descended. Talon was more animalistic in his approach, opening his mouth and roughly sucking my clit inside.

"Oh, my, fucking shifter," I cried, needing to claw at something, but I couldn't. "I'm so sensitive," I sobbed. "I don't think I can take much more of this."

"You can and you will," Slade ordered, his tone filled with command.

He leaned down and he kissed me, until all I could taste was us, so sweet and musky. Another release tore through me as Talon lapped at my fucking pussy like it was his full-time job.

"How are you both so good at this?" I whispered weakly, collapsing in a heap, wrung out and oversensitive. "If I didn't know you both, I'd suspect you lied to me about your experience." Or lack thereof.

Slade's grunt was a warning, and I took his advice and shut up. He despised liars, and I wasn't really accusing him of anything, but shutting up was still the way to go.

"One more until she's ready for us," Slade said to his twin, and as Talon slid his hands under my ass to lift me higher, I caught a glimpse of his anticipation filled expression. The dragon was about to feast.

*Wait, ready?* This was all to get me ready for sex? I was about to be ready to pass out or die, but at least I'd go as one satisfied shifter.

Talon took that challenge seriously, his teeth pressing against my aching clit.

Slade growled. "Come for us."

My thighs shook, and a release ripped from deep in my spine. Darkness closed in on me so rapidly that I might have actually lost consciousness for a few seconds. My brain came back online when I was lifted and turned onto my stomach. Slade's scent was strong behind me, and Talon resituated himself to my front.

"I will claim you as we did in the past," Slade murmured, pressing his hand against my back and tracing a fiery path until he reached my ass. "You will submit to me, Omega. You will submit and accept my claim."

My core clenched, the ache of emptiness surprising after so many orgasms.

When Slade ordered me to submit in that deep, raspy tone, I would have done whatever he said. *Yes, sir. No, sir. Fuck me in the ass, sir.*

"Emmeline," he called, more bite in his tone. "Will you submit?"

Trembles racked my body, my limbs were heavy, but there was only one correct response here: "I will submit to your claim, Alpha."

He'd proven many times that I held the power everywhere else but in the bedroom.

I had what no one else in the world did—I was his exception.

He could be the ruler here, especially when my reward came with a fuck-ton of orgasms.

"I'm going to last approximately five seconds once I get inside her," Talon moaned with a shake of his head, his pupils blown as he focused on his brother and me.

Slade slid his hands down my ass and parted me slowly until he reached my pussy. The burning tip of him entered me and I cried out, having no idea if I'd actually be able to take all of him. The goddess didn't make mistakes with mate bonds, but at the same time, it felt near impossible.

"Relax, sweetheart," Slade whispered as he pushed through the tight muscles, both of our groans guttural and fractured. "You feel so much better than I imagined."

I shuddered when his first piercing entered me, the bar hot and hard, and as he thrust again, another one followed, and then another. It felt like that piece of steel glided over a million pleasure points with each movement. I'd never experienced anything this intense in my life. There were bites of pain with the pleasure, as his sheer size took time to adjust around, but I knew I was going to come before he even got fully seated.

When I attempted to back against him, his big hand kept me in place. "Stay where you are, sweetheart," he ordered, though his tone was soft and coaxing. "You're taking me so well, mate."

On the cusp of his praise, he thrust harder, sliding another inch and another piercing inside me. I couldn't breathe as the sensation of *too much* filled me. *Too full.* The metal scraped along the overwhelming fullness until I was going to explode.

As predicted, his next thrust sent me screaming into the sheets, and there was a real possibility of suffocation as I lost control. At least there was a possibility until Slade used his impressive strength to haul me higher, and *finally* buried his full length inside me, so deep I swore I could taste him in my mouth. Ashy sweetness.

When I clenched around him, he muttered a string of words in a language I didn't understand, but Talon nodded as if he knew exactly what was said. Slade moved slow at first, seeming to know how much my body could handle before it broke. He kept me right on the edge of release with those slow, firm strokes.

Release hovered so close; tears slipped down my cheeks in my desperation. A part of me was tempted to use my safe word just to escape the torture of being edged by this magnificent asshole. Only I knew it wasn't designed for that, and I wouldn't abuse the safety net.

I also semi-loved being edged, knowing that the release was going to be so satisfyingly glorious.

The pleasure built as a deep, raw ache in my core, and my clit throbbing so hard that I'd only have to graze it to send me over the edge. "Are you ready to be claimed, mate?" Slade murmured, his movements really drawn out now.

I nodded and moaned, completely fucking ruined. I'd never felt like this before, unhinged and desperate, unsure how much more I could handle.

But I didn't want him to stop.

I never wanted him to stop.

As the cresting wave of my release hovered, Slade was barely moving, and I wondered if I could partially shift and stab him with my wolf claws.

His chuckle was low and pleased. "I can feel your fury, Snow. I like that rage. Give me more."

He pulled out of me completely and I almost screamed at the loss. When he lifted me onto my back, he slid his hands under my ass and angled me so he could thrust inside in one rugged movement.

"Fuck me, mate," I demanded, and his eyes darkened as he stilled once more. "Please," I quickly added. "Please claim me until I can't remember my name."

Pacified slightly, he crowded over the top of me, until all I could see was his chest. Throwing my head back, I met his piercing green eyes and my existence unraveled and reformed around this shifter.

As he moved faster, I dug my nails into his shoulders and he huffed out a smoke-scented groan. The delicious expanse of his strong throat captivated me. I wasn't sure how much longer I could hold out not biting him. My gums and jaw ached as the essence of my wolf and his dragon danced between us.

"Please," I begged again. "I will do whatever you say, Alpha. Please claim me." Instinct had me arching up into him to add, "Please, sir."

His pupils flared, and his pace increased until he was driving into me, both of us desperate for the claim. Pressing my nails deeper, I scented his blood, and the bite of pain was enough for him to jerk against me.

When he groaned, the sound sent me hurtling off the cliff. I came so hard my release drenched our thighs. Slade roared my name as his jaw elongated, the dragon blooming with his impending release. I tilted my head back to give him free access and his bite landed on top of my shoulder, beside Hunter's and above Talon's.

I immediately knew it was the deepest of all the bites, the pain leaving me breathless, but it was quickly followed by pleasure as another orgasm took me under.

In the throes of this, my wolf knew what to do, as we partially shifted to bite our mate back. As we did, sealing the last of the quintet, our beasts rose up together.

Only it was more than just our beasts—it was all of our quintet as one.

In the strands I felt the dominance of Hunter, the calm stability of Finley, and the exuberance of Kellan. Along with Talon's steadfast lethality.

Our quintet. *Finally as one.*

With that thought, everything went dark.

# CHAPTER 9

EMME

Rumbling voices roused me, and disorientation lasted a brief second, before I scented my mates and remembered exactly what had happened. *We formed a complete quintet.*

The perfect circle of shifter power was sealed, and I'd been so overwhelmed by that *and all the damn orgasms* that I'd passed out cold. My eyes fluttered open as I heard a growl in my mind followed by, *Little mate, are you okay?*

My brain froze, and as I fought panic, I tried to figure out why there was a voice in my head.

*Little mate?*

*Wait.* Not just any voice, but one I knew well. *Hunter Reeves was in my freaking head.*

*Ah…* I tried to direct a thought toward him through my panic. *I think so. Are we really communicating like this?*

There was a brief pause, and I swore I could feel relief wafting from the entitled alpha, though he was clear across town. *Yes. I think this is part of our bond now. The power surge almost knocked us out, and Slade said you were unconscious.*

Focusing on my surroundings, I found Slade and Talon standing over me on the side of the bed, staring down with confused and worried expressions. "Snow," Slade breathed, and I wasn't sure I'd ever seen any form of panic on his face until today. "Thank the fucking goddess. Are you okay?"

Talon reached out for me, running his hands through my hair, soothing my aching brain. "We've got you, sweetness. We won't let you go."

*Emmeline,* Hunter said, his voice filtering in once more. *Can you hear me?*

I shook my head, trying to deal with the internal and external conversations happening at the same time. *I'm okay. But we need to figure out this mind-speak. It's making me dizzy.*

His essence retreated a fraction, and as I focused internally, I realized that I could see all of our beasts. In my fucking mind.

They were gathered together, my wolf center of the pack. Hunter's beast started to retreat step by step, revealing more of Finley's bear and Kellan's wolf.

With that, they poured themselves into the bond.

*Pretty mate, you had us worried.*

*Do you need us there, darlin'? Just say the word.*

My stomach swirled, and I lurched to the side of the bed and vomited through the pounding in my head. From the corner of my eye, Slade disappeared from view, only to return with his phone in hand.

"Get out of her head," he snarled down the line to someone. "You're hurting her, and until we figure out how this mind-speak works, try to keep your essences to yourself."

The other beasts all backed away until my wolf stood alone, and it was then I noticed a shimmering boundary around us. Leaving me in the center. *Me as the heart.*

As the alphas distanced themselves, I was left with relief and distress at losing their energy. But my stomach did stop swirling, and the pounding in my head eased as I sucked in deep breaths. My wolf moved restlessly, and I urged her to step over the shimmering boundary toward Slade, deciding to test a theory.

*Can you hear me?* I asked him, and in our quintet, his dragon lowered its head to caress my wolf. There were thick strands of energy that connected him to Talon, but at the same time, they were their own entities. Two sides of the same coin.

*Yes, I can hear and feel you.*

When I backed away, the flow of his energy eased, and I knew it'd take some practice, but I already got the sense of how this connection and mind-speak would work. "I can feel you all," I said out loud. "And I think as long as your beasts don't rush my wolf at once, I won't be vomiting all over the place."

"It was too much," Slade agreed. "And while it appears you are the one who can control the connection, I could push through your barrier if I wanted to. Not that any of us would force that on you."

With a wave of his hand, the vomit disappeared, and I collapsed back on the bed, filled with mixed emotions. I brushed my fingers over the new mark on my shoulder, which already felt completely healed. The fastest one yet. I attribute that to the bristling strength of my beast as she stood with her pack. Any weaknesses I'd fostered growing up outside the cities and unable to shift regularly, were gone in the face of a complete quintet.

"Are you okay?" Talon asked as he helped me into a sitting position, supporting me against his firm side.

"I think so," I murmured, still feeling like my rattled brain hadn't quite settled.

Slade stepped in between my legs, and it was impossible not to notice that he remained naked and semi-hard. Or was that how his dick always looked?

Wouldn't put it past him… A shower *and* a grower.

"Come back to us, Emmeline," he said gruffly. "We're not pushing in your head, but we are worried."

"I'm fine," I repeated. "I feel stronger and more *whole* with the quintet sealed. It was just overwhelming to have all the power and voices in my head at once."

Slade lifted his hand and brushed down my cheek. "Your essence is definitely stronger, your beast too." He leaned closer. "That bonding was beyond my wildest expectations." His lips brushed over my cheek, and the casual touches had me wanting to curl up and sigh. "My dragon is urging me to capture you in our den and never let you leave. Fair warning."

As he pulled away, my eyes locked on the bite I'd left on his shoulder. The only scar on his bronze skin. *My bite.*

Possessiveness rolled through me like a shiver down my spine. As if he'd felt that sensation, Slade's eyes darkened, and he brushed over his bite—the largest of the five I wore.

"You're staring with a Talon-like intensity," I whispered.

Talon laughed, completely at ease with my assessment, and Slade bestowed his famous lip twitch on me. "You have no idea," he murmured. "No fucking idea how closely I've watched you. Pretty much from the second you were dragged into our world. And now… now I can feel you in my essence. I can track you with my beast. There's nowhere on Earth you could run that I wouldn't find you. You don't even need that jewelry, as there's a much larger, more vicious dragon around your throat." He grasped the necklace that I hadn't taken off since that track day.

His confessions might have been concerning if I wasn't as equally obsessed with my alphas. "I can find you too, Scary Shifter," I reminded him. "You're all mine."

I tilted my head back to meet an amused gaze staring down at me, and I found myself brushing my fingers over the scar on Talon's cheek. I hated the reasons for the scar, but I loved every part of this dragon. "You and I have some unfinished business, Tal."

His mirth faded under an inferno of heat, and the ravenous stare he bestowed on me had my thighs clenching. "You should probably rest," he ground out, and I could feel the strength it took for him to say that. Our new bond was allowing some of the alpha's thoughts and emotions to reach me, no doubt due to my lack of experience in knowing how to keep our beasts locked down.

Twisting in his hold, I hugged him closer. Or he let me, since there was no way I could move a mountain of dragon shifter against his will. "I feel better than I have in years," I said, scratching my nails over his short hair, which got a very purr-like rumble from him.

Turned out dragons could definitely purr. My big scary kitty beasts.

"I'm stronger and more capable than I was twenty minutes ago," I reminded him, "and I don't want to wait another second for us to seal the final strands of our bond."

Slade backed up a few steps from us, as if he was giving Talon and me our chance to really bond. I put my full focus into the newest, but no less important, member of my quintet.

"Hey," I whispered, running my finger over his scar again. His throat worked with each touch, and our gazes were locked. "I want you to know how happy I am that we made it here. We're stronger than ever, and this feels right."

"I love you," he choked out, and the depths of his feelings existed right there in his beautiful, broken expression.

"I love you," I said with force, and I shifted my wolf toward his beast, so he could really feel me as well.

Slade's scent blossomed at the exchanged words of love, and I wondered if he was thinking about the fact that *we* hadn't said those words to each other. I didn't even have to ask to know Slade had never said them to anyone, and even though I loved the stubborn bastard, I didn't want to force the declaration before he was ready. He showed me with his actions every day anyway.

"I love your strength and bravery," I continued, pressing my hand into Talon's face. "I love that you chose me. Without asking for anything in return."

"I'm still not a good shifter," he said, expression open and calm. "I'm an assassin at heart, built of the cold mentality of my race, but not for you. You're the best part of my life. *My reason for existence.* There's nothing I wouldn't do, and no one I wouldn't kill to keep you safe."

I kissed Talon so hard I almost knocked him back onto the bed. My joy at finally bonding surged through me, until I was exploding with happiness and desire.

Slade's heat moved farther from us, but I was too consumed to look his way. Talon sprawled back and lifted me on top of him. I spread my thighs to straddle him, but even on top he didn't let me take the lead or control the pace.

Gripping my hips, he slowly thrust, parting me with each slide of his hard length. I hadn't really had enough recovery time after Slade, but as Talon pushed deeper, my core pulsed and ached with intense pleasure.

Talon's pupils were slitted and dragon-like as he growled, "I understand why males go to war over their female." He lifted himself to capture my lips in an unhurried, intoxicating kiss, and all the while he slowly drove inside me. "They kill and die for just a taste of the heaven you offer to us."

His smoky scent blasted through the bedroom, mingling with mine and Slade's. The only way this could get better was if my other mates' scents were here as well.

Moans slipped from my lips as I trembled above him, the sparks of pleasure taking me over. I wasn't fully seated yet, having only managed to take about seventy-five percent of his length.

Talon's grip on my hips was firm; he held me in place as he controlled the pace. Like Slade, he took his time to learn what I liked and didn't, watching me closely and adjusting with each of my moans.

When my eyes fluttered, and my walls pulsed around him, his expression turned satisfied. Both of my dragons were fast learners.

The duality of intense pleasure teamed with the slight burn of being stretched too wide had me panting and seeing stars. Talon slid a hand down my front over my breasts, before he reached my clit. When his thumb moved over me gently, he thrust, and it was enough for me to finally slide down that last quarter to seat myself fully.

*Goddess above.* It was too much. It was everything. It was going to be my undoing.

My alphas would be the beginning and end of me, just as I'd always expected.

Talon took his time, but unlike Slade he didn't edge me. If his expression was any indication, he was barely holding on himself, and when my body tightened around him and I cried out, he drove himself deeper. Impossibly deep. This shifter was rearranging my internal organs, and I was here for it.

My first orgasm spilled into another and another until I shook and collapsed on his chest. Talon held me when I couldn't hold myself, thrusting up into me with the force of… well, a dragon. As the green in his eyes flashed brighter through the darkness, his dick swelled until I was about to burst. I cried out as he partially shifted and bit me again, reconfirming our bond.

My wolf pushed through my daze to shift our jaw, and with Talon attached to my shoulder, I latched on to him. We'd come a full circle, and the hate that surrounded us in that first bonding was now filled with love.

Slade rumbled from somewhere in the room, and when my wolf and Talon's dragon burst into my mind's essence, Slade's beast followed. For a split second in time, the three of us were as one. We were perfect.

Until everything changed.

That circle around my wolf exploded with a new power, one that had been hidden beneath us the entire time. As the icy slap of energy hit me and my beast, I managed to keep my eyes open long enough to see that I wasn't the only one to lose consciousness this time.

# CHAPTER 10

## HUNTER

I slowed my pacing to glare at the shifter-witch crowding my entryway.

"You know we only have until the next full moon to destroy the witch who cast the curse," Constantine said, his eyes manic as he wrung his hands. "We've already wasted near two full days."

This fucker stood in *my* house, wearing clothes provided by *me*, and then had the audacity to start demanding *we* take action. "You were the one who informed us that Emme wouldn't have access to her power without securing her quintet. We will not rush this for them. They deserve their time together, and if you try to interfere, I can promise you that two dragons will tear you to pieces before you even set foot in the apartment."

Not that I'd let this annoying asshole make it that far.

Pursing his lips, he ran a hand through his hair, which was clean now but still tangled. He'd also refused shoes, yapping on about how the Earth energy was absorbed better through his feet. Fucking witches.

Not that I should be harboring so much animosity toward their kind when my mate was a quarter. But she was the exception. The rest of them could burn for all I cared.

"Since we have time to kill, explain it all to me in detail," I said. "Everything you know about what Jewels did, and what will happen if this curse comes to pass."

He let his hands fall to his sides, breathing deeply before rough words spilled from him: "Everything I learned is from gossip, and a few of my own spells. It's not fact, but I think I've pieced most of it together." Since he was the only witch I'd found since the attack, his word would have to do.

"Jewels has been planning this for near two decades," he continued. "She bided her time, worked with Fletcher to destabilize the shifter community, built up the allies she needed for her plan to work, while she waited for the harvest blood moon. It's a powerful night for the Wiccans, and it's the reason she hasn't acted until now."

Hence why my former *and now dead* best friend showed up two nights ago. To kickstart her plan.

"So, she was waiting for the moon, building bonds with shifters—including my fucking pack—while cementing herself as an ally. She had Fletcher doing her dirty work in the background so he'd be the clear *bad guy*, and all the while she was moving everyone around like her own personal chess board… But not Emme?"

Constantine nodded, expression souring. "Yes, from what I've deduced, Emme was Fletcher's plan, not Jewels. She doesn't care about your mate. She had much bigger shifters to fry."

Apparently, an entire fucking world of them.

"Why did she target us, then? If it wasn't about Emme or our quintet?"

He shot me a look like he couldn't believe I'd asked such a stupid question, but I needed him to give me every damn detail so I'd never be taken by surprise like that again.

"As I already said, she needed a shifter connected to Fletcher's bloodline to end him. That was the only way she could not only void the binding alliance her witch line had with him, but the energy of his death would be strong enough to power her curse. Along with the moon of course. She was leaving nothing to chance."

"And this is such a strong, unbreakable curse, that the only way to stop it is to take Jewels out before it comes to pass. Since she's harboring it in her body."

He nodded, no hesitation.

"How does Emme unlocking her magic help us, then? From what I can tell, this really has very little to do with her. She was just in the wrong place at the wrong time when she got Fletcher's attention, who's dead now."

Constantine squeezed his eyes closed, and when he opened them, they were shiny. "Emme exists because I fucked up. I fell in love with a shifter—her mother. I didn't expect we could have a child. I was supposed to be an anomaly, a quirk in nature and genetics, never to be repeated again. When she fell pregnant, I had no choice but to leave, weakening myself to keep them both safe."

"Wouldn't it have been safer for you to stay and protect them both?" I suggested with a bite in my tone. The very thought of Emme not existing almost destroyed me, and more than that, the way she grew up alone was squarely on this asshole's shoulders.

His citrus scent turned bitter. "Emme and I were a beacon together, as our magic bounced off each other. Even though she wasn't in touch with that side of herself, it was there in her essence. At that stage, I didn't want to release her power, so I left. I broke Morgan's heart, and the best parts of her, since we were a scent match. She at least heeded my warning to run for a few years, before it all wore her down. When Fletcher got hold of her, I just placed more protection on Emme to hide her magical side and left them be. I always watched from afar though."

"Even when she went into the human world?" I said, my rage a burning hole in my chest. "Alone and without any packs around her…"

He shot me another incredulous stare. "That was where she was the safest. Shifters and witches would kill us if they knew what we were. We're not supposed to exist. We'd be viewed as a danger to them all." He eyed me closely. "Emme is an omega who could share her power without losing herself. From what I've seen, she doesn't have the same weakness as other omegas."

He confirmed what we long suspected: "All omegas can share power with alphas?"

"Yes," he said, "with bonds or scent matches. But if they share too much, it will eventually steal their beasts and will to live. They'll lose their essences and become human. Fletcher figured that out quite quickly in his experiments. He powered himself and his pack for years on stolen omega energy as they simulated scent matches. No real scent match would ever be able to drain their mate and live with themselves."

I sure as hell wouldn't want to take a sliver of my mate's energy. Not even if I was actively dying. "And you believe Emme will be exempt from these same limitations?"

His shrug told me everything. He didn't know for sure, and I wasn't willing to risk her.

"We'll beat Jewels without taking any of her power," I decided. "Just the simple act of sealing the quintet completely will increase all of our powers and beasts."

His expression remained unreadable as he met my stare, before flinching at the dominance of my beast. "Yes, let's hope it's enough. If she could share her essence with you all, then you'd also share her resistance to magic. For the dragons especially, that would make them near indestructible."

They were already near indestructible, which would have to be enough.

"Okay, so we're working on the assumption that the witch, her coven, and any shifter allies will go to ground for the next twenty-eight days, correct?"

Constantine nodded, rubbing his right hand up and down his arm, as if he were cold. *Pathetic.* "Yep, absolutely. She knows she only has to stay alive until that curse is complete, and everything she's been fighting for will fall into place."

"Can we use magic to track her?"

He paused before letting out another one of those exaggerated breaths. *Was this fucker deep breathing or some shit?* Probably another part of his connection to the Earth.

"That's my hope," he said when he was done being Zen. "But we need to find an anchor for the spell. Something connected to Jewels or another witch she could be hiding with."

That wasn't going to be an easy find. Jewels was too smart and devious to just leave a trail of crumbs. I'd never fully trusted her, but she'd managed to worm her way in closer than any other witch. Her patience and overall affability had gotten her exactly where she wanted.

This was her home stretch after years acting as a sleeper agent in our cities.

I might hate the bitch, but I'd give her credit for a plan well executed.

"I'll let you know when—" A twinge along the bond cut me off. I jolted as a surge of power flooded my veins, and my beast howled.

Constantine raised his eyebrows as if he'd felt the boom of energy, but I knew it was from my pack. As the entitled alpha, I was innately connected to all their essences, and with another surge of power, all five beasts stood beside my own in my mind. With Emme right in the core of us.

Kellan and Finley skidded into the room a second later.

"Holy fuck, did you feel that?" Kellan shouted, his hand pressed to his chest as he threw his head back. "So much power. And Emme is…"

My wolf stepped into the center with Emme's white beast, and with that her thoughts flooded into my head. I lifted my hand to cut Kellan off, and when his tanned wolf tried to shuffle into the circle too, I crowded them back.

Slade's dragon brushed over my flank. *Snow briefly lost consciousness.*

His voice in my head almost sent me spiraling, but I kept it together as my black wolf prowled up to the white one. Slade stayed with me, and while I had no idea how to communicate this way, I used the same approach as I had with my wolf: to talk like it stood in front of me.

Turning to the dragon, I asked, *Is she okay?*

*I'm not sure if any of us are okay. But we are alive.* The reply was in a register too deep for our bipedal form, and I knew I addressed them both.

His dragon backed up then and I focused on my omega. *Little mate, are you okay?*

There was a pause and then she replied, her voice growing higher with each word. *Ah. I think so. Are we really communicating like this?*

Instinct was all I had to answer that, along with the knowledge that our quintet was all but complete. *Yes. I think this is part of our bond now. The power surge almost knocked us out, and Slade said you were unconscious.*

She withdrew from me, and when I couldn't handle the silence any longer, I tried again.

*Little Omega? Can you hear me?*

Her tone was rougher. *I'm okay. But we need to figure out this mind-speak. It's making me dizzy.*

Without hesitation, I pulled away, but my retreat opened the pathway for Finley and Kellan. Their beasts poured into the bond, pushing through the circle around Emme.

I couldn't hear what they said to her, as if we all held our own unique connection to our mate. Along with one to each of our brothers, since Slade had spoken in my mind too.

When my phone rang, I wasn't surprised by the caller. "Get out of her head," he snarled down the line. "The mental communication is hurting her, so until we figure out how this mind link works, let's keep our essences to ourselves."

As I hung up the phone, I relayed this message to Kellan and Finley in a harsh command, and they backed away from Emme too. Letting the quintet essence settle.

"They bonded," Finley breathed, his cheeks flushed as he shook his head. "The power is fucking intoxicating, and we can mentally communicate now."

He turned to me, and his bear approached my wolf at the same time. *Can you hear me?*

I nodded, and double checked I wasn't linking to Emme again before I answered. *Yes, you speak through my beast, and I can hear you.*

"When I tap into the quintet power," I said out loud, "I mentally see all six of our beasts. Emme is in the center of us, and we can all connect to one another."

"Holy fucking shit," Kellan crowed. "This is group chat on steroids. No one can pretend they forgot their phone or leave the chat. In. For. Life."

"We couldn't hear what you said to Emme," Finley added, his expression concerned.

"I couldn't hear you either," I confirmed. "It appears that we have to direct our thoughts toward a specific member, at least for now. I get the feeling Emme is the one who will be able to open us up as a full group, if and when she gets used to the new bond."

"This is a good sign."

Constantine's statement captured all our attentions; I'd forgotten he was even in the room.

"Your connection is stronger already," he continued, and he looked pleased. "You communicated across the city for starters, and it will grow with time. Even I can feel it." He waved his hands, in the same manner most witches used to search for magic. "Once you start to work on that bond, and keep building up your beasts with Emme's magic, you'll be near unstoppable."

"No one is building up our beasts using her magic," I snarled, and he completely ignored me.

"Can you feel her magic?" he asked enthusiastically. "Push in behind her wolf and search for it. That's where I had to bind it, since her beast was more dominant."

Currently, the only thing I could feel from Emme was a surge of pleasure and need. "I don't think she's quite finished sealing the bonds," I noted dryly. "I can't sense any magic though—"

The jolt of her release cut me off, and the bond was flooded with a burst of energy, one filled with ice and fire at the same time.

My knees slammed into the ground, Kellan and Finley right beside me, and it took every ounce of my strength to keep from passing out. Constantine's magic flooded the room, acting like a Taser, jolting us all back to reality.

"We've got to get to the apartment," I bit out, hauling my aching bones up. "I think her magic finally unleashed."

I was halfway to the garage already, with my brothers and Constantine right behind. I tried to connect with Emme through her beast, but there was no response, and Slade didn't answer his phone.

No doubt they were unconscious after that surge, just as we'd have been if Constantine hadn't been here to help us. My pack was unconscious, vulnerable, and possibly hurt.

We had to get there and figure out what the hell just happened.

And make sure it never happened again.

# CHAPTER 11

FINLEY

No one said a word as we raced for the garage, and I knew I wasn't the only one inwardly focused on the bond. Like with Hunter, I could see my pack mates, and that the three who weren't with us were unmoving and unresponsive.

Constantine's expression remained reserved as he followed us, but he didn't ask any questions.

He knew better than to delay us with his curiosity.

My bear raged as we pawed at Emme's wolf, desperately needing her to be okay. She was alive, that much we could tell, but in her current unconscious state there was nothing else to learn. When she was asleep, I could feel her moods—yeah, I was a proud bond stalker —but today there was only silence at the end of our connection.

"She's okay, right?" Kellan's voice rasped on the final word as he slid into the back of Hunter's Flying Spur, leaving me to take the passenger seat.

"She's alive," Hunter growled, starting his vehicle and near shifting into drive in the same movement.

Constantine was seated beside Kellan, and none of us bothered with seatbelts as Hunter tore out of the garage. The temporarily patched walls from when Talon had burst through in his dragon form were almost joined by a Bentley shaped one, as Hunter took the exit so fast he must have scraped his roof on the opening garage door.

When we emerged into our street, a familiar black jeep came into view, and Hunter barely avoided a collision. It wasn't until Kellan leaned forward and gasped, *Mom*, that I realized why it was familiar. It was his brother Julien's car, and sitting clear as day in the passenger seat was their blond-haired, blue-eyed mother, Danielle Jackson.

Hunter repositioned us beside the other car, and Julien lowered his window immediately. "Is everything okay?" he asked when our window was down too. "Mom and Dad dropped by for a surprise visit."

Through our pack bond, I felt the surge of joy and worry from Kellan. "I'm so fucking happy to see you, but we've got a bit of an emergency. We'll be back soon."

His mom was the sweetest lady, looking not much older than us. The Jackson brothers got their coloring from her, and their size from Conrad, their alpha dad.

"Rocket," Conrad called, his gruff voice strong even from the back of the car, "what's the emergency? Can we help?"

Kellan gripped the edge of Hunter's chair. "Emme and the dragons bonded. There was an explosion of energy, and we're heading to check they're all okay."

At the shocked expression on Danielle's face, Hunter took off, calling over his shoulder, "We'll see you when you get back."

We'd already wasted too much time. Kellan's family would just have to wait.

"Did you know they were visiting?" I asked him as we raced from the street, the still smashed security gates allowing us a quick exit.

Kellan sank back against his chair. "I had no idea. They've been asking to visit for ages, but I kept putting them off. We've had too much shit going on, and I didn't want to risk their safety around us. Clearly, they decided they were done waiting."

"You should be grateful for that," Constantine mumbled, rubbing a hand over his wild mane of hair. "Not everyone has a family who cares enough to show up for you."

All of us shot him a *shut the fuck up* stare. "I am grateful," Kellan bit out with an uncharacteristic snarl, "but as I said, it's dangerous around us at the moment. If I could send Emme and my brothers away too, I would. But unfortunately we're the only ones aware of what's happening, and who might be able to stop it."

That was a huge *might*. We couldn't wield magic, we didn't know how to counter a spell, and unless we tracked Jewels down and killed her before the curse enacted, there was no stopping this from happening. But he was correct that we were the only ones aware of the issue.

"As long as Emme and the twins are fine," I said, still searching our bond for her. "The rest can be worked out."

"What exactly happened in the bond?" Constantine asked finally, and while I sensed his gaze on me, I didn't acknowledge him. "I felt a surge of energy, and it was definitely magic, but I couldn't tell more than that. If I didn't give you all a boost of adrenaline, though, you'd have passed out."

"It was like our bond overloaded with power," Hunter explained, dominance leaking from him so strongly even my bear wanted to retreat. "I think they went down under the surge."

Constantine mulled his information over for a minute, and I was hit with an urge to spear him on the end of my claws and shake him until he spoke. He'd already left Emme alone with evil alphas for most of her life, so he had better step up now and make himself useful.

Before my beast decided he would make a great snack.

"As a near perfect mix of wolf and witch," he finally said, "my magic is innately connected to my beast. One can't survive without the other, and while I'm not as powerful in some ways as a full witch, in others… my beast boosts my strength. Emme is less witch than me, which made it easy to suppress her magic behind her beast. As I expected, the final bonding of your quintet likely burst all that containment to pieces. Emme's magic could be running free for the first time in twenty-plus years."

"I'd thought there was a faint buzz of magic when I was first hit," I said, remembering the sensation.

Kellan moved behind me, and I turned to find him eyeballing the witch-wolf. "For a half witch, you're damn strong. Who are your parents?"

Constantine met the blazing blue gaze of my brother without flinching. Kellan might be the sunniest of our quintet, but when he let the darkness seep from his soul, even I exercised caution. "Both long dead. My father was an *Alterni* witch, which was one of the originals. Just like Termaine. There are none of us left now, outside of Emme and me. My mother was an ultimate alpha, before the formation of shifter cities."

The silence was heavy as Hunter continued racing through the streets, his wolf's rumbles never letting up. "How old are you?" I asked, doing some mental math. Shifters lived for a long time, but ultimate alphas hadn't been around for a near century.

"Old enough," he said simply. "My parents were old when they had me, and I've lived for a long time after that. I've seen a lot of battles, and I'm worried about this one. It brought me out of hiding, didn't it? For Emme, I will stand on the right side of history."

Yeah, we'd see. Words were cheap and easy, as I knew all too well. When I'd set out to prove myself to my mate, after fucking up spectacularly, I knew what to say to make her believe I'd changed. But that wasn't enough. Actions held a lasting truth, and I would always use them before words with my pack. Until Constantine proved his loyalty, there'd be no trust from me.

Hunter screeched to a halt out the front of Slade's apartment and all of us piled out, leaving the Bentley on the street, doors open. As we entered the building, my bear pushed lightly, wanting to shoulder some of my stress. But I didn't need to rely on him the same way as I had before.

We were a proper team now, both of us able to take on stressful situations. It was no longer his sole responsibility to protect me, and our new dynamic was one of my favorite parts of my healing journey. Along with finally bonding Emme.

Hunter entered the code to the building so fast that it didn't register the first time, and he cursed his own damn technology before the lock finally released. As tempted as I was to use the fire escape stairs, Slade was in the twentieth-floor penthouse, which made the elevator the fastest route. We were forced to stand there, our beasts growling as we waited for the doors to open.

Kellan started reciting lines from the book he was reading to keep his mind calm, and I went over the last game we'd played against the *Silver City Groundhogs*. Despite their unusual choice of name, they were one of the higher ranked in the league, and I'd been surprised at how easily we'd won. We had another game tonight and were supposed to be at the rink in a few hours—

The ding of the opening door cut off all thoughts except those of Emme, and after we all pushed inside it took less than a minute to reach the twentieth floor. Slade's penthouse spanned across the entire level, and no one could access it without a code.

At least they hadn't been vulnerable and passed out where the general population could reach them. "Can you feel them in the bond yet?" I asked as we entered the apartment.

"No," Hunter shot back. "But they're alive at least. Let's hope the magic just knocked them out."

Constantine trailed us through the halls until we reached the main bedroom, where we found three naked bodies sprawled.

I moved in front of the witch-wolf to block him from seeing the scene. No one saw our mate naked except us. Especially not a male who was virtually a stranger.

Hunter growled over his shoulder. "Out," he snapped through his beast's fury. "We'll call if we need magical help."

To his credit, Constantine backed up quickly, his scent fading when he left this wing of the apartment completely.

I was right beside Hunter and Kellan, and when we reached Emme, I pressed my hands to her chest. The sear of her warm skin under my touch brought so much relief—she was alive and brimming with energy.

"They're filled with power," Hunter said, blinking down at our mate. He leaned over and ran his nose along her throat, scenting her closer. "It's intense."

It was clear that Slade and Talon were the same, their essences so strong that even without touching them I could feel their beasts. "It's all of them," I noted.

"They're burning up," Kellan added, his expression falling. "We need to do something. Share out the power somehow."

Instinct had me stripping off my jersey, shirt, and jeans. "Pack huddle," I suggested, and the others followed suit by stripping off.

The bed in here was huge, which meant we had more than enough room. Hunter placed Emme in the center, and I slid up behind her. My bear rose to join as we wrapped her in our arms, silently begging her beast to come out and play with mine.

Kellan helped Hunter haul the two massive dragons into the bed, and as their scents rose around us, all I could smell was pack and sex. It calmed my beast in a way I didn't expect, and somehow felt right.

Hunter slid in behind Slade, which was the safest option with our touch-shy pack mate. The dragon would flip if he woke up to anyone else touching him.

We were all naked, but hey... what was a little naked cuddling between pack mates to save our lives. Focusing on the omega in my arms, I thanked the fucking universe when her pulse finally started to settle. "It's working," I murmured, and Kellan let out a huff, like he could finally breathe.

"They're sharing the magical energy. Their beasts are starting to move in the bond," Hunter confirmed.

Heat spread through all of us, and the contented rumble of my bear grew louder. There was no way this situation should encourage sleep, which was difficult for me at the best of times, but the longer we lay there in a pack huddle, the more relaxed I grew until eventually I drifted off.

# CHAPTER 12

EMME

For my entire life I've felt my wolf in my soul. Our essences have always been connected in such a complex way that you could never truly separate one from the other. Sure, there were years she was no more than a whisper, but from the first moment we shifted together, she was a strong, connected entity inside of me.

Two parts of the same soul.

And only ever us.

When our quintet sealed, those final strands from Talon securing our power in a way that felt unbreakable, a new energy had raced through my veins and shattered everything I had ever known.

It was no longer just us.

The icy bite of magic rushed through the quintet, and instinct told me that it had been there inside me the whole time, hidden behind the majestic strength of my wolf.

The completion of our bond had unlocked my magic, and now it was a wild, untapped source of power inside me. All of my pack was there as well, their individual strengths joining my new power. Dragons, wolves, and a bear ebbed and flowed with the force of the magic in our essence.

It was a current I couldn't fight against. I had no idea how to control such power, though it had clearly always been contained within me.

As I battled the surges of magic, warmth wrapped around me,

warmth filled with mocha, vanilla, cherry, cinnamon and caramel scents.

*Our pack had come for us.*

As the six of our beasts huddled together, the magical shitstorm started to calm, and we found a new normal within our quintet. Consciousness returned in slow increments, and with it, my magic continued to settle. While it was a wild, untamed energy, it also held hints of curiosity as it poked at me and my wolf, finding us a solid team. The magic didn't know where it fit, and to be honest, I had no idea myself.

It felt new and out of place—only it wasn't. It had been with me since birth too, just caged and hidden behind my beast. Constantine was responsible for that, I didn't even have to ask to know.

*Darlin?*

The grumbly whisper in the mental connection had my wolf turning toward her bear, who towered over us protectively. Our bonds shimmered in a beautiful golden-pink shade, and when I stroked the link to the bear, I felt his energy. Gruff but soft. Finley held a strength that would withstand the ages, as ancient and solid as the earth itself.

Kellan prowled closer, his tan coat glistening with golden strands as I felt his unwavering warmth surround me. Always sunshine in shifter form.

*Are you okay, little omega?* The hugest of the wolves, black as night, stepped forward and into my circle of power. As was his right as entitled alpha.

I was the center of them and controlled the quintet, but Hunter stood a close second.

*I'm okay.* I felt strangely at peace in this new normal.

On either side of us two dragon sentinels guarded their treasures, near identical except for a slight variation in color. We stood as a pack in our essence, all of our beasts and bonds visible, and it was the most spectacular thing I'd ever experienced.

*Can you feel the magic?* I asked, sending the question to all of them. My wolf tilted her head back to nose against the magic, which continued to try to find its place.

There was a rumble from Slade, which would have shaken the ground if this entire conversation wasn't happening in our minds. *We feel it. It is ours, just as you are ours.*

My wolf left the magic alone to prance on the spot, preening from his verbal claiming. My magic flared as well, as if every part of me enjoyed those words. It was a lot though.

My wolf slid back toward her protective circle, and the beasts around her stilled.

*We controlled the connection.* With that thought, I opened my eyes to find myself in a completely different—but no less enjoyable—huddle.

Whiskey eyes, thick dark lashes, and the slightest glimmer of a dimple were my first sights. "Hey there, baby," Finley murmured softly, his brows furrowing as he took me in. "We lost you for a second there."

Swallowing against my dry throat, I tried to shake off the weird sensation of magic in the air. There was no scent of sulfur thankfully, but the tingles remained in my limbs. "When we bonded," I rasped, "my magic exploded." I attempted to clear my throat.

Not even ten seconds later, a few droplets of water landed on my lips, and my gaze shot up to find Talon beside the bed. He held a glass of water in his hands, and a moment of remembrance passed between us. I didn't want to linger on the memory of the underground bunker though.

We weren't the same shifters any longer.

We'd moved beyond that trauma and pain and our reward had been love, strength, and *apparently magic.*

His chest rumbled and, in my mind, his dragon leaned toward me. "Did you just pick up on my thoughts?" I asked him.

Talon nodded. "Yeah. Occasionally your stronger thoughts drift across to me. Or maybe to whoever you're thinking about. It's as if your wolf isn't quite blocking all the time."

*Great.* That was just freaking great.

"I really need to learn how to stop that," I muttered.

Finley cupped my face. "We want every part of you," he told me. "Especially your thoughts."

With a shake of my head, I pushed myself up to find I was still naked, and no doubt covered in all the bodily fluids from Talon and Slade.

Hunter propped himself up on the bed, and Slade was beside him. Kellan's face appeared on the other side of Finley, his hair tousled as his heated gaze dipped to my tits.

*Crap.* I was far too naked for our current situation. Even if I had dreamed of this moment, albeit under different circumstances.

The smirks on *all* the alpha's face indicated that they'd picked up on my dirty little fantasy.

"I hope she never learns to block us out," Kellan said wistfully, crawling over Finley to plant a kiss on my lips.

My cheeks were hot, which didn't halt the strong waves of desire flooding through me. Who would have guessed that I'd just had sex with two virgin dragon shifters.

A sentence that had probably never been uttered before.

"I agree," Hunter said, his smirk going nowhere. "But now is not the time for us to experiment with whatever *pack huddle* our mate has in mind." His eyes were nearly black, with a solid ring of gold around the pupils. "For now, we have to figure out how to deal with this new magic, return to the pack house to find out why Kellan's parents are here, and then get you boys to your hockey game."

*Hockey.* Such a normal part of our lives, even if it felt like years since I'd made it to a game. Despite the deadline looming over us, Hunter continued to make our regular lives a priority, as if he had all the confidence we would still have this reality after the next full moon.

"Wait, Kellan's parents are here?" I asked, leaning forward to grasp Kellan's hand. "Your parents are in Golden Claw?"

From the stories he'd told me, Kellan's parents were incredible shifters, and the sort of family we all wished we'd been born into. I'd wanted to meet them for ages, but the timing wasn't the best with everything happening. Not only were we dealing with new pack bonds, magic, and the fact that my *father* had popped up in our lives, there was a curse about to destroy the very fabric of the shifter world. Actually, *now* might be the best time after all.

Who knew what tomorrow would bring.

"Well, I'm guessing I should probably shower," I said with a low laugh, trying to act nonchalant while sitting naked, covered in *a lot* of dried bodily fluids.

To my surprise, Slade lifted me from the bed and hugged me tight against his broad chest. Talon was the only alpha who didn't react to his casual touch. Hunter and Finley and Kellan all wore shocked expressions.

"I'll get our mate cleaned up," Slade said shortly, ignoring everyone as he strode into the bathroom and closed the door behind us.

"I'll be able to do that too, right?" I said, and for the first time I wasn't filled with dread at the thought of having magic in my veins. "Manipulate the world around me without needing to touch it."

His chest lifted as he rumbled, and it was an amused sound. "I get the sense there's very little you can't do if you set your mind to it, Snow."

I pressed my face against his chest to breathe in his sweet and smoky scent. "I've missed you."

Slade paused by the shower, the water turning on with a few touches of the control panel.

"I'm sorry I pulled away from you when Talon first arrived," he said, and I was relieved he didn't pretend not to understand what I meant. "I was fighting a battle against my guilt and fear. Guilt that it was my family who stole and hurt you, and fear that it was only the beginning of what being involved with us would do to you. But understand this, mate." He lifted me off his chest so I could drown in his brilliant green gaze. "There hasn't been a moment, from almost the first second I laid eyes on you, that I wasn't completely obsessed. I claimed you long before we sealed our bond, and there was nothing on this Earth that could have come between us. I would have destroyed it before it even tried."

"You watch me," I stated.

"Every second of every fucking day."

"And the photos on the wall?"

His stare remained unflinching. "I needed all of you. Even the moments I wasn't there for, including your younger years. I procured every surveillance photo I could find, and then I deleted them all from the web, so no one else could ever have them. They're mine, just like you are."

I knew he included the rest of our pack in his ownership, but that was where it ended. There was possessive, and then there was *Slade possessive*. They were not the same thing.

"There's no other shifter for me," I assured him. "Just our pack. Now and always."

The satisfaction in his gaze had me wanting to wrap myself around him. Slade was far too sexy, and this slightly tousled, just-dragged-himself-from-bed look, had me struggling to keep my hands, *and lips*, to myself. Now that I knew what being with my dragons felt like, there was no putting that desire back in its box.

It had taken on a life of its own, and I was thoroughly addicted.

"I don't think you quite understand how addicted I am," Slade said, answering my thoughts. *Get it together, wolf.* Her blocking was worse than ever. "In fact, you're about to get fucked again. Right now, sweetheart. You have one chance to use your safe word, and then all bets are off."

My scent exploded, and I swore I heard Kellan's groan from the bedroom, but I was too far gone to care how close the rest of our pack were. "Yes, sir," I breathed.

His dragon flashed in his gaze, and we were under the stream of heated water so fast that I was dizzy. He pressed me back against the tiles, and when I attempted to lift my legs around his waist, he used his weight to keep me still.

He buried his face against my throat and snarled, "Mine."

I choked on my moan as he bit into his claiming mark once more, the jolt of pleasure and pain strong enough to throb in my core. "Are you going to do that every time we're together? Bite me over and over?"

My desperation to arch against him had me gasping, but he was too heavy to move.

As his corded muscles held me in place, leaving me helpless under his strength, I realized the importance of the safe word. Not that I could ever imagine a situation where I'd use it, but it was good to know.

"Every fucking time," he promised, and the rumble of those words almost sent me tumbling into Orgasm Land. Goddess, he hadn't even really touched me yet, but apparently all it took was a deep, guttural promise.

Slade's laughter, always so unexpected, sent vibrations over my sensitive skin. Slowly, ever so fucking slowly, he lifted me higher. The scent of my arousal was thick in the air, and my breaths were harsh in the quiet bathroom.

His first thrust was unhurried, just a parting of my thighs. I didn't get a chance to adjust before he thrust again and again, until every decadent inch filled me. The heat of his shaft, and the brush of those metal piercings against my sensitive walls, had sparks darting through my veins.

This was like magic, and my essence filled with all the energy.

My low, husky groans followed each thrust, and all words turned to gibberish, as my ability to speak diminished. It was a surprise I could still breathe with this intense pleasure-pain drowning my senses.

"I'd have waited a thousand years just to touch you once," Slade said, the serious undertones of his words breaking through the pleasure fog. "You're the reason I exist, Emmeline Anders. You are my fucking reason."

"Slade," I moaned. "You're my reason too—*goddess!*"

"There's no goddess here," Slade whispered, and he was absolutely right as he pulled all the way out and slammed back into me, hard and fast. As his powerful body filled me it took seconds, *fucking seconds*, for me to come screaming.

Throughout my climax, I was left with only one thought: I'd endure a fate far worse than death for this pack. I'd endure anything.

# CHAPTER 13

KELLAN

With Emme safe, we left her and Slade to "clean up," and headed back to the house. They'd follow soon enough, and I wanted to chat with my parents.

There was no reason to believe that this was anything more than one of mom's impulsive decisions. They didn't happen a lot, but when she set her mind to something, there wasn't a shifter alive who could change it. Her strength of will had no doubt saved her when she'd been raising three wolf pups determined to destroy her house, plants, and sanity.

Hunter pulled into the garage and said, "I'm going into the office to take care of some shit. We need to fast-track the packages with armored vests and weapons so they're in our allies' hands before Jewels blows everything up."

None of us knew what the next month would bring, or who'd be standing when it all ended, but we were preparing for every possible outcome.

Which meant outfitting as many shifters as we could with magical protection.

"Yeah, it would be good to get that all sorted this week," Finley said. "So we can focus on tracking Jewels."

That sparked Constantine's interest, as he leaned forward. "We absolutely need to focus on finding her now you've bonded in a completed quintet."

He'd been pleased when we'd filled him in on the changes within our pack, and the magic that flowed between all of our beasts. *"You'll be able to share in that energy,"* he'd said, but none of us were willing to try that when it could hurt Emme.

No fucking thank you.

Talon's huge shoulders bumped the witch-wolf, who flinched but didn't protest the dragon squishing him. "I'll check out the compound first, and if it's safe for all of us to travel there, that can be our first place to investigate."

Talon adjusted his shirt, clearly uncomfortable in the limited space, and Emme's bite came into view. It was nice not to want to tear his head off at the sight. *We were growing.* Some of us rather slowly and at an odd angle, but there *was* growth.

Hunter's dominance pressed into me, and in the new version of our quintet, where I could internally see our beasts, the black wolf stood above the pack. "Yeah, I think we should start there too," he said. "So far none of our contacts have come close to discovering where the witch and her allies are hiding."

"We might…" Constantine cleared his throat. "…be able to track her using magic. If we can find a connection to her essence or coven."

Finley scoffed, his gaze dark as it narrowed on Constantine. He wasn't very forgiving of deadshit parents. "Are you even any good at magic? You're only half witch."

There was a heavy moment of silence. "I'm the lone option you've got," Constantine finally said. "And as I told you, while my magic is weaker than a full-blooded witch, the wolf adds an element that they don't have. I can scent magic and track witches through their scent. The individual magical notes are as identifying as a fingerprint."

I wouldn't admit it out loud, not even under torture, but that was kind of impressive.

"I'm also the only one who can teach Emme how to properly access her magic," he added, more bite in his tone. "Which is important when you have no other magical allies."

Hunter grunted, and he didn't sound pleased. "Emme won't be put in any danger. I don't fucking care about the outcome of not having magic on our side. She's the one we all protect, end of story."

My wolf howled at the very thought of our mate being hurt, and I pushed down those swirls of darkness that wanted to tear through the world until we destroyed every threat to Emme.

"And no more council meetings," Hunter added. "Outside of the few entitled alphas I still trust, the rest are useless and most likely Fletcher's spies. We need to approach this as if we can trust no one other than our immediate pack and families. Understood?"

"Yep," I said, tempering down my rage. I might prefer not to dwell on the shittier side of life, but I could absolutely take the low road if necessary. Real fucking low. "Those assholes are all but dead to us."

"Dead as their fucking dominance," Hunter confirmed. "Okay, I need to get to the offices. You all hold down the fort here."

When we hauled ass out of the car, I leaned down to speak to him through the open door. "Will we see you at the game?"

Hunter nodded in an impatient jerk of his head. "Yep, I'll be there to keep our pack safe. Update me if anything happens in the meantime. And make sure you bring your parents tonight, annoying pup."

I loved that bossy fuck, but there were days I could just… "You got it, Hurricane."

Emme's name for him was so fitting, and I'd have been mad not to come up with it, but it made sense that my perfect, precious Shortcake would be the nickname genius.

After Hunter left, Constantine muttered something about heading to the library for research. We apparently had a ton of history books in there. Who knew?

All I knew was our romance section was woefully underrepresented, though Emme was helping me amend that oversight.

I had no idea why Constantine was wasting his time; as far as I could tell no one ever learned from the past, since they kept repeating it. There was literally no fucking point in studying it.

Still, I might change my tune if *old* Connie did find anything useful.

When we entered the house, Finley clapped a hand on my shoulder. "Get your family over here and I'll make the snacks. It'll be good to catch up with everyone."

Talon hesitated beside us, and I barely managed not to laugh at his expression. Poor bastard looked like he'd rather be locked in the basement prison again than play happy families. "You don't need to hang out with us," I said, waving him off. "We'll just find you before the game, since it appears we're showing up there in full pack style."

His scar twisted as his lips pulled into a grimace. "Yeah, I'm not the alpha to introduce to your family. But I am looking forward to hockey since I've heard it's violent."

Finley met my gaze, looking as pleased as a bear with his face buried in the honeypot, AKA Emmeline Anders. "There are times when it's gloriously violent," he said, and his smile was positively feral. Crazy fucker. "You'll love it."

Talon's interest was definitely piqued as he nodded, his eyes brighter. It was the first time I'd seen him show an interest in anything other than Emme. He took off upstairs soon after, and I pulled out my phone to text Julien.

Within minutes, there was a knock on the door, and I opened it to find Mom front and center, Dad right behind her. Julien and Tyson followed them in as well, and when I spotted little Lachlan in my brother's arms, my face split into a genuine smile. Julien's son was adorable, and I was shocked at how much bigger he'd gotten since the last time I saw him.

He'd recently turned one and had just started walking and getting into everything.

I'd always wanted to be a dad, and staring into eyes that were eerily similar to mine had my wolf howling. It would be even sweeter to stare into arctic blue eyes.

*Fuck.* We couldn't let Jewels win. We had to destroy her so that all the babies got to grow up, and I got to breed my mate for the rest of eternity.

"Kel, my baby," Mom crooned, distracting me from what was really not an appropriate train of thought around my parents.

Her firm hug always transported me right back to my childhood, and the million times she'd been my comfort. Dad cocooned us both, his strength unwavering, just as it always had been.

"I've missed you both so much," I said, my voice all raspy as I tried not to cry like a pup. But after finding my pack and Emme, I was more than ever appreciating the love I had growing up. "Thank you for making the effort to get here, but you know we would have sent the jet."

My parents and their quintet were well off, but had nothing on my pack. I enjoyed being able to provide for them, and often sent care packages home with the most outrageous shit in them.

Case in point…

Mom's hold loosened as she shot me a glare. "Kellan Jackson. Don't think I've forgotten the new car that showed up in my driveway last week. A two-hundred-thousand-dollar sportscar is not an appropriate birthday present."

Dad chuckled and patted me on the shoulder. "Now you've got her started."

Mom's little growl was adorable. "On top of that, you know we're more than capable of booking commercial flights to visit you. Truth be told, if we waited for you, I doubt I'd see you for another twelve months."

I couldn't even argue that point, but in my defense, I'd been trying to protect them. "It hasn't exactly been that safe around me lately," I said, my amusement fading under our fucked-up reality. "I don't want you all getting hurt in the crossfire."

Mom's glare deepened, and dad's chest shook, reminding me that he was a highly trained enforcer who could probably take out everyone in this house. Even the dragons. "If our children are in danger, then we're in danger," he told me.

Julien pushed further into the room, since we'd left them half out in the cold. "We updated them on the fight with Fletcher and the witches," he said, closing the door behind him. "You said there's more going on, so we're here to find out what that is. Considering the bad guy is dead, we're all confused about what else is waiting in the wings."

The need to keep my family out of this battle was an all-consuming desire inside me, but we all carried mom's stubborn streak. They wouldn't leave until I told them everything. Tyson was already heading for the living room, ruffling my hair as he passed. I reached out to tickle Lachlan when Julien followed.

Mom linked her arm through mine to drag me along, giving me zero chance to escape.

Dad was at our backs, always the protector. Even though I stood two inches taller than him now.

I ended up on the long couch, squished between my parents.

I was the baby and had spent my formative years protected, loved, and spoiled. My brothers were right to beat the crap out of me whenever my parents weren't looking; otherwise I'd be in-fucking-sufferable.

Well, more insufferable.

When Finley entered the room, Mom jumped to her feet and hurried toward him. She launched herself at the bear, and Dad saved us from wearing a tray of drinks and sandwiches by grabbing it out of Finley's hands.

Mom wrapped her arms around him, and I smirked at the soft expression our Care Bear wore. "You look amazing, Fin," Mom said as she pulled away. "There're less shadows on your face, and I'm so pleased by that. I need to meet this lovely Emme who is caring so well for my boys."

The pink in Finley's cheeks had me itching to switch all his chat names to Bashful Bear, but now wasn't the time. That was a later fun.

Dad placed the tray on the table and got to work handing out beverages for everyone. Mom had tea, Julien and Dad coffee, Tyson had his usual energy drink, and baby Lachlan got milk. Finley and I had our pre-game protein smoothies, or *glasses of sadness* as Emme would call them.

"Okay, spill everything that's happening with your pack," Mom commanded as she blew on her mint tea, made with only the freshest of herbs. The gardener in her would accept nothing less.

I took a long sip of the protein shake, enjoying the hint of honey. "Okay, two afternoons ago we were attacked right here in the street."

It took me twenty minutes to go over what happened during the street-battle, what we knew about Jewels, and the fucking curse that was set to take down shifters by the next full moon.

The only part I left out was Emme's magical side, since that was her secret to reveal when or if she was ever ready to. By the time I'd gotten them up to date, Mom looked horrified, and Dad was clutching his mug hard enough that small cracks had formed around his grip.

"Jewels has been playing the long game," Finley said with a dark growl, "waiting for the blood moon and the power of Fletcher's death to initiate her curse. We have around four weeks to stop her, or all of us will lose control of our beasts and be under the direct influence of magic. Her magic to be specific."

"Why did she target you?" Julien asked, letting Lachlan down to the rug, the little wolf wobbling around to test his limits.

"They needed someone from Fletcher's line to destroy him," Finley said. "And Fletcher wanted Emme's power. She's an omega, and as such, can share her power with bonded alphas."

Jewels had tried to maneuver and manipulate every part of our lives, even to the point of tearing the dragon twins apart. All in a bid to control and destabilize us, which left us ripe for her fucking picking.

# CHAPTER 14

EMME

S lade kept a spare motorcycle at his apartment, safe and secure in the underground parking lot. After a thorough reminder of how much I enjoyed shower sex, we were dressed in our original outfits, and I accepted the helmet he held out to me.

"Are you sure you'll be fine with me plastered to your back?" I checked, eyeing the Honda as I slid the slightly-too-large helmet over my head.

"You're the exception," he said, flipping up my visor to reveal my eyes, which he stared into as he secured the strap, his movements quick and skilled.

When he was satisfied that I was strapped in properly, he gripped the front of the helmet and pulled me in closer. "Now get on the bike, mate."

His voice dropped low over the word *mate*, and my insides swirled as his bite tingled. He swung his leg over first, settling in front, and I managed to hop on behind him. At first, I attempted to keep the tiniest distance between us, but he wrapped his hands around my thighs and tugged me firmly against his back.

There was a real intimacy in riding with someone like this.

Bodies fully aligned.

Heat seeping into my essence.

Dragons burned in a way that had me desperate to consume their fire.

Slade grunted, going all alpha on me, and I wrapped my arms

around his waist, hands linking over his firm abs. For a few heartbeats, we just existed together, his huge frame shielding mine from the world in front of us.

The engine kicked over smoothly; there was a solid thrum of power beneath us. "You want to go fast, Snow?" he asked, his voice even deeper than the bike's rumble.

"Yes," I said, lowering my visor. *Always.*

His dragon shifted in our bond, but he stayed out of my mind, allowing my wolf to keep the block in place. Even if the occasional thought still slipped through. It was going to take time to adjust to these changes within our quintet, but the closer connection didn't upset me.

In fact, I was hoping we could use it to win this fight.

As an omega, I already knew I could share my energy... but what if I could share magic too?

The ride back to the house was a blur of speed, warmth, and... peace. Slade and I didn't communicate, but his dragon remained close in our bond. He nuzzled and adored my wolf like she was precious, and in his own way Slade had treated me the same way from almost the first days we met. He might not use the word *love*, but he showed me in more ways than one.

When we pulled into the underground garage, he parked by the other bikes, and as I went to jump off the back, Slade held my thighs once more. He got off first, his head tilting as he loosened my helmet strap and then removed it.

I shook out my hair, which was no doubt a hot mess after everything I'd put it through today, and he cupped my face. "You always look beautiful," he told me, and the way his gaze ate me up was a blazing fire.

My voice was lost in the raw need pulsing within me. How was this beautiful, magical, mythical creature my alpha?

He wrapped his hands around my waist and lifted me off the bike, setting me on shaky legs.

"It doesn't bother you at all?" I asked him, barely finding my voice. "Touching me so freely?"

Slade took a second to consider my question. "Touch used to bring internal chaos and pain, but when you or my twin touch me, all I feel is harmony. It's calming to the dragon and soothing to the alpha." He leaned down until our lips were mere inches apart. "With you, it's even more than that. Your warmth sparks against the flames of my beast, and it feels so good. You never have to ask for permission to touch me."

Through the bond, I felt how much he meant that statement, which propelled me to slide my hands up his sides until I reached the stubble on his cheeks. As I scraped my fingertips across his face, Slade sighed, the sound filled with relief.

I dropped my hands soon after, and he linked our fingers together, as if he couldn't stand *not* to be touching me now. "Come on," he said. "Kellan's family is upstairs, waiting for us."

That reminder jolted me into a slightly panicked state, and with one more attempt to straighten my hair and dress, I walked with him out of the garage.

In the living room, Slade let me go first, and I took in the cozy scene. Kellan was squished between two shifters who looked so much like him there was no way to mistake them as anyone other than his parents. His brothers were there too, and on Julien's lap was the cute blond baby I'd seen twice now—once at hockey and another time in the street when we were under attack. He'd always reminded me of Kellan, which made perfect sense since he had to be his nephew.

"Shortcake," Kellan said, jumping to his feet and racing over to sweep me up into his arms, like it had been days since we were parted. "We've been waiting for you."

Despite our audience, he pressed a kiss to my lips, his fingers threading into my ratty hair as he pulled me closer. Finley joined us too, wrapping me in a bear hug, and I was calmed once more by their scents and presence.

"I'll grab more drinks," Finley offered as he pulled away, allowing Kellan to lead me to the couch.

His mom, who stared at me with the sort of intensity usually reserved for my alphas, was standing and waiting for us. I took her in, noting that she was very pretty, with blond hair and blue eyes like her sons. She also wore a warm smile that made me feel instantly at ease.

"Oh, our beautiful Emme," she crooned, and to my shock she reached right out and hugged me like this wasn't the first time we'd met.

I'd received many hugs since coming into this pack, and almost all of them affected me in different ways. But a mom hug. I'd never had one of those before.

I fought down my emotions, noticing that Danielle Jackson smelled like the lightest spray of violets. She was quite a few inches shorter than me, but I felt small and protected in her firm embrace as her beta energy soothed my omega.

When she sniffled, my eyes burned until I squeezed them closed. "I've waited so long to meet you, gorgeous girl," she whispered against my shoulder. "You are such a precious gift to our family. To our Kellan."

My wolf howled, and I barely held it together. *Gift.* I hadn't been a gift to my own family. It was astonishing to have a virtual stranger make such a heartfelt statement.

"She's the fucking best thing that ever walked into my life," Kellan murmured, brushing his arm over my shoulder. "Can I have her back now, please?"

I couldn't see him, but I heard a low snicker from one of his brothers. Even his dad released a deep chuckle. "You're going to have to learn to share her son, just as your brothers did with their mates."

Kellan's mom sniffled again as she pulled away to look me over. "I'm Danielle," she told me, though I already knew their names from Kellan. "But I'd love if you might consider calling me Mom. Or whatever you're comfortable with."

I wasn't sure how I felt about her offer, but it was lovely of her to make it in the first place. "Thank you, and it's so nice to meet you. Kellan told me how amazing his childhood was, and I wanted to say just how proud you should be of the boys you've raised."

Her eyes were shiny as she squeezed my hands. "Goddess, you really are the sweetest. I've always wanted a daughter... I might take you home with me."

Kellan groaned, and looked pleadingly at his father, who took pity on him and wrapped his mate up in his arms. Danielle sank back against the burly alpha, her expression filled with joy.

"I'm Conrad," he said, his wolf dominant though it had no effect on me. "We're sorry to just drop by unannounced, but Danni couldn't wait one more minute to meet you. Along with ensuring her baby had fully recovered from the magical attack."

I found myself genuinely smiling at them both. "You're always welcome here. I'm guessing the guys have filled you in on what we've been facing lately. The only reason I haven't insisted on meeting you sooner is I'd hate for you to be in any danger because of me."

Julien, who'd just jumped to his feet to keep a wobbly baby from crashing headfirst into the coffee table, said, "I'm sending my pack and Lochie back with Mom and Dad. I know they're no safer there from the curse, but I feel like Golden Claw could end up front and center of a war." He shifted Lachlan closer to the couch.

"You should go too," Kellan said, guiding me down to sit beside him on the couch, his palm wrapped around my thigh. I got the sense he was barely stopping himself from pulling me completely into his lap. "I want all of you out of the danger zone."

Julien snorted, as if that was the dumbest thing he'd ever heard. "Rocket, you're crazy if you think I'm leaving my baby brother alone. I'll be here if you need me."

"Me too," Tyson said. "My mate is staying too, but we don't have any babies to consider. Golden Claw is our home, and we will fight for it."

I appreciated everyone taking this seriously, but I hated the thought of anyone else we cared about going into battle. We'd already lost Marcus, and that was one good shifter too many.

How many more would we lose before this was over?

Needing a subject change, I said, "As much as we should discuss the witch, there's one thing I have to know first." Kellan raised an eyebrow at me, the slightest hint of a smile on his lips.

"How did you get the nickname Rocket?"

As I asked the question, Finley returned with my coffee and Slade's tea. The dragon had remained back near the entrance, giving me time to bond with the Jacksons.

Finley handed me my sweet, milky heaven with a kiss on my cheek, and I thanked him before taking my first, perfect sip.

"Anytime, darlin'," Finley murmured, the nickname still sending shivers through me.

Slade continued to silently observe us as he drank his tea, and Finley sat to finish off his cup of sadness, all green and healthy. There was nothing unattractive about my mates, but that drink was a tick in the negative column.

"So… Rocket?" I repeated, looking at the mostly blond family.

Julien snorted. "Kellan was such a shit of a kid," he said, before shaking his head when his son toddled over to us.

Lachlan held out his hands for Kellan and chanted, "Ke, ke, ke."

My ovaries nearly exploded when Kellan leaned down and

scooped up the little cutie, cuddling him against his chest. "Your son doesn't think so," he fired back at his brother.

*Okay…* Kellan with a baby was too fucking hot for me to handle.

When Golden flashed me a smirk, I realized my emotions had slipped through the bond. "It suits you," I whispered near his ear, and his eyes got all shiny.

*One day, Shortcake*, he mentally said, his wolf nosing against mine.

The thought of having kids with my pack was enough to send terror and joy through me. It was a secret wish for the future, that I hoped we'd get a chance to fulfil.

"He was definitely spoiled, and Mom's favorite," Tyson continued, relaxing back into the couch as he reminisced. "He got away with everything, and we were the ones who got our asses kicked."

Danielle gasped as she shook her head. "I don't recall any of you ever getting a beating, even when you deserved it. Your daddy has too gentle a soul."

Conrad snorted before he coughed to cover it up. This was the alpha who'd trained my mega-skilled, weapon's expert of a mate. Yeah, I wasn't sure there was much *gentle* in his soul for anyone other than Danielle. The way he looked at her was exactly how my pack looked at me.

Like there was no other shifter in the world.

Julien eyed his mother with scrunched brows but didn't call her out. "Anyways, one day when he was about five, Kellan was out in the back yard. He climbed this huge oak tree, and no matter how many times I told him to get down, he ignored me and kept climbing higher. When he reached the top, I taunted him and asked how he planned on getting down."

"You told me it was much harder to climb down than up," Kellan said with a laugh, rubbing a hand over his face. "I told you that you were wrong, and I was a rocket that would land at your feet."

"And land you did," Tyson added with a snort. "You plummeted out of the damn branch headfirst and almost gave us a heart attack."

"But you caught me," Kellan said, bestowing his brilliant smile on his big brother. "Stopped me from breaking my neck, before you then proceeded to kick me in the ass, screaming…"

"You spoiled little shit," Julien burst out. "And we called you Rocket ever since, to remind you of the first stupid decision you made."

"But not the last," Kellan conceded with a sheepish grin, reminding me of how he'd driven around the racetrack like a shifter with a death wish.

On my other side, Danielle moved forward, shaking her head. "He has a free spirit, and I wasn't about to tarnish his light by trying to cover him in bubble wrap."

"You were the exact parent Kellan needed to grow into our Golden Boy," Slade noted, his voice soft. "We are grateful for his light too."

Kellan's smirk grew. "Okay, then. We have our squishy Care Bear, and our fluffy little drago—"

Slade's growl reminded the room he was a deadly killing machine, and Kellan took the warning seriously by immediately shutting up.

"Yep, still stupid," Julien noted with a shake of his head.

"Still Rocket," Tyson added to the sound of laughter.

I was fairly sure even the *fluffy little dragon* joined in.

# CHAPTER 15

EMME

The next few hours felt so normal that I briefly forgot the crisis we were facing. The Reeves pack were right—Kellan's family were everything good in the world. From his bubbly, kind, and sweet mother to the stoic and calm silence of his father, not to mention the way the brothers ribbed each other with a million inside jokes but never made me feel like an outsider.

It was nice to just bask in their comfortable glow.

Slade eventually left to beat up his enforcers, but not before reminding me he'd be waking my ass up for dawn training. Everyone else departed soon after, to get ready for hockey tonight. I was thrilled to watch our Celtic Wolves take on the Greenville Demons.

It had been too long since I attended a game.

"Hunter will meet us there, so you're driving over with us, Shortcake," Kellan said after we'd waved off his family, who would also meet us there.

"Sounds good to me," I said. "I've just got to get my jersey on, and paint your numbers on my cheeks, and then I'm set."

Finley and Kellan pushed in on either side of me, their alpha dominance washing over my tingling skin, leaving my legs like Jello. "We had a special jersey made for you," Finley murmured, his voice deepening as his scent spiked. "Florence left it on your bed."

Desperately searching for moisture in my mouth, I swallowed roughly. "You guys had a jersey made?"

When they nodded, curiosity pushed through my breathless state.

Which was how these alphas always affected me. Popping up on my toes, I pressed a kiss on Finley's lips first, and then Kellan's, before I took off up the stairs. They attempted to grab me but I got away. I was on a mission, and their warm laughter followed me all the way to my room.

Inside, their scents were strong, and tingles fluttered across their bites as the bond shimmered in my mind. Their beasts were closer, so my wolf was all but pressed against them, and we could have communicated if we wanted, but instead chose to just let our essences dance together.

Until we were almost one and the same.

Our full quintet was a complete circle, with no beginning or end. All sharing one power.

Pushing aside the curiosity of *sharing power*, I focused on the pile of neatly folded clothing on the bed. Above all of it, though, was new piece of origami.

I lifted it, examining what was clearly a flower. It took me a minute to recall the name: lotus. The dark pink lotus was intricate, and I couldn't figure out how many pieces of paper Finley had used to make it, but it was more than one. My pulse fluttered as I sent a happy sigh toward my bear. *Thank you, mate. I love all these heartfelt gifts.*

Kellan's wolf butted in closer to mine, as if he wanted to see what I held, and I sent him a mental image of the flower. I didn't expect that to work, but to my surprise, he yipped. *Did you ever unfold any of them, pretty mate?*

Finley's bear bellowed with that, and it was clear he'd heard those words too. But he didn't say anything. All I got through the bond were waves of his love and gentleness.

*I've never opened them.*

Kellan's wolf nudged me again, and I retreated from the bond, re-positioning my beast so she was blocking the conversation once more. It had only been hours, but already I'd figured out how to single out and communicate with the alphas, mostly due to trusting the instinct of my wolf.

I focused on the lotus once more before deciding it was far too intricate to unfold. This would have taken him hours to create. It was so delicately perfect, I refused to mess with it. Moving to the drawer of origami, I slid it open and swapped out the lotus for the horse.

Finley had made this one for me on the day we went to therapy together, and as much as I loved it, I wanted to know what might have been in his heart that day. It took me many minutes to unfold the paper without tearing it, marveling all the while at how tiny some of the folds were. Finley might be a huge bear, but it didn't show in the dexterity of his fingers.

A truth that made me one *very lucky* omega.

As the paper unraveled before me, the occasional word appeared, and when I finally had the creased paper open, there was also a drawing in the middle. It was my face with a pair of familiar hands cupping my cheeks. Such a beautiful and simple line sketch and written along Finley's hands were tiny words—*adore, cherish, crave, desire, need, want, love, mate, peace.* Love, peace, and mate were repeated multiple times. Above all of that, almost like the title of the piece, was a single word: HEALING.

His feelings for me coated his arms, but the sketched version of me couldn't see them, as my eyes were closed. *Oh, Finley.* My beautiful bear.

My eyes were wide open now, and I wouldn't be closing them again. Not ever.

Wanting to keep this with me, I slid it into my bra, leaving it close to my heart. Finley's bear pressed in against my wolf, waiting for me to let him in, so he'd know what piece I'd chosen to unravel. I sent him a mental picture of the navy horse, and a huge rumble shook the bear's chest.

*Not what I expected, but I should have known you'd be drawn to the one where I left most of my heart.*

*I'll keep it safe for you*, I whispered back. *I love you, Grouchy.*

There was not even a second delay from him. *I love you too, baby. I'll keep every part of you safe. Now get your jersey on and get that sexy ass downstairs. We're waiting for you.*

I felt the caress of his bear, and then I was once again alone in my essence. Or at least my wolf was, standing in the center, with beasts quiet and dark around her.

When my focus returned to my room, I moved toward the pile of clothes finding jeans, socks, a tank, and the new jersey. I quickly ditched my tights and dress and had another quick shower, though Slade had already *cleaned me thoroughly.*

I pulled on the underwear and jeans first, followed by my bra. Not worrying about the tank, I held up the jersey, smiling when I saw that on the back they'd had *Jackson* and *Thornton* printed, with their numbers below, both in separate circles. Beneath the numbers was a single word: *Ours.*

It was a clear claim, and I wasn't remotely upset about it.

There was no universe in which I'd ever be upset about carrying their claims. I wore their bites proudly on my skin and loved the new scars that adorned me.

Which reminded me that Finley had almost finished drawing up a quintet concept to tattoo on me. After I'd finally seen his third tattoo, which was on his right thigh—a crown wrapped around a beautifully intricate snowflake, representing his *Ice Queen* nickname for me, I wanted my own tattoo.

Sliding the jersey on, it fell to mid-thigh, custom made to hug my body. It was thicker and warmer than my usual ones, and they'd also left a matching scarf and gloves in the Celtic colors.

Once I was dressed, I brushed and braided my mop of hair, drew their numbers on each cheek, and dotted some gloss on my lips. Wrapping myself up in all their thoughtfully provided gifts was heartening, especially with their scents clinging to them. For tonight at least, I looked like a shifter without a care in the world.

No one would know that I feared the way magic would steal everything from us tomorrow.

As I started down the stairs, Kellan, Finley and Talon were already waiting for me in the entrance hall. The dragon's gaze locked onto me, and I enjoyed his unwavering stare. Heat rose from him, and I was suddenly too warm in my hockey gear.

Now that we'd sealed the bond in all ways, a new craving tore at my body to claim them all again. Over and over. Circumstances prevented us from having a true honeymoon period, a time when most packs holed up in their bedrooms for weeks. But that didn't mean I wasn't feeling all those drives and desires to hide away with them.

Talon's boots hit the bottom step. "Sweet Honey," he breathed, his voice a whisper of a prayer.

"Tal," I gushed, basically throwing myself into his arms as I skipped the last few steps.

He caught me with ease, barely even rocking back. "I missed you, mate," I said, our bond thrumming strongly as his dragon's snout caressed my wolf's flank.

"I don't like being apart from you," he admitted. "I don't like not being able to see you. Darkness creeps in around the edges of my mind, and I don't want to go there again."

Wiggling my arms free from where he had them pinned against my sides, I cupped his face. "You can find me anytime you need. In our bond, or out here in the real world. I'm always available when you need me."

Kellan and Finley hovered closer, as if drawn forward by my words. Talon, to my surprise, turned to include them in the connection. "We all need you in our own ways," Kellan said, his smile slipping until he no longer looked his normally cheery self. "I hope we don't take too much from you, Shortcake. You need to tell us if we're pushing too hard, because without limitations, there's a real chance we could devour you whole."

Finley rumbled until his bear was visible in his gaze. "Whatever time and energy you have for us, will be more than enough," he said. "We're all grown alphas, and it's not your job to ensure our happiness. Just having you in our lives makes us whole and happy. You will drive yourself crazy constantly trying to keep us all functional. Trust that we'll come to you if we are in real need."

Talon looked between Kellan and Finley, a thoughtful expression tugging at his face, as if he hadn't considered that before. Unable to help myself, I leaned in and kissed the taut skin of his scar. "One," I said, "it is my job to ensure your happiness. And two, please find me if you need me. Trust that I will speak up if it's ever too much, but I can't imagine a time when I wouldn't want to be close to all of you."

Even with five mates, there was never a sense of *too much* or being overwhelmed. If anything, I missed Slade and Hunter, and wished they were here with me too. My greatest wish right now would be to wrap five alphas around me, crawl into a huge, soft bed, and maybe never come out.

As that thought filtered out through my pack, there was a rumble from the beasts, along with an overall feeling of satisfaction.

Here in the entrance hall, I got kisses and hugs from all three of my mates, and then we headed for the garage.

"Constantine's not coming?" I asked, not sure if I cared or not.

We'd had very little time to get to know each other or build any sort of relationship thus far. I might have misgivings about him being in my life, but I knew I couldn't avoid him forever.

"He's researching," Finley said as he opened the door to the Benz for me. "He said he'd see us after the game."

*After the game.* Where all normalcy would vanish, and we'd once again be fighting to save shifters and our cities.

Not that I was going to think about the future until I absolutely had to.

Living in denial and all that.

Worked like a charm.

# CHAPTER 16

EMME

On the drive, the guys explained the rules of the game to Talon. The dragon's eyes lit up when they described their defense, and the ways they were allowed to check their opponents.

Kellan got us to the hockey arena in record time, pulling into the already crowded parking lot and sliding into his spot near the players' entrance. Finley opened the door for me and took great pleasure in *helping* me from the car, my body sliding down his as he gripped unrepentantly.

This lighthearted, flirty side of Finley was utterly addictive and intoxicating. Especially when he growled, "You're welcome, darlin'," to my thank you.

At the entrance just behind the security who kept out the average hockey fan, Kassidy, Danielle, Conrad, Julien, and Tyson waited for us.

Kellan walked into his mom's waiting arms, and I found it odd to see a shifter so comfortable around his family. There was not the slightest sign he expected to be hurt or rejected by them… just embraced by unconditional love.

It was the sort of love I'd never known until I met my alphas.

As we headed inside, Kellan filled his family in on the other team's stats, and I found myself walking arm in arm with Kassidy. She wore a Wolves jersey too, with Finley's name and number on it. I'd seen her in Kellan's too, as she swapped them frequently. She told me it was whoever was her favorite that day.

"Have you heard from Cora?" she asked as we followed everyone down a well-lit but empty hallway. Everyone except Talon, who remained protectively at my back.

"Not really," I said, my excitement over tonight fading. "I tried to see her today but didn't make it past the start of their street. We just left them with food and our love." My voice dropped lower. "I really want to kill that fucking witch."

Kassidy's breaths were shallow, as the mild sea breeze scent she always carried deepened. She hadn't known Marcus well, but she grieved for our friend. "We will kill Jewels," she decided, as if already manifesting it. "I don't care what it takes. She cannot be allowed to exist, let alone control our beasts." My pack weren't the only one prepared to die before letting a witch control our beasts, even as I hoped it wouldn't come to that.

When we reached the t-section which branched off into the lockers or the main stadium, we nearly collided with other Wolves players. They all wore suits, like Kellan and Finley, and I could feel their high energy as they got into their gameday mindset.

Front and center was Christian, Kellan's bestie, who I hadn't seen for ages.

"Strawberry Shortcake," he crowed, racing right for me.

He almost collided with Talon, who moved like a damn ninja to stand in front of me. Talon was an expert at remaining still and calm, until he snapped into action and you found yourself dead at his feet.

Christian, who was no doubt well aware of our newest pack mate from Kellan, managed to avoid a collision. By the time I peeped around Talon's broad shoulders, the wolf shifter was backing away slowly, hands held up in front of his chest as his sports bag swung by his side.

"Sorry, Alpha…" He squinted an eye, and then turned to Kellan, who wore an expression of amusement.

"Talon," he reminded his best friend. "I told you about him, moron. Did you hit your head while off playing in the sand?"

Christian mocked a furious expression, while keeping one cautious eye on Talon. "I was helping my mom's pack in Hawaii. The sickness almost took them all out." He shrugged. "Though, to be fair, there was a lot of digging in the sand."

He continued to back away until he collided with Kellan, who slapped a hand on his shoulder. "Good to have you back, brother. Are you ready for the game tonight?"

"Uh huh," Christian said, sounding distracted.

To no one's surprise, his focus remained locked on the quietly vibrating dragon.

When I tapped Talon's shoulder, his chest rumbled once, the tremor tingling through my fingers, but he must have decided that Christian was no real threat and eased up just enough for me to view the rest of the shifters.

Including a semi-familiar face that I hadn't seen on this team before. It took me a beat to remember the huge Viking-looking shifter's name... Henderson.

*What is he doing here?*

Kassidy must have noticed where my curious focus was directed. "He just joined the team," she murmured near my ear. "Trace Henderson. Apparently, our GM thought he was too good a player to leave on another team. He offered up a trade to get him."

Finley and Kellan didn't really acknowledge the Viking as they caught up with Christian. When Henderson's gaze landed on me, it lingered for a few seconds, but other than mild curiosity he showed no other interest. At least none that got my guard-dragon moving.

The Viking alpha had sharp, masculine features, intense gray eyes like a storm at sea, and full lips that were flat and unsmiling. When his stare skipped past me, it locked right on Kassidy. And that was where it stayed.

Kassidy cleared her throat and he didn't react at all. "Can I help you with something?" she asked, her gaze darting around like she was uncomfortable under that penetrating stare. It was clear she wanted her question to sound annoyed and abrasive, but the breathiness in her tone betrayed her.

Kassidy had called him hot the first time she saw him, and up close he was magnetic. Not like my alphas, but there was certainly a unique strength in this shifter that most alphas didn't possess.

Henderson must have felt the same way about Kassidy—she was drop-dead gorgeous, so I wouldn't blame him—or she'd triggered his beast to take control. His stare was unwavering.

There was a lot of wolf in his sea-storm eyes, and when he took a step toward her Kassidy flinched. "Can I help you?" she repeated, this time managing to inject a decent bite into her tone.

Kassidy was an alpha, and though I hadn't seen her really use the force of her dominance, as Hunter's sister she did pack a punch. Henderson shook his head, his expression falling into confused lines.

"What's happening?" I whispered to Talon, before remembering he was usually more clueless to shifter interactions than me.

To my surprise, he didn't even hesitate to answer. "They're mates —scent matches, if the flare of their beasts is any indication."

His statement sent a quiet shockwave through the hall as everyone looked between the two shifters. Henderson took another step forward as his confusion faded into determination. It was a look I was well acquainted with, one that had started with Hunter Reeves the first time he scented me.

"No," Kassidy breathed, shaking her head. "No. I don't have mates. I don't have scent matches. I don't care that he smells like fresh air and first rain in the desert. I hate rain and deserts. I hate mates."

Despite this very blunt statement, which told me there was a lot more to unpack with Kassidy than I'd ever realized, Henderson's expression didn't change. The glint of determination remained, and that slice of obsession blazed in his eyes. I still hadn't seen him smile, but this was another Hunter if I'd ever seen one.

Kassidy backed up and I could tell she was about to turn tail and run. That was, after all, another look I recognized.

Before she could make her escape, Hunter appeared in the hall that led to the rink, and he got right in Henderson's way. The two of them stood eye to eye and seemed an even match, though one was a hypocritical bastard because he'd let no one get in his way when he was coming after me.

"You need to walk away," Hunter said without inflection. "Give her some time."

He pulled a business card from inside his suit jacket and handed it to Henderson. "Call me tomorrow and we can talk more. For now, you've got a hockey game to focus on."

The other shifter glanced at the card like it was a bag of shit, and though it felt impossible, his expression grew even harder until he looked like he was carved from granite. Thankfully, the rest of the team managed to get him moving toward the lockers, even as his gaze remained on Kassidy until they disappeared from sight.

When my friend breathed a heavy sigh, one might think it was all relief, but I heard the sniffle that followed. Kellan distracted me by giving me and his mom a hug, before he dragged Christian off toward the lockers.

Finley also closed his arms around me in one of his all-encompassing bear hugs. "I'll talk to him," he murmured. A kiss followed, and I momentarily forgot the hallway drama.

"He joined the team two weeks ago," Hunter said from nearby.

Finley nodded as he pulled back from me. "Yeah, the paperwork took a bit to finalize. I'll find out whatever I can to see if he's a good match for Kassidy." His gaze met mine, those whiskey eyes sparkling as a dimple appeared. "Though the goddess rarely makes mistakes."

Me and my current life were living, breathing proof of that.

Kassidy choked out her next words. "No. No… no mates. I can't live through it again."

Pain and fear were threaded through her shattered expression, and while she'd hinted at a tragedy in her past, I had no idea what had caused her to live alone and without a pack.

Whatever it was, she'd clearly been hurt. Badly.

"Come on, Kass," Hunter said, wrapping his arm around her and leading her toward the stands. "Let's watch some hockey. Scent match or not, you don't need to make any decisions today."

Part of me wanted to roll my eyes and ask him where this reasonable side was when *I* was the one running from my mates. As if he'd heard that, he shot a smirk over his shoulder, and in the bond his wolf eased against mine. *I would chase you to the ends of existence, little mate. Don't ever forget it. And kill anyone who got in my way.*

*Lucky I enjoy a little chase*, I shot back, and he answered with a satisfied rumble, before his wolf backed out of the bond once more.

"Always riling up our entitled alpha." Talon sounded amused. "He likes when you sass him."

Hunter had never made that a secret. When I sassed him, he took great pleasure in fucking me until I couldn't remember my name, let alone make another smartass comment.

Talon stayed close as we entered the main stadium, the noise extra-loud after being in the relatively soundproofed halls. It was so noisy I expected the stands were already filled, but it was early; only about thirty percent of seats were taken.

"They're an enthusiastic crowd already," I noted.

"We can use the corporate box," Hunter offered, his worried glance shifting to Kassidy.

As much as I loved being in the crowd and really feeling the action, a little anonymity might be exactly what she needed tonight.

Kassidy shook her head though. "No, I want to watch from down here. Emme prefers it too."

Warmth lit up my chest at her caring enough to notice this about me. "Don't stay down here on account of me," I blurted, ignoring Talon, who grumbled about me not getting whatever made me the happiest. "I haven't even seen the corporate box, and I'm happy to sit up there."

Kassidy, finally starting to shake off her shock, planted her hands on her hips. I took in her full badass alpha wolf glory, all decked out in combat boots, black leather pants, and her Celtics' jersey. "Nope," she said with a snap. "I'm staying down here. I'm also going to need nachos, a beer, and some form of chocolate. Stat."

"Done," Hunter replied, his mood lightening as his sister pulled herself together.

Knowing my mate, Florence and Gerald were out there already ensuring we were delivered the highest quality hockey snacks. Especially with the Annandale pack away from their jobs as they grieved Marcus. My eyes burned, and I fought to push the sorrow aside to focus on hockey.

The next hour was spent sandwiched between Talon and Hunter, one who mentally updated Slade, while the other sent him messages. Slade's dragon also checked in with my wolf, and I was pleased that distance wasn't an issue with our mental communication.

It came in handy with how often I forgot my phone.

As the crowds piled in, I chatted to Danielle, who had pulled an actual cross-stitch out of her bag to do while she waited. I was fascinated watching her create a gorgeous pattern of flowers across the surface. *Was she even real?*

Danielle loved to talk, and conversation was so easy with her. She told me stories of Kellan over the years, along with a list of her favorite plants, and what book she was currently reading. The next time she excused herself to use the restroom, Slade's dragon surged in our bond, as if he'd been waiting for a lull to push forward. *Everything okay, Snow?*

*I'm totally fine, bestie.*

Besties who pranked each other. I missed that side of our bond, but I wasn't complaining about where we were now.

*Mate*, he growled back. *We are mates, which is a much stronger bond than besties.*

As I composed my best rebuttal to that statement, he added, *Though, I suppose we are that as well. We're soulmates. Best friends is part and parcel of that.*

Oh goddess. I was suddenly feeling a little hot under the collar. *I'm honored to be your soulmate and best friend, Slade Riverson.*

He was silent for a beat, as his beast nuzzled against my wolf, in what felt like a very loving stroke along my side. *Are you sure you're not hurt? I can feel some discomfort.*

As if he conjured the pain with those words, I felt a mild throb in my lower back. Were these plastic chairs a little harder than usual and I hadn't noticed while I was caught up in my chat with Danielle?

*I'm probably just sore from being claimed by two giant dragons co—*

I cut myself off, but the damage was already done. Talon coughed out a smoky laugh beside me, and since he wasn't in my communication with Slade, I had to assume he'd heard that through his twin connection.

Slade joined him not even a second later, and his deep raspy laughter had me feeling warm all over, until I was a puddle about to melt on the floor. I'd waited a long time to hear him laugh like that, and I was not disappointed.

*You were made for us, Snow. There's no part of me... or Talon, that you cannot take. Keep that in mind for the next time the three of us are together.*

I spluttered out loud and my wolf stepped away from the dragon, breaking the connection. Not that Slade couldn't have blasted his way through again, but thankfully he respected my need for privacy. Even as his warm laughter continued to echo through my mind.

Hunter slung his arm around my shoulder and pulled me closer, and I wondered what they saw in the bond while I was privately chatting to the other alphas. Could they see the way our beasts drifted together, while they remained more on the outside?

*Yes*, he said softly, moving forward in our connection, while making it clear I still wasn't very good at blocking my stronger thoughts. *That's what I see.*

I shivered as his teeth grazed the shell of my ear. "You smell like the sweetest candy treat," he murmured out loud, his right hand sliding up to wrap around the base of my throat in my favorite power move of his. "What did our dragon say to get you so hot and bothered?"

"Sandwiches," I blurted out, flustered as hell and relieved that Kellan's parents hadn't returned yet. "He was talking about a dragon sandwich."

His laughter drew not only my attention but that of shifter groups around us. Golden Claw wasn't used to seeing my pack express amusement so freely, but when darkness chased us around every corner, a moment of levity was exactly what we all needed.

# CHAPTER 17

EMME

The hockey game was a demolition. The Wolves burst onto the ice with a vengeance, and by the third period the score was ten to one in their favor. Kellan had a hat trick under his belt, and so did Henderson. Every time the Viking shifter scored, his gaze flashed to Kassidy, who was resolutely pretending to be very interested in the giant screen at the top of the arena.

Kellan beamed at me when he scored, and my heart fluttered with each blown kiss as he skated closer. Finley also beamed in my direction whenever he smashed one of his opponents into the side. When he spent two minutes in the penalty box, he alternated between watching the game and me. As if I could have any doubt that he loved us both.

Being here to witness my alphas playing a sport they were so good at, especially when they showed off for me, was honestly foreplay. Nothing could change my mind.

When there were only a few minutes left, Kassidy rose from her seat beside Hunter. "I think I'm going to head out before the rush," she murmured, her gaze flickering down to the ice before she tore it away once more. Henderson was on the bench, which meant he had time to watch her like she was his source of life.

Hunter rose too, then paused as he glanced down at me. "I'm totally fine," I said, shooing him out to follow her. "I've got Talon, Fin, and Kellan."

"They'll have press after the game," he reminded me, looking torn.

It was clear he was about to sit again, and I noticed Kassidy already sidling her way along the row.

"She has me," Talon reiterated with a lazy smile. "I'll tear the fucking head off anyone who touches her. You know that."

Hunter's eyes burned gold as his beast rose up. "I already know you'd choose me every time, Alpha," I whispered. "You should go after her. She needs you tonight."

The growl of his wolf was loud enough to turn more than a few heads around us. "I love my sister, but you always come first."

Just as I expected, but my answer remained the same. "Go," I said, pressing my hands to his abs. "I'll meet you at home."

He leaned down and cupped my face. His lips were soft as his tongue slid against mine. His dominance spilled into our kiss, and my beast rolled over in my mind, *choosing* to submit to her alpha. "I love you," he stated, loud and uncaring about anyone overhearing. "Stay in touch." He tapped the side of my head gently. "And remember, Slade is out there patrolling with his enforcers."

By this point, Kassidy had reached the end of the row, and Henderson was back on the ice, ignoring the game as he followed her path. She resolutely pretended not to notice, and even when he slammed his hand against the glass, Kassidy barely reacted.

Only those close would notice how stiffly she held herself, her shoulders a touch higher than usual. She was just as aware of Henderson as he was of her.

Hunter reached her in a few seconds, his broad shoulders blocking her from sight. They were gone by the time the game ended and our team did a *salute to the fans* with their sticks raised in the air—minus Henderson, who was already off the ice. I had no doubts he'd be at the newly-repaired gates of the family compound tonight.

Hunter wouldn't let him in though. Not until his sister was ready to deal with this new, unexpected, and clearly unwanted revelation in her life.

Normally, I'd be the perfect shifter to ask for advice on dealing with determined, scent-matched alphas, but since I'd all but caved to mine, unquestionably enamored with the obsessive way they loved me, I couldn't help her here.

"We're going to stay with Tyson tonight," Danielle told me as she got to her feet, her mate hovering close by. "Tell Kel to call us tomorrow. We're heading back home the day after, but we hope to see you again soon for a longer visit. Welcome to our family, Emme."

She leaned in for another hug, and I almost laughed at Talon's alarmed expression when she all but nudged him out of the way. Generally, everyone feared the dragons too much to get close, but not Kellan's mom.

"It was so amazing to meet you," I said, trying not to let my sniffles free at her welcoming me to the family. "When life isn't quite so chaotic, I'd love to spend more time with your pack."

"Keep us updated," Conrad ordered, his serious expression reminiscent of Kellan's when he was in alpha mode. "We'll be out here as soon as you need us. This isn't your battle to fight alone."

Kellan would never put them in danger, but I appreciated the offer. "Thank you," I said softly, making no promises.

As Danielle squeezed me once more, her hold tight, I felt that same twinge low in my back. Despite my smartass remark from before, there was no way it was sex related. My shifter healing would have fixed that up by now.

I was fairly sure I knew what was going on, and while the timing sucked, a little period pain wouldn't hold me back from finding that fucking witch and eliminating her from the world.

Talon and I remained in our seats until most of the stadium was cleared, before we exited as well. Finley and Kellan checked in soon after, telling me they were more than happy to skip out on their media obligations and head home with us.

*Stay. You don't know if you'll even be able to make the next games. Your coach deserves your time tonight, and I have Tal.*

Their reluctance filtered through; their beasts moved uneasily, but they didn't argue.

*You take the car, darlin'*, Finley said.

I relayed this out loud to Talon, and as he glanced around at the vehicles and shifters filling the parking lot, his distaste for the chaos was clear.

"Tell them to keep the car," he said. "I've got a better way for us to get home."

The twinge in my back was joined by butterflies in my stomach as I considered the only possible travel option for a dragon shifter.

*Car is yours, Grouchy. Tal will get me home.*

The bear and wolf caressed my beast, before they backed out of the connection, giving me a brief flash of them stepping into the press room.

"Come on, Honey," Talon said, the shortened nickname purring from him. "I've been waiting a long time for this."

As we moved through the crowd, most shifters gave Talon a wide berth. More than a couple did a double take as they tried to figure out who the Slade doppelganger was. It was a big city, and the information clearly wasn't everywhere yet.

After what had happened in the street, most of the council and enforcers knew. Hunter had told them all to go fuck themselves, along with a warning that if any of them tried to come after Talon, our pack would tear them into little pieces.

The threat had held up so far.

Trust was thin these days, and I was happy with our decision to stick with our pack and a few loyal friends and family. Which didn't quite include Constantine, at least not for me yet.

Ignoring his existence would end soon though, as I needed his help to learn how to control the tendrils of magic floating freely around my essence. Eventually, it would force its way out of me, and I'd be foolish not to prepare.

When we moved beyond the crowds, Talon led me to a patch of cleared land on the side of the arena. The ground was icy, only a few threadbare trees around us. Talon's smile flashed in the shadows as he pulled off his leather jacket, followed by his shirt, revealing firm skin over taut muscles.

Despite the near freezing temperatures, I burned up at the sight of him shedding clothing. His gaze remained on me as his scent filled the air, all sweet and smoky. When he ditched his boots and pants, completely commando beneath the denim, the bond between us thrummed strongly. As the connection blazed, my thighs trembled and barely kept me standing.

I was unable to tear my gaze away.

*Mine.* My mate. One I'd claimed in all ways today and wanted to do so again very soon.

"You're magnificent," I whispered, the words slipping out.

His huge chest lifted as a feral growl escaped him. "*You* are magnificent, mate, and my most precious gift." His voice was a tantalizing murmur in the still air, and my feet moved to bring me right against him, huffing in his scent like I needed it to live. And maybe I did.

His clothes fell from his grasp as he wrapped me in his arms, and we stood under the moonlight for many beats of my racing heart. I sensed that Talon would never be the first to let go, so I eased back, and he used that space to reach down and grab his jacket. He pulled the thick, heavy leather material over my shoulders and zipped it up to hide my jersey. "It will be cold up there. Let me know if it gets to be too much and I can fly lower."

Before I could respond, he took more than a dozen steps back. The scent of ozone filled the air as he called on the shift. I didn't look away as his beast emerged from the man, leaving a huge, darkly captivating dragon perched before me.

The once midnight of his scales were greener now, but you couldn't really tell in the shadowy night. As he stepped forward, I fumbled for the rest of his clothes, but he growled, and a familiar voice filled my mind. It was a mix of Talon and beast. *Leave them. Climb on me, little mate.*

The dragon was intense, as was to be expected, and my wolf wasn't the only one who shivered and fought the desire to roll over and expose her belly. In our essence, the dragon stroked his snout along my beast, and out here, in the freezing night, the real creature did the same to me.

When he reached the front of my jeans there was a huff as he growled, *You're fertile.*

Flames burst to life in my center, and that ache in my back eased up under the touch of dragon heat. "Yes, thank you for pointing it out. But as you know, I'm taking the brew to prevent pregnancy."

The dragon huffed again, filling the clearing with smoky maple. He didn't sound impressed by my responsible actions, and I found myself chuckling. "Don't tell me you have a breeding kink like Kellan? That boy reads too many books."

Another rumble, and his voice returned to my mind. *We would be honored if you carried our youngling. But not while this world is in peril. We will destroy the witch first, and then we will breed you.*

Well, fuck. His statement had those licks of fire turning into an inferno, and even though I wasn't sure I wanted babies yet, the way he'd said that was really freaking hot.

As I melted into a puddle at his massive, clawed feet, he used his head to guide me around his left side toward his front leg. Even bent as it was, there was no way I could climb his limb, not even when he lowered himself to the ground. I'd been able to race up his giant tail when he was Slalon, but this was a whole different task.

Stretching my leg as high as I could, I still needed a boost from his head to be able to make the height. My breath came out in rapid gasps as I scrambled to keep my balance on what I assumed was his knee, only to have a random gust of cold air almost send me tumbling back off.

Talon caught me again on his snout, and then remained behind me until I reached his broad back. The scales weren't as slippery as I expected. His natural heat seeped into me, and with his guidance I found a spot where I could comfortably sit near the base of his neck, spreading my legs wide enough to slot in on either side of him. There were spikes down the crest and at the base of his neck, which I used as handholds, careful not to cut myself on their lethally sharp ends.

"Let me know if I hurt you," I said as I tried not to squeeze too tightly.

I got a scoff in response. *Silly mate. You could never hurt me, and even if you did, I would accept the pain as mine. Just as you are mine.*

Okay, the dragon was as destructive as the man.

A beat later, his wings spread out on either side of him and I had to adjust my seat again. Swirls of excitement and anticipation raced through me, knowing this was the fulfilment of a promise he made long ago. I would teach him to drive, not that he'd really needed much help, and he would take me flying.

Ever since I'd found out one of my mates was a dragon, I'd been curious about how it felt to fly. It was so foreign to my landbound beast, and from the outside appeared more magical than even magic itself. Pure freedom.

With the first powerful thrusts of his wings, Talon lifted us from the ground, and if I hadn't had my handholds, I'd probably have slid right off his back. After tightening the grip of my thighs, I found stability as he got us airborne. In less than a minute we were soaring above the trees and stadium, the dark wintery sky spanning out around us.

A ripple of his energy tingled along my thighs and into my butt, straight from the beast himself. I wondered if he'd just used his magical abilities to keep us concealed. The higher we climbed, the colder it grew, but between Talon's jacket and the dragon's natural heat, I remained toasty warm.

Golden Claw spread out below us and the sea of lights was stunning. Off in the distance I caught sight of the Thenguard and Reeves offices, which stood higher than all the rest. I had no idea what had happened to all of Sorenson's properties, now that he was dead and his pack was lost to whatever Fletcher did to them. For now, the lights remained on, as if everything was running normally.

Talon banked to the left in a slow, gentle swirl before he flapped his huge wings. The breezes picked up around us as he moved across Golden Claw, and I was finally starting to understand why Slade hadn't been able to describe this experience. It held a fraction of the thrill of driving fast, but was unique all on its own.

Through all of it, though, there was this unfathomable awe. We hovered above the world.

*Like gods.*

No wonder dragons were arrogant. They'd definitely earned it.

# CHAPTER 18

EMME

By the time Talon landed smoothly in front of our house, my body felt weightless, while my legs were heavy, as if they refused to walk after experiencing the thrill of flying. It took a full minute to adjust to being grounded, and Talon didn't rush me, letting me have all the time I needed to find my equilibrium. Eventually, I was able to slide off his huge back, and his head stayed with me all the way down to my thud of a landing against the front sidewalk.

He returned to his bipedal form in a flash, and I threw myself into his arms, exploding with all the emotions—joy, excitement, fear, and so much love for this shifter who continued to demonstrate that we could be more than our upbringing.

We could rise above our circumstances in life.

Talon had spent countless years acting as the nameless weapon of a psychopath, an assassin who was never taught to question anything, which was the scariest part of all. This shifter had only ever known forced loyalty and false truths, but he hadn't let that define his future. Sure, his future had been helped along by a life-changing bond that rearranged our very cells and essences, but the choices that brought him to this moment… they were all Talon's.

"Thank you," I gushed against his throat, and he wrapped me up tighter, burying his face in my hair. "Thank you for fighting so hard to be part of this pack. For trusting and accepting us. For being mine."

His voice broke on a rasp. "Thank you for existing, Emme."

We stood there long enough to give the street a great view of his naked butt, which had my possessive side all riled up. When I attempted to hand Talon his jacket, he shook his head. "You keep it, mate. It looks better on you anyway, and I enjoy seeing you in *my* clothes. It's another sign that you belong to me."

"The bite on my neck is an even clearer sign," I reminded him with a laugh, but since I also enjoyed wearing their clothes, I didn't object.

"The bite is my favorite," Talon agreed, his eyes darkening to a deep black. "I'd like to claim you again and again, and mark all over your soft skin."

Only a claiming bond was supposed to leave a scar on a full-strength shifter, but my alphas certainly enjoyed testing that theory.

When we made it inside, Hunter strolled in from the kitchen, and I was surprised by Talon nudging me in his direction. "Go to our entitled alpha," he said. "He needs to tell you about Kassidy."

He brushed a kiss across my lips and then strolled out of the room. I watched his perfect muscled butt until he was all the way up the stairs, and while Hunter's scent grew stronger, he didn't interrupt my drooling.

I turned to find him wearing an amused smirk. "You really are the perfect match for us," he drawled in that deep rasp. "I'd have worried that five alpha males might end up being too much for you, but so far you've handled us very well."

My cheeks heated, even though I knew he spoke of more than sex in that statement. Still, my mind was naturally designed to flop around in the gutter when it came to *handling* my mates.

Hunter's smile faded. "Just remember that you have all the power here, little omega. Don't let us take more than you have to give us." It was the same warning I'd received from my other mates earlier. Clearly all of them were concerned about it.

"We've only been a completed quintet for half a day, therefore my experience is limited, but I don't think there's anything for you to worry about."

I stepped into him, needing to see his concerned expression eased. "I'm glad you're our entitled alpha. I wasn't sure at first, with how dominant and demanding your beast is, but you're levelheaded and truly care about your entire pack. I might be the heart of this quintet, but you're the structure that holds us all together. We'd just be a pile of blood and organs on the ground without you."

Hunter arched an eyebrow. "Eloquently put, Emmeline. Please, tell me more about the massacre that would occur without me."

I tapped him on his chest, and he straightened to his full height, leaving me to tilt my head back to meet his gaze. "Nah, I wouldn't want you to get a big head. Yours is just the right size for your body."

With a wolfy grumble, he wrapped an arm around me and drew me into his side, moving us toward the kitchen. The house was quiet with Finley and Kellan in press, Slade patrolling, Talon upstairs, and I could only assume Constantine was still researching in the library.

The relief I felt at not having to deal with him yet was far too great, but as I'd thought earlier, the avoidance of my *father* could not go on much longer. Not with the magic swirling inside me. It hadn't burst out yet—thankfully—but surely it was only a matter of time.

I'd always heard that magic was as volatile as our beasts, and neither could stay trapped for long. A theory I didn't really want to test.

The kitchen was warm, with low lights illuminating the cabinetry. There was a large platter set out on the widest of counters, and Hunter directed me toward a stool, his fingers tracing along my biceps in a teasing movement. When I sat, he leaned down to run his nose up the curve of my neck, his teeth grazing over his bite. My thighs clenched against the sudden pulse in my core. It took less than a single touch for these alphas to reduce me to a soaked, needy mess.

"Baby girl," he murmured. "Let me feed you while we talk about Kassidy."

It was on the tip of my tongue to mention that the hunger inside me couldn't be sated by food, but the mention of his sister halted that line of thought. My friend had gone through a lot tonight, and I wanted to be there for her in whatever way she needed. All of which would be made easier with more information up my sleeve.

"Did she get home okay?" I asked, as Hunter slid into the chair beside mine, pulling the tray closer. Florence had left out a charcuterie board for us, and Hunter took his time loading up a small side plate with cheeses, cured meats, crackers, and fruit.

As I let a deliciously creamy goat cheese melt across my tongue, Hunter relaxed until wafts of satisfaction reached me through our bond. "Yes, I left her at home," he said, "where she's locked in and ready to sleep away this new revelation."

Knowing she was alone bothered me, though it appeared to be her preferred state. "Did you tell her she's welcome to stay here?" I asked around my next bite, which was aged cheddar that tasted like heaven. *Rich people* cheese was the best. "I hate the thought of her being alone and freaking out over Henderson knocking on her door."

Hunter noticed my blissed-out cheese state and added more of it to my plate. "Yeah, I offered, but my sister is a stubborn shit. Always has been. She's also a strong alpha, and Henderson won't find her presence at home any more welcoming than it was in the arena."

I barely managed not to roll my eyes. "Oh wow. How weird that she's a stubborn and strong-willed alpha. Especially when the rest of her family is chill as fuck. Maybe she's adopted...?"

Hunter playfully narrowed his eyes on me. "As much as I love your sass, brat, don't make me take you over my knee. That's more of a Slade kink."

A shiver traversed my spine and I almost choked on the strawberry I'd just shoved in my mouth. "You all have a one-track mind."

"And you love it."

The alpha had a point.

As Hunter continued to add food to my plate, I decided to fix one for him too. His big body stilled when I started to fill it, and that confusion remained even as I slid it across the counter to sit in front of him. "It's my job to feed you, little mate," he said with a huff.

Shaking my head, I leaned over and snuggled into his side. "An omega can look after her alphas too. It makes me happy."

His scent deepened, and there was a very contented rumble rocking his chest. "I don't think anyone has ever looked after me in my life, but I find when it comes from you I quite like it."

My heart squeezed, and I was more determined than ever to keep showing up and showing my love for them. "Well, get used to it," I rasped around my tight throat.

Hunter dragged his plate closer and *fuck* the satisfaction I felt when he started to eat what I'd selected for him... *Was that how they felt feeding me?*

"Why is Kassidy so concerned about a mate bond?" I asked, settling in to enjoy our time in the darkened kitchen, just the two of us. "Unless that's prying too far into her business. I do prefer to hear it directly. I just don't want to say something that might hurt her when I don't know the full story."

Hunter shook his head, chewing on a slice of apple. "You're not prying. You're family, and you care about Kassidy. We're lucky to have you in our lives."

He spread soft cheese on a cracker next and held it out to me. It had been at least ten seconds since I'd taken a bite, which was far too long for this entitled alpha. As I opened my mouth so he could slide the offering inside, he made that very satisfied sound again.

"It all goes back to Fletcher, of course," he continued. "As you can imagine it was worse when we were younger and had neither the strength nor financial means to fight back against him."

It had been bad growing up with my mom and the Rogers pack, but Fletcher seemed infinitely worse. At least most of the time I'd just been locked in my room and ignored.

Hunter huffed, and mocha scent surrounded me. "There was an alpha wolf who lived on the property beside ours," he said. "Jonas. Kassidy developed a bit of a crush on him when we were younger, which exploded when their beasts emerged. Jonas reciprocated, and while they showed no sign of being a scent match, my sister didn't care. One day, Fletcher caught wind of her sneaking off to hang out with Jonas and he had him killed. There was no body found, but his room was torn up, and there was enough blood that it was doubtful anyone could have survived. Kass was never the same again. She swore off mates and packs after that. While Fletcher was alive, she'd never risk losing anyone she loved again."

"Fletcher is dead now though."

Hunter nodded. "Yeah, but I think enough time has passed that she's too scared to risk it, full-stop. There's always a danger out there, and I don't think she'd survive the loss of someone she loved again." The low lights flickered over the serious planes of his face, turning his expression darker.

My wolf rose up to rumble, and I felt the same fury. "I'm glad you got free of that evil shifter before he completely destroyed you all, even if you do still wear the scars he inflicted." Internally at least.

Hunter and Slade's success had given them the money and power to walk away from Fletcher and take their family and friends with them. Kassidy worked for Reeves Industries in their distribution division, and I had no doubt she was paid very well for her time.

"That was the tipping point for me," he growled, hands pressing against the counter as his anger and frustration filtered through the bond. "I'd have killed him if it came down to protecting them, but it felt cleaner to leave. At that stage, he was a powerful alpha in our community."

Powerful and evil. "There are many days," I bit out, "that I wish we could bring that piece of shit shifter back from the dead and kill him again. Just more painfully."

Hunter cupped my face, rubbing his thumb over my cheek. "Such a violent little wolf. I love that about you."

Violence wasn't in my innate nature as an omega, but the moment anyone threatened me or mine, I was all female rage. "It's a tough situation with Kass," I said, wishing that my friend wasn't in pain. "I don't think there's anything we can do other than be there for her. Support her decision. And offer our opinions *if* she asks for them."

Hunter let out a sigh, and just like violence wasn't in my nature, *not taking action* definitely wasn't in his. But he didn't argue with my assessment.

I leaned toward him, and he released me long enough to nudge my plate forward, which was filled again. *How in the…?*

"Eat," he commanded, and when I huffed and grabbed another slice of meat, he picked up the newspaper that he hadn't gotten to this morning.

He shook it open, and I caught sight of the front-page article, my eyes widening as I choked for the second time tonight. Thankfully, the ham slid down the right pipe, and I managed not to die over the headline: *Thieves Destroy Old Jim's Prize-Winning Magnolia Tree Orchard.*

Hunter lowered the paper and raised an eyebrow as he stared at me, but I was too busy trying to read the full article.

*Old Jim has reported the loss of one of his rare cross-bred magnolias that pollinate and flower all year round. "I'm devastated to find it has been pulled up from the ground in one hard yank…"*

Hunter dropped the paper, cutting me off, and my gaze darted over to where *Steven*, my magnolia tree, was growing quite nicely in the kitchen. We'd repotted him into a massive stone planter and had him over near the window for sun exposure.

When I continued to gawk at the paper, Hunter turned it over and quickly read the article himself. Before I could ask *What the fuck are we going to do?* his husky laughter rang out through the kitchen. "Don't worry about Steve," he said, shaking his head like he couldn't believe we had given our plant a people name. "We'll keep you and Fin out of the slammer. Bribe the proper authorities."

I snorted, before clearing my throat. It wasn't funny that Finley had drunkenly stolen poor Old Jim's plant, but I sure as shit wasn't giving Steven back. He was mine, and I was possessive of my things.

"I've already sent him a generous donation," Hunter informed me, opening the paper once more. "Anonymously of course. He's much better off now, and he has the means to grow many more Steves. You'll be fine."

"There's only one Steven," I muttered, before I reached out and gave him a hug. "But thank you. You're always looking after us." He didn't say anything, but I felt how pleased he was through our bond.

"I think I might get ready for bed," I said around a yawn. "We've got a big day tomorrow, and apparently it starts at the crack of dawn, with Slade's training."

My muscles ached at the thought, but I hadn't given up on wanting to hold my own in a fight. Whether that be physically, mentally, or magically. *Apparently*.

Hunter nuzzled me and breathed in my scent once more. "Okay, little mate. Just remember that the sleeping schedule kicks in tomorrow, since we know you'll want to be with the twins tonight to reinforce the new bond."

*Sleeping schedule*. Right, that was happening.

"What if I wanted all of you around me?" I teased, even though it was actually the truth.

Hunter's expression dimmed until he was all predator. "All of us want to sleep with you," he said softly. "You're the heart of our quintet, and you always decide."

With that power bestowed on me, a shiver traced down my spine, and I dropped a kiss on his cheek before I scurried from the room.

Wondering how I'd make it all work.

# CHAPTER 19

EMME

During my shower, a deeper cramp hit, and by the time I got out my ovaries and uterus ached. A smear of blood came away on the towel I used to dry myself, but thankfully this time I had all the supplies in the world.

Opening one of my bathroom drawers, I grabbed the period disc and underwear, unsure how heavy my flow would be tonight. My skin was irritated too, so I dressed in my softest pajama set and headed out of my room with full intentions of filling my hot water bottle. Only to find myself turning in the opposite direction and taking the stairs *up* to the third floor. My feet slowed outside Slade's room, and I knew why I'd inadvertently sought him out.

He'd been the one who'd eased my pain last time.

Not to mention, I hadn't been able to shake the memory of the twins sprawled in that bed together. That night hadn't been the right timing to crawl in between them—Finley had been calling me, and the twins needed a few nights to properly cement *their* bond. But now… they were my newest bonded mates, and I needed them tonight.

When I stepped through their doorway, I blinked at the sight of them already on the bed. "Snow," Slade drawled, his green gaze locking me in place. "We've been waiting for you, sweetheart."

My breaths came out slow and heavy, and I couldn't bring myself to move. "Weren't you patrolling?" I managed to ask.

He canted his head, taking a long, leisurely glance along my body. "I could feel that you needed me, so I cut the night short."

The twins were positioned against the headboard, their wide shoulders taking up almost the entire width. "Come to us," Talon commanded, and before I could think I was moving.

When my toes hit the frame of the massive bed, I all but toppled forward, forgetting I held my hot water bottle. The faceplant into the cloudlike mattress didn't hurt, and I huffed at the laughter over the top of my head.

"Some days I wonder how you're a shifter," Slade said, slipping his hands under my armpits and slowly dragging me up the bed to face him. Drawing the hot water bottle from my hands, he tossed it to the side. "Your coordination and stamina are *unique*, that's for sure." As the alpha who trained me, he had a ton of evidence to back that statement.

I opened my mouth to defend myself but Talon interrupted with a growl. "I smell blood. Are you injured?"

Both of them examined me closer, and their intense heat was soothing to my pain. Slade's nostrils flared, but he quickly ascertained there were no injuries. "You have your period," he noted. "Your fertile time is coming to an end for another season."

I doubted Talon had much experience with fertile times or periods, and with that in my mind, I was already bracing for how he'd react. I'd heard there were males who didn't handle it well or got grossed out. It would take him time to get used—

One of his hands slid down to cover my stomach, and the other across my lower back. "We feel your discomfort, Emme," he said. "You're staying with us tonight so we can soothe you. Whatever it takes." He looked toward his twin. "I read that orgasms can help omegas during their period. Is that correct?"

*Goddessfuck.* Did I just burst into flames?

The ache in my uterus flared when it spasmed, my lower half unsure if we were shedding our lining or preparing to be bred. *Who said it couldn't be both?*

"As nice as an orgasm would be," I managed to say, sounding almost normal. "I'd prefer not to cover you both in blood. I can be quite the heavy bleeder for the first few days."

As Slade was well aware. Not that he appeared to care, as he followed his brother's lead and slid his hands across my sides until their heat infiltrated my entire core. "We're not turned off by blood," he said, his accent deepening. "You just let us know what you need."

There was a ruckus at the door, and my bites pulsed as my other mates all but tumbled inside. "She *needs* to kiss us goodnight," Kellan declared, the first in the room, with Finley right behind him. "And you two big bastards *need* to get on board with larger beds, and pack huddles from here on out."

There was no real bite in his tone, as they all knew I'd spend this night with the twins. It was hard not to stay with all my alphas though, especially Finley, who struggled to sleep by himself. I'd been with him for the last two nights, and he'd crashed out completely for the first time in weeks.

As if he'd heard that thought, the bear knee walked from the end of the bed, ignoring the rumbles of the dragons as he pulled me from their grasp.

He wrapped me in a bear hug. "Now that our bond is complete, my soul is at ease," he said softly, soothing my worries. "I can reach for your essence anytime I need, and my bear is already inching toward your beast. I want to sleep with you, don't get me wrong, but you don't need to feel any guilt. Enjoy your slumber in the dragon inferno."

My lips parted and he kissed me thoroughly. Kellan dipped in a beat later with a slow, tender touch against my lips. "See you at training, Shortcake," he murmured in a teasing tone. "You've got weapons with me, after Slade destroys you on a soul-deep level."

"Then magic with Constantine," Slade added, not denying the *soul-destroying* comment.

I groaned at the very thought, especially while I had my period. "Aren't we heading to the compound tomorrow?" The hint of hope was easily heard in my question, and Kellan snorted.

"Only you'd take Fletcher's creepy lair over magic training."

"Magic training *with* Constantine," I reminded him.

Talon shook his head. "I need to do some scouting first, make sure the area is clear. I won't put you all at risk. If everything is good though, we can head there the next day."

The dragon's energy pulsed strongly in our quintet bond, and I was starting to wonder if that happened when they were doing their own *twin* communicating.

"The next day works," Hunter said, the last to enter the room. His nostrils flared. "You're bleeding."

I forced myself not to roll my eyes at their overprotective nature;

I'd barely been alone in weeks and was clearly uninjured. "I'm fine," I said, meeting his blazing gaze.

"She's got her period." Kellan figured it out quickly. "Everyone needs to go easy on her tomorrow."

So far, none of my alphas showed any sign of being remotely squeamish about periods, which was... unexpected. But really damn nice.

"They'll be here every six to eight weeks," I said with a shrug. "As long as I'm not knocked up of course."

That statement had scents flaring, and in our quintet energy, all the beasts pressed against my wolf. No thoughts really accompanied it, but we were absolutely in a pack huddle. "That day will come, Emmeline Anders," Hunter said in a low, soothing burr. "Now, let's get you to bed."

The alphas who weren't sleeping in here tonight kissed me one last time and then headed off to do their own thing. With exhaustion pressing in on me, I crawled in between the dragons, and Slade wasted no time stripping me out of my pajamas, leaving me in just black period underwear.

"Much better," he declared, his gaze dragging down my bare breasts. "I want to feel your skin against mine."

Talon grunted his agreement, and I cursed the timing of bleeding when I really wanted a few of those promised orgasms. A thought that immediately filtered through the bond.

Slade's smile grew, and his eyes were a blazing green fire as they burned into my soul. "Talon's offer stands. We aren't worried about a little blood, but we can use the shower if it makes you feel more comfortable."

My stare darted toward the bathroom door. I swore it was an involuntary movement. Not that Slade cared as he hauled me up in a flash, and by the time I sucked in a deep, ragged breath, we were in the bathroom.

Slade stripped my underwear from me, and then two naked shifters crowded me back against the wall. The cool tiles were a blessed relief as steam and dragon heat covered me until I burned. Talon stroked down my stomach, his fingers sliding inside me without hesitation, only pausing when he hit the edge of the disc. "What's that?" he asked, blinking down at me.

"My period disc," I rasped, my core aching as my legs trembled beneath me. "You can leave it in if you'd like. According to the instructions, the disc should contain blood without limiting sexual activity."

"Remove it," Slade ordered, and Talon curled his fingers in to hook on the edge, somehow knowing the exact way to catch it and pull free. There was no way it should be as erotic as it was to watch him slide the disc from me, blood slicking down my legs to land on the white tiled floor. But here we were.

True to their word, neither of them looked remotely turned off by the blood, and I shouldn't have been surprised. I'd watched them tear Fletcher to pieces only two days ago, and not one of the alphas had flinched at the blood that had covered them.

"Stop thinking so hard," Slade murmured near my ear, and while there was a brief annoyance at his arrogant ass trying to force my *thoughts* to obey him, my mind did weirdly clear.

My wolf obeyed her alphas in a way that the human side of me couldn't.

When Talon sank to his knees, I gasped and tried to back up, but I was already plastered against the wall. "No, not like that," I choked out. "Put the disc back in before you stick your mouth—"

My words were cut off by his tongue on my clit, then my head spun until I couldn't remember my objections. Slade tilted my head back and captured my lips, his hands reaching out to clasp mine and keep me pressed against the wall. As sparks of pleasure took me under, I decided that it wasn't up to me to protect grown shifters from a little blood.

If they didn't care, then I *did not care.*

After taking both of my hands into one of his, and positioning them above my head, Slade used his other hand to slide two fingers inside me, moving them in time to his brother's tongue stroking my clit.

They were both gentle, as if they sensed how tender and sore I was in my core. A pain that all but vanished under the maddening swirl of a tongue meeting slow thrusts of a hand.

My moans were so loud that not even Slade's kiss drowned them out. I parted my thighs wider, hovering on the edge of what felt like a devastating release. At the first roll of the orgasm, my knees buckled, but I already knew they'd hold me up.

Neither of them slowed, and when my release shattered through me, I gushed all over Slade's hand. They continued to touch me until I was spent, relaxed, and completely pain free. There wasn't a ton of blood from what I could see, with the shower taking care of most of it.

After that, Talon lifted me out from under the stream and dried me off. Neither of them looked away when I inserted my disc again, and I got the feeling that they'd be asking to do that job next time. With my backup underwear on once more, I crawled into bed between them, half drifting off before my head hit the pillow.

As they cocooned me between their naked lengths, their palms landed on my stomach and back, the heat easing any cramps the orgasm hadn't taken care of.

I fell asleep so fast that I barely caught their goodnights.

Sleeping between my dragon sentinels was the safest place in the world, and I knew I would rest easy.

# CHAPTER 20

TALON

Until recently, my life was one of servitude, with brief moments of interaction with other shifters. Most of whom I either worked for or had to kill.

There was no true connection or bond in my life.

All of which changed the moment I set my eyes on a terrified, *unexpectedly* perfect omega.

As much as I wished to take back our first meeting, I was too selfish to ever risk not tying her to me in all ways. Every moment spent with Emme, sleeping beside her, touching her soft skin, and drowning in her scent calmed and healed my beast and me.

Now we cared about more than just our task and the destruction of shifter cities.

We cared about our mate and the entire pack of alphas in my quintet.

The transition from wanting to please my *captor* to wanting to protect my family had changed me on a level that felt essence-deep. Touching Emme all night soothed ragged edges that I never even knew were there until I had the *after* to compare to. Along with my twin's proximity, I'd never slept so well in my life.

*You heading out soon?* Slade's voice was a low hum in our bond, neither of us needing as much sleep as Emmeline, but unable to leave her comforting presence in our bed.

We were tangled around her, just as our beasts were pressed against her wolf in the bond.

*Yeah, it'll take me four or so hours to fly to the compound, and then I need to scout the area. Assess the danger.* I paused, as a worrying thought hit me. *Will Emme be in pain from our distance. Our bond isn't new, but this full connection is.*

He was silent for a moment, his fingers tracing gently over her stomach, soothing her pain. *I don't believe so. There's no evidence of any strain now we're all bonded in a complete quintet. With the ability to communicate and share energy fully in our grasp, we're never really at a distance.*

His logic was undeniable. *You have sensed the way we can share our essences now too? Her magic feels similar to the energy our dragons use to control matter around us.*

Slade's green eyes flashed, the darkness of the room not enough to restrict my sight of him. *Agreed. Our essences are all flowing together, along with her magic. I've experimented and pulled a little into myself, and it tasted like all of our beasts. Emme hasn't fully figured out how to control it yet, and when she does, she could possibly block the share, but none of us could block her.*

We would never want to block our heart.

The silence extended, and it was comfortable and warm. Warm was the oddest concept for one who'd lived such a cold life.

*What if the witch is there?* Slade asked, a flicker of concern bleeding into those words. *Maybe I should come with you. The others can keep an eye on our mate while we're gone.*

My beast reared up at the thought of one of us not being here with the pack. *In this situation I don't think it's necessary. It's only scouting. If I was planning on attacking, then it would be worth the risk to remove us both from the pack.*

Slade wanted to argue, but this time I had logic on my side. My twin loved logic. *Yeah, that makes sense. I'm also not ready to fully trust Constantine. Not yet. Still, I find myself uncomfortable with you leaving.*

There was that damn warmth again. *I'll be careful,* I assured him. *This is just a scouting mission. I shouldn't have to get close enough to trigger any magical alarms.*

Long before the light of dawn filled the room, I dragged myself from Emme and Slade. As she slept, I brushed my lips lightly against hers, relieved that she already felt less exhausted. She'd needed this healing sleep—we all had.

The strength of our quintet pleased me, and I enjoyed the magic flowing through our beasts now too. *I thought I'd hate the foreign feeling of magic inside her, but it feels like ours. She is ours.*

Slade's words resonated deeply within me and my dragon.

*Always ours. We have magic too, and all of it works together.*

*Yes.*

When I'd first met my twin, there'd been a strong rift between him and his beast. This volatile, roaring chasm of pain that neither of them were able to cross. Now that we'd reformed our twin soul bond, that chasm was gone, and in its place a sea of tranquility.

My rift with my dragon had never been as deep or enraged, but it existed all the same. We both enjoyed this new feeling of power and *peace.* I'd never experienced anything like it before, and I would not give it up easily.

After drawing the covers over Emme's bare shoulders, I forced myself into the bathroom to get ready for the day. On the street, in the predawn chill of the winter day, there was no sign of shifters. A light dusting of snow had fallen overnight, and as I glanced around at the picture-perfect scene, it was hard to believe our world could be torn apart in a matter of weeks.

Thank the goddess I hadn't ended up helping Fletcher with his master plan. While part of me still saw the reason in what he wanted to do, a stronger part now knew that it wasn't my place to make a life-altering decision for all shifters.

*Even as a dragon,* I never would.

Shedding my clothing, I placed them into the small bag with elastic sides attached to my leg. It was specially designed shifter equipment that would expand during my shift, allowing me a change of clothes when I reached my destination. I'd used these *Expanbags* many times in the past and had no fucking idea they'd been invented by my entitled alpha. Hunter created the prototype four years ago, and it was one of their best sellers.

For all of Fletcher's complaining about his son's company, which had surpassed his by hundreds of millions of dollars, he'd certainly taken advantage of their products. Especially their weapons and defensive items.

Just as I was calling on the energy to shift into my dragon form, I felt the spark of my mate through our bond. When she burst through the front door, I was ready and waiting for her. Slade must have gotten one of his shirts over her head to hide her nakedness from prying eyes, but her arms weren't through the sleeves yet as she sprinted forward and launched herself at me.

"You can't sneak away to do dangerous scouting and not say goodbye," she choked out against my chest, which felt like it was caving in at the devastation in her tone.

"I'm always with you, Honey," I said, breathing in her sweet scent. "We don't think you'll get any kickback or bond strain now that we're a completed quintet, but I'm going to keep an eye on it. Let me know if you feel any unease."

"I will," she said, her gaze piercing as she pulled away to examine me in a way that had my alpha roaring. "Please be careful." She shivered when the breeze drifted between us.

Slade appeared in the doorway, and there was a surge of his beast heating the air so Emme didn't freeze.

"I will return to you," I promised. "No matter what it takes. You don't need to worry. There's very little in this world that can threaten me."

Emme didn't look convinced as her bottom lip trembled. "Just remember that magic has taken you down before. Don't be overconfident. Scout and return, and we will face whatever is there as a pack. That's where we're truly strong, now our essences have joined."

Reaching out, I helped her get her arms through the sleeves of the shirt, wanting to feel them wrapped around me. "Was in a bit of a rush," she mumbled, her cheeks pinkening to match the end of her cold nose.

My dragon growled, pushing once more to snatch our adorable female up and steal her away to a cave high in the mountains, safe and hidden from the world. Where no one could touch her again.

Except there was no safe or hiding from the curse. It would come for us all, and there was only one way to stop it.

Needing another taste before I left, I swept her feet off the ground, and when her arms wrapped around my neck the world stopped for just a beat. We kissed until my dragon roared in my head, wanting to bury in her softness. My dick was a hard length between us, which we were both ignoring.

I stroked my tongue against hers, inhaling her sweetness. Goddess, I wanted to drop to my knees once more and worship at the altar that was Emmeline Anders. Only this wasn't the time or place.

"I love you," I said. The *easiest* words I'd ever said. "I fucking adore you, Honey."

She pulled away breathless, her expression lighting up. "I love you too," she said, with so much warmth that my heart cracked again. I never knew a shifter could have such a full, intense feeling in their chest and not die from it.

Brushing her messy hair back, I cupped the side of her face. "If my twin is too hard on you in training today, I will kick his ass for you. It would do *everyone* well to remember that I can kill a shifter in at least a hundred different ways."

Slade scoffed, but through the bond I felt his amusement. My twin was the only shifter who could give me a run in a fight, and I was looking forward to testing myself against him one day.

*I will destroy you without even breaking a sweat, brother.* Yep, he was definitely amused.

"I can handle Slade just fine on my own," Emme sassed, shooting a soft smile over her shoulder. "And he always goes easy on me. He may not say the words, but I know he loves me."

Our mate had grown confident within the quintet bond, reading all of us on a level much deeper than what we showed the world.

Slade's growl filled my mind, straight in our twin connection. *Love is such a pathetic word to use for what I feel. People love kittens and food. They love walks in the park and television shows. What I feel for our mate is beyond all love, obsession and idolization. I would not survive or exist without her, and she wants me to call it love.*

His tone was filled with fire as he raged with each sentence, and I barely contained my smirk. *Doesn't matter if the word is pathetic. She wants to hear it from you.*

He better give our mate what she wanted, or I really would beat his ass.

"Slade loves you," I confirmed, ratting him out. "He loves you in ways that are far beyond a single word."

Emme's smile was broad, and her eyes shone like crystals, icy in color but somehow still filled with heat. "I know. He shows me every single day how he feels, and it means more than the words themselves. But he'll say it eventually too. We all fall back on *love,* as it's the best we've got."

My twin growled and muttered, "We'll see," as he crossed his arms over his bare chest.

Emme popped up on her toes for one last kiss. "I love you," she murmured again, as if to prove her point. "Please stay in touch."

With one last deep breath of her scent, I let her go, and she hurried back up the stairs. Slade scooped her off her feet as she passed him, hugging her shivering form to his chest.

When she relaxed against him, I dug deep for the strength to call on my beast and shift. The change was fast, and I shot into the sky, aware that if I didn't leave now I never would.

It was far harder than I expected to race away from Golden Claw, but thankfully there was no strain in our bond. Emme's beast remained strong and vibrant, and the connection swirled even with distance.

I'd never have expected to enjoy living in an overdeveloped city of metal and concrete, and for the most part I didn't. But I certainly enjoyed the pack I'd found myself in.

Over the next few hours, my beast took control, and outside of checking in on the bond, I lost myself to the freedom of flight. Emme was training now, and through Slade I marveled at her skills. In both hand to hand and with her blades, she was learning exceptionally fast, and with each lesson her confidence soared.

When familiar landscape started to appear, I slowed and let the clouds shield me from view as I assessed for danger. Finding none.

On the ground, I shifted back and pulled my clothes on. Wasting no time, I took off along a rather underused path into the compound, using every skill I possessed to remain undetected.

There was no sign of life in the area, no scents, sights, or sounds. It also looked rundown, with the grass, browned from frost, sitting at uneven lengths. Fletcher would never normally allow his surroundings to look so unkempt, but since he was dead, that didn't mean there weren't still others inside.

Using the back entrance, I moved past my old quarters—a prison far worse than the one I'd found myself in at Reeves pack house. At least there I'd had company and my mate nearby.

The top level of the compound was where Fletcher and his son lived, but there was no one inside today. I'd never been into the lower facility before, but I knew the entrance was a concealed door near the garage.

As I got closer to it, there was an echo of a thud from below, so faint that I doubted anyone with weaker senses than a dragon would have heard. Another thud followed by a groan, and I sensed a shifter down there. *One of Fletcher's captives?*

Not that I was going to open the door to find out today. I had no idea how many might be below, trapped and waiting to die. Getting back to my pack was my only concern today, along with keeping my promise to Emme that I wouldn't take any unnecessary risks. There was very little a shifter prisoner could do to hurt me, but it would be better to return with the full quintet tomorrow. Just in case it was one of Jewels' well-laid traps.

She might not be here in person, but it didn't mean there weren't dangers here of her making.

All of which we'd find out tomorrow.

# CHAPTER 21

EMME

My breaths wheezed in and out, and I spent eight long seconds deciding if my rib was cracked or just bruised. The pain wasn't horrific, but if the past twenty-plus years had taught me anything, it was that it shouldn't hurt to breathe.

Slade's face appeared over the top of mine, his bulk blocking out the cloudy sky above. "You destroyed Horton, Snow. You should be proud of yourself."

With a groan, I rolled to the side, and for once he allowed me to pull myself to my feet. Through our bond, I could sense that he wanted me to prove to myself that I could get up from the battle. A battle I'd lost, but only by the minutest of margins, since Horton was as injured as me.

"My essence is so much stronger," I said, lifting my water bottle out of the snowdrift. "I can move—" I gulped down an icy sip— "faster, and my reflexes were so quick that I could track his movements as if they were in slow motion."

Slade nodded, a pleased expression on his handsome face. "Today you've proven to be overall better at shooting, handling your blades, and in general hand-to-hand. Our incomplete bond had been holding you back, little mate. But you're finally reaching your full potential."

"All she needs to add in is magic," Constantine called from nearby, where he'd been patiently waiting for his turn to instruct me. The alpha had stood there in the cold all morning, watching silently, never pushing his time on me.

I gulped down more water, my gaze still locked on Slade, his pleased expression fading to annoyance. I wouldn't have been surprised to find him debating the importance of Constantine's existence. Unfortunately, he was still quite important. A conclusion Slade must have also drawn as he exhaled an annoyed gust of smoky air.

My magic had been surging on and off during my training, assisting with reflexes and strength. But it hadn't burst from its cage. My wolf remained the strongest side of me, standing front and center of the quintet power—and the magic. A magic I still needed to utilize, whether I liked it or not.

*Just say the word, Snow. He can disappear as quickly as he arrived.*

That was my dragon, giving zero fucks about any shifter outside of our pack. My wolf brushed closer to his beast, allowing our communication to continue internally. *Appreciate the sentiment, Scary. But let's table that conversation for later.*

Out loud I added, "Okay, let's do this magic thing. I want to be my strongest self against Jewels, and I can't imagine that won't require magic."

Finally giving Constantine my undivided attention, I found him looking just as disheveled as the day he arrived. His hair remained tangled, which seemed odd without a beard. I had no idea if he couldn't grow facial hair or if he just hated it, but it was the only kempt part of him.

He was at least wearing shoes today, which was important during these icy mornings. Even shifters could lose toes to frostbite if they pushed their healing capabilities too far.

His clothing, all of which came from Kellan, was clean and slightly too big. There was nothing about him that suggested he was a strong or dominant alpha, and I wondered if for him the magic tempered the wolf somewhat.

"You hide your true essence well," I noted flatly.

He shrugged, and it was once again an almost nothing movement. "I've had many years of perfecting a forgettable persona."

"Why?" I knew so little about him, and since I could no longer pretend he didn't exist, I was ready for information.

His expression softened just enough that it made me feel weird. "Because I shouldn't exist."

I almost took a step back like that had been a physical blow. I'd felt that way about myself many times over the years, like I shouldn't be here. Having to hide and run meant I never got to find the life I would flourish in—until of course, it was thrust upon me.

Constantine continued, his observant gaze no doubt picking up every one of my reactions. "I spent many decades watching my parents—your grandparents—suffer because of a love that was bigger than their two different species. Once they were gone, I learned to blend into the background and live with humans. They might sense that I'm different, but since they don't believe in the supernatural, they assume it's due to my eccentricities."

He waved his hand over his hair. "Hence the hobo-like appearance I've adopted. You'd be amazed at how easily they ignore those of us who are a little... *worn out.*"

"I lived amongst humans for a near decade," I reminded him, "and they're not all bad."

A lot of the staff I'd worked with in restaurants and cafes had been quite generous and kind to those in need. Those without homes. Those struggling. More than once they'd pooled money to help friends out of bad situations, or to get a coat for someone who didn't have one for winter. Still, there had been a few who'd avoid and outright mock the humans they believed were beneath them. So, he had a point too.

Humans were multifaceted, just like shifters.

Shifters made their judgements based on power. Everything in life had a hierarchy, and it was never nice to sit at the bottom of it. As an omega, I knew that all too well, but luckily the goddess gave me a kickass pack to boost my credibility.

As if he'd heard that thought, Slade pressed in closer, and I relished the touch of his energy along my skin. "Who were your parents?" I asked Constantine. "What witch line are we from?"

"Alterni," he said, and I shook my head, having never heard of them before. "It's one of the ancient lines, just like Termaine. Once upon a time, our two clans were the largest and strongest in the world. Now, though, we've all but died out. There's just us and Jewels left."

Okay, there was zero chance Jewels knew about us, then. She would hate to have another ancient and powerful line still alive, especially when we were blended with wolves. There was no way she wouldn't have tried harder to kill me had she known...

"My mom was an alpha wolf," Constantine continued, "one who was very powerful. She was born in Europe, and at the time they weren't forming quintets and instead had large packs. She was the Ultimate Alpha of hers, which was almost unheard of for a female. You come from a strong line on both sides."

"Did Fletcher know about my heritage?" I asked him, wondering how Jewels couldn't have known. "Was that why he was waiting for me to shift and designate as an omega…? To see if I also had a magical side?"

For the first time, my father's expression fell, and his scent turned bitter. Citrus had never been my favorite to start with, and when you added rotten orange, it was even worse. "I believe Fletcher knew most if not all of who we are," he confirmed. "Your mother followed my instructions for a few years, but after she fell in with the Rogers pack, she was under their control. She would have told them everything."

"Why did Jewels not kill Emme immediately?" Slade asked, following the same train of thought I'd had before. "That witch would never tolerate another original line running around when she wants to be the top power."

"Either she doesn't know or she doesn't care," Constantine said with a shrug. "Though that's unlikely. The most probable scenario is that Fletcher didn't want to share the power of an omega-witch."

He was dead now, so his intentions no longer mattered. Jewels, on the other hand, still very much mattered.

"How did your parents meet?" I asked. As a shifter who'd always been kept in the dark about my history and family, I wouldn't waste this opportunity to learn more about them.

"I could find no evidence of your origins," Slade said, his warm fingertips tracing softly down the back of my right arm, sending goosebumps over my skin. It was such a casual touch, and yet it had a devastating effect on me. "There's nothing in our history or reference books."

Constantine's expression tightened, and no one could miss the pain as he spoke. "They met during a war of course. Shifters have been battling witches forever. Probably as long as shifters have existed. They were both injured, and found themselves in the same cave. Instead of following their instinct and destroying each other, they helped the other to survive, and then…" He shrugged. "Fell in love, I guess. They snuck around for years, and after the war was over, Mom found out she was pregnant."

We already knew Constantine was old, so this had to have

happened many decades ago. "They're no longer alive, right?" He'd basically said that before, but I wanted confirmation.

He shook his head, and there was an ache in my chest as I watched him stand so alone. Just as I'd been for many years. Before my pack.

"They died before you were born, both from aging-related illnesses. Witches and wolves have similar long lives, and those two lived longer than most. I still don't know how they managed to overcome the rules of nature and produce a child, but apparently we are an anomaly."

Even in nature, there were animals that occasionally slipped through the genetic cracks and found a way for incompatible DNA to stitch together.

"So, Jewels targeted our pack simply so we'd be in position to take out Fletcher when she needed him gone?" Slade asked, seeking confirmation of our working theory. "It had nothing to do with Emme, or the fact she's our fated mate?"

"As far as I know, nothing to do with Emme," Constantine confirmed, his grief fading away as if it had never been there. "She needed Fletcher's blood-related family to take him out, so she could not only break free from him, but also use his energy to enact her curse. Fletcher was powerful from his stolen omega essences."

My stomach lurched. "Wait," I said, holding a hand up. "I thought omegas could only share with bonded mates?"

Mom had said she was a scent match, which I knew was bullshit, but they were bonded.

"Technically true," Constantine confirmed. "But rumor was that Fletcher figured out how to simulate fake bonds and scent matches. I'm assuming he also wasn't opposed to forcibly biting omegas during his experiments. There were many ways he could steal their essences."

A shudder ran through me, and Slade snaked an arm around my waist, as if we both needed the anchor. "I'm lucky he didn't try that with me," I whispered.

"I'll bet that bastard was tempted," the dragon growled. "Only he had bigger plans for you. One that would power his greatest weapon."

Constantine rubbed a hand over his face, his eyes holding a weariness that only years of pain and suffering could bring. "Yeah, he wanted Emme's power, but Talon was his shot to destroy the cities. He made the choice to boost his weapon's strength instead."

I had never been happier for him to have underestimated Talon's true nature.

"Emme turning out to be your mate," Constantine said, "was the worst thing that could have happened to Jewels *and* Fletcher. She was the chink in both plans, and neither of them knew it until it was too late."

And the largest reason they hadn't known, especially Jewels, was due to Constantine keeping me safe, hiding my magic from the world.

Slade snarled, his big chest heaving behind me. "We're going to be her downfall. I don't care how powerful she is, or how long this has been in the works, Jewels won't win. The entire world will burn before that happens."

I'd be right there lighting the first spark.

"I believe the reason Emme is your mate," Constantine said, his focus moving between us both, "is that with her Alterni magic in your combined essences, you will be strong enough to stop the witch's plans."

It was my turn to scowl. "That's not the sole reason." I refused to accept our bonding was only about Jewels and saving the world.

Slade was right there with me. "Emme is the perfect match to our beasts and souls," he said, a warning snap in his words. "The heart of us all. Anything else is just an added strength from the goddess, as she knows who her most capable soldiers are. Emme would be ours even if we'd all been born human with no magical ties."

The urge to spin in his arms and crawl right up his big body was so strong that I had to grit my teeth and plant my boots. There was no time for that. But all the love rocketing around inside of me had to go somewhere.

Constantine didn't argue with us, and oddly, looked happy with our declarations. "As much as I wished differently, I knew to hide you at birth, to keep you safe, until you were strong enough to keep yourself safe. I'm sure it means nothing to you, after my years of silence and absence, but I'm proud of you, Emmeline. You're a gift from the goddess, and our one chance to save shifters."

All along, I'd rejected any concept of being the *chosen one* in this battle, and despite his take on it all, I still believed that. This was real life and not a book, and I had my pack surrounding me, showing that if anyone was *chosen*, it was all of us.

"I guess it's time for me to learn how to use my magic, then," I declared, forcing a lighter tone.

As if the very thought excited my magic, tingles raced down my hands and through my center. It wasn't the first time I'd felt them, but now I recognized exactly what was happening: my witch and shifter sides were merging to fill my blood with energy.

Constantine's slow smile was my only warning as he flicked his hands up, facing his palms toward me. A warm tingle raced over my already heated skin, and magic fizzed inside me, as if it had been shaken up suddenly.

"We start by bringing your magic to the surface and then forcing it out into the world."

Slade pulled away from me, and even knowing I had to face this alone, I hated the loss of contact.

He turned to shout at his enforcers still training. "Everyone out! We're using dangerous energy, and I don't want any shifters hurt." Not to mention my magic was still a closely held secret that not even his trusted team would know about.

No one questioned Slade, the most dominant shifter here, leaving without another word. "And none of you better mention Constantine to the council," he added. "Those fuckers don't need to know what's happening here." He received salutes and cheers in response, and then the field slowly emptied.

With Kellan and Finley having left for hockey training a few hours ago, it was only the three of us now. Ready to learn magic.

# CHAPTER 22

EMME

I'd thought my first shift, when my wolf and I were virtual strangers, had been the toughest transition in my life. But today, two hours deep into my first magic lesson, I was once again on the ground breathing through what felt like cracked ribs.

Magic was going to be my toughest transition. I could already tell.

Slade had been forced to do intense workouts on the other side of the field, so his dragon didn't growl and threaten to snap the witch-wolf like a twig every time Constantine had to attack me with a spell. Beyond my ribs, the real travesty here was being too winded to even admire Slade's firm ass as he trained.

"You're fighting against the magic," Constantine said for the fifth time, yet somehow still not sounding irritated with me. "Whenever you get close to drawing on it, your wolf steps in. Since that side of you is the strongest, it slams the magic down. You have to learn how to mingle both sides of yourself. Turn them into allies."

*Do we really need this guy?* I projected into the group, sending the message to all my mates for once.

*Want me to kill him for you?* Slade offered, his dragon all puffed up in the bond, smoke billowing from his lethal jaws.

I laughed, fairly sure he was half joking.

*Not even close to half,* he drawled.

Talon's laughter filtered through as well, and when I caught a glimpse of sky, I knew he was still flying. There'd been no strain from our bond, but it didn't mean I wasn't missing him.

I hated any of my mates being away from me.

*I vote we kill him too,* Finley chimed in, his bear rearing up with a bellow. *Emme survived just fine without him.* Just fine was probably a stretch since Constantine had been keeping me magically hidden.

*Aw, Shortcake. Come home so I can rub your shoulders... and other parts of your body. You need to relax, and I haven't finished my weapons training.*

Hunter's beast released a warning growl, as if he wanted to jump on Kellan and tear him in two. *If you mention your weapon, annoying pup, you'll be neutered in the same breath.*

I snorted out loud, relieved at least that having all of their voices in my mind hadn't brought on the nausea and headache again. Constantine was watching me closely, but didn't say a word, as if he knew I was focused internally with my pack.

*You don't have to use your magic if it feels wrong to you,* Hunter said, always the voice of supportive reason. *We're strong enough without it. Maybe there's a reason you've never had it in your life before now.*

A great point, but there was one part I needed to clarify. *It doesn't feel wrong,* I admitted, and it wasn't as painful as I expected to acknowledge that. *It's familiar enough that I must have been interacting with it all along, even if only in small increments. It was enough to build a bond. I just need to figure out how to release it.*

After so many years of being caged by Constantine and my beast, that was always going to be the hardest task. *Thanks for your unwavering support,* I said as my wolf brushed by each of their beasts. *I'm going to try again.*

My mental block returned so I could focus, but I felt their reassurances drifting through still.

"Okay, time to call on my magic again," I said out loud, straightening my aching limbs and ignoring the dull throb in my uterus. I wouldn't have much longer before I needed to empty my disc again, so I needed to get this done.

Drawing on the magic, swirls of energy rose until my limbs tingled with the power. This sensation felt like I was being smothered in bubbles, and I wanted to flinch away, but that had only gotten me blasted by Constantine's energy all afternoon.

Blasts I was supposed to be countering.

"Okay, you need to keep drawing your magic around yourself," he said. "Thicker and stronger. Shielding is the first magic we learn, and it's relatively easy. It's just using the energy to coat your skin in a protective layer. You can feel it, right?"

"Yes," I bit out. "I can feel it all over my body, and it makes my wolf want to tear our skin to pieces."

"Push her down," Constantine returned with more fire. "Control the beast."

In my chest, my wolf snarled and raged, but if there was one thing I had experience with, it was controlling her.

*We have no other choice*, I said to the wolf, getting a snap of her jaws in response.

Her unease riled up the other beasts in our quintet, but they didn't push through to communicate again. We all had to deal with our discomfort if we wanted to be able to take on a witch.

With one final snarl, my wolf finally backed off, giving the magic its first real chance to grow. Constantine murmured under his breath, and I could soon scent the slight tinge of sulfur in his essence. For the most part, both of our magic-scents were hidden by the shifter essence, but this close there was a faint waft.

"I'm going to use a low-level blast of energy," he warned me. "It's basic magic. No real finesse, but it can knock your opponent off their feet. Your job is to counter that energy. Block it with your own."

Sure, that sounded easy peasy lemon fucking squeezy. "It's not basic magic to me," I reminded him through gritted teeth, already cranky, sore, and about to bleed through my pants. "Which you'd know if you didn't just toss me to the wolves, literally, and fuck off out of my life."

Constantine's expression hardened. "You're feeling sorry for yourself, and I'm not saying you don't have reason, but it's not going to win this fight. I did the best I could, and I would make different choices now that I know your destiny. But I wasn't blessed with foresight. All I wanted was to keep you safe. This training is another way to keep you safe."

He was right, and even knowing I was being a bitch, I couldn't help that comment. Still, I wasn't usually the type to dwell on my hardships, and I didn't want to start today. "Yeah, you're right and I'm sorry," I muttered. "Hit me. I'm going to try and block it."

With my wolf still subdued, I could really force that icy swell of power to expand. My body felt too full, and I kept waiting for it to burst from me in a violent display. Instead, the power slipped free, a shimmer of golden energy that had Slade slowing to watch us.

"More, Emme," Constantine said, his eyes lighting up at my display. "You're still holding back."

My teeth literally ached from the amount of magic surrounding me. I wasn't sure there was any more energy to expel. As only a quarter witch, maybe this was all I had to give.

"Are you drawing on your pack and wolf?" Constantine asked suddenly, as if he'd just figured out what I was doing wrong.

"You told me to control her so the magic can go free," I bit out, my teeth starting to chatter. "And how would I draw on the pack? Their energy is their own."

His magic swirled hotter, and I recognized the signs of his attack. *This is going to hurt.*

"You don't push her away, just make her less dominant," he said. "You must join all the sides of yourself if you want to be strong. Your witch, wolf, and omega sides. The omega can share power with her pack, as you very well know."

Deciding that instinct would have to be the guide here, I released the reins of my wolf, and stopped blocking the pack bond. My wolf rose to join the already powerful waves of magic, and along with that were the five other beasts. Bear, wolf and dragon essences swirled until I wasn't sure which energy belonged to who.

No one in my pack spoke, but they also didn't hold themselves back from me, as if there weren't any part of them off limits to me and my wolf. As terrifying as it was to think I could hurt or drain them, I also knew we couldn't play it safe. Not if we wanted to win against Jewels.

When our essences were just one huge swirl of magic and shifter, I pushed it against my already tingling skin. Constantine released his attack, which looked like lightning as it shot from his fingertips, and I shoved all of my pack at it. Six beasts, leaping together.

Our quintet collided with Constantine's spell, and it shattered so loudly that birds flew off squawking in the forest miles from us. Constantine slammed into the ground, and for once I didn't lose my footing. There was no pain, and for a brief moment, I wondered if I could fracture the very earth I stood on with the energy I held in my hand.

"Dial it back, Emmeline," Constantine shouted, but not only did I have no idea how to do that, I also didn't want to. This was pure power. With it, I'd never have to be afraid again. No more kidnapping or losing people I loved.

No more enemies lying in wait to take us out.

"Snow," Slade roared, the magic so loud that I barely heard him. When I turned his way, I could see the outline of golden beasts in front of me, as if they were partially superimposed over my skin. Not just my wolf, but all of theirs. *Ours.*

"Sweetheart," Slade continued, in front of me, his hands held up placatingly.

It was such an unexpected position to see the dragon shifter take, that a fraction of my brain snapped out of my power-induced haze. "You need to bring our quintet back into our essence," he continued. "Separate out the magic. Let our beasts free."

The thought that I'd caged them against their will horrified me, and I immediately let all magic slip back inside. It released like an elastic band that had been stretched to fit us all, everything springing right back into place with my wolf standing center of the quintet.

My five mates surrounding me.

Collapsing to my knees, I gasped in air, as if I'd been unable to breathe for many minutes. Slade crouched with me, wrapping himself protectively around my body. "Our beasts burst from you," he whispered, and I felt the tremor that rocked through him.

My head jerked up so fast I almost headbutted him. "Are you weaker?" I rasped, running my gaze over the parts of him I could see. There was no indication I'd hurt him, the dragon looking as virile and gorgeous as ever. "Did I steal your power and weaken your beast?"

His laughter was low and soothing. "Not even a little. You used our power, and then you released it back to us. I've never seen literal spirit animals fight magic the way you just had us fighting it."

"I never physically changed into my wolf." It wasn't a question, as I knew I hadn't, but for some reason I needed his confirmation.

"No, you stayed in this form."

My heart was finally starting to calm in his embrace, and with it I gained more clarity. "It was almost too powerful," I admitted. "I didn't want to let it go."

"You'll do better next time," Constantine said, snapping us out of our little bubble as he appeared beside us. Slade rumbled at the proximity, already in protective dragon mode. "You will learn to understand and embrace your magic. I wasn't sure until today that you six would be able to join in such a way. It was quite spectacular to behold."

"Glad I could be of entertainment," I murmured, shaking my head. "But it feels like too big of a risk to ever use their energy in such a way again. I can just combine my wolf and magic."

Slade finally lifted me from the ground, and when he set me on my feet, I found I was more stable than expected. "You will use us," he ordered in his usual bossy way. "Do not protect us at your own sacrifice, Emmeline."

Constantine looked nervous as he fidgeted from foot to foot. "I don't think you have to worry, Emme. Are all of their beasts okay now?"

Focusing internally, I checked in with each of my mates, to find most of them exuding excitement over what I'd done. There was not an ounce of concern about them sharing power, or me possibly draining them into husks. *I didn't even have to shift back,* Talon said, already on his way home as he sent more flying images.

Another bout of guilt hit that I could have drawn on his energy while he was in danger.

When I apologized, he growled. *Honey, you will take from me any time you need to. What's mine is yours.*

*And vice versa,* I added.

Hunter's wolf rumbled. *Not a chance, Emmeline. You will take from us... we will never take from you.*

Grumbling about their stubborn ways, I was still mostly relieved that everyone felt as strong as ever. "They're all fine," I admitted with a sigh. "But since it's still all an experiment, I won't be rushing to do that again."

Slade mulled my words over. "If it makes you feel more comfortable, you can practice with your magic and beast for now, but we can't ignore the possible strength of our full quintet forever."

The fact that we even had a "quintet" with six showed that we were *more* than the average pack.

Still, my concerns remained, as my number one priority was to protect my mates.

Constantine dusted himself off, his face impassive. "Next time, we will focus on you just using your beast and magic together."

I nodded. "Yes, that works for me. Should we try something else with magic now?"

Slade answered with a rumbling growl: "You're exhausted. Magic is new to you and your beast. You're no use to anyone if you burn out. You get one more try on your own today, and then you're done. You can practice anew tomorrow."

*Tomorrow.* As much as I wanted to argue with him, he was correct about the fatigue. It wasn't so much a weakening of my energy, but more the exhaustion that came with learning a new skill.

Slade moved away only a few feet this time, unconcerned by Constantine calling on another spell. My beast and magic swirled in harmony, the merging easier now that we'd fought together as a pack. When the blast of energy slammed against me, they formed enough of a shield to repel the worst of the spell.

No beasts leapt from my skin this time, and Constantine remained on his feet, but it was progress.

"Okay, that's enough," Slade said, a note of finality in his voice. "You need to rest."

"I need to figure out how to track Jewels," I countered. "If I can learn every facet of my magic, I might be able to help Constantine." When he eased forward, I focused fully on him. "You mentioned using something of hers to track the witch…?"

He hesitated, as if it wasn't a simple answer. "Yes, you can usually track through objects, but it depends on where Jewels is holed up, and how magically protected she is. The more time we give her to bunker down, the harder it will be to find her."

It had only been a couple of days since the attack in the street, so we needed to find that item straight away. "Talon's on his way home," I said, turning to Slade. "Did he find anything at the compound?"

"Nothing of Jewels, since the compound was all but deserted. He did detect signs of life in the lower levels, but hasn't checked down there per your request to stay safe. We'll all go tomorrow as a pack."

*As per your request.* Now, that was a sexy statement. Nothing like these alphas keeping their promises to me.

Slade wrapped a heavy arm around my shoulders to lead me from the training center. "We'll see you back at home," he called to Constantine.

I had no idea how the witch-wolf had gotten out here this

morning, but apparently he was on his own getting home. We'd taken Slade's bike, which meant no room for a third.

It was a silent but relaxed walk through the training facility, and I assumed Slade was wrapped up in his thoughts too. When we reached his Panigale, Slade slid a helmet over my head and secured the strap under my chin. His own helmet was on in a flash, and when I moved toward the bike, he wrapped his hands around my hips and lifted me onto the back.

"Are you letting me drive, big boy?" I teased, while pretending to slide forward. I already knew there wasn't a chance in hell, but it was fun to poke at the beast.

I jumped when his voice echoed through my helmet, connected to comms I hadn't known were there. "It'll be a cold day in hell before I'm your backpack, Snow. I'm the alpha. I protect you."

I snorted and pounded my chest. "Me alpha, strongggg. You omega, weakkkk."

Slade's chest rumbled before he shrugged, as if he couldn't really argue with me. I'd never deny that every alpha in my pack was more dominant than me, but I had my own special brand of strength.

"Yes, you do, sweetheart," he whispered in response to a thought he shouldn't have heard, and I flushed over every part of my damn body. "But I have to protect you. It's built into my very essence."

He was stubborn and arrogant, which was partly the reason I started prank wars in the first place. To humble him a touch. It might just be time to bring it back... At least once we defeated the wicked witch.

I was already manifesting her destruction, and with that, Prank Wars would return.

Trademark pending.

# CHAPTER 23

## HUNTER

It had been a hell of a week. Between my father attacking the street, Jewels' betrayal, the death of Marcus, and then Constantine showing up on our doorstep to fuck our day just a little further, I was ready to let my beast loose. Tear it all down.

My wolf cared little for Golden Claw and the rest of the shifters in it. He cared for our pack, our quintet of power, and Emme. Not in that order. My little omega was always first.

My day had consisted of meetings and product launches, but my strongest focus was on our preparations for a war between witches and shifters. Kassidy was heading up a newly formed team that was working on sending out *battle packages* to the strongest enforcer groups across the cities.

All of them would be outfitted with the best tech Reeves Industries had to offer, including our patented armored vests. It might not be enough, but I had to do something.

We didn't really know who was friend or foe these days, so our efforts were being marketed as a *goodwill gesture*. A bonding between the shifter cities. Though we definitely still had some trusted allies out there. Most other shifters would fight on our side, too, as none of them would want to lose their autonomy to witches.

I'd been in the middle of a meeting with our London offices when Emme's magic had burst to life inside me, tearing through my control over my beast, as she immersed him in her spell. I'd barely managed to keep my furious howl from spilling free, before I figured out what she'd done. Our little mate had merged our energies and sent all six beasts out to attack Constantine's spell.

There'd been a long moment when Emmeline had held my beast in her grasp, keeping him beyond my control. He was hers, in all ways, but I hadn't felt weakened. Emme's control over our essences didn't drain us. We were just all part of her attack, even without moving a muscle.

The scariest part was the moment after she'd unleashed our power, when she'd been almost consumed by it. But I'd never had any doubt my little omega would snap herself out of it. Emmeline did not crave more power. She craved peace and stability, which was what I'd work forever to give her.

When I was ready to leave the office for the day, Talon checked in to inform me he was almost home too. I packed up my laptop and paperwork, deciding I needed a few hours with Emme to soothe my ragged edges. I'd never realized what true peace felt like until I was bonded. I'd never had a place I could exist where the noise of our world and my responsibilities just… stopped. Emme was my peace.

As I got to my feet, Casey popped her head around the corner. "Sir, do you have a moment? There's an alpha here to see you, and while he doesn't have an appointment, I think you'll want to take this meeting."

I'd already mentally checked out of Reeves Industries for the day, but curiosity had me pausing. "Alpha?"

She nodded, expression unchanging. "Yes. Alpha Annandale."

My wolf howled at Warrick finally emerging from his pack house. We'd been worried about our old friend. "Send him in."

Warrick entered slowly, looking like he'd aged ten years from the last time I saw him. His clothes were rumpled, shirt half tucked in, a few days growth on his normally smooth-shaven face. I met his bloodshot gaze, and he just stared at me like I was a stranger. "War," I said kindly, not making a move closer since he was keeping his distance. "What do you need? Is everything okay with Cora and the others?" He wouldn't be here while his pack mourned unless something was wrong.

As he continued to stare, I managed to keep my normally impatient nature under control. Give him a moment of grace. If I lost anyone in my pack, I'd have been a raving mess. Well, anyone other than Emmeline. If I lost her, I'd be dead too.

"Where's the fucking witch?" His first words were a rasp of agony, and I felt them all the way to my soul.

"We don't know." There was no point in lying. We had no fucking clue where the witch was, and even with every contact we had out looking, there was no sign of magic.

There wasn't even a regular witch to be found, let alone Jewels.

"She's gone to ground with apparently every other witch in existence. I have no doubt her plan is to stay hidden until the next full moon."

I'd told our closest allies about Constantine's warning, and though Warrick hadn't returned my message, it had come up as read.

A small tic started in the corner of his eye. He leaned back against the door like he needed the support. "I'm assuming you don't plan on letting that stand. You need to figure out how to find her…"

"We're working on tracking her through magic," I assured him. "We'll track other witches too, if we can find an object that would lead us to them. We're going to head for Fletcher's old compound tomorrow in the hopes of unearthing a clue."

His throat moved roughly as he swallowed, and the cry of his beast echoed through my own. "What happens if we don't find her? What's the plan?"

"We will go to war with the witches," I said without hesitation, feeling my beast rising up. "They might control our shifts, but we have other strengths. We will figure out how to fight them and destroy the curse somehow. Or wipe out all witches so no one will ever control us again."

Warrick didn't appear convinced, so I offered him extra hope. "I have a team outfitting select groups of enforcers and warriors. They don't really understand why, but they will come to our aid if we find ourselves at war. We're bypassing the useless councils though."

Warrick nodded, as if for the first time he was also done pandering to their needs. "I want to be part of the hunting parties when you go after the witches."

With that, he stood straight and strong, as if he'd briefly shook off the weight on his shoulders. "Bring me into the planning meetings and keep me updated so I can help in whatever way is needed. You can't trust random enforcers in other cities but you ca —" His voice broke. "We are old friends, and I have to avenge Marcus."

"You will have your vengeance," I assured him. "Every witch can die for all I care."

Except for my mate, but there was no reason anyone needed to know about her unique heritage. Especially not her friend, who was currently on a path of revenge against magic.

"Keep me apprised," he said with a firm nod. "If you find anything, I want to be there."

That much I could promise him. "You'll be the first to know if we discover anything of importance."

With that he stomped out of my office, his dark energy trailing through the building.

Leaving right after, I was tense all the way back to the house, only finding relief when Slade texted that he was on his way home with Emme. The long way, since the lucky bastard had her backpacking with him right now.

As I pulled my bike into the garage, Talon's energy thrummed in our bond, and I wasn't surprised to find him waiting in the entrance hall. We could all mentally check in now, though Emme kept us from communicating as a group. It was clear that one day we'd all freely speak when needed, but for now, Emme held tightly to her control.

"Hunter," Talon called, leaning down to unclip his bag, pulling out clothing. When he was dressed, he looked around. "Where is everyone?"

"Slade and Emme are on their way home from training. Kellan and Fin are at hockey—they've got a few new team members, which means their coaches are forcing longer practices to team bond, and Slade left Constantine at the training facility to figure out his own way home."

Talon's smile was darkly satisfied, but before he could respond, Florence hurried into the room. "Alpha Hunter and Alpha Talon," she exclaimed. "I'm so glad you're both home. I left snacks in the gaming room. I wondered if you might like to… hang out there."

She smiled softly, and I knew she was hoping I'd indulge in my usual place of calm—my place before Emme that was. Florence had been part of our lives for a long time, and knew me almost as well as my pack.

"Thank you," I said, unsure if I was ready to game again after Sorenson's betrayal. "We're lucky to have you." She smiled and half-bowed, before scurrying off.

"Gaming room?" Talon asked, a deeper furrow between his brows. "What's a gaming room?"

Deciding I could at least use the snack, I waved a hand at him. "Come on, I'll show you." On the way through the house I ditched my jacket over a side table and was already loosening my cuffs and rolling up my sleeves.

I wasn't sure Talon would enjoy gaming; Slade had never been into it. He preferred to be online, scouring the web to keep tabs on friends… and enemies. Slade also loved facts and figures. Knowledge was power, after all. He didn't buy into escapism—I'd always been the dreamer, inventor, and fantasy fan.

If there was a sliding scale with me at one end and Slade at the other, Talon fell somewhere between us. So maybe he'd enjoy a little *Call of Duty*.

When we entered the room I'd personally designed as my dream space, he took it in quietly, as was his way. He did show a stronger level of interest than I expected, running his hand over the pool table and turning a few handles on the foosball. When we ended up on the couches in front of the multiple screens, I asked him, "Have you ever played on a gaming system?"

I handed him the controller, and he held it like it was a bomb about to explode in his hands. The device did appear oddly small in his grasp, and I was already preparing for how many he'd crush on me tonight.

"No. I've never even seen anything like this before. What does it do?"

I loaded up my old server without thought, relieved when there was only a slight pang in my chest at the memories of gaming all night with Sorenson. His betrayal cut through any loyalty I'd ever felt; there was no room for his memories in my life any longer.

It helped to focus on Talon, so I taught him the moves while explaining the aim of the game.

"So, you just kill everyone?" he confirmed, and when he smiled, I was reminded that I wasn't the only sociopathic shifter in this pack. The dragons were far worse.

"Yep, this is free for all. No teams. You win by being the last one standing."

His confident smirk reminded me of Slade, and while it was eerie when they did the twin soul thing, it was also… comforting. As if he'd been part of our quintet all along.

"I'm always the last one standing," he declared, cocky as fuck, right before his head got blown off. With a snarl, his body tensed, and there was a creak as he split the edge of the controller.

I barely controlled my laughter. "You might want to camp for a bit until you learn how to sneak around better." My fingers were fast as I took off into the map, and I didn't bother with headphones or mic, since there was no one I cared to connect with.

Talon snarled when he got shot again, hitting the respawn button so hard that I heard another crack. This time his character took off, following my path, firing wildly as he ran.

"Stealth works better than just holding the trigger and hoping for the best," I said, but he wasn't listening, all of his focus on the huge split screen.

His reflexes were next-level, which helped him overcome his lack of skill in taking out opponents, but he also died so many times that he was starting to wear out the respawn button.

"What did you find at the compound?" I asked as we gamed, actually enjoying myself despite his growls and curses.

"Well, there wasn't anyone in—hey, you sneaky fuck!" He glared at me, and it was fair, since I'd just shot him in the head. Forcing my laughter down, I decided this was a new kind of therapy that I was totally subscribing to.

Talon respawned once more and took off, no doubt searching for me. "The witch hasn't been there in at least a few weeks," he muttered, the tip of his tongue emerging from his lips as he knifed a bot. "No scent or magic in the area, and she reeks of both. But there was at least one shifter stuck in the underground containment rooms. We should go tomorrow and explore down there. I've never been to those levels. I suspect that will be where the most important information is held."

He ran around the corner where I was camped, and I shot him again. My move was so fast that he snarled and turned his body to full-on glare at me. For the first time in ages, I laughed freely, and another slice of tension left me.

Talon shook his head, and on his next respawn I noticed him following my screen first, to figure out exactly where I was. Switching guns to my sniper, I went to my favorite tower, and when Talon closed in, I shot him straight between the eyes.

"Motherfucker," he bellowed, throwing the controller into the wall, smashing it into pieces. It took a lot to turn the rather unflappable dragon shifter into a raging inferno. My sperm donor had worked hard to knock any disobedience and independent thought from him.

Until now, I'd never seen anything other than Emme's safety trigger him.

Now we had Emme and gaming.

Talon continued to glare at the split screen and then me, as if he wasn't sure which one had wronged him the worst. Then right before my eyes, all the tension drained from him, and I knew the exact reason. *I felt it too.*

Our mate was here. Her soft, lilting laughter filled the room as Emme caught the tail end of Talon's little temper tantrum.

# CHAPTER 24

EMME

**B**y the time Slade brought me home, he was covered in my scent. There was nothing quite like having both horsepower *and* a dragon between my thighs. *These are a few of my favorite things.*

Slade took a longer path home than usual, and it was the perfect end to a day filled with training and magical revelations. I found a sense of peace knowing that I hadn't hurt any of my mates. Their essences were as strong as ever in our quintet bond.

Their beasts lingered near mine, and I might be imagining it, but there was a new sense of closeness between us that hadn't been there before.

When we walked into the house, I followed the tugging of my bond to find Hunter and Talon in the gaming room, desperately trying to shoot each other. Or at least one of them was desperate, right before he threw the controller into the wall.

To see my rather unflappable mate in this state was hilarious.

Talon was so used to being excellent at everything he attempted to do, including driving for the first time, that he was flummoxed with his lack of skills at gaming.

"Brother, I could have warned you not to go up against our resident nerd," Slade said with an amused huff, close at my back as he'd been all afternoon.

Fighting the urge to lean into him, in case it was all too much for one day, I jolted when his heavy arm snaked around my middle and yanked me back.

I rested my head against his chest, meeting his gaze. "Did you just pick up on my thoughts again?"

His nose traced down my cheek, and *who the hell was this shifter?* Not my usually stoic mate. "Only the ones you scream really loudly through our bond," he murmured, as his lips grazed mine. "You don't even bother to try and hide them. You *and your thoughts* belong to me."

Hunter chuckled, giving off the vibes that he totally agreed. *Possessive bastards.*

That *thought* went freely into our quintet and all three of them released low, husky laughs.

It was almost cute when they ganged up on me. *Almost.*

Hunter jumped to his feet, and within two strides was in front of me, caging me between him and the dragon. "You're our number one priority," he said, going *all* entitled alpha. "We might outnumber you, but we'll never use that to gang up on you, Emme. You hold all the power here, and I hope you know that."

Talon propped himself up on the couch as he turned my way. "Just say the word, Honey. I'll kill any of these bastards and not lose a night of sleep."

Hunter and Slade didn't even flinch at what was absolutely a real threat. "That's disturbing," I noted, narrowing my eyes on them. "Please don't talk about killing each other to make me happy. I can tell you all right now that would be the farthest thing from happy, and we'd probably all suffer from some sort of bond sickness and die."

"Who we killing?" Kellan chirped cheerfully as he strode into the room, practically beaming.

Finley was right behind him, and as our gazes locked, his expression softened, his big body relaxed.

"They're showing their love for me by threatening to kill anyone who bothers me," I told them. "Including you five in my pack."

There was a long beat of silence, and then Finley's big belly laughter set them all off again.

I just shook my head and scowled. "Figures that my alphas would be a bunch of psychos."

Hunter wiped a hand over his mouth, but his smile remained. "I mean, I wouldn't enjoy destroying my brothers," he said. "But you come first."

Kellan snorted again. "I'd take all you fuckers out for my Shortcake."

Disengaging from the alphas, I marched over to the couch and somewhat dramatically threw myself into the soft cushion. My faux-annoyance faded when I noticed the tray of snacks on the coffee table.

Selecting a small pizza roll, I shoved it in my mouth, muttering as I chewed, "Why don't you idiots kill each other in *Call of Duty*." I swallowed the bite. "There's clearly some frustration to work out here, and I promise, I'll be very upset if any of you hurt each other in real life."

Talon, the only one on the couch with me, slid over to settle by my side. "I missed you today," I said with a sigh.

That had him wrapping his arms around me, holding me close in a moment of calm and silence. "I missed you so much," he breathed. "It was a dull ache that had nothing to do with our bond separation and everything to do with not being close to you."

That was exactly how I'd felt too. Burying my face against his hard chest, I just breathed him in. It really wasn't just Slade and Hunter like this… it was all of us. Disgustingly obsessed.

"And proud of it," Talon said with a rumble, once again picking up on thoughts that hadn't really been meant for him.

When we pulled apart, I found myself staring at the split screen, which was paused in the middle of a warzone. "Do you know how to play?" Talon asked, as the others started to make their way over to us.

"Video games weren't part of my life growing up or in the human world," I said. "But I've sat with Hunter a few times and watched him absolutely demolish anyone who goes up against him."

Hunter slid in on my other side, Kellan crashed on the floor between my legs, and Finley pouted briefly, before slumping down beside Hunter.

When I turned to Slade, the dragon shifter remained perched near the doorway. "I'm going to get a workout in," he said. "As much as I'd enjoy seeing Talon smash more controllers, I've had you all day. I can share for a few hours so the others get their bonding time in."

He strode over to trace his finger down my cheek, in a very *Slade* move. "But I will see you later," he murmured, and I nodded.

Before he left, he said to Talon, "We must train tonight too. Emme can't be the only one building strength when we're the perfect weapon to use against magic. We need to ensure our ultimate beast is as strong as possible."

"I'm ready," Talon assured him, and I caught the glimmer of excitement in his expression. "I'll be down in an hour or so."

The dragons didn't need much sleep, which no doubt meant they'd be out most of the night, strengthening Slalon.

For the next hour we focused on eating, gaming, and generally enjoying the company of our pack. That new sense of closeness after the magical merge didn't dissipate, and even Hunter commented on how content his alpha wolf was in our bond. Not that we really spoke about what had happened, but it was still on my mind.

They played a range of games, most of which required them to stab or shoot something, and all of them were good… except for Talon. The dragon couldn't figure out how to make his massive fingers mash little buttons, and it was lucky that Hunter had dozens of controllers in the storage cupboard. Talon went through at least four in the hour.

"You can't be good at everything," I said, patting his arm consolingly. "I sucked too."

I'd only played once, and all of them had refused to kill me. They were my opponents, but they spent the entire round camping and guarding me, so there was nothing for me to kill, and not a single bullet touched me. I shot them, tried to run from them, and still those possessive asses stayed right with me, absolutely annihilating everyone in the field.

"You didn't suck," Hunter argued. "Everyone else died and you didn't have to respawn once."

I narrowed my eyes on him. "Yeah, and that had nothing to do with my skills and everything to do with being mated into a group of over-the-top alphas who—"

"Will never let anyone hurt you," Finley declared with a decisive nod. "Not even in a fucking video game. I'm pissed just thinking about it." He turned to Hunter. "Let's buy this company and destroy this game. That bullet *almost* grazed Emme's arm."

Hunter furrowed his brow like he was seriously considering it, and I pressed my lips together to stem my laughter. They were unhinged, and I wasn't even mad about it.

When a yawn almost took me out, I was reminded once again of my magical training. "Did Constantine get home?" I asked, realizing I hadn't heard or felt him in the house.

Hunter pulled out his phone and scrolled through the security feed. "Yep, he's in his room," he said. "Appears to be sleeping. You can see him tomorrow."

I nodded, accepting that while tonight was a great reprieve from reality, tomorrow we'd be focused on our task of tracking Jewels. Whether we wanted it to be or not, the full moon was closing in on us.

"I'm going to use the restroom and then say goodnight to Slade," I said, jumping up from the couch. The alphas watched me leave, but thankfully none of them actually followed me inside to watch me empty my disc.

After washing my hands, I emerged to find Talon waiting for me. "I might as well train with Slade now," he said, holding his hand out for me to take.

"Sounds like a plan."

"See you in my room, little omega," Hunter called, and I glanced over my shoulder to find my remaining three alphas staring at me with heated gazes. *Whoa.* Juggling five mates was not for the faint of heart, but I wouldn't change it for the world.

Talon's hand was warm and firm in mine as we headed toward the gym, but we didn't make it halfway there before his beast roared in his chest. He swung me around and had me pressed against the wall in a beat. "I missed you so much today," he breathed against my lips, crowding and heating me in all the best ways.

His hands slowly slid down my spine, the path burning. I parted my lips to taste him, and *fuck* he tasted as good as he smelled. His tongue brushed over mine, and I was hit with a sense of desperation that had me climbing him in an attempt to get closer.

He eased back to give me space, and when my legs were wrapped around his waist, the possessive rumbles spilling from his chest were enough to send me reeling. Even fully clothed my core ached and pulsed, and Talon scented how wet I was in seconds. His hands fumbled on my jeans, getting them unbuttoned and halfway down with my panties before I grabbed his arms.

"Periods," I blurted out a breathless reminder.

His gaze was glassy as he got my lower half naked. "I don't care, Honey. I need you. *Now.*"

My core pulsed again. I was so fucked up over him. "My disc is in, so it should keep the blood contained, and I cleaned up after training…"

"Don't. Care."

He wrapped his hands around my thighs and lifted me up above his head. Using the wall for support, he pressed me against it, his mouth landing on my clit. Thank the goddess this dragon was extra-strong even for a shifter.

When he buried his face and rumbled out more of those desperate, needy sounds, I almost came then and there. He lapped at my clit, dragging the tingling bundle of nerves into his mouth.

"Fuck, Honey," he whispered, his voice a husky rasp. "You taste like heaven, spice, and fertility."

"Tal. *Please.*" I started chanting, unable to do more than get swept up in the pleasure, and when I climaxed, there was a gush that would have covered the poor dragon in blood if my disc wasn't in.

I choked out, "I still find it hard to believe you've never done that before… *Your skills*… I might be dead."

He lowered his head to my sensitive clit, still circling it with his tongue, until I was racked with aftershocks. When he finally let me slide down to wrap myself around him again, I felt the pulse of his cock between us. "Let me taste you too," I said, tracing my hands over his shadowed face.

Those shadows lifted as his lips tilted. "I need all of you," he whispered, and a trill of excitement rocked through me.

In a moment, I was facing the wall, my hands pressed against the smooth surface, the head of his cock pressed against the junction of my thighs, and from this angle he felt even bigger. Which was ridiculous.

"I don't think I'll be able to go all the way in without hurting you or breaking the disc," he said in a huff, his lips on my ear. "Does this still feel good?"

He rocked against me, and my head spun at *how damn good* it felt.

"So good," I moaned, my walls pulsing around his length, already building to my next release.

"I want to do this every day until I die," Talon stated, his teeth grazing my neck as if he were about to bite me. "I always knew I'd kill and die for you, but when I'm inside you, I truly understand why love is the most powerful emotion of all."

My core pulsed with each thrust and word he spoke. "Sex and love don't always go hand in hand," I gasped.

"With us it does," he said, fucking me harder, "and it's the best feeling in the world. The pleasure we experience is heightened because we love each other. The bond between us grows stronger each time we come together."

My head snapped back as I climaxed hard, crying out as Talon fucked me through that release and into the next. He groaned my name and his teeth sank into my skin right when he came too. He held me through all of our aftershocks, moving slowly until we were both sated.

I loved that we could exist together like this. Two broken shifters made whole by our bond and pack.

When he finally pulled out of me, I mourned the loss, though my body was achy and overstimulated. Bonus though: there was no period pain to be found.

Talon helped me clean up in the bathroom, and I shooed him out of the room when I emptied my disc again, even though he was quite insistent he could help with that too.

In the gym, we found Slade on the bench press. "Nice of you to join me," he said, lifting one eyebrow as he took in my appearance. "Not that either of you blocked the bond well enough to hide what you were doing."

*Whoops.* "Sorry about that," I said, trying not to laugh, even as my cheeks heated. "We got a little carried away. But I wanted to come and say goodnight before you two go and train Slalon."

Slade grimaced and dropped his million-pound weighted bar on the rack. "We need to chat about that name, mate. It's not your best work."

I shrugged. "Agree to disagree."

I leaned down to kiss his cheek, only to find myself being lifted like the weights and dropped right on top of him. The bench groaned under us but we didn't care, too caught up in a desperate kiss.

The tense muscles under my body were a decent sign that he was slightly worked up from what Talon and I had done in the hall. It also turned me on to know the others had been listening and feeling the effects through the bond.

"No time for that, brat," Slade said as he groaned and smacked my ass. I moaned and arched against him, realizing that with these alphas, I was insatiable.

But, really, who could blame me?

# CHAPTER 25

EMME

After saying goodnight to Slade and Talon, I hurried into my room to change into pjs, before I ended up in Hunter's bedroom. Hunter and Slade had the largest beds in the house, so there was no issue fitting between the huge, boxer-clad alphas, already waiting for me. No one spoke a word as we arranged ourselves for the night, a comforting darkness wrapped around us.

There was no argument about who would sleep beside me, and I was fairly sure they'd decided long before I made it into the room. Kellan and Finley slid in on either side of me, and Hunter settled in beside Kellan, draping his arm over the alpha to touch my thigh, his usual place to claim.

I faced Finley, who also had his arm over me, with Kellan spooning me from behind.

From the second I closed my eyes, surrounded by their scents, to when I opened them the next morning, none of us moved an inch. I'd slept so soundly, and for that brief moment between sleep and waking where everything was a dreamy blur, I swore all our beasts were also mingled together in our essence, as they'd done when I used magic yesterday.

I pried my eyes open to meet swirling whiskey irises, the low light of the morning highlighting gold in their depths. "Morning, darlin'," he murmured in his soft drawl, which sent a shiver all the way to my core.

Periods were annoyingly inconvenient, even if they didn't seem to bother Talon in the slightest. "Morning, Grouchy," I whispered, clearing my throat. "What time is it?"

"Too fucking early," Kellan grumbled from behind me, and I had to laugh that our sunshiny boy got grumpy when he didn't get enough sleep. "I just want to stay buried against my omega, breathing in chocolate and honey, and dreaming about eating all her creamy goodness from between thighs wrapped around my face—"

There was a thud, and I didn't have to turn to know it was Hunter slamming his fist into Kellan's side. One of them growled, and the other laughed, and no guesses were needed for which was which. "Control yourself, pup," came out as an aggravated growl. "Emme needs our care and consideration during her period."

"And orgasms, if Talon's adventure with her last night is any indication," Kellan added matter-of-factly.

My cheeks heated at the memory of them experiencing what happened in the hallway, and not all of that blush was from embarrassment. Apparently my voyeuristic side was growing.

"When I wear my disc, I can have sex and… *other stuff*." The way all three focused on me, not only here in the bedroom but their beasts in the bond, was overwhelming. "But it's probably best if we wait. They should be over in a couple of days."

Instead of the groans and muttered annoyances I expected, I got cuddles and lazy morning kisses that had me never wanting to leave the bed.

Eventually Hunter and Kellan dragged themselves away to get ready for the day, leaving me with Finley. He brushed his nose against mine, and I took the opportunity to really check in with him. "How are you doing?" I asked, breathing deeply to take the full notes of vanilla and cherry into my lungs. "Have you had a chance to attend therapy this week?"

He brushed his thumb slowly over my lower lip and down my jaw. "I'm making every effort not to miss therapy," he said as he continued to caress me. "And I'm doing well, all things considered."

My legs grew restless under his touch, until he eventually trapped them beneath one of his thick thighs. "Our bonding has settled elements of my beast and soul," he continued, his hand in my hair now, tracing through the length. "I've never been this happy before, and considering the circumstances, it feels kind of fucked up to admit that."

"I'm happy too," I said with a shrug. "I'm not going to let Jewels steal that from us. None of us know what tomorrow will bring, so I plan to enjoy every second I have with you five."

He pressed his lips to my cheek, and then kissed my jaw, and then the corner of my mouth. He repeated it on the other side, these soft, feathery kisses that had butterflies erupting in my stomach. If there was one thing Finley Thornton knew how to do, it was adore his mate.

"No matter what happens," Finley told me between kisses, "as long as we're together, I'll be okay. No witch, magic, or curse is going to tear us down. I'd turn human for you, Ice."

My chest ached at that declaration. For a shifter, that was about the greatest statement of love one could make, and as a wave of emotions washed through me, my wolf shifted to allow all of my mates into the essence. Into my thoughts.

*I'd turn human for you, too!* Kellan said in a rush.

*Me too*, Hunter rumbled. *Human and happy about it.*

*Us too*, Slade said. And Talon's grunt of agreement indicated he was fine for his twin to speak for him.

The fact that *dragons* would offer that without hesitation floored me. They were more than just regular shifters, the most magical and mystical of our kind. For them to be no more than a regular human…

*There'd be nothing regular about us*, Slade scoffed. *We'd be exceptional humans and you know it.*

*I'd probably be a king*, Kellan decided, and I couldn't see him, but I knew he was nodding his head decisively.

Hunter scoffed. *You'd be the fucking court jester.*

*And you'd all love me.*

I was laughing as I closed off the mental connection once more and returned my focus to Finley.

He stared at me with the softest eyes, and I was living for these moments with him. "You're definitely the most caring *Care Bear*, Grouchy," I told him as I brushed our noses together, taking in his scent. "And I love you." The whiskey depths darkened, and our kisses went on until my head spun.

We showered together and I let him wash my hair, enjoying a chance to be pampered. I did the same for him, relishing the chance to run my hands through his luscious locks. I even got to scrub over his beard.

"Fuck, that feels so good," he groaned, sitting on the bench to give me easier access.

My gaze took in his broad shoulders and thick chest, and I lingered on that new thigh tattoo. The one for me. He'd marked the crown in pigmented gold, while the snowflake was done in the same icy blue as my eyes.

Finley wore only three tattoos, and all of them held great significance for him, marking important lessons he'd learned, mottos he lived by, and the things he loved.

I was now one of those significant parts of his life, and I doubted my heart would never not skip a beat at the sight of it.

"I want you to tattoo me," I said, tracing my fingers over the snowflake-crown. "I want your hands to be the one to mark me. I want one of the designs you've been working on."

His eyes widened, and I couldn't hold back my laughter. "Yeah, I saw them on your desk, and I love all of it. They're exactly what I was hoping for."

As I traced his thigh again, the length of his cock jumped near my hand, and I couldn't fight the urge any longer. Dropping to my knees, I crawled between his parted thighs, pressing a kiss to his tattoo on my way. His groan was deep and loud, and his shaft pulsed near my face.

I continued to kiss along his thigh until I was finally able to properly taste him, the thick tip already slick with his desire. My tongue darted out to lap at the pre-cum, and Finley's hands gripped the side of the bench. "Baby," he choked out. "I want you so fucking bad."

Tilting my head back, I kissed and licked along the underside of his cock, moving down until my tongue brushed his heavy balls. The whole time, his gaze was super-focused on me, his breaths coming out in little pants.

"Em. Please," my proud bear said, and no wonder begging drove my alphas crazy when I did it. I felt an instant pulse in my core.

Even more, I loved that Finley no longer hid the softer sides of himself from me. He was turning out to be the most open and gentlest of all my alphas now, right up there with Kellan.

Sliding my tongue over the warm, firm skin, I reached his crown and once again lapped up his sweet and salty taste. When I closed my mouth over the head, he thrust suddenly, as if he couldn't help himself.

A low laugh spilled from me, which vibrated into Finley. He moaned and slid his hands into the wet strands of my hair to hold me in place. "I'm not going to take long," he breathed, staring down at me. "Your mouth is a dangerous, perfect place to exist, darlin'. Watching you slide that pretty pink tongue around my dick... such a good fucking omega."

My core spasmed, the walls of my pussy clenching around nothing. The ache in my ovaries faded as I snaked my hand down to play with my clit, all the while sucking harder and taking Finley deeper. Or as deep as I could, which like the other alphas, wasn't too far.

Not that he seemed to mind.

He moaned once more as his focus trailed down to where my hand worked between my thighs; his thrusts in my mouth turned frantic and jerky. The sweet and salty taste washed over my tongue, and my release was so close that I knew we were going to come together.

"Now, Ice," he demanded. "Baby, now."

I cried out as his cock thickened and he spilled down the back of my throat, my own shuddering release blasting through me at the same time. The sensation of our dual orgasm was almost too much to handle, and eventually I was a panting, dizzy pile of omega on the floor. At least until he pulled me up into his lap, rocking me back and forth as the warm water washed over us.

When we finally dragged ourselves from the shower, he dried me off, and left so I could reinsert my disc. A lot of my clothes were in Hunter's wardrobe, and I slipped on a pair of jeans, a maroon hoodie, and dark socks. Finley returned dressed in jeans and a thick red and white flannel button-down.

He held my hand all the way into the kitchen, where Florence and Gerald were bustling around feeding the alphas. "Good morning, Steven," I called, and Hunter grunted from where he was reading the paper at the counter.

"Fucking plant gets a good morning before us," he muttered, but he was amused. I could tell. It was just really deep down.

"Any more stories about illegal activities pertaining to the Reeves pack?" Kellan asked with a smirk as he sidled by to drop a kiss on my head.

I slid into a stool beside Hunter, and he nudged a mug of coffee under my nose that was still steaming. As usual, he'd heard me coming and had it prepared. I all but buried my face in the sweet, creamy depths to hide how overwhelming it was to be loved so thoroughly by these alphas. "Thank you," I managed to say.

He dropped his paper long enough to press a kiss to the side of my neck. "Anytime, little mate. Anytime." He turned to where Kellan had positioned himself against the other counter, near the sink. "And no, there's been nothing else that could be considered Reeves pack related."

Kellan's pout was ridiculous; the last thing we needed was to be front page news again. Though his love of stirring drama was cute. Not that I'd tell him that.

His pout formed into a smirk, and I groaned knowing he'd just heard that thought.

He blew me a kiss, but I ignored him for Florence, who'd just placed five breakfast sandwiches in front of me. "I love you," I sang to her, both of us ignoring the alpha grunts and rumbles in the room.

We'd be on the road today and I'd need my energy, so I polished off the sandwiches then debated if I needed a cookie as well.

Hunter snapped his paper closed and dropped it on the counter. "We're heading to Fletcher's compound after breakfast," he said. "This is our first real opportunity to not only investigate what he was doing there, but also hopefully find an item that we can use to track Jewels or one of her allies. Constantine said that Jewels will have the most magical shielding and protection around her, but she might not have the power to shield everyone else. We can leave no stone unturned."

"Is Constantine coming with us?" Before I even finished asking, my magic pulsed as the witch-wolf entered the kitchen.

"I'll absolutely be with you, Emme," he said with a brief but genuine smile.

As our gazes met, I felt a spark of connection that I hadn't had before I found my magic yesterday. There'd apparently been some bonding between us, or at least between our powers.

We had a long way to go for a real relationship, but for the first time I felt there was a flicker of hope.

# CHAPTER 26

SLADE

When Emme declared that her Panigale looked sad and lonely so she needed to ride it today, I knew I'd be on my bike beside her. Hunter decided to ride with us too.

Finley, Kellan, and Constantine would take the Flying Spur, which had the size for comfort and the speed to keep up. Talon was going to fly, always more at ease in his beast form. If not for Emme, I'd have joined him; my beast was restless but not in the way that he used to be. There was no longer a cold distance between us. Now all I felt was an animalistic restlessness.

"I'm ready," my mate called, racing into the garage, staring at the row of bikes like she'd genuinely missed them.

While the five of us stared at her like the rest of the world didn't exist.

Hunter let out a low rumble, his gaze dragging over her outfit. She'd dressed herself in the boots and gloves he'd had custom made for her birthday. The boots were zipped up over leather pants, hugging her long, shapely legs, and she'd paired them with a black tank and Kellan's jacket.

Her hair was loose around her shoulders, and I craved her like the rarest of treasures. Dragons loved treasure, and she was one I'd kill to keep.

I'd always been proud to be a dragon shifter, but that feeling was nothing compared to how proud I was to have Emmeline as a mate.

"You're wearing my jacket, Shortcake," Kellan crooned, stroking his hands down the back of the thick leather, before he reached forward to grasp both sides, zipping her up.

"It's as amazing as the one that got destroyed," she said, her face falling briefly before she smiled again. "It's so warm and snuggly, while heavy-duty enough to protect me from road rash."

My dragon hissed and I clenched my hands. "The only way the road will ever touch you, Snow, is if I'm dead."

Emmeline gave me heart eyes and I was fucking purring like a damn dragon-cat. *Fuck me.*

She turned toward Hunter. "These boots are the most amazing pair I've ever owned. How are they this soft but also so sturdy?"

Our little omega was discovering the reason custom-made cost at least four times as off-the-rack.

Hunter shrugged like he had no idea. "They look incredible on you."

Emme gave him a hug. "You downplay it, but I can already tell how expensive they were. You all spent far too much money on me for my birthday, but it turns out that I'm kind of in love with everything and I'm not giving any of it back." She clutched her dragon necklace briefly in her gloved hand.

When she released Hunter, she moved toward her bike, only to pause, her hands flying to her hair. "Oh fuck, I need to braid this back and I can't do it with gloves."

"Let me," I said, already moving toward her.

She blinked at me like she couldn't understand those two words, while Talon grabbed one of the many brushes he had stashed around the house for any opportunity that arose to brush Emme's hair. As he ran the soft bristles through her pinkish gold strands, I stripped a hair tie from her wrist. I'd never braided before, but I'd watched Emme do it so many times that I understood the mechanics.

Talon stepped away once her hair was smooth, and I threaded my fingers through the strands, the rest of our pack gawking on like they'd never seen a fucking dragon braid a female's hair before. Her scent surged with each twist, and I had to give myself a very stern talking to since this was not the time to bend her over the back of my bike and sink my cock into her.

I might be new to sex and physical contact in general, but I was a damn quick learner. I also had a new obsession. It was pretty, pink, and under my hands right now. And I wasn't just talking about her hair.

After fifteen seconds I'd figured out the pattern in braiding, immediately finding the motion rhythmic and soothing. "That feels so good," Emme said, tilting her head back.

When her eyes fluttered closed, I understood why my twin was hung up on brushing her hair. There was a strong satisfaction in soothing one's mate. My dragon was a contented beast in my chest.

When I tied off the ends, she murmured her thanks, and we both turned to find our silent and shellshocked pack frozen in place. No doubt it would take time for them to get used to me voluntarily touching another shifter. Or maybe it was the shock of me braiding, though I don't know why any of them would have doubted my ability to do so.

If Emme needed brain surgery I'd have that figured out in a few hours too. For her, there were no limits.

Kellan silently handed me her helmet, his eyes wide as he looked between me and our mate, as if he felt my possessive need to finish getting her ready for our ride.

Locking her in my focus, her expression was soft as she stared up at me. I didn't even need to push into her thoughts to know what she was thinking: *love.*

Stupid word. But fuck if it wasn't the only one I could think of to use.

Unable to cover her face without tasting her one last time, I pressed my lips to hers and she sighed. *Fuck.* I barely managed to tear myself away to slide her helmet on, and after carefully strapping her in, I checked everything twice, before patting her on the ass.

"You stay between Hunt and me," I ordered. "We have enemies out there, and you're more breakable than us."

There was a pause, and through the dark tint of her visor, I caught the eye roll. *Little brat.* Still, she eventually nodded. I enjoyed when she was submissive to my dominance. Mostly because she chose to be. There was no one who could make an omega submit, not even a dragon. While her fire and sass were sexy, her submission got me on a fundamental level.

Constantine broke the silence by stomping noisily into the garage, being the annoying mouth breather that he was. He had shoes on for once, and his backpack was slung over his shoulder. That was the one piece of luggage he had with him when he arrived, and I'd already checked the contents to find a few of his parents' journals and some magical paraphernalia.

Which was most likely why he had it with him today, in case he needed to perform magic at the compound. None of us had any idea what we'd find there, and it never hurt to be prepared.

Hence why the Bentley's trunk was filled with weapons and body armor.

Constantine's arrival kicked us all into gear. Half of the group peeled off to enter the car, while the rest of us climbed onto our bikes. Hunter had already swung Emme's around to face the exit, and through the bond I could feel her surprise and then gratitude at the gesture.

No one had ever taken care of her, but this was her new reality. Now and always.

As I pulled my helmet on, the comms kicked in, and her voice filled my head. "—thank you, Hurricane. I appreciate the assist."

Hunter shrugged as he leaned down to tap his helmet against hers. "Taking care of you is the best part of my day. I love you, little mate."

Emme's words were huskier as she sniffled. "I love you too, Alpha Hunter."

For maybe the first time, I truly understood the reason shifters used those three words in their packs. Sure *love* was thrown around too easily, but it was more than the word itself. It was *how* it was said. I'd just felt the soul-deep emotion between Emme and Hunter as they shared their love. I'd felt the power behind it. It was beyond any power witches could touch; it was an eternal magic that spanned more than our mortal lives.

My first, *and hopefully fucking last*, existential crisis was shelved when engines roared to life in the garage, and I kicked my bike over to join them. Hunter headed out first, Emme followed, and I brought up the rear to keep their backs safe. Talon would remain overhead the whole time, offering a full range of protection for our mate.

In the street, we followed the Bentley's steady pace until we left Golden Claw's borders. Emme eased up her hold on the quintet bond so Talon could give us direction, and when we hit the highway it was time to open up the engines.

Emme's whoop of joy was almost drowned out by the throaty

rumble of our bikes, and my dragon roared at the rush. We kept pace with her, relishing the speed, which was *almost* as good as flying.

"I flew with Talon the other night," Emme said as if she'd heard my thought, though the connection was once again closed.

"I know. I witnessed most of it through Talon." I'd never allowed anyone on my back during flight, but Emme's excitement with Talon had me reconsidering it.

"I will finally concede that a motorcycle comes second to flying. You were both right."

My amusement took me by surprise. "You don't say that a lot."

Hunter let loose a laugh, deeper over the comms. "And I hope you don't make it a habit. This asshole is already too full of himself. Cocky fucking dragons."

Talon might be a literal part of my soul, but Hunter was as well, just in a different way. Which meant he got to make comments like that and not get hurt for it. Also, he wasn't wrong. Dragons were cocky, and it was for a good damn reason.

"I'm appropriately confident," I reminded them.

"You can't deny that," Emme said with a snort. "The dragons definitely live up to their hype."

*And I always will, sweetheart.*

We rode for hours surrounded by engine noises and the occasional conversation that sprang up between us. Emme told us a little more about her years on the run, and how her bike had been an escape from her loneliness and her wolf's need to be with her pack. "She wanted to be in the cities," she said. "She would push me and try to force the shift. Remember that day I ran around my bedroom, unable to stop until we calmed? That was a common occurrence in my day-to-day. Kind of took the edge off."

That day in question was maybe the first time I acknowledged how desperately obsessed I was with this omega. I'd watched the security footage of her wolf circling the room so many times, that it permanently played on one of the screens in my room for a good week. Seeing her distress, the bitterness of her scent filling the house long after she'd recovered, had me wanting to burn the world down just to scorch every person who'd ever hurt her.

Emme still had no idea that every night for weeks after that I'd sat by her side in the dark, keeping her as safe as I could, craving a touch

I wasn't sure I'd ever feel. All while fearing my beast would destroy the best thing to ever come into my life.

"You never have to worry about that again," Hunter said, dragging me from those darker memories. "Not even with this new attack on shifters. We will keep you safe."

Emme scoffed. "Fucking war, it makes no sense to me. How are there any winners?"

"There aren't," I confirmed. "But if I've learned anything from our history, it's that you need to take whatever chances you can get for happiness. These darker days can drag on, and our souls aren't designed to live in the dark forever. Even the smallest snippet of light helps to get us through."

Ahead, the Bentley turned into a gas station, and I indicated to follow.

Emme let out a sigh. "Yeah, I don't want to feel guilty about enjoying myself. The truth is, we have no idea if we're going to be able to win this time. I hope we do, but there are no guarantees. I don't want to miss out on these last days, if that's all we have left."

"These are not our last days," Hunter growled, spilling dominance. "We will not let that bitch best us."

Kellan pulled up beside the pump, ready to gas up his car, and Emme followed to the next.

"What do you think of Constantine?" she asked, turning to watch her father hop out of the car. "I don't get bad vibes from him, but I'm also hesitating to get closer."

The shifter in question looked in our direction—he was always sneaking glances at his daughter, whenever she wasn't looking his way. I'd been keeping a close eye on him, and so far there were no red flags, though he was well-versed in hiding his true identity...

"From what I learned during my research, which granted, was much easier with his name and heritage, most of his story checks out. He was trying to protect you by magically hiding your witch essence. I don't believe he's here to betray you, but at the end of the day, I trust no one except our pack."

Emme nodded, but further conversation was cut off by Finley wrapping his arms around her and lifting her from the bike. He had her helmet off in a beat, rubbing his hands over her cheek. "Missed you, darlin'."

Emme's happiness was a balm filtering through the bond and soothing our alpha beasts. All of us needed her in different ways, and somehow she was able to provide that for each of us.

Now we just had to ensure we did the same for her.

Starting with finding and destroying a witch, and giving us all a shot at a future.

# CHAPTER 27

EMME

According to Talon, the compound was so isolated that if we'd used the jet to get there, we would still have had to drive for a few hours anyway. Hence the decision to road trip across the state and into Idaho. A decision I was more than happy about, as it was my first real chance to test out the Panigale. *The power and handling…* oh my goddess.

The bike was everything I'd hoped it would be and more.

All expectations had been met and exceeded, and it was exciting to know we still had plenty of hours left to our destination.

"You need to eat, Shortcake," Kellan said as he exited the gas station, hands full of snacks. I rescued a few that appeared to be teetering on the edge of falling. "You can't eat while you're riding, so now's your chance."

Hunter had gassed up my bike while I used the restroom—Slade had checked them before allowing me inside of course. Now Kellan was handing me food, while Finley had drinks.

For weeks now these alphas had been caring and catering to me, without ever expecting a single thing in return. I was possibly the most spoiled shifter in history, and it felt overwhelming *in the best ways.*

"Slade and Hunter need to eat now too," I said, offloading some of the sandwiches and snacks their way. Or trying to, since neither of them would take them.

Kellan hooted as he whisked me over to sit in the front seat of the

Bentley, the others following us. More than a few humans glanced our way, wearing expressions that were a mix of awe and fear. They probably wondered if this group of huge and scarily lethal males had kidnapped me. I hoped my smile accurately represented that I was *exactly where I wanted to be.*

"Eat up, Emme," Kellan said, nudging the snacks in my lap. "I have no idea what most of this is, but these were what the attendant recommended."

All of them looked confused, as if they'd never seen a Twinkie, Snickers bar, or pack of Skittles before. Come to think of it, the only junk we'd had in our house was either shifter specific, or homemade. I couldn't wait to see these alphas racing through the streets hyped up on fake sugar.

Constantine, who remained off to the side watching the five of us closely, caught my attention.

"You've never been around a properly bonded pack before, have you?" I asked him, assuming that was what drew so much of his curiosity.

His smile was brief. "No. My parents weren't in a pack, and I've all but been a nomad since they died. I hoped to find a family with your mother, but once she got pregnant I knew I couldn't stay. It was a brief dream."

My nose wrinkled at the thought of anyone ever wanting to be in a pack with my mother. "Why would you want her? She was the most narcissistic bitch I've ever met. Excluding Jewels of course. She cared about no one but herself and treated me like I was an annoyance at best and a curse she needed to be rid of at worst. You know she told me you wanted her *to tear me from her womb*. It was her favorite bedtime story."

My father's only reaction was to release the faintest of sighs. "She knew I wanted you more than life, but when I left her... It was the first step of breaking her. Then whatever that pack did... whatever they stole from her essence changed her fundamentally. I saw her the day you were born, when I warned her to keep moving to hide your hybrid nature. She was happy on that day, and very much cherished being a mother."

I'd never known her to be happy or caring, but after experiencing true love with my mates, I understood how losing that could break a shifter. Followed by what Fletcher and Blaine's pack put her through.

It wasn't that I excused her actions, but I did at least understand them better.

"I still can't comprehend how you could have left your child," Finley grumbled, his stare hard and cold. "If you kept tabs on Emme as you say you did, then you knew how they treated her. You must have seen she was at risk. It's pure luck that the Rogers pack didn't forcibly bond Emme and steal her essence, same as they did with her mother."

My wolf howled and moved closer to the bear. Finley was triggered by parental abuse, but while he was clearly upset, he wasn't losing it. Therapy and bonding continued to help him manage his darker emotions.

"I would have stepped in had Emme been in real danger," Constantine said shortly. "I'd never have let them truly hurt her. I spelled the damn mechanic's workshop so she'd be safe there. I did keep an eye on her, and when Morgan died, I ensured she could go free."

*The mechanic's workshop.* It had been the only place I'd felt safe for years. "You did keep me hidden in the human world. My getting caught was just a series of unfortunate events."

Constantine swallowed roughly, rubbing at his temples as if this conversation pained him. "It's clear that the goddess decided it was time for you to fulfill your destiny. Not even I have the power to take her on."

Hunter shifted forward. "You'd have kept her from us, wouldn't you? If the goddess never stepped in?" His expression wasn't as hard as Finley's, and through our bond I picked up tendrils of understanding and empathy from the entitled alpha.

"If it meant that Emme was never vilified or hurt by the packs or witches, I'd have kept her hidden forever." There was no hesitation in Constantine's statement. "Our kind has many enemies, and I hadn't even really known about Fletcher and Jewels at the time."

Clearly, once my mother told Fletcher about my hybrid nature, I became very important to his plans. All of which Constantine saved me from.

"I owe you my thanks," I said suddenly, and he startled like I'd slapped him. "Fletcher would have destroyed me in his quest for more power, but you kept me safe for years. Even in your absence, you were a far better parent than Morgan."

His cheeks pinkened, and he opened and closed his mouth a few times, before shaking his head. Giving him a second to pull himself together, I focused on unwrapping a sandwich and eating quickly, while the alphas chatted softly.

"Whatever Jewels has planned after the curse can mean nothing good for the shifter world," Hunter said to Slade, rubbing a hand over his jaw.

Slade nodded. "Nothing good. She's waited a long time for this to come to fruition, and if it's set to control all of us, it's a heavy curse."

This jolted Constantine back into the conversation. "It's one of the most powerful of magics," he confirmed.

"How did you even find out about it?" Kellan asked him, still examining a Snickers bar.

"Everyone with active magic felt her draw on the power to cast the spell. There's no witch who wouldn't have felt that."

Except for me apparently. "I didn't feel anything," I said, taking a bite of the chicken and mayo. "The only time I ever felt magic before the full quintet bond were those faint tingles in my hands."

"Your magic was locked away," he reminded me. "You probably did feel it, but it would have registered as a weird flip in your gut."

I had a sudden thought: *Do you think magic was how I blasted you across the room?* I asked Talon, who remained high in the skies above.

The dragon's reply was immediate. *Yeah, I already had an idea you might have magic in your blood with how excited Fletcher was to claim you. But I expected it to be more like dragons. Not witches.*

*Yeah, that makes sense. I wish it was more like that.*

There was a caress of his dragon against my wolf, and then he withdrew to continue his sky patrol.

I didn't bother to tell Constantine I'd briefly accessed my magic in a moment of pure survival; it was really a moot point now that the full bond had shattered all locks on my magic.

The alphas encouraged me to finish up my snacks, and they wolfed down whatever was left, before we hit the road once more, this time with more focus on getting there as quickly as possible.

Out front, Kellan pushed the Bentley to its maximum capacity, and we all needed to take a moment to give thanks for the power of a W12 engine. When we closed in on the compound, Talon directed us down isolated, rougher roads, which we were forced to slow along.

*It's very remote,* he confirmed when my wolf backed up for easier quintet conversation. *But there are no immediate dangers. I've already scouted ahead, and it's as deserted as it was yesterday.*

The chain-link and wire fence came into view first, spanning high into the air. There was nothing welcoming about this compound, and I shivered as Talon directed us toward the front gate, which had been blasted open.

We drove down a short dirt path to reach the dwellings, with the main building made up of gray walls and squat shapes. When I pulled my bike to a stop, Talon landed beside me. I swung myself off the bike, my aching legs briefly faltering, but he was there. I wrapped my arms around his snout, which allowed me to give him a hug as well, before pressing a kiss to the side of his nose.

Talon's massive chest rumbled. "You're so gorgeous and scary," I cooed at the beast, and there was another satisfied vibration from him. "Thank you for leading us here."

The dry heat of his scales left me nicely warmed, and I jumped at the rough scrape of his tongue over my cheek. "Whoa, that texture will take some getting used to."

After the dragon released a rasping gurgle that must be its version of a laugh, there was a pull of power, and I had a naked human Talon in front of me. His tongue swiped over the same spot his beast had, and my core clenched. "Naughty dragon," I murmured, shaking off the thrall he had me under. "No time for that."

Talon smirked, entirely unrepentant. Slade handed him a pile of clothes, and he dressed quickly, sliding on combat boots to finish his badass, SWAT look.

"Come on, let's get this shit over with," Kellan said, eyeing the side of the industrial building which looked like it was designed to withstand the strongest of attacks.

Not wanting any distractions, I nudged my beast back in to block the connection. Our energies meshing wasn't anywhere near as overwhelming as it had been the first time, but with all of us still getting used to it, I wouldn't take any chances in dangerous situations.

Talon led us to a side entrance, and we entered a large kitchen, which bore a slightly musty smell. It hadn't really been long enough for decaying food, unless Fletcher had been away from here longer than just the days since the street battle.

It took us twenty minutes to check every room on the massive main level, finding no shifters or evidence that could be used. All that remained was a multitude of bedding on the floor, none of which held any personal essence, as it was clearly used like a drop-in zone for Fletcher's army.

The door that led down into the sublevels was thick and reinforced, with steel layered so not even shifter strength could easily bust through. It took two partially shifted dragons multiple attempts to break it down.

"They're rather useful, these twins," Kellan noted, and he wasn't the only one who looked impressed.

As we descended into the lower levels, my stomach churned, and I had to clasp my hands together to keep from picking the edges of my nails off. If I made myself bleed, the alphas would lose their shit and now was not the time.

Talon was first into the creepy basement, with Slade right behind him. I ended up in the center of the group, with Constantine in front of me. Weirdly, his scent was soothing for the first time. There was a note of comfort and familiarity in the citrus tones, as if he was finally a shifter I trusted.

When we exited the stairs, it was nothing like the creepy, dank interior I expected. We stepped into what looked like a laboratory or research facility, all white and sterile. But whatever comforting scents were around me faded under the stench of this area. I barely managed to hold in a gasp, and covering my nose did little to dull what had to be a dead body or five.

On silent feet, we pushed farther inside, the whole scene eerie as the fluorescent lights above flickered on and off. We moved past rows of stainless-steel tables, some of which were covered in scientific equipment, before reaching a series of cages lining the far wall.

Cages that weren't empty, though there was nothing alive in any of them.

Which explained the smell.

Hunter blocked me so I couldn't stare upon the death, but the scents suggested there were varying levels of decomposition here. Many of these prisoners had died while Fletcher was very much still alive. That sick fuck had left them in with the other prisoners, decaying right in front of them.

"Evil piece of shit," Hunter growled, and even with my wolf blocking it, waves of his rage simmered in the bond. He prowled along the cages, double-checking there was no one alive.

When he paused halfway along, his stare unnatural and pointed, I called out. "Is there someone alive?"

His throat moved as he swallowed, before he shook his head. "No, but when this shifter was… I called her Mom."

The sense of horror and dread flooded me so suddenly that I almost threw up. My stomach was already weak from the death-scents, and just hearing him utter those words…

"Hunter," I choked out, attempting to get to him, only to find Slade blocking my path.

"Give him a moment," he murmured, and I swallowed around the lump in my throat.

Hunter didn't linger, already returning to us, his expression neutral. "She was a shit mother," he said, hard features softening as he met my stricken gaze. "Fletcher clearly thought she was a shit wife too, since she ended up in there. Either way, they both got what they deserved."

Toneless or not, his wolf flashed in his gaze, but before I could offer comfort, there was a shuffling on the tiles behind us. My pack spun and fell into protective stances around me, obstructing me from even seeing who was out there.

Popping up on my toes, I caught sight of an emaciated shifter as she stumbled around the corner. One I recognized immediately. "Chelsea," I gasped, taking in the changes. There was no weight on her skeletal structure, and she'd aged twenty years since I saw her last.

When Slade's dragon rage filled the room in a roar, the air crackling with heat and intensity, she glanced briefly between us before her eyes rolled back in her head and she fainted.

# CHAPTER 28

EMME

Talon moved first, striding toward the frail bundle of omega. He leaned close but didn't touch her, which had my wolf howling in appreciation.

Kellan lifted one eyebrow as he smirked. "We like jealous Emme," he said in a side-whisper, like it was a secret.

I scoffed. "Chelsea is half dead, and a traitorous, lying bitch. I'm not concerned."

My possessiveness wasn't because I didn't trust my alphas. Not only did their actions demonstrate I was everything to them, but I could literally *feel* it through the bond. Nope, my possessiveness was because I loved them and claimed them as mine.

Any shifter with half a brain knew the rules... you don't touch other shifter's mates.

"She's definitely half dead," Talon confirmed, straightening and scowling as if her unconscious presence annoyed him. I wondered if he was remembering her forcing me to bite him during our first meeting. He held blame for himself as well, but there was plenty to go around.

*It was not your fault, mate.* I kept that just between us in the bond. *You were a victim too.*

Slade's hug was tight and unexpected, as he clearly heard my words through Talon. "I will kill her for you," he bit out in a rasp of dragon. "Burn her until she's ash, and you will never have to see her face again."

In his powerful embrace, I felt a touch less brittle. These alphas were healing traumas one at a time, and facing this shit with them by my side made it almost easy.

When Slade released me to head for Chelsea, Hunter stopped him with a hand on his chest. There wasn't even a flicker of unease from Slade at his brother's touch. "We need to extract information from her first," Hunter said, eyeing the omega with distaste too. "Then she can die."

There was not a chance in purgatory that any of these alphas would suggest a trial by Alpha Council for Chelsea. We were done with them completely, choosing to play by our own rules now. In our rules, she'd screwed up so badly that there was no saving her. Her actions could have cost me my life, and if what I picked up at the time was accurate, she'd had no idea what Fletcher had planned for me. She hadn't even cared to ask.

He could have killed me or worse… bonded me to Blaine.

It was only pure luck, and maybe a little magic dust from the goddess, that kept me from losing everything.

Slade huffed at the fact that he had to wait to avenge me, but he trusted Hunter to be the more levelheaded when his dragon's rage took over. Personally, I enjoyed the side of him that lost control and killed any threat around us. Not that I'd admit it.

The bright green of his gaze snapped in my direction. *I will kill anything that even breathes wrong around you, Snow.*

My block was as faulty as the flickering lights above us. *That's the sweetest thing you've ever said to me, Scary.*

Slade tilted his head and looked rather pleased that I was slightly unhinged too.

While most of us waited around Chelsea, Finley and Constantine wandered off to investigate the rest of this level. I kept tabs on the bear through our bond, worried when he was out of sight in this horror house. Hopefully Constantine would spot any magical traps before they were sprung.

Finley hurried back a few minutes later. "I found Fletcher's office."

Slade and Hunter eased up on eyeballing Chelsea and headed toward Finley.

"Keep an eye on her," Slade called to his twin, and Talon nodded, arms crossed and expression hard. "And don't kill her yet. Hunter is right, we need to wait for answers first."

Now Talon just looked annoyed but didn't do anything other than lean against one of the stainless-steel tables.

Curiosity had me following the alphas down a white hall into the office. A cold, impersonal office. The metal desk held a laptop and a few folders, which Finley was riffling through. There were two filing cabinets which Hunter approached, and Slade went for the computer.

"Have you found anything of importance?" Slade asked as he booted up the device.

Finley's expression was grim. "These are notes from his omega experiments. Not to mention alphas, betas, and deltas."

He opened a folder which had a bold, black title on the cover: *Experiment 34. Forced bonding 8.*

Inside, I could see a pinned photo of a pretty blonde omega female. She was smiling, her blue eyes lit up as if she were truly happy. A few flips through the pages told a completely different story. More photos, each of them showing a deterioration, until the last photo she was barely recognizable. "There are experiment notes for each stage," Finley muttered, and I heard the clank of his teeth as he ground them together. "In this case, he bonded her to two alphas, simulating a scent match, and was able to strip her of her powers. Only the alphas couldn't hold on to the additional strength long enough to be useful." He read a bit more and shook his head. "He noted that it took a completed quintet to form long-lasting power. He was also making adjustment to how they simulated scent matches."

"There are more in here," Hunter said, his words shaking with his fury. "Folder after folder of experiments. Some dating back twenty or more years."

Slade's keystrokes were heavy against the laptop, the heat in the room giving away his fury, but he hadn't said anything yet.

"He always planned to control us," Hunter said, each word filled with his rage. "We all have folders in here. Each of us was groomed in a different way to create the alphas he wanted. He didn't care that we hated him, he knew he could control us through Emme. And he planned to control Emme through Talon and Jewels."

"Jewels was the nail in his coffin," I said, shaking my head. "Amazing that for all of his research, he never saw her betrayal coming. Which derailed his entire plan."

"Talon helped fuck him up too," Slade finally spoke, voice flat, though I caught the lick of pride over his twin. "He was on Fletcher's side, but what that pathetic excuse for an alpha didn't realize was that it's impossible to fight Emme's purity. Fletcher never expected Emme to forgive Talon for his actions and show him the meaning of a true pack. *Emme* and Jewels were the nails in his coffin."

Slade's praise meant so much that it was hard not to react. Somehow, I managed to keep my voice even. "Now we just need to find the nail in Jewels' coffin."

Slade returned to his typing. Finley was finished with the folders on the table, and had taken to reading over the dragon's shoulder.

"What did you find?" Hunter asked them as he piled files on the table.

"This is the online account," Finley said, his voice brimming with the burr of his bear. "He held fifty-eight omegas over a thirty-year period."

Fifty-fucking-eight. We were so rare to begin with, and fifty-eight of my kind had been experimented on and were dead at Fletcher's hands. "Is my mother's file in there?" I asked, my voice cracking even though I was mostly anger. "Is mine?"

Finley leapt over the desk and wrapped me up in one of his perfect bear hugs. "She was subject forty-five," he said as he held me. "Chelsea was fifty-seven."

He paused, and Slade's voice slowly filtered through the room, a deep, raging rumble. "You were fifty-eight, Emme."

Just two of us still alive, out of almost sixty omegas.

Finley tightened his hold, and despite the hollow, choked-up feeling inside of me, I was comforted. "What… what did he say about Mom?"

I didn't care about me since I was free and Fletcher was too dead to hurt me again, but I wanted to know what had happened to her. Finley pulled away so I could see Slade, who was scanning the screen. "Subject forty-five is a naturally born omega," he started in a factual tone. "Age: thirty-nine. First located with a possible hybrid shifter-witch. Four-year-old daughter suspected to be the same. Paternal line has vanished but will keep this subject locked down until daughter comes of age. Plans: manipulate a full quintet bond, scent match with new spell. Pack: Rogers pack."

Slade's chest rose and fell roughly, his words cutting off until he eventually continued.

"These are his first real observations: *My son wants to build his power and will allow me to observe and take blood and vitals every six months to document the various ways an omega can be used by alphas. The duration of this experiment will be approximately ten years. Or until the daughter presents as an omega and confirms suspicions. So far, Subject forty-five has not confirmed her parentage. If the daughter is a witch-wolf, we will bond her to one of her real scent matches. Testing indicates it's one of my alphas. The dragon—"*

My gasp was loud cutting Slade right off. "How can you test for a scent-match at such a young age?"

I couldn't remember anyone testing me for anything, but most likely it happened when I was asleep. Or maybe too young to recall. The very thought had shivers running down my spine at the violation of it.

"Fletcher was dabbling in magic and experiments far beyond what was ethical," Hunter said, still in that cold, unemotional tone. "He didn't care how much pain he caused shifters, all in the name of playing goddess."

Swallowing roughly, I clung to Finley until I was sure my nails would be cutting into him, but he never made a sound. Just held me together. "I wish there was an experiment to bring him back from the dead so we could kill him slower. That was far too fast."

The rumbles of beasts around me, both internally and externally, indicated that everyone agreed with me.

Slade returned to the screen. "There are hundreds of pages of observations from your mom and the Rogers pack. He was finessing the process, and he figured out how to keep all of her stolen power within that pack. The scent match mimicking was also improving." He paused for a beat, blinking at the screen. "Did you know Fletcher was bonded to your mother, Emme?"

I grimaced, hearing those words but not really processing them. "That's not... that's not possible?"

Hunter shifted closer to Slade, reading over his shoulder now. "He figured out how to split essences," he murmured, as if he couldn't quite believe it either. "He must have learned that from Talon's presence in our lives."

Fletcher had been everywhere, manipulating everyone in a bid to control the shifter world like a giant chess board of life. Only he hadn't quite kept all of his pieces together and one stabbed him in the back.

*Could the same happen to Jewels?* Was there a piece out there that she'd forgotten about, positioned perfectly to take the queen down?

"No wonder Mom was so drained in the end," I said, feeling detached from the emotions that should have gone with this information. "Do you think he planned to do the same with Talon and me too?"

The detachment ended with that thought, and I almost lost control of my howling wolf.

*He's dead. He's dead. He's motherfucking dead,* I reminded myself.

There was no way he could ever hurt anyone again.

"I would say there was a strong chance." Slade and his unwavering truth left a bitter taste in my mouth. "Your mother appeared to be the dress rehearsal for her daughter." He waved at the computer. "We owe Constantine more than we realized, since there's record here of Fletcher spending millions and using multiple witches to try and track you. Whatever Constantine did, he wiped you from the alpha's radar."

Which no doubt saved me in the end, along with my bonding to Hunter and Kellan that kept me from ever being just Talon's.

Finley held me through each revelation as I tried to process all of this new information. Fletcher had been systematically taking omegas apart until he knew exactly what magical essence filled us, and how he could utilize it for himself.

We'd stopped him in the end, but not before it was too late. My kind were all but extinct.

Constantine entered the room, his blue gaze piercing as he examined me. I wondered if I looked as distraught as I felt. "Chelsea is awake," he said. "The others wanted me to get you."

My chest remained heavy and tight as I sucked in a deep breath, while still feeling starved of oxygen. "Yeah, we need to find out what she knows."

Even with all the bombshells, we were still no closer to tracking Jewels.

We might not be able to undo Fletcher's horror-experiments, but we could ensure that we didn't lose our autonomy and beasts forever.

# CHAPTER 29

EMME

Chelsea was propped up against a metal shelf, a blank look on her face. Her matted hair fell over the waxy skin on her forehead. When she managed to roughly lift her head to meet my gaze, I noticed the whites of her eyes were yellow.

"Emme," she breathed, her voice barely even audible, lips dry and cracked. "I've been waiting for you to find me."

The alphas shifted forward as I crouched down in front of her, but no one interfered. "What happened to you?" I asked, running my gaze over her emaciated form. "Fletcher has only been dead for a couple of days. As has Sorenson."

Her current state represented weeks of mistreatment.

When she frowned, small cuts appeared across her cheeks, like her skin was so dry and fragile that she was literally starting to crumble away. I never even knew a wolf could... *decay?* She looked like she was in a state of decay.

"He left us down here for weeks," she whispered, her head falling back in her weakness. "Left me here to watch my pack die after Soren's death. Left me without food or water or hope. I have too much magic running through me now, and it's breaking me apart. He wanted to figure out—" She coughed, her face pained. "—how long it took to break an omega, and if we were more responsive to magic than other designations."

She managed to level her gaze back on me. "Spoiler alert..." Another cough. "...we can handle a lot of magic. We're different to regular shifters as we already hold slices of magic, which is what makes us resistant to dominance. We're closer to witches than any other designation."

None as close as me.

"Why did you not succumb to death when Soren was killed," Hunter asked, tucking the folder he'd brought out from the office under his arm. "If the rest of your pack died?"

Her face crumpled again, and this time Slade let out an irritated huff. "They broke my bond to them. They can do that, you know." Talon had told me long ago, and all the files confirmed it.

"So, Fletcher used magic to break and create quintet bonds and scent matches?" Finley asked, clearly wanting her to confirm it.

Chelsea nodded, her movements slower. "Yes, if you know the right spells, you can do anything. It was another alliance between Fletcher and the witch. They had many."

Hence why Jewels needed us to destroy him; she was bound and couldn't kill him herself.

"There's no way it would have worked on dragons," Slade snarled, his face wreathed in shadows as he glared her down. "You can't fake a true mate match with us. Our beasts would never be confused by magical manipulation."

Chelsea coughed once more. "Hence why he needed to control Talon and try bonding him to Emme."

Kellan leaned closer, his golden glow dulled by the green tinge to his skin. "Do you know how they simulate or break scent matches?" When I released a soft sound of distress, he looked straight at me. "We can never let that happen to our pack. No matter what."

Chelsea's head rolled forward as she fought for consciousness. "Fletcher's research," she whispered. "It's in his research. But it takes magic and a specific spell."

Those words took the last of her strength and she collapsed, her breathing so shallow it was clear she was on her way to joining the rest of the dead in this room.

"We're leaving her down here, right?" Finley said, shooting her a glare. "Whatever magic is shattering her essence is going to take care of her soon enough."

Slade leaned closer to give her a few seconds of his focus. "Yes, her lifeforce is fading. We couldn't save her now even if we wanted to."

She'd already watched her pack die around her, which felt like the worst torture to live through, so I was fine with a quick and easy death for her now.

"We need to find that research on pack bonds," Hunter said to Slade. "It wasn't in the filing cabinet."

"It'll be on the computer," Slade confirmed. "There are thousands of files to go through though, so I'll take it with us back to Golden Claw."

Hunter nodded. "Okay, grab it now while the rest of us search for anything to track Jewels with. It didn't feel like her magic in Chelsea, but she had to be part of these experiments."

With that, all of us searched this level, and with each new discovery my stomach churned, until I barely held on to my gas station snacks. Those Skittles were going to come up in the sort of rainbow no one needed to see. I was doing okay until we opened an entire wing dedicated to torture, with many of the devices still holding decaying shifters.

Yep, could confirm that Skittles reappeared as a gross green sludge.

When I couldn't take it any longer, I headed back to the main room, noticing Hunter standing by the cell with his mom in it. In his hand was the folder that he'd brought from the office.

"Hunter," I said softly.

"My mom was an alpha," he said monotonously. "According to the file, she finally had enough of his bullshit and fought back. He killed her for it. She became another one of his experiments."

He handed me the folder and I flicked through it, noticing that his mom was beautiful, though even in a photo she appeared as cold as I'd expected.

"I'm so sorry you lost your family, Hunter," I said, dropping the file to wrap my arms around him. "No one deserved to die like this, except for Fletcher."

He returned my hug so hard that I gasped. Not from pain, but more surprise. "You're my family," he rasped, his voice suddenly filled with all the emotions. "I can't let anything happen to you, Emmeline. I won't survive it. The world is a better place without my parents in it, and I don't mourn either of their deaths. But you..." His voice broke, and the pain in that strangled sound had me wanting to bawl.

But this wasn't about me, and I would comfort my mate as he'd done for me so many times. "You will never lose me," I said, keeping my voice low and hopefully soothing. "I'm fighting to stay with you and our quintet with every part of myself."

Our wolves howled together, and we didn't pull apart until the rest of our pack returned. Empty-handed of course. Nothing here held enough magical resonance to track Jewels with.

Hunter remained close to my side as we left the compound. Slade had the computer and files, which were placed in the car, and then we watched as the dragons lit the place up like it was the world's largest crematorium. Whatever was left inside would be destroyed, and the souls of Fletcher's victims would finally get to rest in the eternal lands.

Constantine moved closer to me wearing a concerned expression. "Are you okay?" he asked, and I was reminded that they all saw me hurl up my guts. Only that wasn't really what had him worried. "Slade told me that they found files on you and Morgan."

"We learned that the reason I'm even standing here today," I said, watching the flames dance high into the sky, "is because you saved me." I turned to give him my focus. "Thank you. Fletcher couldn't find me due to your magic holding his money and best witches at bay."

He shook his head. "Emme, I would do anything to keep you safe. You're my child."

Constantine spoke with such sincerity that I found the need to offer him the same in return. "And you're my father. I claim our bond."

A smile ripped across his face, so bright he was basically beaming. "I've waited a long time to hear you say that. I'm so sorry I wasn't in your life before now."

"But you *are* here now," Hunter said, his presence comforting at my side. "And when we destroy Jewels, we'll all have many uneventful years to move on from our fucked up pasts. You won't have to fear the wrath of the shifter cities any longer. We'll protect you and Emme, even though I doubt anyone will find out about your hybrid natures unless you tell them. Your beasts hide the magic, and once we wipe out witches, there'll be no one left to sense it."

Constantine's smile somehow got even brighter. "I'd really like a chance at that future."

We just had to figure out how to track Jewels, since all we'd found at this compound were new horrors to add to our nightmares.

"There's something poetic about watching the twin soul dragons, whom Fletcher tore apart, destroy the last of his depravity together," Kellan said, the flames lighting up his features.

"I've never experienced anything like that bunker," Finley bit out with a shudder, his eyes darkening as his bear pushed closer to the surface. "It surpasses finding my dad and brother, and let me tell you, that shit has been centerstage in my darkest memories for years."

As much as it hurt to hear his trauma, I loved that he chose to openly share with us. "As a pack, we will keep those memories away," I said, hoping that was the truth.

Hunter felt stable in our bond now, so I crossed to Kellan and Finley, taking both their hands. It was the first contact we'd had since exiting the building, and all of us relaxed a little more. Their holds on me were tight, all of us adrift and struggling with what we'd seen. In our quintet energy, our beasts remained close enough that they were basically pack huddling.

By the time the dragons were done, there was nothing more than ash left here. It was time for us to return to Golden Claw. Return, regroup and replan.

Hunter met me beside our bikes. "Are you sure you're up to riding?" he asked, his gaze taking me in as if assessing my health and wellbeing.

"I'm more than up for it," I confirmed. "I need it."

Hunter cupped his hand around the back of my neck, his claiming tattoo right there for the world to see. "Okay, baby girl," he murmured as he leaned down and pressed his lips to my forehead. *Gah*, forehead kisses.

Such a simple, quick kiss, which left me desperate to get home and be naked with my alphas.

Our beasts had already shown us the way to heal from the trauma and strengthen our bond, and I would absolutely be taking their very solid advice.

One naked pack huddle coming right up.

# CHAPTER 30

FINLEY

It took days and some intense therapy sessions to deal with what we'd found in Fletcher's research facility. Helped along by how busy we were with no real time to dwell.

Slade was researching, Talon had fight training, Kellan and I were in the midst of hockey season, and Hunter left the city to tear apart his old childhood home in the hopes of finding something we could use to track Jewels. All the while, Emme kept us from fracturing, her soothing presence what we came home to every single day.

After today's early therapy appointment, I spent a few hours in the garage, my hands buried under the hood of my Ford, letting the calming and familiar motions of fixing an engine add to my healing. Emme had been here earlier, and we'd made great progress on her vehicle before she had to leave for magical training with Constantine.

The more she warmed up to her father, the more I let go of my concerns. The witch-wolf had kept my mate safe, and for that I owed him. He'd just better never hurt her again, or he'd soon be joining Emme's mom.

There was a clang behind me as one of the contractors fixing the garage wall dropped metal. It was taking longer than expected to *fill in* the dragon-shaped cutout, but they were scheduled to finish in the next couple of days, which would take some strain off Slade.

The dragon had been all but sequestered in his room going through the files, but he was distracted by strangers in proximity to our mate. As we all were. It split his focus, and fractured his temper, until the only one who could be around him and not fear for their life was Emme.

He'd swoop in like an overgrown bat, steal our girl away for *whatever* he got up to with her, and then come back almost tolerable. All I knew was that when our omega was with the dragons, her mind and essence calmed to the point I was sure she handed all of her freewill over to them.

We all had our kinks, and Slade's was control. Thankfully, Emme appeared well-equipped to not only handle us, but also enjoy our particular quirks. *Thank you, goddess.*

"Hey, bro," Kellan said, wandering into the garage, taking a bite of a shiny red apple. The fact that he refused to admit green was the superior apple color… "You ready for the game? We've got to be there in three hours."

The weight on my chest lightened again. "Yeah, I could use some bash therapy on top of my regular therapy." It was really a day of therapy for me between Dr. Karen, cars, and hockey. Just had to finish with Emme, and it might actually be a perfect day.

"Yeah, fuck… the last few weeks have been a lot," Kellan said, letting out a ragged breath.

I hated when his shining personality dulled—he might be an annoying motherfucker who bounced like an overgrown puppy, but he was *our* annoying motherfucker.

No one was allowed to hurt him.

Kellan wasn't built to exist in the shadows like the rest of us. Even Emme, for all her warmth, held more darkness than Golden.

When I placed my tools back on the shelf, I wiped the grime off my hands with a clean rag. "We should head to the rink early. No one will be there yet, and I think we could both use a free skate."

Kellan's entire face lit up and *fuck* I almost hugged him. He'd love it, of course, but I wasn't a hugger. Still…

When I stepped closer, he blinked in clear surprise, freezing as if he didn't want to spook me. Ignoring that, I followed my instincts and wrapped my arms around his shoulders until a grunt escaped him. The apple hit the floor with a thud, and he was unmoving in my hold for a beat, until his arms banded around me so strongly that my ribs ached.

"Bro," he choked out in a shaky voice. "It freaks me out when you do this shit."

He didn't let me go, though, and I was determined not to release him first.

"Just go with it, Kel," I said. "I'm here for you. You can share your pain, and I promise I will never let you walk through it alone."

"Thanks, Fin," he murmured in a deep, guttural tone. "It's weird when you go all therapist, but fuck… I think I needed that."

My chest ached as my bear bellowed. "Yeah, apparently so did I."

In the end, Kellan wasn't the only one holding on like his life depended on it.

Kellan released me right as Emme's scent exploded through the garage. We both turned to find her standing near the Charger, her beautiful face streaked with tears.

"Shortcake," Kellan called, crossing the garage in two seconds to reach her. "Did you just see Fin in *Care Bear* mode? Did you take a video?"

Despite her trembling lips, she smiled and her whole face lit up. Happiness flowed from her wolf through the bond too. "Only a mental one, which I can share with you anytime you need the reminder."

Kellan met my eyes with a soft gaze. "I'll never forget how lucky I am to have this pack. Fucking blessed."

Goddessdamn. They really were turning me into the softest *Care Bear*. I needed to get out on the ice and smash motherfuckers into the boards. *But first…* "Would you like another skating lesson, Ice? We were thinking of heading down early to blow off some steam before the game. We should be able to get in now before they Zamboni it."

She clapped her hands, the tears no longer falling, though the evidence remained. "Yes, I'm done with magical training for the day. I could use a bit of exercise since Slade isn't free to torture me."

"Hell yes," Kellan whooped. "I've been waiting for my chance to get you on the ice, pretty mate."

Emme patted his chest. "Okay, I just need to change and grab my skates."

She was gone in a flash, and I finished cleaning myself and my work area, before grabbing my gear as well. I wouldn't be back before the game tonight. By the time the three of us were in my truck, heading for the rink, my bear was a contented puddle in my chest.

I loved all my pack, but these two were my peace.

The rink was quiet. It always reminded me of a sleeping bear on game day. Just snoozing away, until it would roar to life a few hours later.

We got changed in the locker room, and when Kellan and I knelt at Emme's feet, each of us taking a skate to lace her up, her breath caught. She stared between the two of us. "Well," she choked out, "this is quite the sight." Her cheeks pinkened as her scent filled the room.

Kellan groaned as he traced his hands up her calves. "You're so fucking sexy, Shortcake. Honestly, I'm going to jump you on the ice."

I slapped his shoulder. "Not that I disagree, but we'll have time for that later. We need to skate now if we want to get out before the Zamboni."

We'd be in big trouble if we fucked it up *after* that.

Slipping guards on all our skates, we helped Emme to the rink. She stepped onto the ice as gingerly as the first time, her feet moving so slowly they were almost stationary. Kellan started to skate laps around her, side to side and then backwards. "Showoff," she shouted as he sped off, his skills far surpassing even mine.

When he returned, she scowled down at her feet. "I suck at this too."

Her adorable little pout had me chuckling as I slipped my hands around her waist, swinging her in an arc. "We'll have you skating rings around us in no time."

Emme's raised brows and narrowed eyes expressed her concern for my sanity, but I was too caught up in being out here with them to worry about it. Kellan came up behind her and I released her to him. Emme collapsed against him and he moved slowly for once, gliding them both around the arena. I joined in, letting the ice and my pack soothe me.

We skated right up until they fired up the machine, then we helped Emme off the ice. She limped between us back to the locker room. "Skating uses muscles I didn't even know I had," she groaned. "Is it normal to feel super sweaty but also cold? It's kind of a gross feeling to be honest."

Kellan and I exchanged a quick glance, and in that one look it was clear we both had the same thought. "Let's get you cleaned up," I suggested, rushing them into the locker room. "You'll feel better soon."

She collapsed against the bench with a relieved sigh. "Thank you, I think I'm going to need a little help until my healing kicks in."

Like we were jacked up on adrenaline, Kellan and I stripped her skates off so fast that she grunted. He moved on to her pants, while I dragged her hoodie up over her head. She looked between us, and confusion tugged at her features, but she didn't say a word.

When she was gloriously naked between us, we stripped our own clothes too, and the three of us walked into the showers, which were state-of-the-art and had near-limitless hot water. The silence was filled with need and desire as we drew her under the spray.

When her soft skin brushed against mine, there was a kick in my shaft, which was already hard and aching. If Emme had glanced down at either of us, she'd know exactly what we had planned. I didn't share as well as Kellan and Hunter, or Slade and Talon, but I didn't have any issue with what was about to happen here today.

Emme moaned as hot water crashed over her from one of the wide showerheads, and I needed to touch her before I lost my mind. My palms slid over her bare skin, and when she rubbed against me, the tightening need in my balls almost sent me to my knees.

"Darlin'," I breathed. "We want you so fucking badly. We both need to be inside you, but this is your chance to say yes or no."

"Yes, yes, all the fucking yeses," she gasped, tilting her head back to give Kellan access to kiss up her throat.

Sliding my hand down her stomach, I drew my finger in a slow circle around her clit and she arched into me. Kellan kept her legs from buckling under her as we continued to explore, and soon I was stroking through a wet mess between her thighs. "Fuck, you feel so good, mate."

Emme moaned again and parted her legs wider. *I got you, baby.*

Sliding two fingers inside her, I curled them to caress her g-spot, while Kellan lowered himself to lap at her clit. It took us less than ten seconds to get her first orgasm. When she gushed over my hand, Kellan rose so he could kiss her, and I dropped to my knees to bury my face in her delicious cunt, which was dripping all over me. *Fuck.* I would gladly take death, if this was how I went out.

After her climax, she was oversensitive, crying out as I slid my tongue into her slick heat, my bear roaring at how good she tasted. My cock kicked against my thigh, demanding entry, and I mentally told it to chill. We weren't skipping the good parts to get to the best part. I'd happily worship my mate on my knees for eternity, even if it meant torture via my aching balls and throbbing dick.

"My turn," Kellan said, nudging me aside.

Emme shook her head, her fingers lacing into our hair. "What are you up to, Kellan Jackson?"

Kellan pressed his face into her core and breathed deeply. "What do you think, Emmeline? I'm worshiping my mate. Goddess be damned, you're my deity now."

Emme didn't like when we cursed the goddess, but she was too far gone as Kellan closed his lips over her clit. I stood to kiss her, and she sucked my tongue in against hers, as if to fully taste her release. Skating and kissing Emme were the only times my brain went quiet and calm, and I was fairly sure I could do this all day every day for the rest of my existence.

When our kiss broke off, she sucked in a deep breath, her pupils blown. She turned toward Kellan as he gently worked her clit between his teeth, and I ended up with her ass right against my cock as she backed up on me. "Please," she begged, moving against me.

I'd never fucked her in the ass before, but Hunter had her well prepared. Moving us out of the direct spray of water, I used the remnants of her release as lube on my cock. Slowly, I pushed inside her, letting her adjust to the stretch, even as the pleasure through the bond came in strong waves. I was barely holding on as she stroked our quintet connection, but I refused to embarrass myself by coming before she did.

When my length was fully buried inside her, I wrapped my palms around the front of her thighs and dragged her body higher for a better angle. With one last thrust of his tongue inside her, Kellan got to his feet, and between us we opened her thighs even wider, drawing them out on either side of her.

"Take her, Kel," I growled, my dick throbbing in her ass. "She wants us both."

I barely moved inside her, but Emme was already sobbing and clenching on me, choking my shaft in the best way. Her words were incoherent as she reached for Golden, and Kellan's wolf flashed in his eyes as a desperate groan of need spilled from him.

Kellan angled himself to slide into her pussy. It was a tight fit between the two of us. "This is how I die of pleasure," Emme rasped, her voice shattered. "It's too much and not enough at the same time. Please move. Please fuck me."

Kellan thrust first, and I went next, until we formed a natural rhythm. Emme's nails dug into my forearm, and the pain just added an extra bite to how good it felt.

"You're doing so well, omega," I murmured, my alpha beast rising to the surface. "You're the most perfect mate for us. Such a good girl, our sweet, sexy mate."

Kellan's moan was guttural, and Emme locked on to him with full focus. "Yes, Golden," she cooed in her raspy voice. "You and Grouchy are such good fucking boys. Taking care of your omega like this."

Kellan's pupils dilated. "Fuck, Shortcake. I'm going to come."

The poor fucker was panting, and I knew exactly how he felt. Praise wasn't one of my kinks, but in this moment, with *this omega*, it had my balls tightening as tingles raced up and down my cock. "Don't come yet," Emme pantingly ordered. "I want to keep feeling this. Both of you inside of me is paradise."

Desperate to give her everything she wanted, we continued to fuck her, and I prayed I could hold out. Emme was so wet that her slick heat covered our lower halves, and I was right there with her in not wanting this pleasure to ever end.

"Yes," Emme cried. "Yes. *Ohmygoddess*. I love you both so much."

Her babbling heightened the sensation, and when my jaw ached with the need to bite her, I just latched on to her shoulder. Without shifting, it wouldn't last like a mating bond, but it sated my beast.

She cried out as her entire lower half tightened. It was the most perfect pleasure-pain I'd ever felt, sending me roaring into a release. Kellan was right behind us, and the three of us panted and moaned through the aftershocks, as close as three separate shifters could ever get.

For many long minutes after, we stayed together under the spray of water.

If it wasn't for the fact that an entire hockey team would be here soon, I'd have requested we stayed like this for the rest of the day.

My perfect peace.

# CHAPTER 31

EMME

After the most intense locker room sex that left me breathless and ready to collapse in a puddle on the floor, there was no time for post-coital cuddling. The boys re-dressed me in jeans, my jersey, and sneakers before handing me off to Hunter. Right around the time the first members of the Wolves entered the room to get ready for the game.

Hopefully they all enjoyed a sweet treat before they played, since our sugary scents were not going anywhere anytime soon. No doubt my possessive alphas were in there growling and demanding their teammates stop breathing.

"I missed you, little mate," Hunter said on a soft sigh. "If this wasn't life and death, I would never have left you."

His plane had landed only thirty minutes earlier, and after a quick stop home to change, he'd come straight to the rink. I was so relieved that he'd finally returned, I hugged him for at least ten minutes straight, out in the hallway of the locker room.

"As long as you're safely back here," I murmured, voice thick. "Did you find anything useful at the old house?"

When I pulled away, I could see exhaustion in his normally unruffled features. He'd worked hard to tear Fletcher's house apart, oftentimes literally. A frustrated huff left him. "Nothing that's immediately useful, but there might be a few items we can work with. I left everything with Constantine and Slade. If anyone can figure it out, it'll be those two."

When we reached the main floor of the stadium, it was only sparsely populated, the game still a good hour away. We ended up in our usual seats with a dozen empty spaces around us, since no one else from our pack was joining today.

It was nice to have some one-on-one time with Hunter; there'd been too little with him lately.

Despite our early entry, food was already available, and Hunter managed to find a shifter to deliver us nachos, two cartons of fries, and a funnel cake. He always knew when I was starving.

In my defense, there had been a lot of *strenuous* exercise today.

"Slade wanted to catch the game with us tonight," he said, looking satisfied when I started to wolf the food down. Pun intended. "But it's more important that he keeps researching Fletcher's notes and helps Constantine with a plan to track Jewels. Or any witch. Talon has fully taken over enforcer training too."

We were all working on the assumption that *all* the magical community was holed up together somewhere. Most likely with Jewels. Find one and we'd find them all.

"I dropped more baked goods off for Cora and Warrick this morning," I said softly around a bite of corn chip that didn't taste quite as good now. "They still wouldn't even let me near the house. I had to leave the basket with the guard stationed at the end of their road."

After what they'd gone through, I wasn't surprised by the extra security, but it hurt all the same to be left out like a stranger. Cora hadn't responded to any of my messages, or returned the missed calls. I knew their time to grieve wasn't about me, but I wished they'd at least let me know they were alive.

"You're doing everything right, Emme," Hunter told me as his hand ran soothingly over my arm. "Just keep showing up. Grief is a weird thing. There's no timeframe on it, but one day they'll remember how you showed up for them."

I nodded, my eyes burning as I blinked rapidly. "It kills me to think that Cora blames me, you know? Her pack wouldn't have been attacked if not for me."

It was my greatest fear, but at the same time there was nothing I could do if they hated me. I *was* indirectly to blame, and I couldn't fault them for having strong feelings about being around me. "No one blames you," Hunter assured me. "They just need time."

And I'd love to give it to them, but time was the one thing we were all running out of. Every second we couldn't find that fucking witch was a second closer to losing our beasts.

The stadium filled eventually, and as the noise level rose around us, my melancholy faded. I let myself enjoy the excitement of being at one of their games.

After I'd eaten all I could manage, Hunter lifted the cartons from me to finish the food off. With each one of his bites though, he'd scoop up a fry or corn chip to feed me, and despite my groaning stomach, I enjoyed wrapping my tongue around his fingers.

It was a fun game we played, his beast rumbling along with the alpha.

On the fifth time, I used a little teeth and his eyes darkened. "You're playing with fire, Emmeline."

My smile grew. "Didn't you hear? I love fire. So toasty and warm."

He leaned closer until I stared into his glowing eyes. "It also burns, baby. Don't forget that."

*Goddess above.* "There's no way to forget with two dragons in my pack," I rasped.

Hunter moved forward so fast that I gasped into his kiss as he swiped his tongue across my bottom lip. "You had a little something there," he murmured, pulling away to leave me lightheaded and craving a firmer touch.

He resumed eating and I was flushed and squirming in my chair, needing him to feel the same uncontrollable desire. Without considering the consequences of my actions, especially in such a public place, I dropped my mental shield and pushed all my desire into our bond. Stroking along our glowing connections. Hunter's scent flared, and I froze as he slowly turned toward me, his eyes as gold as I'd ever seen them.

That was the moment I realized I'd fucked up.

Hunter stood in a flash, and I was over his shoulder just as fast. *I was in so much freaking trouble.*

"Hunter," I choked out. "Wait. Not here, mate."

He was beyond hearing me, and I'd had no idea I could snap his control like this. His hand landed a solid slap to my ass, drawing extra attention our way. Our pack was watched no matter what they did, so of course, shifters were fascinated when they lost it like this.

Scents exploded around us, responding to Hunter's dominance, and with a snarl, my entitled alpha strode from the stadium and out into the cold evening air. Thrown over his shoulder as I was, I didn't immediately see the huge beasts already positioned side by side at the back of the lot, but I sensed them. Whenever the dragons were around, the air was heavy, filled with energy and electricity that felt magical in nature.

Hunter paused at the sight of them, and I felt his next rasp all the way to my core. "You're in trouble now, little omega."

"I have no idea what's happening," I said in a rush. "But whatever it is, we cannot do it in a public parking lot." The breathless nature of my tone didn't give that statement a lot of conviction, but it was still the truth.

"Lie," Hunter rumbled, his beast close to the surface. "I can smell how fucking wet you are, mate. You want this. Right here and now."

*Damn him*. I'd already slammed the connection in our quintet closed, but it was too late.

Kellan and Finley burst out of the stadium, fully dressed in their skates and gloves, sticks still in hand.

"How is this possible?" I muttered, shaking my head. "How the hell did I call you all like this?"

With my question, Hunter started to calm until his dominance no longer filled the air like snowflakes. When he set me on my feet, he kept both hands on my hips, but I was no longer staring right into his wolf's eyes.

Slade shifted into his bipedal form and strode across the lot, all but snatching me from Hunter's grasp. "It's her magic mingling with our mate bond," he said, his words still a deep dragon bass. "We need to be stronger than this. We need to control our beasts."

His pupils thinned, and unlike with Hunter it was all dragon in his gaze, no matter what form the rest of him was in. Deciding that I'd made this mess and now needed to clean it up, I drew back as much energy into my wolf as I could, reining in my magic as well, just like Constantine had taught me. It took effort, since I'd given my need for them complete freedom when I'd dropped all shields, but I could do this.

As the power calmed between us, Hunter rubbed a hand over his face and muttered, "Fuck," before he strode off into the darkness.

"I'm sorry," I whispered, feeling like the stupidest shifter to ever exist. "I'm so sorry. I didn't know that would happen. I didn't know I could even do that."

As my words grew more frantic, Kellan threw his arms around me, uncaring that Slade held me. "Baby, no. You didn't do anything wrong. You had no idea that a bit of teasing would release the wrath of all our dicks."

There was a beat of silence, the snow falling silently around us, and then a rumble of bear laughter broke the tension. To my absolute shock, Slade was next. His hands shook on my skin as he laughed. "A blunt but accurate statement," he finally said.

*Wrath of their dicks.* Honestly, I should be more concerned than I was about what had almost happened. "Do you think you'd have been able to stop if I said no?"

I had no idea why I even asked that. It just occurred to me that I'd almost magicked them into losing control, which was not okay of me. My alphas sobered, and I immediately regretted my question. I wanted them just as badly, and would never have said no.

"I could have," Kellan said, sounding sure. "Your desire drew me out here, but if that desire vanished, then my brain would have been clear enough for consent."

"Same," Finley nodded.

Talon moved closer but didn't shift back. Slade spoke for his brother: "He says that coming to you was an instinctive drive, but it was a drive initiated by you."

Right. *Right.* That made sense.

"I always want all of you," I reassured them. "That question was just a weird random thought related to how strong these pack bonds are, and I guess our desire for each other."

Slade pressed a kiss to my forehead. "And we want you. All of you. In whatever way you're willing to share."

He released me into Finley and Kellan's arms, who quickly cupped my face, one at a time, and kissed me before racing back into the stadium. I was immediately concerned that they'd be late for the game, or their skates would be damaged from sprinting to me.

They had guards on, but it was rough out here.

I hoped I hadn't screwed up this game for them.

When Hunter strode back into sight looking visibly calmer, Slade returned to his dragon form. His and Talon's beasts ran their snouts along my cheeks and then flew off.

Leaving me with our entitled alpha once more.

"I'm sorry," I repeated for him. "I played a stupid fucking game and learned the consequences."

Before I could dig deeper into my worries that I'd fucked everything up, Hunter dragged me against his chest. "You don't have to apologize," he said. "I should have had more control. Three decades of perfecting my control and you detonate it with a single look."

I closed my eyes and soaked up the coziness of his hug. "I think that's the way I can completely share energy without needing to use magic," I murmured. "It was like, I could feel all of you. Everywhere. I could have taken your power or given you mine."

Tonight, I'd completely opened myself up to the five of them and let all our essences flow together in the quintet bond. "I felt it too," he admitted. "But I don't ever want you to use it that way again. Not only did we all lack reasoning and control, it would be easy to drain you. I don't want any of us to accidentally do so. You opened the bond too far."

"It didn't hurt me though," I felt the need to add. "I actually really enjoyed the feeling, though maybe a little too sexually charged for a public venue."

Hunter's hold tightened until I felt a very mild ache in my ribs. "Never again, Emmeline. I don't care if we're about to die, you don't mesh us like that. It clouded our senses and left us no better than rutting, feral beasts." He slowly brushed snowflakes off my face as he caressed it, and I couldn't look away from his serious expression. "What if we'd hurt you in our mindless instinct? What if we drained you until you couldn't recover? There are too many risks and unknowns."

There was not a damn chance I'd ever promise not to share power if they were dying, so I changed the subject. "We should get back inside. I want to see the boys play—if I haven't fucked it up and gotten them benched."

Hunter's stare was resigned, but he didn't call me out on my subject change. "Coach will understand. They'll be playing." He linked our hands together and we walked toward the entrance.

I almost thought I'd gotten away with my segue before he added, "And we will be revisiting this conversation later."

"Sure," I replied, already knowing there was nothing to revisit.

When we reached our seats, they were cleaned of all the food that must have gone flying when Hunter threw me over his shoulder. When countless gazes locked on us, Hunter's chest swelled with a warning grumble, which had them all returning their focus to the game.

A game which was already many minutes into the first period.

To my relief, Kellan and Finley were both out on the ice and appeared to be having the time of their lives. Finley was in full bear-bash mode, crashing the red and orange team into the boards. I had no idea who they were playing, and it didn't matter, since the only team I was interested in was the one in teal, white, and gold.

"Has your sister had any issue with Henderson?" I asked when the burley Viking caught my eye. He wore a 43 on his jersey, and was skating beside Kellan as they fought to get the puck down their end. On the other side of them, Christian stayed close, no doubt good for an assist if needed.

"He shows up every day at the compound gate but has been respecting her refusal to see him," Hunter replied as he leaned back in his chair, long legs spread out as far as he could get them. "He leaves her flowers and gifts, but I don't think Kass has taken any of them."

On the ice, Henderson shot a quick pass to Kellan, setting him up perfectly for a goal attempt. When the buzzer sounded, the stadium erupted, and the alphas huddled together before they skated past the bench to slap gloves with their team.

"I need to catch up with Kass," I said as play started again.

I flinched when Kellan got knocked to the ice, but he was back up in a flash, skating like the devil was on his tail. My daredevil with a death wish.

"You'll see her tonight," Hunter told me, his focus on the fast-paced game. "I invited her around for dinner tonight, along with Kenzo, Warrick, and a few powerful alpha allies. We don't fully trust anyone, but we also might not be able to do this alone. This will be a small, select group to update on what's happening with Jewels."

The game was momentarily forgotten as I stared at him. "Okay, I really didn't expect you to say any of that. You've been adamant that we couldn't trust another soul."

He released a long, drawn-out breath. "I still feel that way, but if we don't happen to win this game of hide-and-seek with Jewels, we need allies to fight the next part of the war. As hard as it is, I have to trust a few in the hopes to save the many."

The buzzer interrupted us as the Celtic Wolves scored again, right before the end of the first period. But my thoughts were consumed by the war that would follow if we lost control of our beasts.

We couldn't let that happen.

No matter who we had to trust.

# CHAPTER 32

EMME

When we ate in the dining room, we used about a fifth of the full table, preferring to remain close together at one end. Tonight, it was maxed out, as multiple alphas filled the chairs.

After their win, Kellan and Finley had raced through press and got home around the time everyone else arrived. Constantine was the only one who'd declined dinner, as he wanted to focus on sorting and cataloguing the items Hunter had brought back. I'd run into him on my way down, and he mentioned an idea of how to track Blaine, which put an extra pep in my step all the way into the dining room.

The first person I greeted was Kassidy, who stood next to Kenzo. After her hug, Kellan's brothers moved toward me for three brief seconds, before rumbles from my pack had them backing up. Suppressing my smile, I nodded at the few strangers in the room, who felt like powerful alphas. They must be the allies we were attempting to bring into the fold.

On my way to my spot at the table, a familiar face had me grinding to a halt. He'd been sitting so I hadn't noticed him until I was almost at his side.

My eyes burned as I stared. "Warrick?" His name was a ragged, broken thing on my tongue.

He stood slowly, and I couldn't see any anger in his serious expression. "Hey, Emme," he replied, and when he opened his arms to me, I choked back my sobs.

As he closed me in his embrace, it felt the same as always. Both of us ignored the low rumbles, which sounded far less menacing than those for Tyson and Julien.

My alphas were making an exception for Warrick, and I appreciated it.

"You're here," I rasped as I pulled back to see his handsome face. "I wasn't sure when we'd see you again."

His eyes were shiny, and there was so much pain in those dark depths that it felt like he'd stabbed me. I wished I could take his hurt away.

"Sorry we haven't seen you, Em," he said, his voice as rough as his appearance. "We've been healing together, as a pack. Cores wanted me to send her love though, and tell you she's thankful for your quiet support. Your cookies are healing, my friend."

My lower lip trembled even as I told myself not to fucking cry—this was not about me.

"I wish there was more I could do, but I wanted you to know I was here. *I am here*. Supporting from the sidelines."

He sucked in a ragged breath, rubbing a hand over his face. "It means a lot. We're lucky to have friends like you and the rest of your pack."

He leaned forward, as if to hug me again, but Hunter's hand on his shoulder slowed the move. "Time for dinner," he said calmly.

There was no obvious warning in the tone, but Warrick smirked anyway. "You're right, Hunt. Let's get to business. I need that witch ended."

When he took his seat again, I raised an eyebrow at my possessive mate. "Subtle," I murmured, and Hunter shrugged.

"Grieving or not, it goes against every instinct to let another alpha touch what's mine. He got one hug. That's the maximum our beasts can handle."

"Overly generous of us," Slade noted, overhearing the conversation. That dragon gave no real fucks about Warrick's grief. He put pack first. Everyone else didn't even exist.

Hunter pulled my chair out for me, and then slid me in under the table. Kellan was on my right as usual, with Slade, Talon, and Finley across from us. Conversation continued until Florence and Gerald entered the room with massive trays hefted across their shoulders. The trays went down the center of the long table, which was already set with plates, cutlery, and glasses.

It was a late dinner, and they'd opted for homemade pizzas, garlic bread, and portioned bowls of pasta. When I saw the meat-filled pizza, and equally meaty pasta, I was happy enough to dance a little in my seat. There was nothing green on this tray, and it was a glorious time to be alive.

Jewels' bullshit notwithstanding.

Hunter piled up a plate for me, and I put a hundred and ten percent of my focus into inhaling my favorite food groups: carbs, meat, fat, cheese.

Cheese was in a group all on its own. Of course.

When the rest of the table—except my alphas—started to eat, I felt through the bond their desires to ask the entire room to pause so I could eat first. "Don't you fucking dare," I mumbled around a bite of bread. "You're acting insane."

Kellan smirked as he took a sip of his beer, and I started to eat so fast I was in real danger of choking. All so my psychopathic alphas didn't snatch slices of pizza from our guests' hands.

Of course, the faster I ate, the more amused my pack of assholes looked, and eventually I had to pause for a breath. And some damn wine.

Is this what they meant by *stress eating*?

A few seats down from me, Kassidy snorted, and when I leaned forward to see around Kellan, I found her silently laughing into her pasta. "I swear," she said, holding her sides, "just when I think I might be ready for a pack, my brother demonstrates the very real reasons why I'd have to kill them all in their sleep."

I gulped down more wine while trying to figure out if I had indigestion or was in the middle of a mild heart attack. "None of them will eat until I'm all but stuffed," I told her. "I know they're about to ask all of you to wait as well. I'm fighting for my life over here so you can eat while the food is hot."

Kellan's bottom lip popped out. "Baby, I would literally die for you. Don't ask me not to ensure your needs are met first."

I patted his cheek. "I would never, hence why I'm turning into a professional eater over here. Everyone is happy that way."

One—or both—of the dragons reacted to that, as heat filled the room.

"No one's happiness matters but yours," Talon told me, his cold gaze trailing along the table of alphas. "I could kill everyone in here before any of them even realized I was stalking their last breaths. It's not too much to ask that they wait for you to eat first."

Every alpha except Kassidy stilled, dropping whatever food was in their hands.

Throwing my arms in the air, I declared loudly, "I'm full. Ignore these alphas. I will personally stand protectively in front of any of you if they so much as breathe heavily in your direction."

For some reason, the males in the room trusted my word, and started to tentatively eat once more. Kassidy continued to chuckle, but I was too busy glaring my pack into eating to glance her way.

Eventually, everyone was full, relaxed, and had topped-up drinks. Hunter placed his whiskey down and addressed the shifters: "Thank you for being here tonight. I've spoken with many of you individually, and you're all aware of the current situation and dwindling timeline we're racing against. As I've explained, I won't be taking this to the Alpha Council, so it's up to us to start preparing for what is to come."

Slade nodded, staring at his brother. "We're hunting the witch named Jewels," he said, picking up where Hunter left off. "She's from the Termaine line and is considered both powerful and unstable. Her family have been directly involved in more than one of our wars. The only way to end her curse is to destroy her before the next full moon."

"Which she is well aware of," Talon added. "Hence why she's working so hard at staying hidden."

"How do we find her?" Warrick asked, his voice brittle. All of him appeared brittle, as if a gentle tap would shatter him. "Do we have any witches in the circle of trust who might be able to help?"

Hunter's beast moved toward me in the bond. *We are not disclosing your heritage. Not now or ever.*

"There are no witches anywhere," he said out loud. "We've had friends and allied packs searching, and no one can find a single magical being."

"They're clearly all together," Tyson muttered, a scowl slashing his handsome face. "They must be combining their magic to keep the shielding strong and impenetrable."

"That's our theory too," Hunter confirmed. "But we might have found a way to track Blaine Rogers. Our assumption is that Jewels' shifter allies are also wherever this magical stronghold is."

"How do you plan to track him?" Warrick asked, his focus unwavering. "Surely if she's got everyone under this protection, his scent or essence will be blocked."

Hunter's eyes darkened. "She might have him under magical protection, but the shifter side isn't hers to control. Not yet anyway. There's a way to track shifters using their blood."

"How do you have Blaine's blood?" I asked.

"You followed my plan?" Warrick answered before Hunter could, and I turned to find the other alpha's gaze filled with fire. "I suggested he check out Fletcher's house, since I figured that a serial killer would have trophies."

Okay, clearly Hunter had been keeping Warrick updated, which made me feel a little better. Even if neither of them had spoken to me about it.

Hunter's expression softened when he met my gaze. "Yes, it was War's suggestion that we check out Fletcher's, but I would have gotten there eventually." His voice grew harder as he addressed Warrick. "As you suspected, he kept samples and tests from all his children. Blaine had a lot, especially from the years he was with Emme's mother. There were a few newer samples that we might be able to use."

*That's what Constantine is trying to do in the library*, I asked through the bond.

Hunter's wolf pressed against my side. *Yes. But not in the usual way of tracking magic. It's specified to shifters, and Jewels' shielding should only have minimal effect.*

His tone told me that it was a long shot, but it was more than we'd had yesterday.

"If the spell works, will you need us all to fight with you?" one of the other alphas asked. From his neutral tone and expression, it was hard to tell how he felt about it. "If this witch does have all the magical community and her ally shifters together, you will most likely be outpowered."

Hunter waved his hand around the room. "This is why we brought you all together. If we end up finding them, we will need *our* allies with us. We really don't know what sort of powerful army Jewels is amassing."

Warrick jolted in his chair. "Wait, what if there's another way to track her? If Blaine's spell doesn't work?"

The room fell completely silent, and he took that as encouragement: "If she's building an army," he said, "they're housed somewhere behind her shielding, right? But shielded or not, they're going to use resources. Be that water, electricity, internet. And if this is a new gathering of hundreds to possibly thousands of shifters and witches, surely there'll be a spike in one of those resources. Can that be tracked?"

Slade slid forward in his chair, his smoky scent growing stronger. "It's possible," he said, and I could see him calculating already. "I'll start searching through all the networks and see what I can find. My instinct says they're close to one of the shifter cities, so I'll focus my search there first to try and find a surge of power that wasn't present a week ago."

Warrick looked pleased as he sank back into his chair, like he could finally relax.

Another one of the alphas, older than us, with brown skin, a bald head, and striking green eyes spoke up. "The more avenues we have to search, the more chances we'll find her." He raised his whiskey glass to Hunter. "My pack is ready to assist in whatever way you need. We received your magically resistant plates and weapons yesterday."

"Excellent, Lionel," Hunter said as he dropped his palms on the table and leaned forward. "Okay, so we know the plan moving forward, and all of us are prepared to move if we track any location. Before we finish up, Slade has some more information to add."

"I've been deconstructing Fletcher's research," Slade began, not bothering to look at the non-pack members in the room. "And while most of it is irrelevant now that he's dead, I will say that he was playing in spaces he should never have ventured, by manipulating bonds and our beasts. All in the hopes of manufacturing an army of shifters who bore strengths and abilities beyond our norm." The silence was heavy as we processed Fletcher playing goddess in his lab of horror.

"From what I can tell, none of his test subjects survived, but he was getting close. I'd say within the next two years, he'd have perfected a hybrid version of our beasts, with wolves the size of a bear. It was lucky that his arrogance blinded him to Jewels' deception, as he could have been a force that destroyed our world."

"Why does Jewels hate shifters so much?" I asked, my mind

fixated on the witch. "Why was she even so involved in the shifter world? I mean, as evil as it was, I understand what Fletcher hoped to achieve, but Jewels' motivation isn't as clear. She already has tons of power and controls the magical world…"

What more could we really give her?

My questions were met with silence, and I wasn't surprised, since the only one with those answers was the witch herself. In the great scheme of things, her motivation probably didn't really matter, but I couldn't stop thinking about it.

Why was she trying to destroy our race?

# CHAPTER 33

KELLAN

After our first official dinner to discuss tracking Jewels' evil ass down, I spent the night blissfully snuggled next to my Shortcake. Hunter was on her other side, with Finley crashed out beside me.

The three of us took turns sleeping beside her on our nights, and then she split her other nights with the twins, who hadn't quite figured out the joys of group snuggles. Yet.

Those big, scaled bastards would come around sooner or later.

Even every second night with Emme wasn't enough.

Finley hadn't really joined Hunter and I with any *other* group activities, choosing to squirrel her away for his own private time, but we were making it work in stolen moments.

Along with learning how to share like good fucking boys.

Before Emme, I'd never really thought about what being in a quintet like this would entail, and now I didn't care as long as she was with us.

"No hockey today," Finley said as the sun started to rise.

Emme didn't stir in my arms, and since Hunter had only slipped into the room two hours ago after helping Constantine, he'd be passed out for the rest of the morning.

"Yeah, Coach sounded like he regretted giving us a day off from training as soon as he opened his mouth." It amused me that we could still piss Coach off, even after all these years. The old bastard probably had strangling us in his permanent spank bank.

"He's put up with a lot from us," Finley said, "and he never takes it out on us during training or games."

"Yeah, he's a decent male, deep, *deep* down under all his roar."

Finley released a disparaging snort, and when he lifted his arm to rub a hand over his face, he cracked me in the ribs. "Shit, sorry."

I waved it off, having barely felt it. "That's a love tap, bro. Compared to that hit from Wilscher last night." Big fucker had deliberately smashed me into the boards, and I'd never seen the check coming.

"True," he said, and his bear was in his tone now. "Should have cracked him harder in that last few minutes."

"You knocked him out," I snorted, managing not to shake with laughter. "You were protective Care Bear last night."

Finley chose to ignore me, but I knew he loved it. "We're almost through the season," he noted, a low hitch in his voice. "Which, weirdly, I'm looking forward to ending."

Most of us looked forward to the break at the end of the season, but I'd never heard Finley say it before. "Is everything okay?"

He shrugged against my side. "I was just thinking about our road trip next week, and how I really don't want to leave Emme."

I'd been shutting that shit in a mental box all week, hoping a solution to skipping our away games would pop up. "I don't think we can go," I said, voicing our reality. "I mean, ten days is less than half the time we have left to track the witch." The problem was, Coach didn't exactly know about our current *life or death* situation, and our excuses to him were wearing thin.

Finley stared into the dark ceiling as Emme stirred. "Coach doesn't know about the curse," he murmured, and I wondered if he'd heard my thought through the bond.

He shouldn't, with Emme blocking, but the occasional one did slip through.

"Makes it hard to come up with a legitimate explanation," he continued. "I just keep thinking we might be done with hockey, you know? How much longer can we carve out the time and dedication required to play at this level?"

There was a brief pang in my chest at the thought of not being on the team. At not being a Celtic Wolf. It had never been my sanity like it was Finley's, but I still loved the sport. Love or not, though, I'd give it up in a heartbeat for Emme. Even with our mate making it clear on multiple occasions she didn't want that for us.

"It's a tough call," I replied, still unsure how I felt. "Either way, the thing with Jewels will be over in a couple of weeks, and I don't think we should make a life-changing decision yet. Of course, if we don't destroy her before the deadline…"

"There may be no decision to even make," Finley noted in a resigned tone.

We had no idea what Jewels planned to do with her power over shifters. Emme believed she hated us, on a true, deep level that would see her destroy us all. How she'd do that was just as unknown, but I got the sense we'd become her mindless army until our usefulness ran out.

"Whatever her plans, I doubt any of them include letting us live our lives in peace," I said, stroking my fingers down Emme's arm as she snuggled closer.

Her ass shifted back into me and my dick kicked hard against my boxers. I'd spent a blissful hour eating Emme out last night while she sucked Hunter off, then I'd buried myself in her perfect cunt until she screamed out her release, and still… I wanted more.

It'd never be enough.

Finley groaned and stretched his long legs out, like they were aching. "She might have communication blocked, but, Golden, I can feel your arousal through the bond. Could you tone it down a touch?"

Okay, then, it wasn't the poor fucker's legs that ached.

"Not a chance," I shot back with a laugh. "I've got all of her soft curves pressed into me, and I can't make it through the day without tasting her."

Emme's light, husky laughter had every part of my body standing to attention. She turned and brushed her soft hand over my bare chest, and then tripped across to Finley's, caressing the bear as well. "Morning, Grouchy and Golden," she murmured, her voice soft. "I was just dreaming about you two."

Goddess above, she was going to be the death of me.

My cock strained hard against my boxer briefs. I wasn't surprised it had already popped up over the band to try to get to its mate.

"What were those dreams, darlin'?" Finley murmured, turning into me to reach her, until I was the one sandwiched between them.

"Were you spread out between us in the lockers again?" He laced his fingers through Emme's, their clasped hands resting on my chest.

We might be heterosexual in this pack, but when you shared, body parts touching was unavoidable. I'd recently learned that I was an excellent team player and didn't have any qualms about sharing her in the bedroom. As long as Emme was the main event, I was an enthusiastic participant.

Just hand me an award for best team player now.

Emme released another burst of laughter and pressed her lips to the corner of my mouth, her tongue swiping out for a quick taste. "You're my best team player, Golden Boy," she whispered, answering my thoughts. "You should have played football, considering how little you care about balls flying toward your face."

My snort of laughter was loud enough to finally wake an exhausted Hunter, who reared up in bed like a raging wolf, looking tousled and half asleep. He took in the room first, checking for danger. The stunned, not quite awake expression he wore set all three of us off into belly laughter.

The kind that hurt my face and had my sides aching.

"What the fuck is happening?" Hunter growled, and Emme kept trying to tell him, but couldn't stop laughing to get the words out.

I managed to say, "Emme was just reminding us about the time I gave you my best assist, and you rewarded me with a black eye via your fucking ball sac—"

"No!" Emme gasped, slapping her free hand over my mouth. "Don't scare him away. Hunter doesn't like his balls slapping anything except my vagina."

That got a groan from Finley. "I swear to fuck, the more proper your terms for body parts get, the more turned on I am."

That set Emme off again. "You want me to describe it in detail for you?" she huffed. "Have a little show and tell? I mean, I can point out the labia and hood of the clitoris, if you'd like. I've heard that one can be hard to find—"

Hunter reached out and hauled her across the bed and into his arms. She was the only one who slept completely naked, and we all got a glimpse of her perfect, tanned butt as she landed on his chest. *Goddess have mercy.*

"None of us need an anatomy lesson, little mate," Hunter rumbled at her, so much wolf in his tone. "We're fast learners, and while I know we already please you, we will continue to learn everything you enjoy. Alone, sharing, whatever our mate needs."

Emme stilled against his chest. Her scent was potent enough to have me cupping my cock to ease the sudden ache. "I could go for some sharing," she said in a breathless rush.

The sudden tension filling the room was all sexual.

"Dibs on your mouth," I said, throwing my hand in the air.

Emme lifted her face to give me a look that said *What the fuck?* "Kellan Jackson. You did not just *dibs* my mouth. You are incorrigible."

I loved when she got riled up, turning her cheeks a delicious pink and deepening her addictive scent. "When it comes to you, baby, I'm incorrigible, irreparable, incurable, irredeemable, unmanageable…"

"Depraved?" Finley suggested dryly, and I nodded enthusiastically.

"Absolutely! The level of depravity I'd hit in regard to loving my mate knows no depths."

Emme's eyes were deep blue as she rested her head on Hunter's chest and gave me her softest stare. It was a stare that could get her anything in the entire world from me. "You're not depraved or corrupt or wicked. You all love me exactly how I need to be loved. You've been healing me piece by piece, and I must have been a very good girl in my past life to deserve this pack."

That reminded me: "Still believe you invented the vibrator?"

Her lips twitched. "It's looking more and more likely."

Finley, who must not have heard her theory before, propped himself up higher. "Look, the vibrator is an excellent invention, but what about cars? Combustion engines? Maybe you had a hand in the early technological age and brought about our change in reliance from *horse* power to horsepower."

Emme considered that, and I could sense her enjoyment over his theory. "Whatever I did, I'm super happy with my *future life* rewards."

I could only speak for myself, but I was confident enough in my pack to know *all of us* were emotionally slammed by her statement. A few months ago, we were Emme's worst nightmare, and now she considered us a reward for past good deeds.

Maybe *I* invented the fucking vibrator, because goddess knows I was one lucky son of a shifter.

Pulling her half off Hunter so she was draped over us both, my hands slid down to her perfect ass. "I love you, pretty mate. More than I can fucking express with words. Now, let me love you."

"Us," Hunter shot out. "*We* will be loving our mate. Together."

We both turned to check in with Finley, and I could already tell by his scent and the feel of his bear in the bond, that he wasn't leaving this room. "I'm in," he rasped.

We all got to bathe in Emme's glorious scent after that, and when she kissed me I also got to taste her sweetness. Unable to help myself, I tightened my hold on her ass cheeks and lifted her until she sat in her favorite chair. My fucking face.

With a moan she clutched my hair, and I slid my tongue through her already dripping slit. *This is exactly how eternal paradise tastes.* "Fuck," I groaned as she arched against me. "You taste so damn good. I could eat you all day."

Her response was to rock back and forth, grinding down on me. Finley moved to slide his fingers into her cunt, while I swirled my tongue around her clit, determined to find this *elusive hood.*

While Finley pumped his fingers inside her, Hunter shifted up the bed to kiss her, playing with her tits at the same time until the three of us had her trembling and on the edge of a release.

My pace had been a slow torment to start, but I was too fucking ravenous to keep it up. Lapping up every drop of her sweetness, she cried out as her thighs tightened on me. Hunter kept her upright as she thrust into my tongue, and then with a final cry, squirted all over me and Finley's hand.

*Oh yeah.* One of us definitely invented the vibrator.

Hunter's chest heaved as he hauled her off me, his tongue buried in her cunt not a second later. He ate her out until Emme fell apart again, and the three of us panted at the sight of her perfect face in the throes of pleasure. The way she threw her head back, full lips parting, as the gold in her hair glinted in the early morning light.

*Forever.* Emme was forever. I could stay here with her for the rest of my life and not have enough. All of us needed to be close to her, and it was about more than just our mate bond. Emme was essential to not only our happiness, but our survival.

# CHAPTER 34

EMME

My morning was spent between three alphas, each of whom had their preferred method of destroying me. Kellan slid his golden dick into my mouth, Hunter claimed my ass, and Finley stepped in as a real team player. Our Grouchy Bear showed no hesitation about sharing me with Hunter during some mind-blowing double penetration.

The three of them worked so seamlessly, it was hard to believe they'd never done this as a pack before. Despite their intimidating sizes, I enjoyed every second of being shared, and my shifter healing had ramped up so that by the time Hunter hauled me into the shower, there wasn't a single lingering ache. Just shaky knees and trembling muscles as I dealt with the aftermath of pleasure overload.

Under the stream of water, Hunter held me, like he'd done so many times in the past. This was our place of quiet, where we found peace and healing.

I leaned against his chest, just soaking it all in.

In our bond, his wolf pressed against mine as well, and I was filled with the sense of safety that was uniquely Hunter. Partly due to him being my entitled alpha, but mostly because he was, at his core, a true protector.

Our comfortable silence remained as he reached for the body wash and thoroughly covered every inch of my skin. His gentle touch worshipped my body in a different way to sex, and I craved the feeling of his hands on me. When he washed and conditioned my hair, his strong fingers dug into my scalp, and I groaned at how good the head massage felt. I couldn't help myself, even knowing how that sound sent them feral.

The fact that he'd literally just fucked me until we both came hard enough to see stars wouldn't change his reaction either. Sure enough, as that breathy sound escaped me, he slid soapy hands down to wrap around my thighs, and in a flash I was pressed against the tiles.

His hard length notched at my entrance, bringing forth more moans. "Are you sore, baby girl?" he asked in a softly dangerous tone, the gold in his eyes bright.

My response was to arch my hips and thrust myself onto the head of his cock. Hunter's grip on me tightened, and then he pressed inside of me, his pace measured. My entitled alpha moved slowly, and all the while his lips locked with mine in deep, drugging kisses. This was the purest definition of lovemaking, and my heart clenched at the sensation of him surrounding me.

I fought the impending orgasm, my climaxes too quick at times. All I wanted was to drag out this moment and enjoy every second of pleasure. Even slow, there was a maddening rhythm to his thrusts, as he pulled all the way out, and then plunged so deeply that I could feel him through every inch of my core.

"Hunter," I gasped as my body pulsated. "Alpha, please."

The gold exploded through his irises, and his pace picked up as he drove into me, shattering me into a release so intense my entire body tensed around him.

"Holy fuck," I groaned, my lungs aching as I only managed a few random breaths of air. "That was…"

Hunter rumbled out my name when he came, burying his face against my throat, teeth scraping over his bite. The pleasure increased until I was sure I would black out.

It took a long time for our pulses to stop racing, and then the cleaning process started all over again. Somehow, I made it through the second time without getting railed against a wall, and I wasn't sure if I was disappointed by that or not.

"I've got to head into the office for a few hours," Hunter informed me when we were in his wardrobe. He was already dressed in a dark suit, and I was drooling over how fucking good he looked.

Meanwhile, I was in my usual uniform of sweatpants and hoodie, damp strands of hair hanging down my back.

"But I'll see you this afternoon," he continued. "Constantine thinks he'll have some real answers soon."

"Stay safe out there," I said to him, pushing up on my toes for another kiss.

He brushed back the tangled strands of my hair. "You stay safe here," he ordered, his brow furrowing as he looked me over. "I'll be keeping an eye on you of course."

I smirked. "It's lucky I enjoy being stalked."

His shrug was effortless. "You say stalking, I say observing without your knowledge."

A scoff ripped from me as I narrowed my eyes on him. "That's the same damn thing."

Hunter's smirk was pretty enough that I almost forgot his arrogant ways.

When we made it downstairs to the kitchen, he grabbed his to-go coffee, and with one last panty-melting kiss, he left for the office. The rest of my pack were seated at the kitchen counter, breakfast sandwiches in front of them, and there was a plate waiting for me beside my coffee and juice.

Florence bustled over, patting me on the cheek as she directed me to a chair. "We heard you coming down the stairs. Everything is still toasty and warm. I also have pancakes."

"Thank you, Flo," I said, my stomach rumbling at the delicious scents in this room.

Slade and Talon wore very similar half-smiles as they watched me, the slight pull from Talon's scar their only difference.

"That wasn't all we heard from upstairs," Slade added to Florence's statement as he took a sip of tea.

Our beasts were close enough in the bond that I knew everyone was aware of my morning activities and none of them had an issue with it. We were a pack, and as the heart of this quintet, I would be *with* all of them.

In truth, we'd adapted surprisingly well considering how new it all was.

Would there be teething issues down the road? Most likely, but I wasn't going to worry about them before they arrived.

"You should have joined in," I said with a cheeky smile, before I pushed up from the counter to press a good morning kiss to Slade's cheek.

The dragon shot me a heated stare, and not only did he not flinch from my contact, he reached out and captured my face to pull me in for a longer, more intense kiss. He pulled away and I was met with Talon, who stood right behind his brother.

"Morning, Honey," he said, leaning down for a gentler but no less powerful kiss.

Both dragons were forces of nature shifting the very atmosphere of the space around them every single time we touched.

"I like the shortened version of my nickname," I said as I sat again in my spot, reaching for the plate of sandwiches and pancakes. There was no more time for conversation as I focused on eating through the deliciousness.

Slade huffed out a smoky grunt. "It's good to see you finally eating like a shifter. A wolf should never pick at food like a baby bird."

His observations were correct, but for most of my life food was scarce. I still wasn't sure I'd ever grow used to the abundance this pack had. "This is the first time in my life that there's more than enough food available. But my wolf has adjusted quickly, and you should all know that I'm spoiled now. I can't go back to rations, so you'd better stay rich."

I laughed so they'd know it was a joke; money was the last reason to be in this pack. It wasn't even on the damn list.

To my relief, all of them laughed too, including Florence. "I second you staying rich," she chimed in, hands on her hips. "I enjoy this job too much to give it up, and you pay better than everybody in Golden Claw."

Slade's eyes were light, which was a good sign he was amused. "Both of you are safe. We have more money than even Kellan can spend, and he has expensive habits."

Kellan scoffed through his chuckles. "Says the dragon who custom-made his Lambo to the sweet tune of three million."

I choked on a bite of sandwich, and Slade clapped me hard on the back to bring it up. "Wait," I managed to say. "Did you say three million dollars for a Lamborghini?"

SVJs were expensive, of course, and Slade's was bigger than usual with other customizations. But three fucking million…

I waited for him to deny it, but clearly that wasn't going to happen. "I'm fairly sure I made that much by mid-day on the morning it arrived."

Talon and I exchanged a glance, and he just shrugged as if to say *rich people are weird*.

True story.

I'd never asked them how much money they made, and even though I had a sleeve of credit cards to use, I found I rarely needed them. They provided everything I needed *and wanted*. Most of the time before I even knew I wanted it.

Talon sipped his tea as he asked, "How much money do you all have?"

The dragon was perched on his stool in borrowed clothing, without a phone or possession to his name. He legitimately cost zero dollars outside of the food he ate.

If there was a shifter here who cared less about money than me, it was him.

Finley shrugged. "Kel and I make about five million a year each from hockey, plus playoff bonuses. Hunter and Slade make about five hundred million a year from the company. Same same."

Kellan cracked up. "I really thought I was going to have big boy money when I got drafted into the NSHL. Then these fuckers came along and reminded me that it's just spare change."

"*We* have," Slade said suddenly, and Talon gave his twin his full focus. "You said *How much money do you all have?* but it's *we*. It's yours and Emme's money too. Pack money."

I leaned over him to high five Talon. "Look at us go. Overnight billionaires."

Talon shook his head as he tapped his hand to mine, the smallest of smiles playing around his lips. I lowered my voice and added, "If you joke about it, it doesn't feel as real and overwhelming."

Finley leaned back against the bench, his expression thoughtful. "I didn't grow up rich, so I think I'd adjust fine if we lost all our money."

"I'd miss affording tech," Slade said, steepling his hands in front of him in his classic thinking pose. "And I'd miss our house and compound. It's comfortable here with plenty of space and a nice yard. My beast enjoys swimming too, so I'd miss the pool. But as long as I had this pack, I could live in a cave. I'd figure out how to outfit it with Wi-Fi."

This pack had been used to power, dominance, and control long before they were rich. If they lost it all, they'd be okay, and I'd be right by their side.

After breakfast Slade and Talon headed out to train. I had training later too, along with a possible session of magic with Constantine. Depending on his progress with the blood-tracing spell.

Until then, I explored the house with Kellan and Finley, suggesting options to fill the time. "Gym? Pool? What about a sauna? Maybe we should watch a movie?" I hadn't been back in the theatre since that fateful first meeting with Finley.

The bear caught my eye, as if he remembered as well. "I need to do something physical. Maybe we can work on your car?"

Kellan bounced on the spot. "I have no idea what to do with an engine other than stare at it, but I'll be excellent moral support."

I was about to agree when a thought came to me. Finley immediately noticed my hesitation. "Did you have another idea of what we could do instead?"

"You didn't hear my thought?" The more I embraced my magic, the stronger I felt I was getting at blocking what I didn't want to be heard.

"Nope," Kellan said. "We can see your beast in the center of us all, but it's quiet in there. We can't even really communicate with each other unless you loosen your hold."

I hadn't realized I was controlling them that much, and I decided to ease up a fraction.

Finley pressed in closer. "What idea did you have for us to do today, darlin'?"

"I'd like to get my tattoo."

His flash of excitement had the broody bear looking almost as cheerful as Golden. "Fuck yes! I've been waiting a long time to get my hands on you and mark my mate."

"Again," I reminded him, laughing at his little bounce of enthusiasm.

Kellan clapped his hands together. "Yes! Can I get mine too? I want that last image you drew of my pretty girl in her wolf form. All majestic and mysterious under the full moon."

Finley pressed a hand to his brother's shoulder. "Depending on how fast I work, I should be able to get yours and Emme's done today." His expression sobered as he looked my way. "Fair warning, this is going to be painful. The magic required to cut through shifter healing takes its toll."

I already knew magic was involved, and there was a flash of

annoyance that we had to rely on witches for anything. Not that I would let it stop me. "Yeah, I can handle it."

Whatever it took to wear our quintet on my skin—as more than bites.

Finley all but swept me off my feet and up the stairs, with Kellan right behind us.

In the bear's room, I was set on the bed while he spent fifteen minutes cleaning up his station, spraying everything down, and pulling out his art and the tattooing gear.

Kellan's design was finalized, but Finley had some new sketches to show me. I flicked between them all, loving so many, which made it a hard choice. There were some with us in our full beast forms, others with our human faces, but I was set on this being about quintet essences.

He hesitated just long enough before he handed over the last sketch, for me to know this was his favorite. It immediately became mine as well.

"This is the one," I whispered, clutching it so tightly my knuckles were almost as white as the paper itself. He'd drawn five beast heads, with the dragons represented as a single entity, all together in a quintet bond. Fire and flames formed around us, and I could feel the magic and love in the one image.

*My pack.*

# CHAPTER 35

EMME

While Kellan's tattoo took a little less than two hours, I sat in Finley's chair for ten very long, very painful hours. Constantine cancelled magic training to keep working on his tracking, and I had to cancel on Slade and Talon, as I was in no condition to spar mid-tattoo.

"You didn't even flinch," Kellan rasped, squeezing my hand. "Feeling your pain through the bond, even if only in the brief moments your control slipped, almost broke me."

His skin had a pallor to it that hadn't been there during his session, so was clearly all about what he felt from me. The worst pain had been when Finley tattooed over my scar; I'd had to tighten up the bond to prevent Hunter from storming home and killing our bear mate.

"I flinched," I said softly, "but a little pain is nothing when I get to wear our quintet on my skin."

Kellan rubbed a hand over his bare chest, gliding his fingers across the very lifelike depiction of my white wolf. "I will admit, it hurt like a bitch, but I love her."

*I loved him.* "You helped distract me," I said shooting him a cheeky smile, "and I think we're both lucky Finley works so fast."

His gun had glided over my skin with the lightest touch, and it was only the magic cutting through our natural healing that caused the pain. After he'd finished, he rubbed a cool gel across my shoulders and upper back, until it mostly felt stiff and tender.

"You're incredibly talented," I told my bear, and he closed the distance between us for a kiss. "Thank you."

"You're welcome," he replied, his smile tired but satisfied. "You were the perfect canvas to create art on. It turned out even better than I expected."

I'd seen bits of it in the mirror, and it was spectacular. My mate was insanely skilled.

"Come on, Shortcake," Kellan said, holding his hand out for me to take. "We can wait for Fin in the theatre room while he cleans up."

When I offered to help, our bear waved me off, so I followed Kellan downstairs. In the theatre, he nudged me forward so he could take in the quintet tattoo visible above my tank top.

"It really is perfect," he said, and I felt the ghost of his touch, though he never made contact.

A shiver traced down my spine, and his scent deepened as he pressed his lips to my shoulder. "You have no idea how fucking obsessed I am with seeing our quintet represented on your skin."

His nose brushed closer to the bend of my neck as he inhaled deeply.

My pulse raced from his tender touches, though both of us knew we were in no condition to do more than cuddle. At least my period was long finished, and I wouldn't have to worry about it for another six weeks or so.

I felt the tugging on my bonds with the twins moments before Slade and Talon entered the room.

"You're in pain," Slade declared as he briskly climbed the stairs toward me.

My nod was brief, so I didn't jar my back. "Yes, it's a big tattoo. It will take a few days to settle."

He responded by gently hauling me up out of my seat, and I found myself holding my breath as he turned to examine the whole piece. For a moment, I panicked that I'd made the wrong decision in having the dragons represented by a single green and black beast. "It's the essence of our quintet," I quickly explained when the silence extended on.

Talon moved closer, his scent adding a deeper smokiness to Slade's. A hand ran down my spine, just under the weird numb pain across my upper back. "It's perfect," Slade murmured, the deep timbre of his dragon in that statement. "This is how our energy looks to me in our bond. A powerful quintet. Fin even used your scar in the design, as part of the tethers between us."

Talon grunted, and it sounded very much like an agreement. "I never understood the tattoo thing," he admitted, voice so close I knew he stood beside his brother. "But this is sexy against all of your tanned skin."

Two hands stroked me now, and it was soothing enough that I sighed in relief. "You're both helping with the pain," I told them. "And I agree. Finley created a masterpiece, and I'm genuinely in love with it."

The clank of Slade's teeth had me chuckling. "Can't be jealous of me loving a tattoo, mate."

"Watch me," he muttered.

Finley entered the room soon after, and he joined the dragons in a few long strides. "I've got a different cream to rub over it," he said, leaning in to spread a cool liquid over my skin. "This has tendrils of magic in it, to give you some numbing relief."

In hindsight, getting myself tattooed in the middle of crisis probably wasn't my smartest move. But we also had no idea how much longer we'd have our autonomy and freedom.

I would be in control of my own actions, and choose my own path, for as long as I had the ability.

"As you should, baby girl." Hunter stepped into the room, and I was glad he'd heard that declaration. Since easing up my hold on the bond, I'd allowed more natural thoughts to flow between all of us.

Hunter had already ditched the jacket and rolled up his sleeves, his forearms flexing as he ran a hand over his face. I hated the fatigue in his features. I could have killed Jewels just for the stress she was adding to his life alone.

"You're home late," Slade noted, and without even glancing at his watch, said, "It's twelve twenty-five." Somehow he always knew the exact time.

Hunter huffed out a long breath as he reached the bar in the back corner, pouring himself a generous shot of whiskey. He gulped it down in one hit and then went back for a second. "Yeah, there was a massive fuck-up with a large shipment of armored vests and weapons. At first I thought it was human interference, but it turned out magic was involved. We lost ten good shifters, and about a million dollars in stock."

That had the others on alert, except for Slade, who wore a resigned look on his face.

"Did Jewels interfere?" I asked.

Hunter shrugged, the second glass of whiskey almost gone now. "Looks that way, though she wasn't out of her protective shield long enough for us to get a reading on her location."

"She's trying to stop us from arming shifters with anything that can interfere with magic or hurt witches," Finley said, his scowl deepening. "Why does she even care if she thinks she's just going to hide out until she completely controls us?"

Another shrug from Hunter. "Maybe she's hedging all bets in case we manage to stop her. Whatever the reason, she's either watching our movements or there's another spy here in Golden Claw."

"Or in Reeves Industries," Talon suggested.

Hunter exchanged a glance with Slade. "Yeah, we've already considered that," he said. "Slade is doing a deep dive into our employees again, but it's hard when most of his time and bandwidth is being used to trace the excessive power usage around the shifter cities."

"I've already found three possible locations from my search," he said. "Talon and I plan on checking them out tomorrow, even though the program will take at least another day or so to finish. Longer if I have to expand the search parameters."

My first instinct was to reach out and grasp on to both dragons, preventing them from leaving my side. Not that I could physically restrain them, but I was confident they wouldn't fight my hold. The thought of them going out there, to possibly encounter Jewels on their own, was terrifying.

"We should go with you," I said, when no one else voiced concerns. "If she's keeping tabs on us anyway, there's no point hiding our actions from her."

"In our dragon form, we can cloak our movements," Talon reminded me. "We should go first, like I did with Fletcher's compound, and then we can reassess our movements as a pack."

Hunter looked unhappy as he continued to hammer whiskey like he was training for a drinking competition.

Slade waved off my concern. "She's no match for us. I hope she finds us so I can be the one to personally tear her to shreds." I had zero issue with that plan, providing none of my alphas were collateral damage in her death.

Needing some normalcy, we settled in after that to watch a movie. I curled up on Hunter's chest, as our entitled alpha needed the most comfort tonight. When my stomach rumbled, Talon headed into the kitchen, returning in twenty minutes with toasted sandwiches.

"Florence prepped ahead again," he said. "These were in the fridge, ready and waiting to be popped under the grill."

He offered me the tray first as I said, "Yeah, we all missed dinner so she would have been stressed about us starving."

Between taking bites of my Reuben sandwich, I leaned back to get comfortable, ignoring the twinge in my back. Hunter adjusted me against his side, taking my weight.

"Eat, little omega," he murmured, his voice steady.

In our quintet, his wolf paced, in what appeared to be a manic back and forth motion.

Shoving half the bread and meat into my mouth, I chewed quickly, wanting all of them to eat too. Once I was done, they finished their food in record time, and I proceeded to fall asleep halfway through the movie.

I drowsily woke as someone carried me up the stairs and placed me on my stomach in the middle of Slade and Talon's bed, their scents strong around me. My other alphas pressed kisses on my cheeks and shoulders as they left.

"Sweet dream, Shortcake," Kellan whispered, followed by Finley, who spread another layer of cream over my tattoo, called me darlin', and left me swooning. Half asleep or not, I enjoyed every second of their pampering.

Hunter's wolf surged against mine, nuzzling down her side, while in the bedroom the alpha kissed my lips. "Sleep well, baby girl," he murmured. "I love you. I'll see you in the morning."

"Love you," I mumbled, sleep already dragging me under again now that Finley's magic cream was numbing my pain.

When the dragons slid in on either side of me, their naked, muscled lengths took away the last of my discomfort. It was blissfully silent and pain free in this bed, and the comfort of having my mates so close took me into a deep, uninterrupted sleep.

# CHAPTER 36

EMME

I cy magic surrounded me, so thick I could taste it on my tongue. It was not my magic, this was bitter, overused, and pulled from darker curses than were safe for any witch to use. It stirred my own essence in response, but my wolf stood in the way to keep us safe from the taint.

At least internally. Externally, I was held and forced to submit to the witch.

"You shouldn't exist," she snarled at me, and despite the harsh tone, and darkness obscuring her face, I knew who it was. "Your kind is an affront to witches. You will be a shifter I cannot control."

In my dream, it was as if the curse had come to fruition. We'd failed and I'd ended up here, in Jewels' clutches. Where were my alphas?

Pain filled every nerve ending of my body as she hit me with a spell. There was no way to halt the screams that ripped from me until my throat ached.

Desperate, I reached through the bond, pushing past the insidious magic that held me immobile, and found my mates. They were alive!

All was not lost. At least not yet.

A surge of fight returned to me, and I searched for a weapon to use against her. I'd come here with the intention of ending her but she'd ambushed me. Or maybe I hadn't intended to be here at all.

The dream kept swirling and changing, but the pain remained as I fought and sliced the darkness, the magic bleeding through me.

*Emme, let us in,* Hunter demanded, his voice in my head.

*I can't,* I replied, whimpering as more pain crashed against me. *She's killing me.*

*I could feel my pack getting closer, but they would be too late. My body only had one more blast of magic in it... The coiled darkness tightened, and as the spell left Jewels' grasp, I closed my eyes and murmured goodby—*

"Emme!" The jolt that woke me wasn't from magic, but Finley's rough hands. "Baby," he said, his touch gentling. "You were screaming."

Choked sobs burst from me as flashes of the dream lingered, reminding me of how close I'd come to death... at the hands of that witch. More than that, as the heart of our quintet, if I died, I'd take all of my mates with me.

Finley wrapped himself around me, with Hunter and Kellan pressing close on the bed too. In the bond our beasts huddled, and I fully opened the connection, allowing Slade and Talon to be part of this. They'd left a few hours ago to investigate the three locations with an overuse of power, and it must have been after I fell back asleep that the nightmare took hold.

*What happened?* Slade demanded. *We could feel your panic and pain, but there was no way to push through our connection. It felt like we were being blocked.*

Growls filled the room as Hunter's gaze snapped to me. "What if that wasn't a dream. What if it was a magical attack?"

With the bond fully open, Slade heard him, and we were all bathed in dragon heat. *We should return,* Talon said. *It's not safe there for you all without us.*

*No,* I said, with more force than was probably necessary. *We're running out of time to stop her, and it's going to take all of our strength. There are no second chances with this curse, and... I'm okay. I'll ask Constantine if there's a way to protect us during sleep. You two need to focus on these locations, to figure out if any of them might hold the witch.*

Their worry lingered along with their rage, but in the end, they stayed on course. Through the bond, Slade sent me a flash of the town they were closing in on. *This is site one. We'll report back soon. Ask your father right now to protect your mind.*

When he pulled away, I limited the connection once more so we didn't distract them. I knew better than to close it fully, as their beasts would lose it again.

Hunter hurled himself off the bed and disappeared from the room, reappearing minutes later with a harried-looking witch-wolf in tow.

"Protect her," our entitled alpha snarled. "She was magically attacked in her dreams."

Constantine's sleepy expression faded, his eyes focused and alert as he examined me.

"Can you release her?" he asked Kellan and Finley, who were still wrapped around me as if they were prepared to throw their half-naked bodies between me and an attack. "I need to assess her energy to pinpoint what happened."

With reluctance, they removed their hands, but didn't back up more than a few inches. "Don't touch her any more than necessary," Finley warned my father, an edge in his tone.

Constantine nodded, showing no sign of being offended. For an alpha, he was rather unarrogant and unconcerned with dominance battles. I wondered if his witch side tempered the shifter side, or maybe it was more to do with his age and years of being on the run in the human world.

"I'm going to touch your collarbone, Emme," he informed me, hands hovering above the sheet I had clutched to my chest.

The fact that any of the alphas were even allowing him to be in here while I was naked showed their level of worry. I mean, he was my father, so it wasn't a sexual thing, but they would always be possessive.

When I nodded, he pressed his warm hands to my skin, a spark of his magic lighting up my own. After our time training together, I was familiar with the surge of his energy, but this felt like an even closer connection than usual, as if our magics realized we were from the same witch line. *Family.*

With my emotions still raw from the dream, and the stress of the twins being far away, I couldn't help the tears that slipped from beneath my closed eyelids.

"What are you doing to her?" Hunter demanded, and my eyes opened to find him pushing against a magical barrier that Constantine must have erected around us.

*I'm okay*, I said through the bond. *The familial ties that come with connecting our magic hit me hard, but he's not hurting me.*

Hunter's wolf snarled until all of his pearly white teeth were on violent display. *He has two fucking minutes. Tell him.*

"Are you okay?" Constantine asked as he ignored Hunter's scowl.

"Yeah, I can just feel our magic is connected."

A soft smile lifted his lips, and I realized how rarely I'd seen him actually smile. A part of me regretted the cold and dismissive way I treated him when he first showed up, but at least we were slowly building a bond. "Our magic is connected to our family line," he told me in a wistful tone. "To our ancestors. We inherit more than magic. We inherit the past and future from them. We inherit the essence of our covens."

I'd never liked magic. Or witches. But in this moment, I felt connected to a coven I hadn't even known existed until recently. "There's only the two of us left, right?"

Constantine nodded, and then winced when Hunter slammed his hands against the shield, reminding us both that his patience was running out.

"He's not going to hold off much longer," I said, though the entitled alpha did back up when I waved him away.

Constantine let his magic flow deeper into mine, probing along the swirls of my energy. "There are tendrils of foreign magic mixed with yours," he said as his eyebrows drew closer. "I can't tell if it was an attack or just a warning, but either way, it's a concern."

He dropped the shield, but they'd all heard him. "How can you ensure it doesn't happen again?" Kellan asked, his expression darkened by worry. His violet eyes assessed me, and I wished there was a way to reassure him. In truth, if any of my mates had been mentally attacked while asleep, I'd be raging and trying to catch and kill myself a witch.

"I can place wards on the house itself," Constantine said. "At least here you'll sleep safely. It's much harder to infiltrate your mind when you're awake, as your own personal shielding is strong. Asleep, we're all more vulnerable."

"Yes, thank you," I said with a shudder at the thought of not being able to sleep for fear of another magical attack.

Constantine pushed himself back off the bed. "Okay, I'm going to start working on it now. As long as you sleep under this roof, you should be safe from dream manipulation. Keep your shielding up through the day though. When you open to the pack, spread that shielding out around them as well. Don't just drop it... include them instead."

I blinked at him, as it had never occurred to me to include them that way. "Right, so instead of dropping our shields, I just expand it out to fit all of the pack."

"Exactly," he said, and then with a nod he hopped off the bed and headed for the exit.

"Thank you," I called after him, wanting to say it again. "We appreciate you helping us out. Not just with this but also Jewels."

Constantine's eyes were shiny as he shook his head. "I've wanted to keep you safe for years, and more than that, I'm sick of having to run. I mean no harm to the shifter or witch communities, and yet I've been shunned from both. I'd love to settle somewhere. Visit you on occasion. For that to happen, the more powerful witches must be taken out."

It didn't bother me that there was a personal reason for him to care about this war. I wanted him to be able to stop running too. I wanted him around so we could continue to nurture these tendrils of a relationship.

"We're going to make sure you don't have to run anymore," I assured him, determined to manifest our victory. We were going to win this battle.

Jewels picked the wrong pack to fuck with. If that bitch entered my dreams again, I was going to figure out a way to kill her.

# CHAPTER 37

EMME

After his assessment, Constantine left us for the library, where he'd set up all his spell equipment. On top of casting protection over the house so we could safely sleep, he was still working on the blood-tracing spell—our plan B if Slade and Talon's search didn't pan out.

So far the first site had been a bust, housing a *very human* protest, which explained away their recent power usage surge.

While they moved on to site two, I dragged myself off to shower and get ready.

"I'm going to assist Constantine," Hunter said after he helped me into the shower. "Unless you need me?"

I always needed him, but there were far more important priorities today. "Go, I'm totally fine," I said, waving him off.

After he left, Finley pressed in through the open bathroom door. "I have therapy," he said, steam wafting around him, "but I can cancel if you need me here."

"Not a chance," I told him. "Tell Dr. Karen I said hello."

He stepped over to the shower door, and I leaned out to brush my hand across his beard, pulling him closer for a kiss. When we parted, I was rewarded with a hint of my favorite dimples. "I'm so proud of you for sticking with therapy," I murmured, keeping it just between us. "I still see *and feel* improvements in your energy and aura. You're doing amazing."

Finley shrugged but couldn't hide his hint of pleasure at my praise.

"Before I decided to heal, I felt like I was living on a boat at sea. One minute it was smooth sailing, and the next huge waves would almost throw me overboard. And while my healing journey won't ever be linear, it's in general so much smoother now. The waves aren't as severe, and they don't take me by surprise. I feel like I might finally be on an even keel."

He dropped his forehead against mine. "Still my peace," he whispered against my skin. "Don't forget to rub cream on your tattoo when you get out of the shower. I left it by the sink."

I only had minimal discomfort today and already felt like his mark was settling against my skin. "Thank you, Grouchy."

"Anytime, darlin'." Then with one last kiss, he left me with Golden.

Kellan smiled, but it didn't quite reach his eyes. "Well, Shortcake. It's just you and me. Whatever should we do with our time?"

Leaning forward, I crooked a finger at him, and he trotted right over. "I have an idea."

"Care to share with the class?" he asked, a spark finally lighting up his eyes.

"Anticipation is half the fun," I said with a smirk, "now get your workout gear on and I'll meet you in the gym."

"The gym?" he rasped, clearly having had other ideas of what we could do.

I laughed and pressed my hand against his chest, all but walking him out of the bathroom, dripping water as I went. When I closed the door on him, there was a thud on the other side. As if he'd dropped his head against it. "No fair, mate," he called out, sounding pained.

With a laugh, I returned to the shower, grabbing up my bodywash to quickly clean myself. There were tons of bathrooms in this house, and somehow all of them ended up stocked with my favorite items, from hair products to period needs. There were even makeup essentials scattered in their drawers. I could essentially use any bathroom in the house and find what I needed to start my day.

I had no idea who was responsible, and while my first guess would be Hunter, it could be any of them. Though I knew for sure Talon was the one who planted hairbrushes in *every* room of the house. It had been too long since he'd brushed my hair, and my beast wasn't the only one uneasy with the twins so far away from us.

After my shower, I smothered cream on my back, using the mirror to make sure I covered it all. I got dressed in Slade's wardrobe—my clothes were in every room too—and was soon ready to find Kellan. Training with our resident weapons expert was exactly what I needed after that unsettling dream. Preparation was the only way to counter this feeling of vulnerability in the face of magic.

On my way out of the room, I passed Slade's row of computers, one of which was running his search. Scanning the data, I noted that it hadn't found anything else of significance, and was about to turn away when a minimized file caught my eye. *Fletcher's research.*

Clicking on it, it opened in what was a blur until I forced my eyes to focus. I had to read slowly, since it wasn't in the font or background color that helped me keep letters straight.

The file appeared to be a summary of Fletcher's notes, focusing mostly on creating and breaking pack bonds. My breath caught at the thought of ever losing one of my bonds. I'd literally have to be dying before I'd break our quintet, or more accurately, one of them would have to be dying.

In Slade's concise dot points, the entire process of breaking a bond was surprisingly simple. The difficulty came from needing magic and permission of the center or entitled alpha, since they were the ones who held strong ties to all the other members of the quintet.

I wondered if that was why Jewels and Fletcher hadn't just broken my bonds to Hunter and Kellan, even when it interfered with their Talon plans. They couldn't without my permission.

Of course, under the right *torturous* circumstances, I imagined a shifter would agree to just about anything to make it end.

Not wanting to know more, I shut the folder down, my gut churning in distaste. Needing to fill my mind with happier thoughts, I backtracked to Slade's stalker wall and ripped the curtains open. Googly eyes bounced back at me, and I felt the slightest, unhinged chuckle creep up my throat as I stared at them. He'd left the eyes, and more than that, he'd added some shelves beside his security monitors, where all the glow-in-the-dark dragons from his room were perched.

Staring down at me.

I loved that he'd kept the items from my pranks. I was still working out plans for prank number three. Most of my ideas would require help from all the pack, but there was no point until we destroyed Jewels. Not a single alpha would mess with the cameras for even a second while we were in danger.

As I turned away, a pinned sheet of paper caught my eye. Mostly as it hadn't been there the last time I'd stared at the stalker wall. The writing was small and boxy, and I couldn't read it clearly until I got closer. As soon as the words made sense, I started to curse under my breath.

Slade had pinned a list of names, addresses, and social security numbers.

All of them human men.

This *motherfucker* had done exactly what he'd promised and tracked down the few guys I'd had sex with. Goddess give me strength. Marching over to his desk, I found a black marker in the drawers, the same shade as what he'd used to ink his murder-list in the first place.

When I returned to the curtain, I unpinned the paper and pressed it against the wall to scribble a huge black line through each name. Underneath I wrote, in my messy, childish scrawl, *NO touching! Don't push me on this one, Slade Riverson.*

After I pinned the defaced paper back to his wall, I left the room feeling much more positive.

In the gym, I found Kellan absolutely whaling on the boxing bag. For all of his lightheartedness, there was a coiled lethality around him when he fought. In this state, no one could miss the deadly weapon buried beneath his golden complexion and easy-going smile.

As I closed in on him, it took real effort not to drool over the sweat dripping down his perfect abs, not to mention those delicious veins popping out of his forearms. Kellan shot me a smirk as he grabbed the swinging bag. "See something you like, pretty mate?"

"I see a lot I like actually."

He growled and released the bag to prowl up to me. His scent was potent, and I almost swooned like a damsel.

"You have no idea how badly I want to fuck you against the wall," he rumbled, his wolf flashing in his eyes until they blazed violet. "Bury myself in your tight pussy. I dream about it, mate. I dream about you. Every. Damn. Night."

My thighs clenched against the pulse that thudded like a drumbeat between them, but I refused to be seduced by his dirty mouth and smoldering stare. "Let's fight first," I said, struggling to breathe through the intensity oozing between us. "If you beat me, you get to claim me."

Kellan's scent deepened, and he palmed his dick with a groan. "Baby, fuck, you're speaking my love language now. Add in some praise and I'm going to be a puddle at your feet."

I waved a finger at him. "A puddle won't win you anything, Golden. You need to bring your A-game."

I wasn't good enough for his L-game, let alone his A, but I didn't want him to baby me. If I was going to improve, I needed to be pushed.

He nodded, his chest heaving with multiple rapid breaths. "I accept. Weapons?"

"Oh yeah."

After stripping off my top to leave myself clad in a sports bra and workout tights, I grabbed my blades from their case. Kellan groaned again, his expression pained, as he looked between me and the weapons. He loved these custom-made beauties, and I was thrilled that Slade had been able to call in another favor and get a set made for his birthday next month.

That we *would* be celebrating because we *would* beat that fucking witch.

She'd already taken too much from us.

Kellan lifted two blades from a nearby shelf, a set I'd seen him practice with many times. He had a lot of weapons in his bedroom, but they were mostly shelf trophies. The ones down here were put to use.

"These are *Stab* and *Jab*," he said, lifting the two, long, thick bladed weapons. I'd modeled his birthday ones on this same size. "They're old friends of mine."

My words came out in a burst of laughter. "Stab and Jab? Well, I guess I don't have to look far for how you chose those names." I glanced down at my pretty pair. "Maybe I need to call mine something too."

Kellan's amusement grew. "Oh yeah, you absolutely do. How else will you shout out their kill count during battle." My Golden certainly had a vicious, bloodthirsty streak in him.

When we moved into the ring and faced each other, his expression turned pinched and worried. "I'm not sure I can do this, Shortcake. What if I accidentally nick you. I know you haven't been learning for long."

"Magic gives me a slight advantage," I reminded him, "and if I battle Jewels or Blaine, neither of them will go easy on me. I need to be pushed past my comfort zone."

He didn't look fully convinced, but he remained in place, dropping lower into a fighting stance. Kellan was an offensive fighter, always striking first, and *Stab and Jab* sat very comfortably in his hands. Even anticipating his quick strike, I only just managed to get my blade up in time to partially block his hit, the force sending a jolt through my arm.

Kellan didn't give me a chance to recover, striking again with his other hand. While I mostly managed to block him, he was too fast for me to do anything other than defend myself. The magic essence inside me rose up as we parried, and I used it to anticipate his strikes.

It helped, but damn he was fast and strong.

"You're pretty good, Shortcake," he said, looking impressed. "For such a minimal time training, you've really developed some skills."

I somehow managed not to beam, even though his praise flowed like a warm hug over me. "Thank you. The blades and magic help, of course, but I weirdly enjoy pushing my body. I never expected that. You saw me try to run without wheezing when I first arrived here, but now…" I paused. "Don't you dare tell Slade."

He chuckled. "Your secret is safe with me, pretty mate. Now, let's get you attacking back."

His strikes slowed as he encouraged me to return attack, calling out directions to improve my power and aim. After an hour, my arms ached in a way that shifter healing wasn't keeping up with, and my tattoo was starting to smart, but it was still one of the best sessions I'd ever had.

When Kellan spun in another ninja move, he swung out sharply, and the next thing I knew *Stab* was at my throat. My heart skipped a beat, and I stilled so thoroughly I wasn't even breathing.

Kellan held my gaze, our chests heaving as we stared at each other, our beasts prowling through the bond. A growl ripped from him, and as he lunged for me, his blades fell to the mat. My weapons dropped too, and I was too far gone to worry about the lack of respect we were showing our tools.

Kellan tore through my workout gear, literally ripping my sports bra down the center, and when my tits fell free, he buried his face between them. I was sweaty as shit, but he didn't care as he lapped at my skin and sucked my right nipple in his mouth, followed by the left.

His hands traced down to slide my sweats and underwear off,

until all I could smell was both of our scents, tinged with the musk of our arousal. He followed the path of my pants, his tongue sliding into my dripping pussy. He lapped at me and then buried his face until he had to be near-drowning down there.

"Fuck me," he groaned, reassuring me he was alive. He wrapped his palms around my thighs, tugging me closer to him. My blood pumped from our fight, and as desperate need coursed through me, I tried to thrust against his mouth, but he remained in control.

"So fucking good," I moaned. "Such a good boy, eating me like I'm your last meal."

His chest shook with the deepest rumble I'd ever heard. He was near-frantic as he licked and sucked, sliding my clit into his mouth until I screamed into a rather dramatic release. Giving me exactly zero seconds to recover, he hauled to his feet, shoved down his sports shorts, and had me pinned against the wall with his cock buried inside me.

I groaned at that burning stretch of his frantic thrust, but it was a welcome ache in my core. I felt him through every nerve ending, as my walls clenched around his length. Kellan slammed into me in the same determined, desperate way he'd eaten me out, and I could do nothing but hold on and pray to survive the wave of pleasure.

I came two times before he buried his face in my throat and jerked inside of me, filling me until our combined releases dripped down our thighs. It took a long time before either of us could walk, and even when we wobbled from the gym, we had to hold each other up.

"Best day ever," Kellan said, keeping me pressed against his side. "I can't wait to spend the rest of my life doing just this with you, pretty mate."

His lips landed on the side of my head, and my eyes almost fluttered closed at how good it all felt. "I'm ready to sign up for a lifetime of this."

Kellan whooped, and then swept me into his arms. "Okay, baby. Let's finish off with pool and sauna. Work out a few of those fighting muscles."

Before I could protest, or remind him it was freezing outside, he took off running with me in his arms.

# CHAPTER 38

## TALON

We'd been flying for most of the day only to be able to eliminate two locations as possible hideouts for Jewels, Blaine, or any of their allies. I hadn't expected it to be easy, knowing that witch always had plans upon plans. Her schemes were layered. Even if we unraveled one, we'd soon find ourselves battling the next.

*This is peaceful.*

Slade's voice thundered in my head and my beast and I concurred with that feeling. Despite not finding anything useful yet, the only part of this day I really hadn't enjoyed was crawling out of bed this morning and leaving Emme. The fact that she'd been attacked in her dreams right after was unacceptable. Constantine had better get his shit together and figure out how to protect her.

At least until we fucked that witch up.

*It's always peaceful up here,* I said. *There's nothing that can compare to the freedom of soaring above the world like this. We're as close to gods as any shifter could be.*

Slade's laughter was low and filled with fire. *Couldn't agree more, brother. The smaller animals of flight cannot reach our vantage point, so they only partly understand.* There was a long pause, before he rumbled with more amusement. *Emme would tell us we're arrogant bastards, and she's not wrong. But we can at least back up our arrogance.*

*Our mate loves us. Including our arrogance.*

We might never have met another dragon, but there was no chance any of our ancestors were lacking in confidence. We knew our place in the food chain.

Right at the top.

*It's nice to be on a mission for my pack,* I told my twin. *I spent a lot of time flying for Fletcher, but there was never any enjoyment in it.*

Working *with* my family changed it all. I had a choice now, and I chose to fight for them.

*This is how it should have always been,* Slade muttered as he released a small blast of fire.

*It will be from now on.* I'd never go back to who I used to be.

As we continued our flight, we checked in on Emme and the rest of the pack. She had us partially blocked, but we could push through it.

*She's training with Kellan.*

Slade's dragon's rumble grew louder as he banked west to reach the third and final location. *Yes, Kellan is very well trained in fighting, but especially weapon work. His father was quite an exceptional enforcer. Our brother might appear cheerful and laidback, but when he fights, even I am wary of his skill and lethality.*

Kellan was the literal definition of *watch out for the quiet ones.* Though in his case, it was the smiling ones.

*It was almost impossible to leave Emme this morning.* My omega was never far from my thoughts, and not having her pretty face in front of me felt wrong. I might have every curve, feature, and all twenty-six freckles memorized, but that wasn't enough. *I've never had anyone in my life that I needed to see on a daily basis. I was alone at least ninety percent of my week. But now I feel adrift when I don't have contact with you or Emme every few hours.*

It was easy to admit my weakness to Slade. My twin felt like an extension of myself and my beast, and there'd never be any true judgment between us.

*Yeah, it's weird for me too,* Slade admitted. *I always had Hunter, and while he was essential to my survival and mental health, you and Emme are the other parts of my soul. Kellan and Finley sit only just below you three.*

He didn't need to justify his hierarchy to me; I completely understood. All of our brothers were important, but Emme was first, then my twin, followed by everyone else.

*Beyond our pack, every other shifter is no more than an ant though. I care nothing for them.*

Slade's dragon nodded. *Agreed.* When he turned again, I followed close behind. *The third and final site is up ahead*. His tone turned sharper as his beast focused.

Sending more of my dragon essence through my scales, I made sure to hide every part of myself. We were up so high that the tips of my claws had frost clinging to them, but there was no discomfort as internal fires kept my center toasty warm.

The first two sites were closer to Golden Claw, but all we'd found were a large-scale protest and a new, not-yet-registered commercial farm. This third site was near Silver City and had taken most of the day to reach. Since Slade expected Blaine would be near one of the cities, this was our most likely location.

We started our descent, and I caught a glint of silver buildings shimmering on the horizon, telling me we were maybe ten miles from the city.

*This is where Blaine sat on the council*, Slade said, dropping faster.

*Which makes it safe and familiar territory for him.*

We landed in a parcel of uninhabited land, shaking off our hours of flight.

*Exactly*, Slade said. *This is also where a lot of his allies will be. It was always my strongest lead, but the others still needed to be eliminated.* My brother was nothing if not thorough and methodical.

Shifting back took an extra second after being in our beast forms for so long. As soon as we were bipedal, we pulled clothes and boots from our storage bags and got dressed.

"Let's check it out," Slade said, taking off at a run. "The recent surge in power was triggered from a spot northeast of us.

"I didn't see any civilization as we flew overhead," I noted, easily keeping up with him.

Slade shrugged. "Me either, but I expect they'll be hidden with more than magic. Possibly camouflaged as well."

We ran through the territory, most of which had the look of an area that had been recently cleared. "From my research, nothing here was connected to Blaine or Jewels," Slade told me, his head almost on a swivel as he tried to take in everything around, above, and below us. "But it's easy enough to hide information under multiple shell companies. I didn't have enough time for the days of hacking it would take to unravel a detailed web of deception."

"I'd rather track hands-on anyway," I said, still not buying into this whole online world bullshit.

Slade just shook his head at me, but he didn't try and change my mind. We were similar in so many ways that it was almost scary, but our upbringings had obviously created more than a few differences also.

"Location is just up ahead," Slade murmured, his voice much lower.

I expected to find a building or sign of habitation but there was still only wilderness. "You're sure this is where you pinged the heavy power usage?" I asked when we stopped, basically right on the coordinates.

Slade's gaze narrowed as he perused closer. "Absolutely. I checked it twice. Which is once more than usual, since I'm rarely wrong."

Striding out in a wide perimeter, I used every extra sense I possessed to figure out what we were missing. "The previous two locations showed immediate reasons for their power registering so high," I called back to my twin as I spun in a circle. "But this… makes no sense. It might be magically shielded or an underground bunker?"

Only, where was the entrance?

Slade did his own sweep, his expression both focused and annoyed. "There's something hidden here," he said slowly. "I can feel the *otherness* on or under this land, but I can't figure out how to penetrate the veil that hides it. It must be magic, but usually dragons wouldn't be fooled by a spell when we stand in front of it."

Magic wasn't my expertise, outside of my innate dragon abilities. I did know our kind weren't susceptible to a lot of spells or normal witchy tricks. "Jewels knows us," I reminded him, "and thanks to Fletcher, has a lot of insider information. She's going to throw everything at this hiding place, especially if she has any of your essence remaining."

Stolen dragon energy was how she'd ambushed Slade in the street, and since Slade's essence was essentially mine, I would also be impacted.

"I'm sick of this bitch always being one step ahead," he snarled, his frustrations bleeding through. "I'm usually the most powerful, but lately I keep chasing my damn dragon tail. I've even screwed up a few times, which never fucking happens. Hence the reason I checked the coordinates twice."

"Jewels knows you too well," I said, wishing I could wrap my hands around that witch's throat and squeeze until her head popped off. *So fucking satisfying.* "You were always fighting a losing battle with her, especially after you dismissed her as a threat long ago. You know everything now, though, which means letting go of your self-anger and moving forward to take her down."

I didn't beat myself up for mistakes. I simply moved forward and never made that mistake again.

My pep talk didn't ease his furious expression, but his essence was lighter. "Maybe we need Constantine for this?" he said, giving the area another glance. "If it's magic, he's our best chance of sensing it."

"Yeah, I don't think it would hurt to bring him in to help." We were running out of time, and if this curse came to pass, my dragon would hit the self-destruct button and wipe all of us from this world. He'd never allow me or any of his pack to be caged by magic.

Not even Fletcher did that to me.

If I needed to shift, I never had to ask permission. Within the compound grounds, of course.

"Come on, let's do a quick aerial search again, then I'll contact Hunter and get them out here." Slade stripped off his clothes in quick, succinct movements, and I ditched mine as quickly. When the items were packed in the bag, I called on the change.

*Can you scent the magic in this form?* Slade asked as we lifted off from the land. *It's stronger.*

Circling above him, I took my time to really breathe in the area, noting a faint buzz of static electricity in the air, along with the sulfur of spells. *There's definitely more going on here than we can see.*

Fire spilled from Slade's mouth. *I can't find even the slightest crack in their shielding to take advantage of. It's got to be the most thorough shielding I've ever come across.*

*Agreed.* Even without an extensive knowledge of magic, I was aware that there was always a point of origin with a spell. It was this point you needed to start unraveling the spell.

*Jewels has to be behind this*, I said, stretching my wings out, which were strong and sure even with our hours of flying today. *She's the only one with enough power for this.*

*Yes, it's looking more likely. We need to figure out how they have power hooked up here, hidden beneath the shielding. I have no idea how far we'd have to travel to find that source.*

I tilted my long neck to take in the silver glow. *My guess would be that city.*

Slade took off toward it, and though the sun was long gone, our vision remained clear. He banked toward the city, hovering over the power station on the edge of town.

*I wonder if they're drawing from here*, he said, examining it from all angles.

*Let's call Hunter*, I suggested. *We can investigate while they fly out to us.*

Slade's hesitation was strong, even in dragon form. *Just Hunter and Constantine, I think. We can't remove Emme from the protection of our house, now we know she can be attacked in her dreams.*

*Will she be safe there without all of us?*

Slade didn't answer immediately, and I was about to ask again, when he finally replied: *Okay, I managed to get a message through to Hunter, now that Emme has eased up on blocking us. He agreed that she should stay for now. She has Kellan and Finley, and as an extra, I'll keep the enforcers around the compound. I really believe we might have the location here, which makes Golden Claw the safer option.*

Emme would be pissed with us, but as long as she was safe, I didn't care. *Okay, we bring them out just to check what we're dealing with before we involve Emme.*

Slade rumbled his agreement. *We'll only be gone another day at most*, he said.

*We need this to be over*, I bit out, resigned to my fate for the next twenty-four hours. *We need the threat to be eliminated and our mate safe.*

Slade's wing brushed against mine, and it was weirdly comforting. *It will end one way or another. We're closing in. I can feel it.*

Part of me knew he was right, while another sensed it wouldn't be as easy as that.

It never was.

# CHAPTER 39

EMME

We were in the middle of dinner when Hunter lurched to his feet and grunted, "Fuck."

His gaze remained unfocused for about a minute, and then he shook it off.

Dropping my fork into the lasagna, I watched him closely. "What's wrong?" I asked, searching through my bonds for Slade and Talon, to find them flying around as they'd been most of the day.

Hunter leaned over and grasped my hand, his eyes thankfully stormy without any gold. "The twins might have found something, but it's being strongly shielded. They want me and Constantine to head for Silver City and help them investigate."

Constantine, who'd managed to make it to dinner, stumbled to his feet as well. He looked exhausted, as if he was already at the end of his magical strength, but there was no lack of determination to help. "Whatever you all need," he said, confirming my thoughts.

"We're coming too, right?" I asked, surging out of my chair.

Kellan snarled as he pushed to stand. "You can't leave us out, Daddy Alpha."

"Pack sticks together," Finley added as he too rose, bear rumbling in his chest.

Hunter sucked in long draws of air, his nostrils flaring with each inhale. "Normally I'd agree, but in light of the magical attack on Emme this morning, we think it's best if she remains here behind Constantine's wards. Until we know for sure what we're up against."

When I opened my mouth to protest, he wrapped his arms around me, bringing our bodies flush together. "The more time you spend out in the world, beyond our protections, the easier you're making it for Jewels to find you."

There was literally no rational reason for Jewels to be targeting me above the others. I'd never been her target before; it was always my pack she needed.

"I'm safest with you," I whispered, my mind rebelling at the thought of more than half my pack out there, beyond Golden Claw's protection.

Hunter held me so tight it was if our bones were imprinting, and I desperately committed the feel of him to memory. "I know, baby girl. I know we're stronger together, but this is just an exploratory mission. More than our house now being warded, here in Golden Claw, our borders are closed to any newcomers or witches. The entire enforcer branch and council would be informed if anyone breached it. We don't have that out in the open. Here, you are safer."

My father agreed with a swift nod. "Yes, I've done everything in my power to make this house the safest place for Emme in the world."

"What if Jewels attacks while the strongest of our pack is gone?" Finley asked, his expression calm though his eyes were tumultuous swirls of bronze and gold. "We already know she's keeping an eye on us through either her own spying technique or another traitor."

Hunter put space between us so he could face Finley. "The odds are that she won't leave her nest to try and take us down. There's no reason for her to risk it, when all she has to do is hide until this spell comes to pass."

I already knew we wouldn't be changing his mind, and I tried not to let my panic bubble into the bond. "How long will you be gone?"

"Not even twenty-four hours," he replied, and when he met my gaze, there was nothing but sincerity in his.

"Okay," I said, pressing my lips together so they didn't tremble. "Twenty-four hours, and not a second more. This is also a scouting mission and nothing else. I don't care if you find half the witch covens of America hidden out there, you don't attack without us. Not to mention all the allies you've been arming. You will not face this alone."

Hunter captured my face in his huge grip. "I promise, little omega.

We just need to eliminate this as a possible hiding place before we can move on to the next plan."

Hunter's intense stare held me captive, and I almost missed Kellan's question to Constantine. "Speaking of next plan, did the blood spell pick up anything?"

My father shook his head. "It wasn't quite finished when I came down here for dinner. I should go and check."

Hunter remained by my side as the witch-wolf raced from the room. "You stay close to Kel and Finley," he murmured. "They'll keep you safe."

"What about hockey?" I asked, letting myself rest against him in both need and exhaustion. "They have an early game tomorrow. Do I stay in the house or go with them?"

Hunter exchanged a glance with the boys, and whatever they mentally discussed didn't come through the bond. "Decide tomorrow," he finally said. "I think you're probably equally as safe in either scenario, with crowds versus being here alone. Make sure you sleep here though, when you're most vulnerable."

There was nowhere else I'd rather sleep than in this house that had quickly turned into a home. We all turned at the clap of boots when Constantine re-entered the room. "It pinpointed a spot near Silver City."

Hunter's face barely reacted, but I felt the flinch from his beast. "Exactly where Slade wants us to go."

My stomach lurched at the thought that they were walking into a trap. There were many likely reasons this was the spot Jewels and her minions were located, and I couldn't shake the feeling that all of us should be going. But for now, I'd play by their rules.

"Scouting only," I reminded him, and he acknowledged *my order* with a kiss. After clapping his hands on Kellan and Finley's shoulders, he headed out with Constantine. "Stay safe out there or I'll kill you," I shouted after them, and Hunter's chuckle followed him all the way from the room.

When they were gone, I sank into my chair, deflated. My wolf howled mournfully, and Kellan's joined in our quintet. "This sucks," he said, slumping down as well. "I understand why they're not taking all of us, but at the same time it feels wrong to split the pack during times of crisis."

Finley was brooding, staring down at his untouched food. "Golden

Claw is the safest place for Emme," he repeated, as if we all needed another reminder. "Jewels can't get within ten feet of its upgraded border security without setting off a million alarms. And it's only for twenty-four hours."

We'd worked overtime to convince ourselves this was a good idea, and I still wasn't convinced. Knowing I wouldn't be able to eat anything else I pushed my chair back from the table.

"We can't run in the forest, but I need to shift. Could we use the back yard?"

Kellan bounced to his feet and hauled me up to mine. "Yes! A little escapism into our beasts is exactly what the healer ordered."

In the yard, we stripped down, and my wolf surfaced so fast I knew it had been too long since I'd let her go free. Kellan's much larger beast crowded in on my right side, and Grouchy Bear guarded my left. We took off into the expansive yard, which was big enough to give the feeling of freedom, without any real dangers. It was much more enjoyable than circling a bedroom.

We ran for hours, until eventually we tumbled into the kitchen starving and exhausted. I patted one of Steven's leaves to say hello, and Finley chuckled, still pleased with his gift.

Florence and Gerald had already left by now, but I wasn't surprised to find our dinners in the oven, set to keep them warm. The lasagna was much more enjoyable the second time around, and I scarfed mine down so fast that only my healing abilities kept me from a scorched mouth and throat.

Kellan and Finley also ate their food in record time, then the three of us drowned our sorrows in cookies, popcorn, and hours of movies. "I'm going to need some lemon tarts," Kellan informed me as he sprawled back, pulling me across his lap, leaving Finley to hold my feet.

"Yeah, I love baking. It would be nice to do it again without the haze of trauma forcing my actions." Both alphas hugged me a little tighter, comforting me in the best of ways.

Halfway through a movie, Kellan, who'd been staring intently at me, completely uninterested in the animated film we were watching, tilted my head back for a kiss. And just like that, I also no longer cared how a French rat could cook.

The three of us got naked so fast that it made my head spin, and the boys took my mind off our missing pack members in a very, *very* pleasurable way. Later that night, as I crawled naked and sated into Kellan's bed, I quickly checked in with Hunter, Slade, and Talon.

*All of you alive and well?* I asked, my wolf moving closer to them. *I'm just about to jump into bed.*

*Safe and well. Goodnight, little mate,* Hunter rumbled. The caress of his beast against my wolf's flank was comforting.

*Sleep well, Emmeline Anders,* Slade said. *I will keep watch over you.*

*Love you, stalker,* I replied, my mumble barely making sense.

There was a deep, echoing purr from his dragon, and I wasn't going to give up on using that word with him. One day he'd say it back.

*I love you, Honey,* Talon told me, no hesitation. *We'll see you tomorrow. Sleep for all of us.*

Conscious thought vanished as I finally let go, snuggled between my alphas.

My dreams were filled with weird energy as my wolf tried to catch her pack, but there were no nightmares.

"You need some more cream on your tattoo," Finley told me early the next morning when I got out of the shower. "I also have time to fix those few lines and colors, if you want?"

"When do you have to be at the rink?" I asked, knowing it was a morning game today.

He glanced at his watch. "Not for another two hours, so we have time."

"Sure, let's do it, then."

Thus far the healing process hadn't been too onerous, and I knew the few tiny imperfections were bothering Finley—even though it looked spectacular to me.

"It'll be a good way to clear my mind before the game," he said, flashing twin dimples.

Kellan remained asleep as we headed for Finley's room.

On the way, I checked in with Hunter, Slade, and Talon. *Any updates? Did you get any sleep?*

*No sleep. We're focused on searching and returning to you,* Hunter replied, and his beast pressed right against me, both of us struggling with the distance. *We might have to backtrack from the origin, which appears to be Silver City.*

I couldn't fault them for being thorough, even though it pained me. *Don't forget your deadline to return home, Alpha.* I was only half joking. A desperate need to get all of my pack back together pummeled into my tight chest.

*I haven't forgotten, little omega,* Hunter replied, and even in our essence he sounded amused. *I'll keep you updated.*

When they pulled back from the bond, I let my beast drift in to semi-block our connection once more, leaving just enough to feel their strong essences.

In Finley's room, he got everything prepped, and I removed my bra and top. "It turned out even better than I hoped," he said as he brushed his gloved hand over the current design. "How have your pain levels been? I didn't pick up much through the bond."

"Truthfully, it's not too bad. I'm getting used to the slight numbness. I expect in a week or so, I won't notice it at all."

That pleased him, and he hummed thoughtfully. "Excellent. Okay, I'm about to start."

For the next hour, he finished up the edges, fixed some color and shading, and added extra details to keep his perfectionist heart happy. As he worked, he told me about his life with Kenzo, and how his family had saved him over the years. "You need to come to Kenz's for dinner one night," he said, brushing the now familiar soothing cream over the tattoo as he finished up. "His teppanyaki is next freaking level."

"Tonight?" I suggested. "After the game? We'll still be in the street at least."

I felt a surge of happiness from the bear so genuine and deep that I almost cried. It was beyond weird to feel emotions that weren't my own, and even weirder to be affected by them. But I loved knowing how happy his current life was making him.

"That would be amazing," Finley said, brushing a kiss across my cheek. "Now, have you decided if you're coming to our game or not?"

"I'm coming," I said, not wanting to be here by myself. "It's a good break from the house, and then we'll all be back later this evening."

Along with the rest of our pack. Goddess willing.

# CHAPTER 40

EMME

The atmosphere in the crowd of a hockey game would never get old. The boys personally escorted me to our usual section, informed security to keep an eye on me and that no one except family was to sit there, then reluctantly left me with hugs and kisses.

"Kassidy is joining me soon," I reminded them, but it didn't ease up their pained expressions.

"Lucky we can keep an eye on you via our bond," Finley said in a low rumble near my ear. "Don't close the connection tightly, Ice."

"I won't," I promised.

Neither of them took their eyes off me the entire way back into the tunnels, even as every shifter in the half-filled seats watched them like they were their gods. They knew better than to touch them though, and my boys made it through without incident.

On my own, I occupied myself with a decent case of overthinking and worry, while checking in with Hunter and the twins. I found their beasts relaxed, as if waiting for something. Deciding to leave them be, I didn't push into the bond. They'd better only be doing a recon mission though, or they'd have one pissed off omega on their hands.

When the warmups started, Kellan and Finley were all but plastered to my side of the arena, doing their groin stretches while eyeballing the heck out of me.

*That's a weirdly intimate level of eye contact when you're ass up and dick down like that, boys.*

When that thought reached their beasts in the bond, Kellan's bark of laughter could be heard even over the noise of the crowd. *I would like to dick you down right now, Shortcake.*

Finley's bear stepped closer to my wolf, and I nuzzled against his side.

*You're not playing fair,* I said, *while I can do little more than window shop in the hockey aquarium.*

This time it was Finley's rumble of laughter that could be heard through the arena. *No more window shopping for you, Ice. You've already made your selections... We're bought and claimed.*

Yes, they were.

*Mine.* The thought rumbled through my beast and into theirs, and I was immediately buried under a bear and wolf pile until I was surrounded in their scents.

There was a burst of chocolate and honey from me, and I wiggled in my chair as shifters turned, their nostrils flaring.

*You're a damn candy store,* Finley growled, and the slam of his hand against the glass had all the curious faces jerking away. *And I don't like the way they're looking at you.*

Kellan joined him at the side. *Don't make us come up there and steal you away, pretty mate. 'Cause I don't give a fuck about hockey right now.*

Narrowing my eyes on him and his relentless stare, I shook my head slowly. *Stay down there and win for me today. Like. Good. Boys.*

Kellan's growl turned into a groan, and I had to cover up my smile when he shifted his hand over his groin. Finley shook his head, but he was smiling again. *Mission accomplished.*

Kellan got straight back into stretches, wearing the most adorable sexy smirk the whole time. It was nice to feel his lighthearted side return in our bond, especially as he started to loosen up and create havoc with his teammates out there. Finley and Kellan were both wavering about whether they could continue their careers, but I didn't want them to give it up.

Not when it clearly still gave them joy, and...

*Abs,* Kellan suggested, keeping up with my thoughts.

I covered my laugh with my hands, so I didn't look like a crazy shifter chuckling away to myself. *As much as I enjoy your ab muscles, Golden Boy, they're not more important than your happiness. That's what I couldn't live without.*

Kellan skated into the center of the rink with Finley right beside him. *You'll never have to live without either, Shortcake. The abs and the happiness are here to stay.*

Warmth washed through the bond, and despite more than half my pack missing, I was content and enjoying the moment.

Hunter's wolf moved in closer to me, and I opened the bond a little more. *We might have found the original source of the shielding*, he said. *We'll confirm it before heading home.*

*Amazing*, I replied. *As long as you're not taking unnecessary risks, then do what you need to find that fucking witch.*

There was a brief pause. *We will come home to you, little omega. Cheer our boys on for us.*

His wolf nuzzled against mine, and that contentment from before grew until I could have curled up in the warmth and taken a nap. *I will. Stay safe.*

Our beasts eased apart right when the wolves left the ice for the short interval before the game got underway. When my stomach growled, I debated if it was too early for beer and nachos. It wasn't lunchtime yet, but it was a game ritual at this point, and no one liked to mess with those. Finley still wore underwear with my face on them, and I always ate nachos when I was here. We couldn't mess with the ritual.

No one touched me as I moved through the crowd, and it wasn't my imagination that the security kept me firmly in their line of vision, most of whom looked like enforcers. When I got into line, I remembered that I hadn't grabbed cash or card before leaving the house; I was so used to being with my pack, who just paid for everything. My alphas were spoiling the independence right out of me.

*We have an account at the stadium*, Hunter said, slipping closer once more.

With the connection remaining semi-open, thoughts crossed unintentionally at times. *That's good to know*, I told him. *At least I won't have to sell my firstborn or soul for food now.*

Hunter didn't find that remotely amusing, his wolf stalking forward to prod at the tip of my snout. *No one will ever touch your soul or our pups. Not even for nachos, Emmeline.*

Snorting under my breath, I drew attention, but everyone looked away just as quickly when they realized who I was. The scariest of my pack weren't even here, but their reputations preceded them. No one wanted to be on their bad side, not if they could help it.

*You should focus on finishing up what you're doing, entitled alpha. You don't have long to make it back and stay within your deadline.*

I felt his possessive touch against my throat, despite the fact that he was half the damn country away from me. *I'll make it in time, mate.*

*I'm holding you to that.* Wanting him to keep his focus, I moved back in the bond again, stitching just a little more shielding between us. Hunter's wolf backed up too, and I felt his attention shift elsewhere.

The intro music started loudly around us, which meant there were less than two minutes until the first players were announced. Thankfully, I was almost to the front of the line. Around me, shifters chatted excitedly about the team, most of them wearing Celtic colors, but there were a couple in the purple, green and white of the other team.

As I shuffled toward the front of the line, a familiar scent closed in on me, and I turned to find Kassidy. "Ah," I said as she threw her arms around me. "It's so great to see you."

When I'd done my daily check of my phone to ensure Cora hadn't replied to a message, I'd had a text from Kassidy saying she'd be here today. None from Cora of course.

"I wasn't going to come, but I didn't want you sitting here alone." Her gaze darted to the ice, and she looked relieved that none of the players were out yet.

"Have you spoken to him?" I asked, knowing who she was afraid to see.

Her cheeks reddened, which only highlighted how drawn the rest of her looked. Kassidy was always gorgeous, but today her skin was paler and there were dark circles under her eyes. She looked like she hadn't slept in days. "No. I can't. I know if I let him in, it'll change everything."

Reaching out to grasp her hand, I squeezed it briefly. "Maybe it could be a good change though? I do understand all too well the fear holding you back. I've been there with my pack, and I almost let it cost me the best days of my life. For me, even if I had died from this bonding, the time I've had with my alphas would have made it worth it."

Kassidy's eyes were shiny as she murmured, "It's not my death I worry about."

We reached the front of the line and gave our orders, putting everything on the Reeves' account. "Thanks, big brother," Kassidy said as she blew a kiss into the air.

Hunter hated that his sister refused to let him financially help her, but she was an independent shifter who stood on her own two feet. Their sibling bond was pure, and I loved that they had each other.

In our seats, we shoved the first delicious bite of corn chip into our mouths as the stadium lights dimmed, and a colorful strobing effect filled the arena. The crowds screamed and cheered, and except for our empty row, the place was packed. Not an empty chair in sight.

"We're heading into the end of the season and the most important games," Kassidy explained, leaning closer so I could hear her over the noise.

"I'm assuming the boys are doing well in the overall rankings?" I'd missed too many of their games, but I was sure they'd won a lot more than they'd lost.

She nodded, and I didn't miss the glow of pride in her tired features. "Oh yeah, they'll be in the top three going into the finals of the Shifter Cup. The elimination rounds kick off after their road trip."

*The road trip.* The boys still weren't sure they could even make it, especially if we were neck deep ferreting out a witch and her evil minions. My hope was that Hunter and the twins found the hidey hole, and we would be able to take them all down before they left next week.

We just needed one break.

When our team hit the ice, I was well into my nachos and ice-cold beer. During hockey was the only time I drank beer, and though I'd never been a real fan, it just worked here.

"It's weird how nervous I still get," I told Kassidy as I took a sip. "And they're so damn good at hockey, that I really have nothing to worry about."

Kassidy had just crammed a big bite of chips and guac in her mouth, so she chewed quickly and swallowed before answering. "It never goes away," she said, wiping her face with a napkin. "I used to watch Hunt compete in motocross trials, and damn I was always shitting myself. Just like with your boys, he was the best, but still… I'd be chewing my nails and tapping my knee for the entire race."

"I wish I could have seen that," I said, imagining Hunter flying on his bike. "Though I'd have been just as nervous."

She nudged me gently. "We could have been nervous together. I'd have liked that."

"Me too," I said, voice turning wistful.

When I first met Kassidy, I'd been worried that she would see me as an interloper in her family and hate me on principle. But she'd been nothing but welcoming. She'd opened her arms and accepted me without question, and I considered her to be one of my best friends now.

The game started fast, and it was immediately rough out there. I'd missed who we were against today, but whoever they were, they were out for blood and on the attack.

Kassidy's nachos lay forgotten in her lap as she leaned forward, her eyes trained on one shifter in particular. No matter how much she denied it, her beast's desire to be with her mate was going to force her to deal with him.

By the end of the first period, the score was one apiece. Though it felt like there should have been ten more points on our side with how many shots they'd had on goal. The other team's goalie was exceptional, and if I were the Celtic's coach, I'd have been poaching him for sure.

Not that ours was far behind, really.

As the players left the ice, a shadow fell over our chairs. I glanced up to find Warrick settling into the seat beside me. I blinked in surprise and elation, even though I wished he'd sat one seat away like he normally would. But I was too happy to see him to suggest it.

"I didn't know you were coming tonight," I said, taking in his bloodshot eyes and generally wrinkled and unkept appearance. "Is Cora okay?"

He nodded roughly, running a hand over his few days of beard growth. "Yeah, I just had to get out of the house and away from the grief." There was a rasp in his voice, as if he hadn't used it in days. "As I was driving, I remembered there was a game on, and knew you'd have these seats. I hope you don't mind."

"You're always welcome," I told him, relaxing only when he shifted a little to the left so we weren't touching. Without my alphas here, I wouldn't be touching another male, not unless it was to save his life.

Packs were sacred; you didn't touch another's mate without

permission. None of my guys had given Warrick permission, and thankfully he was respecting that.

We settled into a comfortable silence to watch the game, my hands clenched into fists on my thighs every time Finley and Kellan were out there. The game continued to be one of the toughest I'd ever seen them in, and when they were closing in on the third period, Warrick finally spoke up.

"Kellan and Finley will probably be in media for a couple of hours. Do you want me to give you both a ride home?"

"That'd be great," Kassidy said before I could answer. "I caught a ride here with a friend, but she's heading out afterwards, so I always planned to head home with Em and the boys."

I could feel her desperation to get out of here and hidden safely behind the compound's gates before Henderson cornered her. She'd come to keep me company, and since it was either go home with Warrick or wait in the locker rooms for the guys to finish up their interviews, I'd stick with Kassidy.

"Sounds good," I said, wondering if he'd answer any questions about Cora on the way home. At least a very brief update about how she was doing, along with Richard and Sierra.

The crowds erupted around us. In my distraction, I'd missed the other team managing to score right on the final buzzer. "Fuck," Kassidy snarled as the score flashed two to one on the Jumbotron. "What a messy game, and our boys still lost."

So much for the beer and nachos ritual. It was an extra betrayal when food let me down.

"They'll beat them next time," Warrick said with confidence, already standing. "Come on, let's get out of here before the crowds get crazy."

*I'm going to catch a ride home with Warrick*, I said into the pack bond. *He's going to drop Kassidy and me back to the compound so she doesn't have to deal with Henderson.*

Slade's reply came through immediately. *Sit in the back seat, Emmeline. You were far too close to him during that game.*

Ah, I loved that despite our new bond, my favorite stalker continued to keep an eye on me through whatever security system filled the stadium.

*I promise*, I replied.

*Just wait for us,* Kellan suggested, sounding a little breathless. That game had been brutal, and he was feeling it. *We won't be too long.*

*I'm going to try and talk to him about Cora,* I told them. *I'm worried about her, but I'll meet you at home.*

Finley's bear pushed forward. *We'll be home within the hour, Em. Coach doesn't need as much of our time as we initially thought.*

*Perfect.*

I had the drive home now to grill my friend about Cora, and hope that she was doing better than I expected.

# CHAPTER 41

## HUNTER

From the moment my plane taxied out of Golden Claw, my wolf had been uneasy, but after the blood spell pulled the same Silver City location, I knew this was our best chance to stop the witch.

To protect our mate.

When we landed on the private airstrip outside the city, Constantine and I shifted into our beasts to track Slade and Talon. He was a medium-sized ginger wolf, and while smaller than me all around, he was so fluffy that it gave the illusion of bulk. It was clear where Emme's gorgeous hair came from. The pair shared many similar traits, including the fact that both were wolves who could wield magic.

Their newly blossoming relationship was complicated, but there was hope for them. Constantine had made his decisions to keep Emme safe and protected the best way he knew how. Her suffering hadn't been part of his plan, and I sensed genuine remorse from him over what she'd experienced in those years with her mother. Hence the reason he was still alive.

I'd have taken him out without a second thought if he meant even the slightest harm to Emme. Slade and Talon probably two steps ahead of me.

As we crossed rugged terrain, his wolf slowed, and it was clear he didn't spend much time in this form. My beast disliked his weaknesses, but we also understood that he'd been working around the clock on the tracking spell and other shit, so we'd give him some grace.

When we reached Slade and Talon, we shifted back, and I pulled our jeans and shirts from my bag. We'd rushed out the door with nothing more than the clothes on our backs.

"Find anything?" I asked Slade as we got dressed. "I don't like being away from Emme for long, so we need to hurry the fuck up."

I'd already checked in on her multiple times through the bond, and while it was a relief to feel her safe with Kellan and Finley, I needed to be back there too.

"Agreed," Slade said. "We have found what we think might be the entrance to their hideout. We traced our way to the edge of the shielding, which is closer to Silver City."

Constantine did a little walk around, twirling his hands in small circles at his sides. "There's definitely a strong magical shield here," he confirmed. "Its old magic weaved in a distinct diamond pattern. Quite reminiscent of Termaine spelling." He regarded the dragons. "It's impressive that you found it, since they also buried most of it underground. The earth itself is our greatest magical interference when it comes to tracing spells."

"We're dragons," Talon said, and that was the whole statement. Nothing more needed.

Constantine's lips twitched, but he knew better than to laugh.

He focused on the ground once more, and then lowered himself so he could press his hands to the dirt. The sun had not quite risen yet, but I could see his focus clearly. "Definitely underground," he murmured as he stood. "Show me this origin point."

Without a word, the twins took off, and Constantine and I had to jog to catch up with them. It took us an hour to reach the outer edges of Silver City, the urban landscape spanning out in the distance. We were in an area with warehouses, similar to where we'd killed most of the Rogers pack a few months ago, even though we were on the opposite side of Silver City today.

Slade indicated we needed to head for a large, rusty-red building a few blocks from us. Everything here was secured behind chain-link fences, but we'd have no issue breaking through.

"My phone doesn't have the right apps for me to dig into who this lot belongs to," Slade murmured as we crept along, "but it stinks like the Rogers pack. In more ways than one."

I nodded, my beast rising to give me extra senses as we moved. "It has the same general look of their other one."

"The magical shield definitely originated here," Constantine whispered. His steps slowed as he tilted his head back. "Oh, there are guards at the entrance."

"We didn't get this close last time," Talon said as he crouched and waved for us to follow.

We ended up near a large bushy garden, blending into the shadows of early morning. From here, we could observe the six shifters positioned near the chain-link gate.

"There are witches too," Constantine murmured, angling his head to the right.

I followed his line of sight to find two females in a roughly constructed, wood-lined watchtower.

Okay, there were eight of them and only four of us, but when you had two dragons, it was like a hundred shifters. We could easily take them out. Still, we had promised Emme we wouldn't do anything risky, and if there were witches here, it was clear we'd stumbled onto something of significa—

My thoughts were cut off as Constantine leapt out from the garden and took off along the fence line. None of the guards had a chance to turn their damn heads before his magic blasted out with enough force that even from back here my beast reacted to the buzz. By the time we reached him, all the shifters were on the ground, and there was a thud as one of the witches fell out of the watchtower.

"Simple knockout spell," he said with a shrug. "They'll be out for at least the next twelve hours, since none of them were remotely prepared for a magical attack. No security or shielding around them at all."

Talon grunted. "That's an oversight which happens when you believe you have all the witches under your control."

Constantine could be the chink in Jewels' plan that she never saw coming.

Slade, who was already moving to hide the bodies, gave Constantine a nod when he started to help. And fuck, that was as much respect as I'd ever seen him show anyone outside of our pack.

Emme's father was winning over more than just me with his actions and willingness to help.

When the bodies were all out of sight, Talon destroyed the locks on the gate and we moved through, closing it after us. On the expectations there could be more security closer to the warehouse, we kept to shadows and trees, but didn't encounter anyone else. It was likely that those shifters weren't supposed to be grouped at the front but had been bored and wanted to chat. Jewels had grown sloppy in her confidence, and we would use every advantage to destroy her.

Inside the building, Constantine ambushed four more guards stationed in the entrance. Like the ones at the gate, they went down so quickly there was no way they'd had a chance to send out an alert. The witch in their ranks had hit the ground the hardest.

"How's your magic and energy levels?" I asked Constantine. "You were semi-drained coming into this recon mission."

I'd continue to call it recon, even as we skirted Emme's rules by entering the warehouse. But we needed to confirm that Jewels was here before we returned with the pack. And if by some chance we ended up facing her today, we would deal with it. Maybe it would be better that way, never having to bring the most precious piece of our quintet into danger.

Constantine waggled his shoulders, as if he was tense. "I'm fine. So far there are no magical protections on these guards, so it's taking almost none of my strength to knock them out. I might only be a half-breed, but I'm from an original magical line."

Slade grunted and waved the witch-wolf on, since he was so far the most adept at silently taking out the guards. He didn't even need to get that close to them.

"The warehouse is a cover," I noted, glancing around the empty space. "They're not using this area for anything, but there's security here? There's no way this isn't her safe house."

It took us close to an hour to find the hidden entrance that led below ground, and when we stood before the dark hole, Slade met my gaze. I already knew what he was going to say—even before the full quintet bond we'd often been on the same wavelength. "You want to get closer and see what we're up against, don't you?"

His response was immediate and without hesitation. "What if we can take these fuckers out now and never have to bring our omega even remotely close to danger? All of this magical protection… they have to be here. We know it, and we are the strongest members of our pack. We can do this."

My wolf twisted in my chest as we considered breaking our

promise to Emme. Slade spoke logic, and with two dragons and a witch-wolf by my side, I couldn't think of much that would take us down, but it still went against my instincts.

"Em, Kellan and Finley are strong," Talon said, as he stared at me, and I wondered if he could sense my indecision. "But they're not going to be much help to us here. We're the ones who can stop this and keep our pack safe, unless of course we tap into Emme's essence, and we don't want to do that."

As our entitled alpha, my entire fucking reason for existence was to keep my pack safe. I cared little for the rest of the shifter world, but for my family I'd step over every moral line that existed.

"Let me put out a call to our allies," I said, needing a compromise that Emme might be able to live with. After the fact of course, as we couldn't run this by her in advance. "We have a dozen or more allies in Silver City, already outfitted to fight magic and enforcers."

Slade held his phone out since I'd left mine on the plane, and I dialed the one shifter I knew would take care of it for me. She answered on the second ring, and I wasted no time on pleasantries.

"Casey, it's Alpha Hunter. I need you to send out these coordinates to the Silver City allies." I rattled them off and then paused for her to read them back to me correctly. "That's it," I said. "Tell them we need them to head this way, outfitted for battle."

"On it, boss."

When she hung up, I had no doubts that backup would be here soon. My assistant was proficient and would not let us down.

"What if we aren't strong enough on our own?" Constantine asked, looking between us. "Emme is going to be so upset that we took this risk without her. I don't want to lose my daughter again. She's only just starting to trust me."

Slade rumbled. "We're strong enough. And as long as Emme is alive, I don't care if she hates us. It won't last forever. One day she'll understand that we will burn everything down to keep her safe, even ourselves."

It was the truth, but I also knew Emme wouldn't want to live without us. Which was what made her so fucking precious. No one had ever loved us the way she did, and we would fight literally the entire world to just feel her soft touch one more time.

Constantine didn't argue, but his concerned expression remained. We all stood at the top of the stairs that disappeared down into the unknown. This was where the shielding really started, and the bursts of magic against our skin were painful.

"You weren't kidding about the earth dulling magic," Talon muttered. A fluttering of scales slithered over his arms before he got his beast under control again.

"It's one of the most thorough blankets I've ever experienced," Constantine said, the unease from his expression creeping into his voice. "Do you plan on waiting for the backup before we go down there?"

Slade didn't bother to answer him, and I wouldn't have been surprised to find that whatever respect the witch-wolf had garnered with his earlier actions was gone now under his hesitation. The dragons feared nothing and no one, and when their mate's life was on the line... He would not wait any longer.

Checking on Emme once more, I found her safe and in Finley's chair, getting her tattoo finished. Their game was an early one today, and I'd already arranged for Kassidy to be there.

If Emme decided to go, she wouldn't be alone.

"Let's just get closer," Slade suggested, his movements uncharacteristically agitated. "We need to know what we're up against. We need to find that witch and destroy her."

My brother was untethering under the threat to his pack, and I already knew he'd destroy half this warehouse if we didn't do something. "Okay, we can move closer, but we don't attack until our backup arrives."

That way I could promise Emme we did everything in our power to win this battle.

Slade agreed with a nod, already striding down the stairs. We all followed behind, and Constantine cast a very dim light above us, which I didn't think we'd need until we were in the narrow tunnel that had been carved into the rock. Down here, the darkness was like a black hole, as if all light had been swallowed.

It took us over an hour to reach the end of the tunnel, and the magic stench was thick enough that we knew it had been constructed by witches. No doubt above our heads would be the very spot we'd met Talon and Slade before; right on the co-ordinates of the power usage Slade had been tracking.

"They're just beyond here," Slade whispered as he came to a halt.

"How many?" I asked softly.

"A lot of them."

Talon pushed in behind me. "What is the plan?"

None of us were using our bond, in case Emme picked up on it, so we had to huddle close and keep our voices low.

"We should wait," I said, infusing my entitled alpha power into my voice. "We cannot risk being outnumbered and not making it back to Emme."

Slade huffed but didn't argue as he leaned against the wall. "Okay. Let's conserve our energy while we wait." He did pull out his phone, and somehow even underground, managed to figure out how to log into a network and check on Emme at the hockey.

"Fucking Warrick," he muttered, right before he stashed his phone again.

"Is Slalon ready?" I asked as I joined him against the wall, forcing my muscles to relax.

Talon answered first. "We're not perfect, but we're working well together."

"We're ready," Slade rumbled softly, the hint of his annoyance still strong. "We'll be enough."

Holding on to that, we all fell silent, our breaths the only noises to infiltrate this desolate tunnel as we waited. Checking in with Emme kept me entertained, as she fully enjoyed herself at the game.

Long after my skin grew icy, and my beast moved restlessly in my chest, the silence was broken by footsteps. We tensed as we waited to see if this was our backup, or those associated with Jewels. When a familiar tea tree scent filtered through, I relaxed and nudged Constantine.

"Light," I murmured. He'd extinguished it when we'd waited here, in case anyone stumbled in or out of the tunnels.

When it flared to life in his palm, I found myself staring at a familiar face. "Will," I said, keeping my voice low. Behind him were dozens of faces, all of them outfitted in Reeves industry tech.

He lifted a bag he'd been carrying and shoved it at me. "Your assistant said you might need some extra gear." The quieter his voice got, the stronger his German accent grew. "We brought all we had."

"Thank you," I said as I took the gear. "If we get out of this shithole alive, remind me to give Casey a bonus."

Constantine and I strapped vests on and pocketed weapons, but the dragons declined. "We'll be shifting," Slade said shortly.

Will nodded, and the bag with the extra gear was left in the hallway at our feet. "You believe this is where the witch is holed up?"

"We do," I said, adrenaline starting to course through me. "We haven't confirmed it, but if Jewels is here, we cannot let her escape. This might be our only chance."

Will's expression was one of determination, no concerns visible. It was harder to see the others, but none of them backed away. "We're here to fight by your sides and save shifters from her curse. Whatever happens, we won't bail on you. Lead the way."

Slade took off, as if he'd barely been holding himself back all of this time. We followed just as fast, and when the tunnel narrowed, we had to move nearly single file to make it through. At the entrance to the bunker or whatever was down here, Slade took out additional security, leaving their dead bodies off to the side.

The entrance was blocked by a heavy door with bright lights on either side of the entrance.

"That explains the power," Talon noted, and I wondered how the hell they'd managed to make this happen. There was no way this had been constructed in the days since the street attack. This was years in the making, even if it had only recently come into use.

The door opened easily to reveal an entrance, already lit up to showcase a wall of weapons. Mostly knives, daggers, and axes. There were also a ton of boots and shoes scattered below.

It remained well-lit as we pushed on, and when we entered the first real room, I almost lost control of my beast at the sheer fucking size of it. The round space spanned out for at least a mile in all directions, with camp beds surrounding the full perimeter. Bedside drawers in between each bunk.

Some of the beds were occupied with sleeping shifters and witches, blissfully unaware that there was an enemy in their midst. Silently, we moved forward, and following our noses, found ourselves in an area containing an industrial kitchen and dining facility.

A dining facility filled with at least fifty shifters, and almost as many witches.

At our appearance, everyone turned to us, and silence descended so fast it was eerie. A low laugh rang out, and from the middle of the tables stepped a far too fucking familiar shifter.

Blaine's grin was lopsided and too large. It made him look even more unhinged than usual. "Well, well, look who stepped right into the fucking shit." His gaze moved between us and our allies. "Jewels was really hoping you'd be stupid enough to try and track her using me. I'm happy to see that she was right. Again."

My gut clenched hard at the thought that Jewels wasn't here, that this was no more than another one of her traps… another plan to take us out. We were vastly outnumbered, especially if you considered how many shifters and witches had been sleeping in the previous room.

"Destroying you, and all of her sycophants, was on our to-do list anyway," Slade said in a calm, unruffled voice. "I'll be happy to tick that one off today."

Blaine threw his head back in another laugh, like that was the funniest joke he'd ever heard. "You might have some immunity to magic, but I have every damn witch left in this country. You cannot take on their collective power."

Slade shuffled us back into the room with the beds, needing the space to shift into Slalon. All of the shifters and witches got to their feet and started to follow.

"You're not going to run, right?" Blaine taunted. "After all your big talk of *ticking me off your to-do list*."

"Where's Jewels?" I asked in the hopes he'd monologue for a minute, so the twins had time to shift. Not to mention, it was still important information we needed. "Why did she leave you here to deal with us?"

Blaine's glee made my stomach swirl, and I fucking itched to tear his head off. "Ah, that's an amazing story. My favorite witch always has plan upon plan in place. In related news, where's your omega?"

At the mention of her name, I tapped into the bond, finding Emme still at the hockey game. She asked about going home with Warrick, and since I needed her safely in our house, I agreed.

"She's safe and sound at home," I told Blaine.

Slade's dragon drifted into her beast too, and then we both shut down the connection. We couldn't have her picking up on what was about to happen here. The air crackled strongly as the twins called on their energy to shift.

"It was brave of you to leave her home unprotected," Blaine said conversationally. "Not that we were surprised. We knew it would happen sooner or later… Especially after *that* dream."

"There's no way for Jewels to get to her," I snapped. "The entire town would be alerted the second she stepped into Golden Claw."

Blaine nodded, as if he completely agreed. "Oh yes, but there's just one little problem with that theory."

When he didn't continue, I clenched my hands and imagined his death. "What's the damn problem?"

Blaine paused. "The problem is…"

Magic exploded around us, and before he could finish, we were under attack.

# CHAPTER 42

## EMME

Warrick was quiet as we left the stadium, the mid-day light enveloping his Range Rover, and despite the packed stadium we managed to escape the crowds fairly quickly. Kassidy had taken the front seat, since I'd jumped in the back like Slade had *requested*.

My friend was tense. I could only assume it was due to seeing Henderson out on the ice today.

The quintet was quiet as well, and when I opened the bond to check on Hunter and the twins, all I picked up on was restlessness, like they were doing a lot of waiting around.

I didn't push any harder. As long as they were safe, I'd give them their privacy, since I expected my own in return. My wolf shifted uneasily but I kept her in place. *Leave them be. They'll check in when they're on the way home.*

In truth, unless Hunter was already on the plane, I doubted he'd make it back within the twenty-four-hour timeframe. But he was still trying to keep his promise, and that mattered as much to me as him making it in time.

When Warrick's phone rang, I jumped about three feet in the air. "Hey, love," he said as he answered, and my heart stuttered when Cora's voice sounded through the speaker.

"Mate, are you on your way home?" she asked softly. "I don't want to be alone any longer, and Richard and Sierra have already gone to their wing."

Warrick shot me a side-eyed glance, and then to my surprise said, "Would you be up for a little company? I could bring two of your lovely friends home with me."

Kassidy shifted to the side, staring at Warrick with a semi-hopeful expression.

There was a long pause, and I tried not to get my hopes up too.

"Actually, yes," Cora finally said, her voice faint. "That would be amazing. I've missed them."

I had no idea how she knew it was us, since Warrick hadn't mentioned our names. Maybe he'd already told her that he sat with us at the hockey, not that I'd seen him grab his phone, but I had been focused on the ice.

Warrick silently asked me if that was okay by lifting one eyebrow and jerking his head. I nodded, desperate to finally see Cora.

"Okay, we'll be home in ten or fifteen," he said, and after a brief pause added, "Put some pants on please."

My heart soared when Cora let out a low laugh. "Can't make any promises. You know how I feel about pants. See you soon."

When the call ended, there was a slightly more upbeat vibe to Warrick's demeanor as he picked up speed, changing directions to head for his house.

"I know we can't possibly understand what you and your pack is going through," Kassidy said, still facing him. "But we're always here to help, even if it's just to get you groceries, or take you out driving so you have a few hours escape. Rely on us."

Warrick's voice was raspy when he answered. "Thank you. It's honestly hard to describe the pain, as it's more than emotional. The physical loss of one of our quintet has destroyed parts of all of us, and while Marcus wasn't the heart of the bond, and we're not all scent matches, it still hurts."

It was lucky he wasn't the heart, otherwise all of them could have died from the loss of the one who bonded them.

"Has it been worse for Richard and Sierra?" I asked softly. "In the way of bond sickness over this loss?"

His nod was jerky. "Yeah, they've been very weak. We feared we might lose them too, as their beasts struggled to deal with their loss."

"I wish there was something we could do to help with that," I said, my heart aching at the very thought of them living through such pain.

Warrick turned and shot me a sad smile. "What you're doing today will help. Cora needs you. We both do." And yet neither of them had even returned a single message since that day in our street.

When he drove into their familiar cul-de-sac, I was reminded of all the times I'd showed up here and gotten turned away by their new security. Today, there were no enforcers, and I finally made it near the house.

Seeing their gorgeous home reminded me of my first days in Golden Claw. I'd been filled with fear and uncertainty, half expecting to be drained of all my essence by the powerful alpha pack I'd found myself part of. A lot had changed since then, and it was so unfair that for this pack it was a change for the worst.

Before his car had even stopped in the drive, I was already out of the car, ready to see Cora.

She stood in the open doorway, wearing a plain blue dress, her face washed out, and dark circles under her eyes. But her smile was warm, if not a little wonky.

"Cores," I murmured, racing up the stairs so I could wrap my arms around her.

She remained tense in my hold for a few seconds, but I wasn't bothered by that. I just kept holding her until she eventually relaxed, her soft sobs ripping through her.

"I missed you, friend," I murmured.

Her sobs grew louder, and when Kassidy's arms came around both of us, we rocked Cora back and forth until she no longer cried. When she pulled away, her eyes were red and puffy. She looked as beautiful as always, but there was a strong sense of fatigue about her, as if grief had worn her too thin.

When she backed up through the doorway, she gestured for us to follow. As I stepped over the threshold she whispered, "I'm really sorry."

There'd been not a single scent of magic until I entered through the doorway, and as the energy encased me full bodily, it was clear her apology was about far more than ignoring all my messages.

"Kassidy, run!" I yelled, but it was too late.

She'd followed me inside, and when I tried to rush out the door again, I was flung backwards by the strong magical essence.

"What did you do?" I croaked, staring at Cora.

Warrick, who'd just stepped inside, closed the front door. Not that it mattered, since we couldn't exit even when it was open. Shivers raced over my skin, and I was struggling to catch my breath. This reminded me of the place in Silver City where I'd been trapped with Slade, and my wolf was howling at the constrictions on us.

"The witch has held us captive from almost the moment she attacked the street," Warrick said, voice near inflectionless. His eyes were dark pits, and there was none of his usual warmth in those shiny depths. "We can only leave when she allows it. We can't bring in outsiders. We are virtual prisoners."

"Why are we here, then?" Kassidy snarled, her gaze darting around as she searched for additional threats. Her dominance was spilling out into the space, but it just bounced back off the shielded walls.

Tingles raced into my hands as my magic reacted to the heavily spelled house, but when I tried to use the quintet bond to reach my pack, all I got was a staticky interference. Our beasts were frozen in place, and no matter how hard I tried to reach them, I kept getting shot back.

Before I threw my full effort into destroying that interference, a tiny blond witch appeared. My world tilted lopsided for a beat, but I recovered almost instantly, snarled and backed closer to Kassidy.

"Jewels," Kassidy raged, and even I almost fell under the spill of her wolf's strength. "They lured us here today to deliver us right to the fucking witch."

I found the strength to glare at Warrick and Cora, who clung to each other near the doorway. Oddly, their expressions were not triumphant. They looked devastated.

No that it mattered. Betrayal was betrayal, whatever way you sliced it.

"You both should have just died at the witch's hands," Kassidy told them, and in that moment she sounded like her brother. *Hunter.* My wolf whined louder than I'd ever heard, and I wanted to join her.

"You know her pack will kill you anyway," Kassidy finished with a huff.

Warrick met both our gazes, and the fact that fucker had the balls to do so when his shameful stare should have been planted on the ground, had red flashing across my vision.

"She holds the rest of our pack, and will kill my twin," he said shortly. "As much as I care about Emme and her pack, I don't care about them more than my own blood. I'm sorry, but there was no other choice."

That had another snarl ripping from my chest. "As I said to Chelsea, who is dead from her betrayal, there's always a choice. You could have let us know what was happening and allowed us to fight with you. You sat in our damn dining room and pledged your allegiance to us."

Jewels' husky laughter cut off his response. "Ah, as if I would have allowed him to tell you of my plan. They're completely under my control, just as all shifters will eventually be. This was a nice little experiment, and I'm happy to report it was a roaring success."

Cora was pleading with me, her eyes filled with tears, but I couldn't bring myself to soften. Right now, I needed to focus on getting Kassidy and myself out of here before we became Jewels' next victims.

"You've been here since the curse was cast?" I asked the witch, needing to buy time until I figured out a plan.

Kellan and Finley would realize soon enough that I wasn't at home, and they'd come right here to Warrick's. But I didn't want them trapped by this psycho either.

In a magical fight, they had very few defenses.

"I figured the safest place to hide was right under your noses," she said, sounding properly pleased with herself. "I stashed all of my witch and shifter allies in another area, knowing that would be where you'd search, while I remained here."

I had no doubts that Hunter, the twins, and my father were in the location of her magical allies.

"Why did you bring me here, then? All you had to do was wait out the rest of the curse and we'd be fucked. None of us thought for a second you'd remain in the city, hidden within the very securities designed to keep you out."

It really had been the ideal hiding spot, which meant she'd only break it for a very serious reason. She'd sent Warrick out to bait the hook, and then Cora called to reel me in. It was a perfectly laid trap and I'd walked right into it.

But what was the reason?

Jewels took a step forward, and I hated that she still looked gorgeous. Dressed completely in black, she was vibing psycho-magic-Barbie, all blond, tiny and evil.

"I honestly wasn't sure if I'd get the opportunity to separate you from your pack," she said, and the smug smile on her face had unease fluttering through me. "But thankfully, with a little hint from Warrick and a bit of a dream to scatter your forces, you all finally followed the breadcrumbs I laid out for you."

She'd orchestrated the search near Silver City, which had been Warrick's suggestion.

"Why am I here?" I repeated, gritting my teeth so hard my gums ached.

Her empty smile grew, and when she no longer bothered to put on an act, it was clear how soulless she really was. She held up a finger. "One: your pack is the only ones who can stop this curse from coming to pass. It was partly their energy and Fletcher's that initiated the curse, and they are essential in destroying it."

I shook my head. "But no one can stop it once the curse comes to pass. All you had to do was stay hidden in this perfect spot. We trusted our friend's odd behavior was just from grief."

Jewels waved that finger at me. "Who told you the curse could only be stopped before it came to pass? It can be stopped at any time by the energy which cast it." She shrugged. "It's just easier before it's enacted."

My heart stuttered in a few weird beats as I wrapped my head around that. Constantine had either lied to us, or he'd been unaware.

"So you need to take them out no matter what?" I whispered, and whatever fear and unease I'd felt before was a thousand-fold now. She would never stop coming after my pack.

Jewels nodded, forcing a fake pout on her full lips. "Yes, and those silly dragons are far too strong together. I knew I should have had them killed young, but I let my sentimentality get the best of me, thinking they'd be great lovers and allies one day."

My wolf raged in my chest, and I barely stopped from shifting.

My magic on the other hand, slipped out before I could stop it.

Jewels lifted a second finger. "And that brings us to reason number two why you're here. You are their mate, the heart of the quintet, and if you die… they will all die."

A third finger lifted. "Even if that wasn't the case, you've just confirmed what I sensed the day you secured your quintet bond. You're an abomination of wolf mixed with witch. You cannot be allowed to survive, so it's a win-win for me to destroy you."

All along, the spy had been Jewels, in this city, stalking our steps. And she knew what I was now. Fletcher had kept me a secret for his own gain, but that secret was out.

Kassidy gawped at me, her eyes wide and glassy. *Magic,* she mouthed, and I swallowed roughly with a brief nod.

I had magic, and I was the heart of this quintet, which meant my entire pack was in danger. Not even dragon genetics could survive the death of the heart of a quintet when we were bonded close enough to mentally communicate.

Jewels was right in saying if she took me out, she'd take them all out.

# CHAPTER 43

SLADE

The explosion of magic from the witches had me drawing on my own energy to connect with Talon's. The joining of our dragons already felt like second nature, even though we'd only had days to practice.

When we stopped fighting the process, the bonding was seamless.

Parts of our minds melded as one, while other parts remained independent. This was different to the first shift when we'd had no cohesiveness and our left and right sides kept trying to move in different directions.

As our enemies rushed toward us, our allies fanned out behind our huge form, instinctively understanding that we offered the best protection from the spells. We moved forward, and I was relieved to feel our essences blending even more seamlessly than they had the last time we'd trained. This unity amplified our strengths, until we were nearly indestructible.

Flames burst from both our heads, blasting back the front line of our enemies. We turned our left head in a wider arc, and the right we moved forward.

*This is a waste of our time,* Talon growled. *Jewels is not here, and we're being forced to destroy any who might be able to lead us to her.*

*They'll never betray her,* I reminded him. *Better that we relieve her of allies. There are powerful shifters and witches here, and we can't have them back her up when we do find her.*

We blasted through another group, more spells bouncing off us, and while some of them left a mark, it wasn't enough to slow us down. Off to the side, Hunter had given up on fighting in his human form and had shifted so his beast could tear shifters to pieces.

So far we'd managed to keep this battle from slipping through the bond to Emme. Our quintet was locked down hard, and her beast wasn't stirring at all. The urge to push into her stasis was strong, just to confirm she was okay, but then I'd lose focus on the battle. Or worse, cause her panic as she felt our fight.

We might have broken our promise to her, but she'd forgive us eventually, provided we all returned unharmed. Hence the need for focus.

Hunter wasn't the only one battling. Constantine sent out waves of magic, while darting behind our body for cover. He apparently liked to fight dirty, his spells leaving his victims writhing on the ground, bleeding from every visible orifice.

The rest of our Silver City allies used Reeves Industries weapons, and while none of them had shifted, they weren't without solid fighting skills. A few had already gone down under spells, and it bothered me to see our allies fall, but there was nothing I could do.

If we didn't give our attention to thinning the numbers, all of us would go down.

More shifters and witches poured into the underground bunker's large, main chamber. In sheer numbers, they had us beat fifty to one, but in the power scale…

We were *always* on top.

Blaine, for all of his early bravado, remained at the back of the group, watching his allies fall one by one. As we crushed their front line, some of the witches and shifters started to back away, but we didn't let them retreat. They'd chosen their path, and now they would die on it.

We pushed harder into the group, using our tail to swing in a massive arc, shattering shifters against the walls. Just when we were starting to make some real headway, Hunter let out a pain-filled roar and our beast bellowed with him. A witch and wolf had teamed up against him, one using magic to hold him, while the bear sank his enhanced claws into my brother's chest, dangerously close to his heart.

We couldn't blast our fire without hitting Hunter, and any attempt to dislodge the bear would only dig those claws in deeper.

*We need to split,* I barked at my twin. *I have to be in my human form to help Hunter.*

Talon accepted this change of plan with the same ease as he accepted most of my orders. I was the older twin, and the only alpha in the world he'd take orders from without question. Not even Hunter had that power.

When our energy separated, it left me briefly disoriented. No amount of practice had eased that transition yet, and I had to ride it out until my brain stopped rattling in my head searching for its twin.

When I reached Hunter, he was motionless on the ground, but I caught sight of his hand gripping the bear, scarcely keeping it from carving out his heart completely. My vision went red on the edges, and the dragon was raging for a kill as we gripped the bear around the throat and broke his neck in one flick of our wrist.

Hunter's breaths were ragged as he stared up at me. His chest was even more destroyed than I expected. That much visible muscle and bone was beyond a shifter's healing, even one as strong and dominant as Hunter.

"Let me try," Constantine said, appearing at my side. I took in his pale, drained features and knew he was running on fucking nothing. But he was our only chance to save Hunter, so I'd take whatever he had left, even if he died in the process.

Talon remained in his dragon form, shifting his bulk to block us, though he wouldn't be able to hold them back for long. "Heal him," I demanded, my voice shot to shit.

There were only three shifters in existence that if I lost, I would lose myself.

Hunter was one of them.

Constantine flinched at my tone, recognizing how far beyond sanity and rational thought I was. Heat spilled from his fingers, and I found myself pushing into the bond to see if Emme was reacting to Hunter's grave injury. Only, her wolf was still not moving, so unnaturally motionless that upon my focus, I knew she was in the middle of some shit too.

Instinct and logic told me that our arrival here had triggered another attack in Golden Claw. Jewels wasn't here, which meant she had to have been there all along. In our fucking city.

No amount of dragon strength could break through the energy that held our quintet, not even to reach Kellan or Finley. Emme was our heart, and whatever controlled her had our whole quintet locked down.

My shredded clothes remained where I'd shifted, and I decided to find my phone, in the hopes of accessing security or contacting someone. "Don't stop healing him until his alpha strength kicks in," I warned Constantine, the witch-wolf so pale he almost glowed.

"I won't," he promised breathlessly, and I nodded my respect.

*Keep blocking them*, I ordered Talon, racing through the crowd, crashing my lethal fist into any who got into my way. *Something is up with Emme and I need my phone to check in with Kellan and Fin.*

Talon's dragon roared out his fury. *I can't feel her in our bond*, he bellowed through our twin connection, the only one still functioning. *We need to return to Golden Claw. She's in trouble.*

Finding my phone, I was relieved to see that the screen was only a little cracked. I took a second to scroll through my security apps, checking Golden Claw's perimeter, our house, and the stadium. *Golden Claw perimeters have not been breached. No magic. No witches. No unauthorized shifters.*

As I suspected, Jewels had been inside already.

Dialing Kellan's number first, and then Finley's, I got no response from either and almost threw the phone in frustration. Talon, who was lost in rage over our mate, blasted so much fire through the room that it felt like a furnace down here. The air was also growing harder to breathe, but he didn't care as he laid waste to the shifters and witches who dared side with the bitch threatening our mate.

On my way back to Hunter, I managed to kill another dozen shifters. By the time I reached his side, his healing had kicked in and his chest was all but knitted back together. "I'm going to help Talon," I told him, as his gold and gray eyes bored into me. "We need to get out of here—Emme is in trouble. I can't see it on the cameras, but I feel it in our bond."

Hunter attempted to sit up, but Constantine stopped him with a hand on his chest. "Don't you fucking dare," he snapped, sounding far from his normal mild-mannered alpha. "You're no use to Emme dead. Heal first, and then we save my daughter."

The snarl from our entitled alpha was filled with the sort of rage that made lesser alphas cower, and I felt the same fury deep in my gut. Moving away from them, I called on my dragon and stretched my wings to get above the masses.

Screams rang out as the witches and shifters ducked down, blindly shooting magic my way, but no one here was strong enough to take on a dragon. Especially not a pissed off one.

Turning my focus on Blaine, I carved a path toward him, ignoring the bite of magic and claws against my side. When I closed in on the pathetic excuse for an entitled alpha, there was for once not a shred of arrogance on his features.

"Wait," he called, throwing his hands up above his head.

I hovered a few feet away, while those around him bailed, leaving him standing alone and shaking. Spells pummeled into me, and they were starting to wear down my natural resistance, but for Emme I'd hold on through a lot worse than this.

"Jewels has been under your noses all along," he burst out, probably expecting me to flip out and lose control. But I'd already figured that out. "She's in Golden Claw, and has been waiting for an opportunity to take Emme out. That omega is your weak link after all."

My beast reared up, but instead of lashing out as I would normally, I let that icy fury settle in my chest. I gave him one more minute to spill information, on the off chance it would be useful, and then decided I could wait no more.

Blaine howled as I blasted him into ash and dust, relieved that dragon fire left nothing behind. There'd be no blood or bone for a spell. No flesh of the pack that once tormented my mate. After what they'd put Emme through, all their deaths were far too easy, but at least they were gone.

Now we just had to save our mate.

My wings extended once more, and I lifted my dragon higher to turn and find Talon guarding my back. *The magic was starting to strain your beast*, he explained.

He'd stepped in to shield me without any hesitation.

*Thank you, brother. Is Hunter okay?*

Talon moved out of my line of sight, his powerful wings gusting wind around the cavernous room. Off to the side, I could now see Hunter and Constantine fighting side by side, standing on a field of dead enemies.

"We've taken this stronghold," Hunter bellowed, and there was no sign of weakness of injury in his voice or energy. "Now, we must return to Golden Claw."

We landed near Hunter and I returned to my bipedal form, the change bringing a wave of fatigue far greater than any I'd felt in a long time.

"Jewels is in Golden Claw," I told them, forcing my legs to stand strong and sure. "She's been right there, under our nose the entire time. And she's gunning for Emme."

Hunter's curse rang out through the cavernous space and he just took off for the exit. Talon and I were right behind him, smashing any witches and shifters we passed. Not that there were many left.

"We'll clean up here," Will shouted from where he stood with a battered group of our allies. "You take out the witch."

Hunter saluted him but didn't look back. While a few might have escaped in the bedlam, for the most part we'd decimated Jewels' hidden army.

Blood, ash, and death coated us, but we didn't care. We had to get home to our omega.

"She's still alive," Hunter said, desperate worry lacing every word.

She was. That much we could tell. But for how long?

# CHAPTER 44

EMME

Jewels' web of magic had clearly been woven day by day since she'd fled from the family compound. It was so thick and cloying that after only a few minutes within its grasp I felt sick. My head spun, and there was a heavy pressure on my chest that made each breath harder and harder to take.

Tendrils of my magic rose as Jewels lifted her hands; this was the moment she planned to destroy me and tear apart our pack.

Which I couldn't let happen.

Kassidy met my gaze, and without words we both took off down the hall. Jewels hadn't bothered to restrain us, knowing we couldn't escape the house. Psychotic bitch probably wanted us to run.

Predators always enjoyed the chase before the kill.

"Do you know your way around this house?" Kassidy huffed as we darted into the living room.

"Yes, most of it," I told her in a rush.

This place wasn't as large as the Reeves pack house, but it was still sizeable, and I'd only lived here for a few days. "She has all the exits locked down," I griped. "Her magic is everywhere."

Kassidy's expression soured. "Yeah. She's clearly spent her time since the battle fortifying this as her stronghold."

A black widow building her nest.

Jewels' laughter rang out from behind us. As I'd expected, she was amused by our pathetic attempts to escape. As we'd just established, this was a nest, and her prey was well trapped.

But that didn't mean we'd go down without a fight.

"If I can get a minute or two to focus on my quintet bond, I can try and get through to my alphas," I murmured. "At least warn them, and maybe they can send enforcers here."

Not that there was really anyone in Golden Claw with the capability to take on a powerful, ancient witch. "How will you get through to them?" Kassidy asked, jerking her head as if she couldn't understand my words. "My phone isn't working, and you never take yours anywhere."

I'd forgotten that she didn't know the full extent and strength of our quintet. "We can mentally communicate," I huffed out as we raced through another hallway. "It happened when we sealed the full quintet. Along with releasing my magic."

I took her by surprise for the second time today. She blinked at me so rapidly I was worried that her brain had short circuited. "Mentally communicating in quintets is like… a myth." It was a whispered statement of disbelief, but at least she was still running. "I know quintets can track and sense each other. They know when the other is in danger or hurt, but they can't communicate. That never happens."

Apparently it does. "You can also never bond six into a quintet," I reminded her, "and wolves don't usually have magic. We're the exception."

Which wasn't always a good thing. The exception brought out the power-hungry fucks who tried to either kill or use you.

My reminder snapped her right out of her shock, and within ten more seconds she was all on board. "Right. *Right.* Okay, we need to give you some time to try contact your pack." She picked up the pace and I stayed with her. We were nearing the back of the house. "Is it possible you could use your magic to break out of here?"

I had absolutely no idea. "I'm willing to try," I said as we both slammed against the glass door that led to the back patio area. The material didn't even flex, magic stopping us from making contact.

Drawing on my magic as Constantine had taught me, I cursed the short amount of time I'd had to train with him. If I was the exception, then I *was* the main character in this damn story, which meant I should be worthy of the role, able to fight my way out of and survive this situation.

There was no *goddessbedamned* way that Jewels was the main character.

*Unacceptable.* She gave off pathetic power-hungry super-villain at best, and evil nemesis at worst.

Which meant sorting myself out so I didn't get us all killed.

Icy power spilled from me faster than it ever had before, pure desperation dropping all of my usual reservations. My magic hit the shielding and bounced back briefly, but I didn't let it retreat. I kept forcing it forward, the scent of sulfur growing stronger, though I got the sense it wasn't my magic but the reaction of Jewels' that caused the stench.

"You'll never be able to destroy my shield," a voice crooned. "It's like hitting a metal door with a spoon." We spun to find Jewels perched in the hallway behind us. "How about I make you a deal? If you stop fighting me and die like a good little wolf abomination, I'll let your friend stroll off into the sunset. Free as an alpha." Her smirk grew as she twirled a blond curl around her finger. "At least until the curse kicks in. But then she'll be in good company with every other shifter in the world."

My gaze briefly met Kassidy's, a snarl tilting up her bow-shaped lips. Girl had the poutiest mouth for an angry alpha that I'd ever seen, and the fact that I even noticed meant I was once again trying to disassociate from this moment.

Kassidy snapped me back into focus. "Do not even fucking think about it, Emmeline. You'll be sacrificing your entire pack."

I shook my head, knowing Jewels was never going to let me go no matter what, and Kassidy didn't deserve to die with us. Without taking my gaze from my friend, I told the witch, "Let her walk out the door and I won't fight you *as hard.*"

Jewels stole my attention as she shifted forward, staring at me in a creepy way. It wasn't animalistic like I was used to, but more alien. *Robotic.* As if parts of her were no longer even remotely human. "Agreed. I didn't need the extra anyway."

With a wave of her hand the doors flung open; tingles of magic raced over my skin. I caught the briefest glimpse of the cloudy sky as Kassidy screamed, the brisk air washing into the house, as my friend was thrown onto the patio. I cried out when her head smashed against a support pole, my hands slamming uselessly against the glass, while Kassidy lay on her side, not moving.

"She'll be fine," Jewels said, joining me at the door like we were just two friends taking in the view. "Couldn't have her running off for help just yet."

She leaned closer to me, and whispered, "Just the two of us. Now go, you abomination. *Run.*"

Taking off once more, I headed up the stairs and straight into the bedroom I'd used when I stayed here. Slamming the door behind me, I engaged the useless lock and headed for the window, which was as secured and sealed as the door downstairs.

For a beat, I imagined destroying the two shifters who had lured me here, but my anger at Warrick and Cora was misplaced. They'd clearly had as much choice as me right now. *None.* Chelsea had been different, as she had the means to tell us what was going on, and chose instead to save herself at my sacrifice.

Heading into the bathroom, I locked that door too and pressed my back against it as I threw my beast at my frozen quintet, attempting to find a crack in whatever interfered with our bond.

My wolf was the only one I could move; the others remained frozen. Even without the curse, Jewels had already figured out how to control the beast—at least on a smaller scale and within her lair.

A bang outside told me that the witch had blasted off the bedroom door, and I backed up from the bathroom door, knowing it would come next.

Jewels cheered when she cleared the opening and saw me pressed against the wall. "I love hide and seek. Want to play again? I've got time to kill."

I hated how confident she was that the dragon twins, whom she clearly feared, would not show up here anytime soon. What had she sent them into?

"You don't think my boys will get here in time?" I asked, almost failing at keeping my panic hidden. The last time I'd checked in with Hunter, they'd been fine, but that was before I got locked down in here.

She moved her head in that alien way again. "They won't save you, abomination. I left every witch and ally shifter of mine in that stronghold. They wove a shielding so strong that I knew your alphas would assume I was there. Then it would be too late. Even if they did survive, they're hours away from here." When she smirked, it was clear how clever she thought herself.

So proud and insane.

"Not to mention, you're about to die, so they are too."

My wolf howled, but shifting wouldn't do anything. All I could do was stand frozen and stare at her, those words running over and over in my mind. *You're about to die, so they are too.*

I was knocked out of my spiral of despair by a blast of magic so potent that pain exploded through every cell in my body. I screamed loud enough to scorch my throat, while skin melted from my bones. If my pack's life wasn't on the line, I'd have *begged* for death.

To my surprise, Jewels eased up before my heart gave out, and I collapsed forward, barely catching myself as I hit the ground. My limbs shook from the aftershocks of pain, though I didn't feel any of the magic now. Even more, there wasn't a single mark on my arms or hands. I would have sworn they'd be covered in burns.

"I don't understand why you hate shifters so much," I huffed, trying to shake off the residual magic rattling through my body. "You worked with our kind for years."

Jewels' expression creased, drawing shadows around her features. "Your race is superior to ours in many ways. Bigger numbers, these nifty little cities to hide out in, all the money and prosperity you could want. Why should you have so much when we have so little? Our numbers dwindle, and covens are all but nonexistent. My family spent decades tied into an accord that mostly benefited shifters. I woke up one day and decided I'd had enough. I'm a patient little witch though, and concocted the perfect plan."

My legs managed to hold me as I got to my feet, determined not to die lying at hers. "But you might have just destroyed the last of your kind by leaving them to Slade and Talon."

She'd put the bulk of her race in a room with two, virtually magic proof dragons.

Her chuckle was without any worry or remorse. "I'd rather be queen and ruler of shifters than part of our weak covens."

As I stared into her coldly excited expression, I knew the truth. She didn't just hate shifters… she hated her own kind as well. "That's why you didn't care when we were taking out witches during the battle. You just left them there to perish."

That got me a nod and shrug. "Yeah, pretty much. Your dragons probably just wiped out the last of our kind, which means I now have no competition. Once you and your pack are gone, there are none who will ever be able to stop me."

Her wrist snapped out and I was hit with another blast of magic that slammed me back into the wall. I slid down to thrash near the toilet, unable to escape the pain. *Lovely.*

Beside a toilet was *exactly* where I imagined taking my last breath.

The burning sensation had me screaming again, and I cursed myself for giving her this satisfaction. My wolf surged inside my essence, fighting to break through the stasis on our mates, and when Jewels rattled me a little harder, my magic finally found a gap in her spell.

Slade's voice echoed in my mind so quickly, I knew he'd been slamming against our quintet bond. *Snow!* he roared as my pain bled into him. I was far too weak to try to hide it from him, as I scraped against the tiles hard enough to break nails. *Where are you? What's happe—?*

Jewels' magic eased up, and the connection between our beasts faded with it. And just like that… I wanted the torture. I wanted to feel them for however many moments I still had.

"Are you ready for it to be over, abomination?" Jewels whispered, leaning down to clutch my face, drawing it up so I had to stare into her eyes. My chest heaved as I sucked in breaths, but never actually felt my lungs fill. "Would you like me to make the pain stop? You and your mates will be together forever in eternal paradise, where no one will ever hurt you again."

As appealing as she wanted that to sound, I wasn't done with this life yet. Not when I'd only just started really living. I would never just roll over and let this bitch choose my destiny.

"Not yet," I bit out between clenched teeth. "Got a little more torture in me."

That appeared to cheer her up, as she chuckled lightly. "Amazing. Let's continue."

It was when she hit me for a third time that I gave myself over to the magic, embracing it as I let my essence flow into the pain. My wolf vibrated harder than ever, and this time the disruption to the block let in more than just Slade. All five of my mates flooded the bond, their voices a balm that damn near soothed the painful magic.

*Mate, we're coming for you*, Hunter rasped in a deep, desperate voice. *Hold on for us, baby girl. Just hold on.*

*You are strong enough to best her, Snow*, Slade said on a rumble.

Talon growled, and I caught the snippets of *murder* and *love*, but he was beyond real words.

*Shortcake,* Kellan's mental voice was graveled and low. *We're outside but we can't get in. Enforcers are here too, but we need you to help us enter the house.*

Finley was last, and there was so much sorrow in his essence that tears unrelated to magical torture leaked from my eye. *I will follow you, darlin'. Whatever happens. I will follow you.*

*I love you all,* I managed to gasp. *I'm sorry for what has to be done.*

Just knowing they were here with me in these last moments was enough, especially as I mentally braced myself for what had to come next. The idea had been hovering at the back of my mind, and while I was terrified, I couldn't let them die. I refused to allow this bitch to kill my pack and damn the entire shifter world to her insanity.

Jewels chuckled louder than ever, her power surging as she prepared to steal my lifeforce.

*Emme!* Slade shouted, as he felt me ready myself. *Do not do this, sweetheart. Do not—*

It was too late for him to stop me.

I started to chant the spell that had lived rent free in my mind from the moment I read it on Slade's computer. As if it knew this moment was going to come for us all.

*Mate, please no,* Hunter howled, and with that, I felt him gathering up his energy, his wolf charging at mine. He wasn't the only one either; the others hurled their essence into my beast, and I was too focused on the chanting to do more than allow their power to flow into mine.

Out in the bathroom, Jewels, who clearly recognized the spell— since she wrote it—launched herself at me. But she was too late.

My soul screamed in anguish as the coldest magic I'd ever felt severed through the ties of my golden bonds, cutting my pack off until I felt nothing except the swirl of the essences they'd sent into me before.

To an orchestra of howls, roars, bellows, and tears, I shattered the quintet bond, leaving my wolf alone in my mind once more. The agony of their loss hit me so hard that it made the witch's torture feel like tickles.

Severing a bond like ours brought forth the sort of pain that destroyed one's sanity, and I was relieved when my mind blanked out, and darkness stole me away.

# CHAPTER 45

FINLEY

*S*he broke the bond.

The anguish of losing our quintet connection was so immediate and debilitating, that Kellan and I slammed into the ground.

We were outside Warrick's place, where we'd been trying to smash through the windows. Enforcers raced around us, having been sent here by Slade, but they couldn't see what attacked us. It was all internal.

As the voices of my brothers faded, my bear was alone once more. The weakness in my veins felt like death, and it was more than losing my pack, it was the depletion of essence that I'd shoved at Emmeline right before she severed the bond. None of us had hesitated to share our power with her as she took on the witch, and with the connection gone, I hoped she'd held on to that part of us all.

Emme used to fear that we'd steal her power, and it felt right that we'd gone the opposite way and given her everything of ourselves.

*Alone.* We were so fucking alone. *Everyone leaves.* Everyone dies.

*Emme.* Emme was gone.

Half my soul was missing as I metaphorically bled out on the ground.

*Not dead! Our mate. Not dead.* Through the bellows my bear spoke, which he did so rarely that it snapped me from a fraction of my despair.

My biceps shook as I pushed myself up to stand, finding Kellan clawing at the ground as he too started to emerge from a state of debilitating shock. We were surrounded by enforcers, all of them protecting us as our bond got shredded.

"Alphas," Horton snapped, "what happened? Were you attacked by magic?"

I waved him off. "Try and destroy the spell on the house," I snarled, half-feral. "We are fine."

With one last worried stare, they obeyed my order and left Kellan and I alone.

My brother scrubbed a hand over his face to wipe his tears. "How did she do that?" he whimpered.

I had my own tears, which I completely ignored. "She must have found the research from Fletcher's notes. But how she did it is less important than the fact that she's on her own in there." Ragged snarls spilled from me, my voice shot to shit. "She's on her own in there with that fucking witch."

Kellan sobbed and rubbed his hand over his cheeks once more, fighting for composure. "Jewels was trying to take us all out by killing Emme, wasn't she? Emme just saved our fucking lives in place of her own."

I nodded, gritting my teeth against the pain crushing my chest. "Yep, and Jewels is going to be out for blood."

With a few ragged inhalations, Kellan finally pulled himself together. He stood taller, staring up into the window of the Annandale pack house. "We sent our energy into her, and considering how drained my beast is now, hopefully Emme is packing power. It has to be enough to keep her alive until our brothers get here, right? *Right?*"

We were existing on hopes and fucking dreams, and all I could do was nod.

Even surrounded by allies and enforcers, none of them could break through this shielding.

We needed Slade and Talon.

As Kellan pounded against the wall, moving up and down the perimeter in the hopes of finding a point of weakness, I called Hunter. But his phone didn't even ring. Slade's either.

In my desperation, I tried Casey. "Alpha Finley," she said, answering on the second ring.

"Have you heard from Hunter?" I asked his assistant.

She hesitated for a beat. "Not for a couple of hours. Have you tried his phone?"

A growl escaped me that was so loud I swore I heard her jump on the other end of the line. "Yes, I did. It isn't even ringing. Can you track him?"

"Of course," her reply was instant. "Is there anything else I can help you with in the meantime?"

A derisive rumble of laughter left me. "Not unless you have a means of cutting through a magical shield."

Casey completely ignored my sarcasm, her reply as professional as always, "Yes. Alpha Hunter was working on a prototype that might do that. It's here in Reeves—"

I hung up the phone and moved my ass over to where Kellan had started to scale the wall to reach the second floor. His beast was as weak as mine though, and he could barely keep his strength up long enough to pull one hand over the other.

"Kel," I called, and he glanced down, arms visibly shaking. "Casey said Hunter has some sort of prototype in the office that might be able to cut through magical shielding."

He let out a yelp as he released the side of the building, and I managed to break his fall before he broke his neck. We both stumbled our weak asses up.

"We need to get to the office," he said. "The enforcers are here if Emme makes it out, but it's more likely she won't unless someone destroys the shielding."

My gaze lingered on the side of the house, not wanting to be so far from her, but Kellan was right.

"She will hold on long enough," Kellan declared, and I wasn't sure who he was trying to convince. No doubt both of us.

I called out the plan to Horton, who waved us off as I followed Kellan to his car. The Bugatti roared to life, and for once he didn't give the engine a chance to warm up, tearing out of the street. "Emme will hold on," I repeated, needing to say it out loud too. "If the witch wanted us dead, she can no longer use our bond with Emme to do it. Surely, she'll now want to use her as bait, right?" For my own fucking sanity, I had to believe that was her next plan, and not that Jewels would realize that by killing Emme she'd effectively destroy us all anyway, bond or not.

Kellan's eyes were wide and dark as he raced through the streets.

"That new plan would make sense. We just need this prototype weapon to work."

"And hope it's easy to use since the tech-bro side of our quintet are currently unavailable."

"We'll figure it out," Kellan said, determination lining his golden features.

He broke every traffic law in the city on his way to Reeves Industries, and when we slammed to a halt out front, we took off inside, leaving the vehicle doors wide open. The front desk staff called out welcomes as we raced past, which we ignored on the way to the private elevator.

This was used exclusively by the top-level staff, and we burst into the foyer to find Casey waiting for us. Her face was drawn, and I skidded to a halt at the sight of tears on her cheeks.

"Alpha Kellan and Alpha Finley," she said in a rush. "I tracked Hunter. Did you hear what happened?"

Kellan shook his head, eyeing her closely. "No, we haven't heard from them."

She twined her hands together over and over. "I—I'm—I don't know how—I—"

Despite our lack of time, I found myself adopting Dr. Karen's manner of calming, as I held both hands up in front of me. "Breathe in and out with me," I said, exaggerating my breaths so they were slow and steady. When the panic faded from her gaze, I nodded. "Okay, now start again and tell us what you found."

"His plane went down," she choked out, swallowing roughly. "I confirmed that they lost tracking and signal—" She glanced at her watch. "Maybe twenty minutes ago."

*Twenty minutes.*

Kellan glanced at me. "When Emme broke the bond."

We'd all been annihilated from the force of our loss, but Hunter didn't fly his own plane…

"Slade and Talon," I murmured, coming to the only logical conclusion. "Their dragons lost control."

Casey stared between us, and I wasn't sure how much she followed, but she didn't interrupt us.

"We need more information," I said, unable to focus on my brothers while Emme was in danger. "Can you find out everything that happened?"

Casey's drawn features were once again a mask of professionalism. "Emergency services are on their way from multiple cities, and I believe humans are on scene too. There was nothing I could do to stop that. I'll update you within the hour as I learn more. Will you be making your way there with Omega Emme? I can arrange another plane."

I shook my head so hard my neck cracked. "Emme's in trouble too. We're here for that prototype weapon you said Hunter was working on."

Casey straightened, her focus intense. "It's in Lab One. I'll take you."

No questions. No wasting our time.

There was a reason she'd survived working with Hunter for so many years.

Her heels clacked on the floor as she hurried off, and none of us spoke. The news of the Reeves plane going down was clearly not widely known, as the office staff went about their normal day. I tried my best not to think about whether our pack mates were alive or not.

The fracturing of our quintet had severed all connections, even those between us, and I couldn't feel any of them. My bear was all I had inside myself, along with a heavily frayed sanity. He pushed me to release him, but I couldn't shift. There was no Emme to bring me back, and I wasn't sure even my therapy and healing would be enough to save me from the bear's protection today.

We descended into the lower levels via an industrial elevator, stepping out into a cool, silent room, heavy with the scent of disinfectants. Everything down here was state-of-the-art, with a filter and ventilation system designed to keep out every known contaminant.

It wasn't always necessary for Hunter's and Slade's inventions, but they would never risk a cross-contamination.

We moved past zones that were clearly being used for the testing of armored vests and other magically resistant weapons. Casey led us through a series of locked doors, using fingerprints and retina scanners at each checkpoint.

"I suspect this is a dragon labyrinth," Kellan joked, though his voice was flat. "Designed to prevent even the staff from finding what they need."

Casey shot a look over her shoulder, sniffling lightly. "Alpha Slade never cuts corners on safety. All of your tech is protected."

Of course it was. The dragon protected what was his, and his beast must have been losing it at Emme in danger once more.

The prototype was housed in a small lab, the door labeled with a sign that read *Magic Disruptor*.

"Their aim was to invent a laser which could disrupt the natural order of magic," Casey explained, waving her hand toward a piece of equipment sitting on a pedestal. It looked like a cross between a nail gun and a mini jackhammer. "Magic is composed of matter, like everything in nature, and it can be disrupted with the right tools. This uses magical frequencies, along with a physical swing, to shatter the natural order of a spell."

When I stepped closer, she stopped me with a hand on my shoulder. My bear immediately erupted into growls, which had Casey removing her offensive touch.

"No one touches me but my fucking mate," I bit out, my voice so low I was surprised she understood the words.

She understood my intention at least, backing up quickly. No matter how great Hunter's assistant was, I'd kill her if she touched me again.

"Apologies, Alpha Finley. I was just going to say that it hasn't been properly tested." She continued to back away, until she was almost out of the room. "It's nowhere near ready to be used."

I lifted it to let the solid weight rest in my hands. "Doesn't matter. It's our only chance, and we will risk it. Do you know how it works?"

She shook her head. "No, I wasn't here for any of the preliminary testing."

Which meant she was of no more use to us.

Kellan followed me from the room, and when we passed some of the other labs again, he grabbed a few of the armored vests and Taser S weapons. "We might need the extra help," he unnecessarily explained.

"Whatever it takes to save our mate," I said, my hands twitching on the disruptor as my bear grumbled.

*Hold on, darlin'. We're coming for you.*

# CHAPTER 46

EMME

The slap of magic against my face roused me. I jerked my head up to find myself sprawled on the bedroom floor, my hands bound in front of me by shining magical strands. Jewels stood over me, slapping my face and neck with bursts of energy.

"Bitch," she snarled as my wolf howled, the emptiness inside us near debilitating.

Every part of me hurt, but the physical held nothing on the emotional. In fact, I'd never felt more physically strong, and it took mere seconds for me to recall that my amazing, incredibly self-sacrificing mates had sent their energy into me before I severed the bond.

Leaving me powerful but completely devastated over the loss of our quintet bond.

I hadn't truly realized how warm and safe I'd felt in their cocoon of beasts, our quintet essence always surrounding me, until it was gone.

Now I was alone. *Eternally alone.*

"You think you're so clever," Jewels hollered between strikes, the hits barely registering. My magic was naturally shielding me, and it appeared she had no idea how much power was coiled inside me, waiting to be released.

She paused and sucked in a deep breath, muttering to herself: "Never mind. I just need another plan. I always have more plans. I'm the queen of plans."

She was the queen of *desperately-in-need-of-therapy-or-prison.*

In the midst of her rants, I began to make my own plans.

I hadn't thought past severing the bond to prevent her from destroying my pack, but now I felt there was a chance to take her out. I was not only *very much* alive, I had so much energy racing through me that it might even be a match for her.

All along a part of me had been waiting for my alphas to save me today, as they had done so many times before. But maybe for once, I would get to be the one to save them. To fight for my pack, and hope that in the end, we could all live and re-form our quintet.

Jewels focused her full attention on me. "I won't be able to destroy them through you any longer, but there's no way they didn't feel that fracturing of the quintet. They'll come for you. You went from the weak link to the bait. Fitting for an abomination."

It was as if she'd completely forgotten her fear of the dragon twins and now believed she could take them on. "I do have a little of their essence left," she pondered, tapping her finger against her lips. "If I focus on the dragons, lock them down one by one, I might have a chance."

There was no way to miss the thread of desperation in her tone as she grasped at the very limited advantages she still possessed.

I attempted to push myself higher, my bound hands making it difficult. She dropped her boot on my shoulder. "No, abomination. You're not going anywhere."

When she slapped out with her magic once more, I smirked up at her, and she screamed before landing a much more potent hit. It knocked the air from my lungs, and all amusement fled along with my ability to breathe. Deciding I'd wasted enough time letting her tire herself out, I drew on the magic that felt like it was a storm in my chest, and was about to release it when two wolves leapt into the bedroom.

Jewels turned to deal with the intruders, but she was too slow. The beasts landed against her, and their claws found traction as they tore into the witch. Neither did a ton of damage against her shields, but they did manage to crack through a few places to make her bleed.

Cora and Warrick's attack gave me enough time to burn off the magical ties on my wrists and get to my feet. Jewels knocked them both down as I stood before her.

"Bitch!" I shouted. "Why don't you take on someone your own size!"

The wolves weren't moving, but they still breathed, which was a relief.

Jewels crossed closer to me, looking disheveled and manic. The whites of her eyes were shattered with red lines, and for once her outside reflected the evil within.

"No shifter is my size," she huffed, taking another step forward. "Not in any way that matters. You *are* mine to control though, and I've decided that none of you will even breathe without my permission. I intend to finish this how I started—as the strongest being alive, one step under the goddess."

"Easy to do when you've destroyed all witches and caged shifters," I said, pointing out that essentially she'd cheated her way to the top.

Jewels' slow smile was fractured too. "None of them will be missed. Did I ever tell you that my family kicked me out when I first came into my powers? My mom had an affair, and when my father found out, they disposed of me like I was trash."

I no longer gave a shit about her tragic backstory. All of us had them, and it hadn't set us on this sort of path of destruction and death. I gathered up my power, knowing I'd only get one shot at destroying her.

"You wouldn't know this, but a young witch on her own often meets a violent end. It's a deplorable world out there for us. I experienced things that I wouldn't even wish on you, and I consider you to be a stain on both races."

*Blah blah, whatever.*

For the first time, real emotion shone in her eyes, and I still didn't care. "I survived. I grew stronger. I reinvented myself and came back to claim my coven, killing my mother and her mate in the process, which allowed me to take over her pact with Fletcher. Step one of my plan to destabilize the entire magical and shifter world. I have plans for everything. Plans on top of plans on top of plans. Hence why I'm still alive, while every other disloyal and fucked-up witch is dead. All in the plan."

"You hate witches more than you hate shifters." It wasn't a question.

Jewels released a deep, husky laugh. "Despite the evidence to the contrary, I don't hate shifters. They treated me far better than witches, and your pack are a real favorite of mine. It will hurt to destroy them, but sacrifices must be made for the greater good. Rest assured, I will rule the packs fairly, and as long as they don't betray me, they'll retain some freedoms."

Right, and her little *They won't breathe without my permission* two minutes ago was all just a slip of the tongue. We all knew the truth: if she eliminated our pack here today, she'd be the ultimate power, and she'd destroy everything.

Not even humans would be safe from her need for power and control.

My wolf swelled in my chest, standing alone, but filled with the essences of our pack and magic. Feeling my alpha's energy inside was no doubt all that kept me sane, but I couldn't hold on to them any longer.

I opened my hands and released the hold I had on my beast. The force of her slammed against Jewels, knocking the witch to the floor. Even free, my rage didn't abate, growing until it swelled against my skin. By instinct, I fell into my usual fight position, hands flexing as I wished for my blades.

Unfortunately, this wasn't a superhero movie, and I couldn't call my weapons to me, but that was okay… I had inbuilt weapons. A wolf and magic.

Jewels bounced back to her feet, hands held in a clawed position as she released another spell. This one felt heavier, with a strong sulfur scent, but my wolf was with me, and she prevented the attack from landing. We shot back pure, unfiltered energy, and while I didn't know many spells yet, my wolf's instincts gave weight to our attack. Jewels' shielding didn't stop my beast as she hit the witch's shoulder, tearing through skin, muscle, and bone.

"How are you so strong?" she screamed, holding her arm close. "How does your wolf work with the magic? It's impossible."

I was the monster of her own creation at this point. "I'm an abomination, remember?" I taunted. "I have the magic of witches and shifters behind me." As I took her in, I shook my head. "You're looking a little tired there, Jewels. Did you expel too much power to shield this house and then attack me? Whoopsie."

I swung and roundhouse kicked her straight in the side, relieved that despite my limited magic training, my fight skills were decent. My hit slammed Jewels into the bedside table, and she landed with a clatter on the floor.

When she got to her feet, I was disappointed to see her shoulder already healing, indicating she still had plenty of power. I had to finish this off soon. My borrowed essences might feel unlimited, but that was far from the truth.

Her next spell, filled with green flames, cracked through my shield to slam against my chest. My heart stuttered for a few beats, and my wolf melted against my skin, her essence easing the irregular arrhythmia, which allowed me to suck in a few deep breaths.

"How?" Jewels screamed, the whites of her eyes almost completely red now. Her expulsion of power was literally bursting blood vessels. "That should have put you into a coma, followed by a slow, drawn-out death. But you're still fucking here."

And here I would stay. "You underestimated me because I wasn't pure enough for you," I said, letting my loathing for her seep out. "My hybrid nature is what gives me unique strengths that you can't counter." I was a perfect blend of two races, both of whom were built from the magic of the moon goddess. A goddess who sided with shifters *and* witches—a fact I'd temporarily forgotten in my hatred of their kind.

"You can't kill me," I declared, feeling that truth. "You cannot use magic in the same way against me because of my wolf, at least not until your curse comes to realization."

Which was why she'd wanted this curse in the first place, to overcome any natural resistance shifters had to magic. Once she controlled their beasts, she'd control everything.

*Yeah, not on my fucking watch.*

Drawing on my magic and beast once more, I gave the predator side of my soul her full freedom. My wolf knew how to hunt and kill, and I could trust her to lead the way.

We stalked forward, my vision a mix of human and wolf, though I remained in my bipedal form. This felt as close as one could get to shifting without actually changing shape.

When I reached Jewels, she threw up a shield, but I chose not to use magic for my first attack. I hit her with my fist. She wasn't shielded against a physical attack, and I cracked her cheek hard enough to break bone. Then I slammed into her ribs, followed by her shoulder.

I hit the bitch until she was a mass of cuts and blood, which forced her to put her energy into healing rather than fighting back. Any spells she did shoot my way were weak and unfocused, my shielding having no issue against them.

*End it*, my beast said, and I slammed my fists into Jewels' chest.

I'd been aiming for her heart, but she rolled at the last second and I grazed her ribs. She struck back at me and landed a half decent hit that knocked the breath from me.

Forcing air into my lungs, I moved fast enough to compete with Slade, and this time my hit was true. Right in the center of her chest. Magic exploded down into my fingers, and with the jaws of my beast following, her chest cracked.

I didn't stop there, sending the full force of my strength into her, only easing up when I held her shredded heart in my hands, its beat slowing until eventually it stopped.

Leaving the witch dead at my feet.

# CHAPTER 47

KELLAN

The streets turned into my own personal racetrack once more as I focused on weaving in and out of traffic. Finley remained silent and tense in the passenger seat, clutching the prototype weapon that neither of us had a clue how to use. But we'd figure it out.

*Hang on, Shortcake. We're coming for you, baby.*

Finley dialed Hunter and Slade again, but both went straight to voicemail. "They have to be okay," he said. "I refuse to accept any other option."

"They're tough," I said through gritted teeth, which didn't hide the shake in my tone. "Slade and Talon could have shifted mid-air and saved them. Their phones were destroyed, but they weren't."

Our quintet was too goddess-blessed to be torn apart forever. What Emme did might have felt like she'd ripped through a house made of wet paper, but we could fix it.

Provided we all survived.

No way would the goddess let this be the end of us.

Drifting around a corner, I almost side-swiped a fucking moron who pulled out without checking the road. He flipped me off, but I was already gone, forgetting his existence.

Finley clutched the weapon with one hand and the edge of his seat with the other, looking slightly green. "I never question why you win all the track days," he murmured. "Unlike family game days, where I know you cheat like the asshole you are."

I snorted, surprised to feel even an iota of amusement on a day like today. "I never lose when it's important."

I took another corner too fast and slightly overcorrected, but it was nothing to get us back on track. When Warrick and Cora's house came into view, I screeched to a halt out the front, and we were out of the car in a second.

At the front door, which was still barred by thick magic, we both examined the weapon. The enforcers weren't anywhere to be seen, but I could feel their energy around the back of the house, followed by heavy thuds of what sounded like metal on wood. They were doing their thing, and we had to do ours.

"This looks like a piece of tech they brought home a few years ago," I said, recognizing Hunter and Slade's work. I tried to keep up with Reeves Industries as much as I could. "It has a similar control panel. Do you remember the robot Slade brought home for security?"

Finley nodded as I opened the panel to examine the internal components. "The one he trashed after it fucked up his commands."

"Yep, that's the one. It looks like this works off the same basic power concept."

Finley took the full weight of the prototype so I could fiddle with the switches, and relief hit when it whirred softly to life. "My bear doesn't like it," Finley grumbled, his face paling. "There's an element of magic attached to this device." I could feel it too, the whir settling uneasily within my poor, grieving wolf.

"What do we do now?" Finley asked, his muscles bunching as he struggled to hold the device wreaking havoc with our beasts. He wasn't the only one fighting an urge to smash it to the ground.

I pressed another familiar button and there was a pop as the front opened to reveal an emerging half circle, like a satellite dish, on the nose of it.

"I think if we press that to the door," I said, noting the design, "and I initiate the energy, it should blast through the shield."

Finley turned to the door. "Okay, let's do this and save our mate."

We moved slowly, and when the dish was flush with the wood, a *pop* sealed it instantly. Finley tugged on it once, but it was stuck tight. "It suctioned right on," I said, nudging him to release it.

"Well, then, crank it all the way up and we'll hide behind the car," Finley said as he opened his hands and stepped back, leaving it against the door.

Hoping my basic knowledge and guesswork was right, I cranked the dials for power and hit the countdown to initiate. Twenty flashed up in red numbers, and then immediately dropped to nineteen.

Finley dragged me down the steps and behind my car, where we pulled on the vests, in anticipation of racing into the house. That and the Tasers were all we had, and I hoped it would be enough.

I silently counted in my head as that clock made its way down to zero. Finley started to mutter under his breath: "This better not be like those stupid-as-fuck movies where they try to set off explosives and then nothing happens, so they have to go and check, only to get themselves blown up."

"Yeah, fuck that noise." But I'd totally check for Emme.

We were out here without a damn clue, hoping this crazy plan worked. There was a reason that device was a prototype and not in production yet. It no doubt had some real kinks. And not the fun kind.

The whir of the prototype got louder. I could feel vibrations from here as the hairs on my arms lifted. "Something is definitely happening," I whispered, bracing myself behind my car... right as the front door opened.

Lifting from my half crouch, I blinked stupidly at the doorway where my mate stood, staring at two of her alphas hiding behind a Bugatti like weak-ass fucks. She was covered in blood as she stumbled forward, and we were running toward her as fast as our legs could move.

"Emme!" Finley shouted. "Get away from the door!"

With his shout, she noticed the prototype, but thankfully I got there in time to shut the power off before any of us exploded. The whir and vibrations eased immediately, and everything felt calmer as we all stared.

Emme's eyes were wide and very blue as she took us in, like she couldn't believe we were here. When the first tear slipped down her cheek, all three of us crashed together, until Finley and I wore as much blood as she did. Blood that thankfully, my wolf could scent, was not hers.

"Darlin'," Finley crooned, as I choked out, "Shortcake."

Emme sobbed against my chest, and I might have shed a few tears myself.

Having her in my arms like this, safe and whole, was everything I'd been praying for. It was overwhelming in the *best damn ways*.

When Emme pulled back, as if she needed to see us once more, I had to ask, "Is Jewels…? Do we need to get away from the house?"

She shook her head, her lips trembling. "She's dead. She overestimated her own strength… and underestimated my ability to use wolf and magic together."

Finley was practically beaming at her as he cupped her face. "Here we were trying to save the day," he said, "and you, our perfect mate, destroyed her all on her own. Not that I ever expected anything less, but fuck I feel useless."

A small snort escaped her, and it was the cutest sound I'd heard in a long time.

"Do you want me to go back inside so you two can bust in and rescue me?" she asked. "'Cause I'm happy to do that."

Nudging her playfully, I forced a teasing tone. "Could you, pretty mate? We're all hyped up with nowhere to go."

She squinted at me, and there was no bond for her to read, but she somehow knew what I really sought. "You want to check on the witch, don't you?"

"Confirmation would be good for my beast," I admitted. "But I suspect the enforcers are inside now too, so they'll be upstairs."

Emme nuzzled against my throat, and then Finley's. "You both smell amazing," she whispered. "Like home and mates." When she choked out more sobs, I rocked her back and forth in my arms. "I'm so fucking sorry I had to break the bond, but she would have murdered us all. I couldn't risk you dying."

She reached up as if to rub her bites, but her skin was smooth and unblemished.

Breaking the bond had stripped it all away. Her face crumbled as she felt the unmarked skin.

I cupped her pretty face and drew her closer, my lips pressing against hers. Her sweet taste filled my mouth, and my wolf eased up on his relentless howling. "We will fix it," I assured her. "Whatever it takes."

Finley kissed her too, and Emme melted into his bear hug, letting herself collapse momentarily. "I was worried that your bear would think I'd abandoned him again," she whispered.

Finley's hold tightened as if he would never let her go. "We understood why you made the choice. Don't get me wrong, I'm still pissed you sacrificed yourself for us, but since we would do the same for you, I won't hold any anger. You're so precious to us, Emmeline. We honestly couldn't live without you, so even if she did kill you and we then killed her, we'd all follow you. I meant that when I said it."

Emme shook her head, her breaths rattling harder. "The thought of you dying is enough to send me into the sort of spiraling panic attack that not even Dr. Karen could get me out of."

Finley bopped her on the nose. "Same, Ice."

A reluctant smile crossed her face, then she straightened her spine, showing the grit and emotional strength that had gotten her through many hard years. "Okay, let's check on the witch and enforcers. Oh, and I forgot to mention Cora and Warrick too. They got hurt in the fight, but were stable when I stumbled down here. We should call some healers for them since they did try and save me—after they led me into the witch's trap of course."

With that revelation, I debated whether we should burn their fucking house down with them in it.

Finley and I both growled, the menacing sounds filling the street. Emme's smile was more like a beam as she patted our chests. "We can rage about them later, when I've told you the whole story. For now, let's check on Jewels. You've got me paranoid, even though I held her dead heart in my hands."

"Explains the blood," I said with a low chuckle. "Our violent little mate. I kinda like this side of you." I kinda *loved* all fucking sides of her.

Emme tried to hide her smile. Tried and failed. "At least checking on her will kill some time until the rest of our pack returns."

Finley froze, and I forced myself to breathe normally. There was no point in breaking her heart until we got an update from Casey. For now, there was still hope they'd all survived.

Emme didn't notice our weird reaction as she was heading back inside. "Okay, come and rescue me, big guys," she called over her shoulder.

As soon as she was out of sight, my wolf howled loud enough that it spilled from my lips. Finley and I crashed into the house, to find Emme waiting near the stairs. I could hear footsteps on the second floor, and I loved that she hadn't gone up there with strange alphas.

"My heroes," she called, beaming at us.

My arms went around her, and I hauled her up against me,

needing to feel every inch. She wrapped her arms around my neck and legs around my waist. "Upstairs, mate," she ordered, and my chest caved in at her using that word, despite our broken bond. Fuck, who cared? We would always be mates, even if we could never bond again.

Emme directed me upstairs, and I followed voices to find a dozen or more enforcers in a room on the second floor. They were standing around what looked like an actual massacre.

"Baby," Finley breathed, his eyes wide as he took in the carnage. "You tore her fucking heart out."

I set Emme on her feet, keeping one arm around her as every alpha in the room snapped to attention. "You did that, Emme?" Horton asked, smiling far too friendly-like.

"About to be a second massacre if you don't stop that," I warned him. I might not be Slade, but he heeded my anger and shut that shit down.

Emme snorted. "So dramatic."

"We have called in healers and the council," another enforcer said, standing very straight and rigid as if we were still under attack. "You all should wait outside for them."

Not wanting Emme to have to stare at death any longer, I took their advice and left the room, keeping one arm around my mate, while my brother stayed behind us.

"How did you take her down?" I asked, when we were back outside, inhaling the fresh, brisk air.

"You shared your energy with me," she said simply, her breaths slow and steady. "I was filled with all of our essences, so, in a way, we all tore her heart out. Between my magic, beast, and the quintet essence, she was no match for us. Jewels thought she was facing a weak omega abomination, but I was more than she ever expected."

I dragged her against my side, which dragged Finley too, since he was wrapped around her. "You've always been the strongest of us all. What happened when you first left the arena? We were on our way home when Kassidy called us and said we needed to get over here as Jewels was holding you hostage."

Emme's sigh was loud. "Oh thank the goddess Kass is okay. I checked for her outside when I first came downstairs, but she was gone."

"More than okay," I said, "she had to go to healers for a quick check, but her vitals were strong."

Our omega nodded, the relief clear on her face. "Jewels has been here since the battle in our street," she said. "Warrick and Cora didn't betray us in the same way as Chelsea, as Jewels kept them locked down and only allowed them out to further her plan. They also burst in that room to save me, risking their lives."

"I'm not in a very forgiving sort of mood," Finley said shortly. "I'm not sure I care that they *came good in the end*."

"Let's burn their house down once they're out," I suggested, not remotely joking.

Finley nodded decisively. "We should be burning the witch's body anyway. Her magic will linger in the blood and bones, and I don't want her resurrected ever. In any way."

Emme pressed her lips together, but a smile still appeared. "I have no idea why I get turned on when you act like bloodthirsty assholes. But I do."

My dick stood at attention like we'd been called a good boy. I was about to say fuck it and take her right here amid death and destruction. Emme snorted and held her hands up. "Down, boy. Plenty of time for that later." She looked up and down the street, and in the distance I could see more enforcers making their way toward us. "Did Hunter and the others say how long until they'd be back? Jewels kept blabbering on about how they were going up against the rest of the witches, and I'm worried about them."

My chest tightened, and when the silence extended on for a few seconds too long, Emme looked between the both of us. "What aren't you telling me? They're okay, right?"

Finley's expression was shattered as he held her tight, his words gentle. "Emme, love... their plane went down on their way back here. We haven't heard from any of them since."

If I thought Finley looked shattered, it was nothing to the way Emme's face crumpled. A sobbing cry tore from her throat. "No!" She shook her head aggressively. "No, they wouldn't go down from a fucking plane. *No!*"

She clawed at her face, scratching her skin, and I reached out to capture her hands. Tears burned my eyes as I tried to reassure her that they were tough enough to survive a crash, but I couldn't speak. I had no idea if our quintet was intact, and Finley hadn't even told her the worst of it.

Her breaking the bond was what set that plane crash in motion.

A truth that would destroy her.

# CHAPTER 48

EMME

The look of astonishment on Kellan's and Finley's faces when I opened the door and found them crouched behind the Bugatti would stay with me forever. Their handsome, perfect faces… jaws ajar and eyes wide.

Still, it did very little to ease the relentless throb of our missing bond, which grew more painful with each second.

Especially now they'd told me that they hadn't heard from Hunter, Slade, and Talon, and the plane had gone down. *They're fine.* No simple plane crash could kill my mates. *Never.*

*Oh goddess.*

We remained in a silent huddle as more enforcers and healers showed up to the Annandale pack house. "What was the weird thing stuck to the front door?" I asked them, as a way of distracting myself from my howling wolf and dark thoughts.

Kellan offered the answer. "It was designed by Hunter and Slade to disrupt magical shielding. It didn't work of course, but we were desperate for anything that might get us in to you."

I loved them for trying to save me, but I was also thankful they couldn't get in. Jewels wouldn't have hesitated to wipe them out, as the two least resistant to magic. Though, with our bond intact, they might have had my magic to help them.

"The spies this time were our friends," I said, shaking my head as I stared over the gathering crowd of shifters. We remained off to the side, waiting for Hunter's assistant to give us an update. A few minutes later, two council members and two enforcers approached us. I knew them all by face, but their names eluded me in my agitated state.

"Alpha Kellan and Alpha Finley! Can you tell us everything that happened…"

Both the boys released animalistic sounds, reminding the council to tread very carefully. "Our mate, Emmeline Anders, is the one who saved the whole fucking city," Kellan bit out, not remotely trying to be polite.

Finley nodded. "But since we don't want you even looking at her, we'll explain."

They filled them in on what they knew, in short blunt statements.

"If you need more information from us, it'll have to be later," Kellan finally said. "Our pack needs us, and we have to go—"

My wolf jolted and her howls died off to be replaced with an excited whine. A beat later, Kellan's wolf was rumbling happily, and Finley's bear was in his eyes. My heart stopped at the sight above us: two dragons charging through the air, moving so fast that they were a blur.

Pushing my way into the gathered crowd, who were losing their shit at this majestic sight, I raced for the end of the street. Kellan and Finley on either side of me. Any shifters who got in our way were barreled over by my hockey-playing badass mates, and it was nice to know that while I could take care of myself, I didn't always have to.

We were a team.

We were a pack.

When we cleared the crowds, I sprinted like my life depended on it, tears streaming down my cheeks in thick, hot rivulets. I'd been trying my best to hold it together until we knew what the verdict was from the rescue team heading for the plane, and all of that suppressed emotion burst out of me in a gush of relief.

The dragons landed smoothly. Hunter was on Slade, while Constantine perched on Talon's back. A cry echoed up from my chest, and it was a mix of human and beast, a broken, jagged call.

*All of my family was safe.*

My fucking world didn't end today.

It. *Didn't.* End.

Hunter hit the ground at a run and scooped me into his arms as the dragons circled us, cutting off Kellan and Finley. My entitled alpha's chest rumbled so hard it shook my entire body. He didn't speak, choosing to bury his face in my neck. He took long, ragged breaths, and I was bawling like a fucking baby.

Big gulping sobs.

Snot everywhere.

A fucking mess.

"Omega… baby… mate… I love you." Hunter's rapid, desperate words spilled into me as he held on so tightly my ribs ached. Any lingering pain from Jewels was gone, and I welcomed his firmness against me.

The heat of the dragons enclosed us, and for the first time in hours, I felt warm and safe.

When Slade's snout glided down my spine I choked on more tears, and while there was nothing of our bond left, I could feel how badly his beast needed the reassurance I was alive. Talon's too. Hunter didn't release me, but he did rearrange our positions so I could also hug their dragon snouts, coating their scales in tears. Both beasts released a purring rumble that was one of the saddest, most soothing sounds I'd ever heard.

The dragons eventually allowed Slade and Talon to return to their bipedal form. There was an electric blast of energy in the air, leaving me with two massive, very, *very*, naked shifters.

Slade didn't remove Hunter from me; he just wrapped his arms around both of us, and I could *feel* the desperate relief from him as he clung on, Talon joining in on my other side. "I love you," I choked out. "I love you all so fucking much. For a brief second I was facing this world without you, and I would not have survived it."

Slade and Talon buried their faces against my neck, and all three alphas just held me. Breathed me in. Reassured all of our beasts that we were still here. Alive. *Together*.

As our scents mingled, that dull echoing ache that had existed from the second I broke our bond started to heal, just enough so I could breathe without feeling like there was a puncture in my lungs. And my heart.

After what felt like the most therapeutic hours of my life, though it was probably only ten minutes, the alphas finally stepped back. All three of them stared at me as if the world around us had ceased to exist.

I met Hunter's blazing gold eyes, Slade's piercing green, and finally the bisected black and green of Talon. Their gazes were heated and feral. If dominance worked on me, I'd be crushed under what they exuded.

"You're in so much fucking trouble, mate," Slade rumbled, his voice dropping to that unattainable dragon pitch. "You broke our quintet bond."

Hunter grunted. "Oh yes, our bratty little omega," he rasped, the bass in his tone sending shivers down my spine. "You never were great at following orders."

Talon just rumbled as if he was beyond words, and I reached out to capture his hand.

"I'm so fucking sorry I put you all through that," I said, and I was relieved when they backed up enough to allow Finley and Kellan into our circle. Well, they were the circle, and I was the wolfy in the middle. Surrounded by five alphas.

*I really liked that number.* New favorite number

"I wasn't even sure I could go through with it," I said, my voice wobbling as I tried not to cry again. "But Jewels was going to kill me to take you all out, and I couldn't let that happen. She had me, our bond, and the house locked down with magic. My only hope was to destroy the quintet and disrupt her plans." My limbs trembled in time with my voice as the pain flooded me. "When that magic severed our bond, it felt like I'd carved out my own heart. Then I was forced to keep carving it up into pieces."

Hunter's nostrils flared as he took a few fortifying breaths. "You most likely saved all of our lives, little omega. Jewels would have killed you before we could get back here, even going as fast as we were."

"We were locked out of the house from her forcefield," Finley added. "No matter what we tried, or how many enforcers joined us, we couldn't get inside."

"We tried to use the disruptor prototype," Kellan added with a sheepish shrug, "but it didn't seem to work. I have no idea what we did wrong, but in the end, Emme saved herself... and all of us."

Even without our bond, I felt the pride beaming from Hunter. His right hand slid up to my throat, cupping his claim there as he leaned down and softly pressed his lips to mine. I almost blacked out from how fucking good he felt and tasted.

"I never doubted your strength for a second," he purred, after what was a chaste kiss for him, but still leveled me with its intensity.

Before I could reply, Talon stole me from our entitled alpha, and his kiss was fierce. His hands cupped the back of my head as he demanded entrance, his tongue dancing with mine. The ashy sweetness of his touch had my head spinning, and I was gasping for air by the time he pulled away.

Slade, my scariest and hardest-to-crack alpha stepped into me, blocking out the rest of the world. His eyes shone, and I could have sworn a tear lingered on the edge as he stared into my face. "I thought we lost you," he whispered, and when his voice broke, my heart fucking broke. *Again.* It felt like the moment I severed our bond was happening all over again. "When you broke the bond, our dragons went ballistic, and we burst through the walls of the plane."

I jerked my head toward Finley and Kellan, wondering if they'd known *I* was the reason for the plane crash. Their shuttered expressions gave away their guilt.

*Sorry*, Kellan mouthed, and I decided that we had more important shit to worry about than their need to protect my feelings.

"Your father cushioned us from the explosion with magic," Slade continued, bringing my attention back to him. "Even as tapped out as he was from our fight in the underground bunker. We left the pilots and crew near the wreckage and raced back here. All the time fearing we'd be too late."

*Your father cushioned us.* I hadn't had a chance to even see Constantine since he'd slid off Talon's back, but I owed him a huge thanks.

He'd saved my pack and therefore my life.

"I want to hear about the fight that you guys promised me you wouldn't get in," I said, narrowing my eyes as I reminded them I wasn't the only one who'd broken a promise. "Then I'll tell you about Jewels, Warrick, and Cora." I sniffled, wiping my eyes on my sleeve. "I can't believe that in my quest to save you all, I almost killed you via plane crash. I promise, the irony is not lost on me."

Slade cupped my face, his big hands catching the rest of my tears. "You made the logical choice at the time. Don't punish yourself. The goddess knew what you were doing."

When he kissed me, my knees buckled, and he grasped my thighs to keep me from falling. Flexing his strength against my skin, he drew me slowly up his body until our faces were the same height. When he tilted his head back, a feral smirk lifted his lips. "I will be getting my mark back on you, Snow. To-fucking-day."

*Yes.* YES. All the yeses.

# CHAPTER 49

EMME

As badly as all of us wanted to escape from this street, we couldn't quite leave yet. We watched as Cora, Warrick, Richard, and Sierra were whisked off to the healing wards, and the Alpha Council assured us they'd all be questioned and dealt with appropriately.

Slade almost torched them where they stood, but my hand on his chest managed to keep him in check. "Please, it's complicated," I said softly. "Let's take some time before we decide how we feel about what happened."

With a huff, he settled for glaring at their retreating medical stretchers.

Moving past the feeling of betrayal wouldn't be easy, but it had been against their will, and in the end, they'd risked their lives to save me. At least the healers had assured us they would be fine once the last of the magic left their bodies.

Jewels was brought out of the house to be examined on the front lawn, and once the council was satisfied with our statements and the evidence from the enforcers who'd been here, they allowed Slade to incinerate her via dragon fire. We managed not to reveal my witchy side, and everyone left believing it was simply my training and quintet strength that allowed me to take her out. Which wasn't a complete lie. It *had* helped.

When Jewels was no more than ash, her remains were sealed up to be disposed of in the darkest corners of the globe so the witch could never taint our world again.

Constantine appeared at my side right around the time we celebrated the Jewels bonfire, and I threw my arms around him. "Thank you," I murmured, and weirdly I let myself rest against him as if he'd always been there to shoulder my burdens. "You've been saving me for years. I'm sorry I didn't show more gratitude when you first appeared on my doorstep."

His faint citrus scent was comforting now, and I lost myself in his hug.

He wasn't as vital to me as my alphas, but he did feel like family. The first shifter outside of my pack to ever do so.

"It's been my greatest pleasure to finally be in your life," he said in a husky rasp. "With all the American witches dead, there's no real threat left for either of us. So…"

"No more running?" I asked as I drew away.

He nodded, a beaming smile turning his whole face into sunshine. "No more running. I might even get the chance to settle into a true pack and live out the rest of my life with the sort of happiness I see in you and your alphas."

"I'd love that for you," I said, meaning every word of it. I doubted Constantine would ever risk having another child or even find an omega who could carry our unique genetics, but that didn't mean he couldn't find happiness.

"How did you really destroy Jewels without your pack?" Constantine asked, all but whispering the question into my ear.

I eyed each of my mates, heart pounding hard in my chest. "I still had them with me, since they don't follow orders either."

Their energy was a gift I would be returning to them, so they'd once again be at full strength.

By the time the council was finished with us and the street was cleared, I was wrecked enough to fall asleep in Kellan's lap on the way home. I woke an indeterminate time later to find myself clean and clad in one of Hunter's shirts, the late afternoon sun filtering through the partly open blinds. The alphas had put me in Slade's bed, and I wasn't alone.

*All* of my pack was here.

Our combined scents filled the room, and my wolf rolled over like a contented pup. Our pain wouldn't completely fade until all of their beasts stood beside her, but for now, this was more than we'd ever expected to have again.

Lifting my head to take in the scene, I was between Hunter and Talon, with Kellan and Finley cuddling my legs across the bottom of the bed, as if none of them had wanted to let me go even in sleep. The only one missing was Slade, but I knew he'd be nearby.

I found him in a chair watching me. No, watching over all of us. Our protective sentinel.

Needing to pee, I extracted myself from the alphas, patting them all gently until they settled back down. They were exhausted, their normal dominance just a low hum. I assumed they would remain that way until I returned their energy.

When I slipped off the bed, Slade rose and followed me without a word, straight into the bathroom. "I'm not peeing with you in here," I said with a snort of laughter, attempting to shove him back out the door.

He just smirked. "Actually, you are, and you better get used to it. I'm literally not taking my eyes off you for at least twenty fucking years."

I bounced from foot to foot, before throwing my hands in the air and yanking down my panties to drop on the warm seat. I had to avert my eyes as stage fright froze my bladder, but in the end, I was far too desperate to hold it in.

True to his word, Slade never took his eyes off me, leaned against the door as if to stop anyone else from entering. When I was finished, I washed my hands and dried them on a towel, before padding over to him.

His palms wrapped around my thighs in his favorite position, and I was lifted until I could wrap my legs around his waist. He walked us back into the bedroom, the soft breaths of my pack soothing my inner wolf. Slade settled into the wide armchair, his arms still around me, warm hands pressed against my spine. I dropped my knees on either side of him to get comfortable, before all but collapsing against his chest.

We remained like that for a long time, the fire of his dragon burning into me. Every now and then he would stroke his hands up and down my spine, and I was calmed by his steady heartbeat. We didn't speak a word, but it felt healing nonetheless. By the time the others started to stir, the rumble of my stomach was loud enough for everyone to hear.

Slade reluctantly returned me to the bed, where my pack dragged me into their arms one by one for hugs and kisses. After believing I'd lost everything, to have them all like this was overwhelming. Once again, my eyes were leaking like a damn tap.

Hunter licked my tears right up. "Every part of you belongs to me, little omega," he said.

The guys bundled me into sweats, and when we reached the kitchen I couldn't wait to eat until my stomach hurt. Florence had left meals in the fridge, which Finley got heating immediately, while Slade fixed us drinks.

I ended up with a creamy and sweet cocoa. None of them would let me lift a finger as they moved around in the kitchen. "You're spoiling me," I said, sitting at the counter and enjoying all the flex of tanned skin and muscle around me. Every alpha except Slade was shirtless.

"You deserve to be spoiled," Kellan said as he dropped a kiss on my cheek. There was real happiness on his face, the sort that had been missing for too long. "I predict that within the month, your arms and legs will forget how to work."

I rolled my eyes at him. "That's not a good thing, Golden. You're going to have to let me walk eventually. My wolf will bust out in rage if you don't."

He shrugged like he wasn't convinced he had to let me do anything. Even worse, none of the others spoke up to disagree. "Obsessive bastards," I murmured, but there was nothing but love in my tone for them as I leaned my head on my hand and sipped the delicious cocoa.

"I can't believe we almost lost this," I whispered, briefly closing my eyes against the pain.

The bustle and chaos slowed as all five of them faced me. "We didn't even come close," Hunter said, holding my gaze. "No matter what happened, we would have crossed dimensions to come after you. There's no escaping us, Emmeline Anders. Not even death would steal you away."

My scent grew stronger, and my wolf howled. "We're going to be unbreakable soon," I said, making another promise. "We'll never be parted again."

Slade's dragon rumble made me feel stronger than ever, as if I'd just gotten his stamp of approval. His respect meant everything to me, especially when it came from my actions and not the scent match we shared.

When the timer dinged, a steamy plate of paella was placed in front of me. I was too hungry to let it cool, shoving a spoonful into my mouth, burning it in the process. "Ah, hot," I gasped, waving my hands across my smarting tongue.

It was already healed by the time I took my second bite, and I could really savor the spice, flavor, and perfectly cooked chicken. The alphas didn't have to worry about burning their mouths, of course, each of them waiting for me to finish before they even started.

"Tell me what happened in Silver City," I said, scraping up the last grains of rice. "All I know is that you broke your promise not to do more than just scout." I shot the three culprits what was supposed to be a stern look, but I wasn't really angry. They made it home to me, and that was all that mattered. Still, I had to add, "We're even, then, on me breaking the bond, right? No punishment necessary?"

Kellan laughed around a bite of chicken, and just that sound alone lifted my spirits. "You tell them, baby," he said, nudging into me once more.

"We did break our promise, little omega," Hunter drawled. "And we're sorry we did."

He placed a plate of warm chocolate chip cookies in front of me and topped up my cocoa.

"Our initial plan was to simply confirm we had Jewels' safehouse," he continued, "and we honestly thought we did, right up until Blaine told us she wasn't there. We made sure to call in backup though, and didn't enter until they arrived."

"We didn't want you to be near danger," Slade said with a shrug, making no apologies.

Not that I expected he would. His arms crossed over his chest as he gave Talon a run for his money in keeping his unblinking gaze on me. "Once we entered their domain, we had no choice but to fight. The entirety of the witch population and all her shifter loyalists were down there. It was an ambush that had been set up in hopes that we'd stumble into it. And we did."

Just like Warrick and Cora's place. Jewels hadn't been kidding when she said she had plans on top of plans.

"She wanted you all to find it," I told them. "Warrick was at the planning dinner to plant the idea and send us down the path of her design. She knew you all would try and keep me safe until such a time there was no other choice. That was why I kept having such a bad feeling about us separating."

Hunter grunted his agreement. "I had the same feeling, and the entire time I was flying away from you, all I wanted to do was return. No doubt the way she attacked you in your dreams was to ensure we'd try to keep you protected at home. She's clever, and that's the only compliment I'll ever give her."

Hunter was spot on about the dream. In the end, we'd all been in danger but had managed to survive, which was the important part.

"It's scary how many witches and shifters you battled. If you didn't have the dragon's resistance and backup…"

"She underestimated all of us," Talon said, his body relaxed, but I knew he could snap into motion in a heartbeat if needed. "She expected that by removing your strongest alphas, you'd be the weak link she could exploit."

That was absolutely what she'd thought. "She was afraid of Slalon," I told them. "More than that, though, you three could have destroyed her curse at any time."

Finley shifted forward. "Any time?"

*Oh whoops.* I'd forgotten to reveal the most important part of all. *The motive.*

"Yeah, that's actually what sent her into this plan to start with, rather than just laying low until the next full moon. Since it was Slade, Talon, and Hunter who destroyed Fletcher and set this all in motion, there was some sort of kill switch they could hit even after it came to fruition."

There was a scuffle from the doorway, and a voice rang out. "What?"

I spun in my chair to find Constantine with a genuinely shocked expression on his face. "I don't understand how that's possible. A fulfilled curse generally cannot be easily undone."

I shrugged, relieved that he hadn't given us false information. "I don't know the finer details, that's just what she said."

Constantine continued to blink, before shaking his head. "There's always something new to learn about magic. Much of which will be lost now that she's wiped out half of us. At least all the ones in America."

"No more threats to shifters though," Hunter said, looking entirely unrepentant that an entire race was dead. "Shifters will just have to adjust without magic to aid them, but they'll figure it out."

Oh, right. I'd forgotten about the different spells that we used in our day-to-day, especially those for birth control and healing.

"Constantine and I will be able to supply all the magic this pack needs," I said, relieved that we wouldn't be completely without it. I might not like aspects of magic and witches, but I was coming to accept all sides of myself.

"We sure can," my father confirmed, and more than a few of my pack looked satisfied. They loved having all the power, and I trusted them never to abuse it.

"We should tell you what happened on our side," Finley started, before going on to explain how they left the game, and then Kassidy called them, half-hysterical.

"Did you hear if she's out of the healers?" I asked, turning to Hunter. "Is she okay?"

He propped his hip against the bench. "Yeah, she's more than okay. She's back home safe and sound, but mentioned that she needed to kick your ass for sacrificing yourself for her. Not quite sure if she's kidding or not."

My laugh was strained. "She's not," I said. "I didn't like what I had to do, but I would do it all the same way again, so she won't get an apology from me."

Hunter shook his head, and I wondered if he was praying to the goddess for the patience needed to handle me through our years of being mated.

My pack stayed together in the kitchen long after Constantine retired to bed, filling in all the details of the three separate situations we'd been in.

"I think the most shocking part of the whole experience," I added around a yawn, "was opening the front door to find two stunned face alphas hidden behind the car."

Kellan grimaced, looking positively pained. "Honestly, not our finest moment. But we were concerned the prototype was going to explode and leave us scattered in pieces around the front of the house." Hunter didn't offer any reassurances that that wouldn't have been the case, which confirmed they'd made the right choice.

When I yawned for the second time, Talon lifted me from my chair, cradling me against his chest. "Let's get you to bed, Honey." He pressed his lips to the side of my head. "We can sort the rest of this out later."

We all ended up back in Slade's room—his bed was the largest so it made sense. No one argued with the sleeping arrangements, with Slade sliding in on my right, Talon beside him, and Finley on my left. Kellan took Finley's other side, and Hunter hauled a mattress into the room to sleep at the foot of the bed.

I was cozy in the heart of my pack, and even though we hadn't made it to the claiming yet, I knew it would come tomorrow.

I had never felt more protected or safe as I drifted off to sleep.

# CHAPTER 50

EMME

While we might have taken the afternoon and evening to just exist with each other, none of us were willing to let another day go by without reforming our quintet.

The next morning we woke early, ate breakfast together, and all the time I had an alpha by my side. Hunter showered with me, Finley helped me pick out my nicest jeans, a blue shirt, and a black winter coat. Talon brushed my hair and then Slade braided it, while Kellan read to me from his latest obsession, which was a vampire fated mates story.

My heart was full of so many squishy feelings; it felt a lot like they were courting and loving on me before we bonded.

I was whisked downstairs soon after and deposited in the front seat of the G-Wagen. Hunter drove, with Finley and Kellan in the back, while Talon and Slade decided to fly. Their beasts needed to work off an overflow of energy.

When we left the street, I turned to take in Hunter's gray suit and white button-down. He looked a lot like he did the very first day I met him, where his beast had driven him to almost claim me in that council chamber. His thick hair was nicely styled, and the shades of gray in his eyes were light and filtered with gold. "Your essences are stronger," I noted, as his dominance filled the car. "How are you feeling after sharing your strength with me?"

"We're recouping the energy already," Hunter said as he took his eye from the road to watch me. Which no longer caused a panic attack.

"There's nothing to worry about, little omega. In a true scent match, essences can be shared without repercussions."

Kellan and Finley leaned forward, and I welcomed their touch against the side of my neck and shoulder. "I want to return energy to you after we bond though. Even after taking out Jewels, I'm more powerful than I was."

Kellan stroked up under my jaw with a gentle touch. "Keep it, Shortcake," he said. "We want you to be so powerful that no one will ever think to hurt you. Our little witch killer."

I snorted, hoping that nickname wasn't about to stick around. "Do any of you think it's weird how easily the council just accepted that I was strong enough to kill the witch? I mean, I'm glad, since we don't want them to know about my hybrid nature, but still…"

Finley grumbled and his hand on my shoulder flexed. "They know they can't take us on, and you also saved their asses from the wicked witch. They won't question a good thing, at least not for a while."

No doubt there'd come a day when someone put the pieces together to find they didn't quite fit, but I wouldn't worry about that until it happened. We were living for the now. Yesterday had shaken all of us in a way that was permanently imprinted on our psyches. Not just losing the bond, but the brief moments we'd thought we lost Hunter, Slade, and Talon.

As much as the alphas had been stuck to my ass since then, I would have freaked if they were far away as well.

"I do have to say, you all look incredible today." I brushed my fingers over the cuff of Kellan's dark blue suit. Finley wore a deep, rich burgundy, and I was legitimately surrounded by the hottest alphas I'd ever seen, dressed up to claim our bond back.

By the time Slade and Talon joined us, I might as well just send up the white flag and surrender. Maybe that was why my bra and panties were white today—the usual white flag of surrender in my world.

"I should have worn a nice dress," I huffed, glancing down at my clothes. They were my best jeans, but still, far from fancy.

Kellan's hold slipped down my arm until our fingers were interlocked. "Why bother when you'll be naked soon enough? Clothes were optional for the entire bonding, but since we'd have to kill any shifters who saw you naked on the drive, it's better for Golden Claw that you at least wear something."

Their dirty mouths didn't make me blush as much these days, but every now and then they managed to bring a rise of heat to my cheeks. Mostly, it was desire that had me all flushed, and I remained in an overheated state all the way to the nature reserve and sacred grounds.

When Hunter opened my door, the winds felt particularly icy as they whooshed in. "When does it start to warm up here?" I whined a little, sick of the chill now.

We were well into February—Kellan's birthday was soon.

"We'll have false spring next month," he offered as he helped me out. "Then it'll get cold again for a while before the real spring sets in." I generally loved snow and winter, as it was my wolf's favorite, but I was ready for some sunshine and warmth.

"Can't wait," I murmured around chattering teeth, which eased when the alphas surrounded me with their bulk and natural heat.

Slade and Talon emerged from the edge of the tree line, also dressed nicely in black slacks and matching black button-downs. They were always beautiful and godlike, and when they dressed head to toe in black, they looked gigantic.

As they strode toward me, and I took in all their glory, a needy whimper slipped from between my pressed lips. Slade's gaze snapped to mine, as if he'd heard that sound.

"You okay, Emme?" Hunter asked, and I huffed.

"You're all hot as fuck, and I'm over here looking like—"

"If you say anything less than a hundred out of ten, I'm going to spank your perfect little ass right here," Slade responded with a slow smile, as if he was still somewhat amused. Before I could recover from that statement, he wrapped his hands around my waist and hauled me over his shoulder.

I tried to glare at him from my perch across his broad shoulder, but he appeared unfazed. The rest of our pack joined us in a march across the grounds, and I leveled that same glare on each of them. "None of you better get used to hauling me around like this just to get your own way. I know how to fight now… And I have magic."

I'd zap their asses without a second thought. Just a minor spell, of course; no one hurt my mates, not even me.

"You know you're the boss, baby girl," Hunter said, and as the entitled alpha that was an official statement. "But since we love to touch you and take care of you, I doubt any of us will stop carrying you around. Within reason."

Slade grunted his agreement, and it was so quintessentially alpha that I was filled with what could only be described as burst of warmth. It flooded into my wolf, who was relaxing in the comfort of her pack and scents.

We ended up in a different hut this time, one with a second room that was almost all bed. Big enough for a quintet plus a few.

I stared down from my vantage point upon the tower of Slade, and my pulse was damn near racing. "It's finally clicked that we'll be performing all parts of the bonding here."

Slade's slap against my ass was firm, even over the top of my coat and jeans. He rubbed across the spot, and the fire which followed was both external and deep in my core.

Wave the damn panties. We were going down.

"You're not leaving this cabin unbonded," he said with a rumble, "and our quintet will never be destroyed again."

"I promise," I murmured, hoping it was one I could keep. I wasn't sure the end of the world could convince me to go through that pain again, even knowing we could reform our quintet later. Or so we hoped. Today would be our telling point.

Slade didn't set me down until we were in the main room, candles already positioned for the circle of energy. When I'd broken our quintet, I'd done more than cut *my* ties to them all—I'd cut their bonds with each other as well. For the strongest quintet we could have, they would join in brotherhood first, and then all of them to me.

My heart slammed in my chest as they started the ritual, which was a repeat of last time, with chanting and the earthy scent surrounding us. It may have been wishful thinking, but it felt like the buzz of their connection was stronger. All I could guess was that this time all five were coming into the bond as equals, and I really loved that for Talon.

When the essence of their beasts rose, a sigh expelled from me with so much force that it caught their attention. But fuck, there'd been more than a small part of me which feared I'd broken the scent match magic beyond repair. This proved that all I'd done was disrupt it for a short time.

The goddess did not forsake our match.

After their part of the ceremony was complete, the alphas abandoned every pretense of formality, encircling me like hungry predators. "It's time, little omega," Hunter purred, reaching out for me. "And I will be going first, as is my right as entitled alpha."

Slade grunted, and there was a lot of dragon in his piercing green gaze. "For the first time ever, I feel the urge to challenge you for that role, brother."

Hunter's smile never wavered. We all knew Slade wouldn't actually challenge him, but I appreciated his need for me all the same. When Hunter extended his hand once more, I placed mine against his palm without hesitation.

With a gentle tug, I fell into his arms. "If you have any objections, baby, now's your time to speak up."

My wolf rose until a purr rattled in my chest, which was pressed against Hunter. My fingers crept down his shirt, unbuttoning it slowly along the way. "Not a single objection, Hurricane. But I do have some requests."

Gold flared in his gaze, and my skin heated at the intensity of five other gazes on me, even as I remained mostly focused on Hunter.

I pressed my lips to his chest I'd just revealed, caressing the hot skin below. "You will claim my ass, Hurricane, while Kellan takes my pussy. You can bite first, but I want Kellan to claim me just after." Their scents exploded, and I had to shrug off my coat before I overheated and died.

"Deal," Kellan burst out, ignoring Hunter's annoyed snarl of a reminder about who was in charge.

"What next?" Hunter asked, returning his focus on me.

"I'd like to suck Finley's dick," I rasped, clearing my throat, "while you two finish inside me. Then he gets to fuck and bite me too."

Hunter nodded with each point, as if he made mental notes, while Finley's low, pained moan was accompanied by a spill of cherry and vanilla through the hut.

"Slade and Talon will claim me last," I continued, unsure where this bold, dirty-mouthed side of me was coming from. But I didn't hate it. And if their scents were any indication, neither did my alphas. "Then our quintet will be complete."

By the time I blinked, Kellan was naked, and the others were damn near close. Clothes littered the floor, and their scents were heavy in the air. Hunter's chest was one big rumble as he hauled me into his arms, and in a move so fast it made my head spin, I was on my back, a soft mattress beneath me.

"This is a new bed," Hunter murmured, as the scent of clean sheets wafted up around us. "We will not claim you on a mattress that's been used by any other pack. No other scent has ever touched this surface, and none ever will after us."

"We need this bed at home," I gasped, arching against him. "So we can all sleep together."

His wolf flared deeper in that gaze, and even without our mental connection, I *knew* he liked that idea. Hunter covered me with his body, pressing me down into the pillow top. He laced his fingers with mine, and then brought my hands above my head, holding me in place.

His first kiss was soft, and so was his second, but by the third he was kissing me like he might die if he didn't consume me. It had been too many days without my alphas' touch, and the throbbing need between my thighs was instant and intense.

Me voicing my wants and needs had acted almost like foreplay, and we were all more than ready to go.

The bed dipped as the others joined us, and Hunter shifted his weight back so they could touch me too. Their firm hands were everywhere, and I moaned as they stripped away my clothes, setting my nerve endings on fire across each piece of skin they revealed.

Kellan lifted my surrendered panties to his nose and breathed deeply. "Fucking hell, you smell so good," he groaned, and then when he threw them to the pile, it really did look like my white flag of surrender waving one last time. "But you taste even better."

He buried his face in my cunt with a relieved sigh, as if he hadn't been able to wait another second. The glide of his tongue, soft at first, but firmer over my clit, had me arching off the bed. Or at least I would have, if the others didn't hold me down under their touches.

Hunter kissed me again, his tongue caressing mine, until all I could taste was mocha goodness. I couldn't see the others, but there was a maddening glide of a big hand along my stomach, pressing against erogenous zones that set fire to my veins. There was also a scrape of callused thumb across my nipples, followed by a mouth closing over the tip. *Goddess.*

With all of that, Kellan only had to drag my clit gently between his teeth before I was screaming into my first orgasm.

None of them eased up, and my hips lifted to thrust harder against Kellan's mouth.

"Please, claim me," I demanded, tearing my mouth from Hunter's to clutch the sheets. "I need to feel our bond. I need you all in my essence again."

The alphas backed away a touch, except for Hunter, who released a feral growl so deep I felt it in my core. When he flipped me over to my stomach, I caught a glimpse of Finley kneeling on the side of the bed, his hand wrapped around his thick length as he slowly stroked himself. Slade and Talon were off the bed now, clad in black boxer briefs. They weren't touching themselves, but there was no hiding their erections.

Those two seemed the type to enjoy the bite of pain as they tormented themselves while waiting.

I gasped when Hunter lifted me, holding me high enough that Kellan could slide right under, before I was lowered right onto his broad, golden chest. When I arched against him, Kellan leaned up and captured my nipple in his mouth.

Clutching two fists into his hair, I dropped my head back and groaned. "Fuck, you're such a good boy, mate. You made me come, and now you're playing with my tits. You deserve a treat."

Kellan's hips thrust against my wet heat as he panted, his violet eyes begging me to put him out of his pained misery. "Baby, please," he groaned.

When Kellan begged, I wanted to give him everything he needed.

Hunter's heat pressed against my back, and he slid his fingers through the mess between my thighs. His fingers dipped into my ass, a slow press against tight muscles; he worked me until I was crying out soft moans.

Tilting my hips forward, I rubbed against Kellan's hard length, but he didn't enter me. Not when Hunter was to be first. We just tortured each other, which was almost as much fun.

When Hunter was satisfied that I was lubed up enough for him, the thick head of his cock replaced his fingers, and it was a slow, delicious press for him to enter me. "Holy fucking fuck," I cried, probably half tearing out Kellan's hair from where I was gripping him like my life depended on it. But he didn't complain.

If anything, he felt even harder against my stomach and clit, and I was using him for all the delicious friction. When Hunter was fully seated, he lifted and angled my pussy so that Kellan could finally enter me.

The two of them together always took a few seconds to get used to, and the bite of pleasure-pain only added to the heady sensations flooding me. Kellan's breaths came out in heavy rasps as he rolled the sensitive peak of my nipple around his tongue. My breasts ached, each nipple so hard that even just a scrape was too much sensation to handle.

Pleasure shot through my core and into my gut. My next orgasm was already barreling toward me, and neither of them were even moving yet.

"Hunt," Kellan rasped. "Start moving, brother. I'm not going to be able to last long."

Same, Golden. So much the same.

It was more than how good it felt, it was that for the first time since breaking the bond, I didn't feel empty inside.

Hunter set the pace, and as they alternated their thrusts, I came almost instantly. I managed to release Kellan's hair before he became bald, but I needed something to hold on to.

Which turned out to be one big Grouchy Bear.

Finley caught and kissed me, and my core spasmed around both alphas who held me in their thrall, controlling the speed of our claiming. "Oh, she liked that," Hunter groaned.

"I want more," I breathed.

Pleasure filled me until my vision blurred and darkness danced on the edges. Finley pulled away long enough to position himself so his rigid length was level with my face. Opening my mouth in a desperate need to taste him, I gasped at how good the weeping end of his cock tasted. It held a hint of vanilla and salt, which catapulted me right into another release.

The gush from between my thighs soaked us all, and Kellan reached down to swipe his hands through the cum, sucking it from his fingers. "Whatever you're doing, Fin," he groaned, "keep doing it. Our girl likes that."

Kellan's thrusts turned jerkier, and if the sheen of sweat on his forehead was any indication, he was about to lose control. "I'm pretty sure I've clenched my ass cheeks into new fucking muscles to keep from coming." He sounded pained. "You better hurry the hell up, Hunt."

Hunter replied in a low murmur, but I was too busy sliding my tongue up and down Finley's shaft to register the words. "Dammit, darlin'," Finley said, threading his fingers into my hair, and tightening his hold as he thrust deep down my throat. "You're going to kill me. Fucking hell."

Kellan was literally panting, and Hunter's response was to thrust harder and faster, until that slow build of another release was no longer slow. When I came again, Hunter and Kellan followed, and Finley's cock popped out of my mouth.

Hunter gave Kellan a minute to finish, and then he lifted me off him, my core clenching on the sudden emptiness. I was on my back in the next breath, and Hunter thrust his still hard cock back into my ass. "I love you," he said, and I clutched on to his thick biceps to keep myself grounded. This was too intense, and I wasn't sure I wouldn't lose myself today.

"I love you," I whispered back.

Hunter's gaze darkened, then the gold of his wolf flashed around his pupils. "I'm going to claim you now, omega," he said in a deep, hypnotic tone.

When his face partially shifted, his teeth cut into my shoulder. His bite landed in the exact spot he'd claimed last time, and my gasp was filled with joy and relief. My wolf rose up to join his, and I bit him too, relishing the taste of Hunter in my mouth, along with the tendrils of him joining my essence.

As we clung together, more than one part of him buried inside of me, the world slowed and noise ceased. I was lost to the claim as our beasts caressed each other, and when we orgasmed together, there was a sliver of peace in my chest that hadn't been there this morning.

After kissing all over my face in soft caresses, Hunter reluctantly released me to Kellan, who slid into my pussy as if he'd never left it. These alphas had an intense refractory period, which meant they could fuck me as much as I needed.

Which apparently was a lot. My previous highest orgasm count was definitely about to be shattered tonight.

"I love you more than existence, Shortcake," Kellan whispered over and over, until his jaw elongated with the partial shift. He sank his teeth into his spot, and I bit him back.

Mine and Hunter's beasts were soon joined by a bouncing tanned monster, and weirdly even without the full quintet bond, none of the beasts disappeared.

They knew their home, and no one was dragging them away ever again.

# CHAPTER 51

## EMME

When Kellan reluctantly left me, Finley was there so fast that I bounced on the bed under him as he pounced. He captured my lips, and the kiss was one of those slow, intense touches that had me forgetting that anything else in the world existed.

Finley released my mouth and slid his hands under my ass to drag me completely beneath him, his broad chest blocking out the world. He smiled softly at me. "Hello, darlin'," he said, and thrust inside me in one firm movement.

My oversensitive core spasmed, and I wrapped my arms and legs around him, holding on. Finley was always powerful and controlled during sex, but today there was an additional element to his thrusts, an almost animalistic drive, as he got caught up in the need to claim his mate.

His desperate, unhinged expression had my walls clenched hard around him. Whenever these alphas unraveled from my touch, it turned me on like nothing else.

"Fin," I cried, my nails digging into his shoulders. His eyes locked on mine, and his obscene lashes did nothing to hide the swirling whiskey depths. "I love you," he declared. "I will always love you."

The building tide of pleasure exploded, but Finley held my gaze and I couldn't close my eyes. "I love you so much," I sobbed as my overstimulated and tender body fell apart.

Finley groaned out my name, and there was a spark of his bear as he partially shifted. His jaw elongated right as he leaned down to claim me beside Kellan's mark. My wolf pushed up so I could claim him back, swirls of magic and shifter essence rising around us.

In my essence, Grouchy Bear stepped up to join our pack.

The beasts nuzzled and frolicked together, and when Finley's bear ran his paws all over my wolf, as if to reassure himself that we were together once more, I started to cry.

Finley's eyes were shiny too. "Fuck, that feels like coming home," he whispered, and that was exactly how it felt for me too.

Kellan, uncaring that his brother was dick deep in me, leaned over and kissed me right on the lips. "Have I told you how pretty you are when you come?" he murmured. "I could watch that pink flush spread over your luscious tits and up to your throat all damn day." His pupils dilated. "Your freckles pop and your eyes turn into this piercing blue." He groaned, pressing his lips to mine again, as if he couldn't help himself. "I'm getting hard just thinking about it."

This was the point Finley had had enough, nudging him away. "My turn, annoying pup."

With a huff, Kellan pointed his finger at his brother. "Only Hunter gets to call me that, and only because he's our entitled alpha. I will beat your ass."

There was that glint of steel in our Golden, and Finley knew well enough to heed the warning.

"Enough."

That snap from Slade shut them both down in an instant. Kellan reluctantly retreated and Finley slid from my body, after giving me one last kiss.

At this point I was a mess, my core ached, and there was cum everywhere. None of which appeared to bother Slade as he pressed his palms against my stomach, holding me in place. "Mine," he murmured in the same tone as his last barked command.

Talon sidled beside him, and I stared up at my dragons with all my love and need.

"Yours," I confirmed, and all the beasts of the quintet howled or bellowed, their voices joining us.

"Ours," Talon and Hunter countered.

Slade's hands wrapped around my thighs as he slowly dragged me toward the edge of the massive bed where he stood. I ended up on my knees before him, and taking the opportunity to freely touch him, I traced my fingers over the dragons on his chest.

Pausing at the dark space between them. More evidence of our bond breaking.

Slade captured my chin in his hand, tilting my face up so I could see him fully. "It will return," he said in that low vibration of male and dragon.

"I need it back, and I need our bond too." My fingertips brushed down to his nipples, the rings catching on my nails.

Slade's husky rasp reminded me that he enjoyed a bite of pain in his pleasure. I dug my nails into the ridges of cut abdominal muscles. Talon was too far away, so I waved him closer, and when I had them both before me, I explored as I'd done during our last claiming, and they let me touch until I had my fill.

My attention was eventually fixated on the thick beads of pre-cum dripping from the slit of their dicks, poking above their boxer briefs. Needing them fully naked, I hooked my fingers in the elastic and pulled them down.

"She chose with *and* without hardware," Kellan murmured to Finley, and he'd get no argument from me.

Grouchy snorted. "I don't know how they don't break her."

"Shut the fuck up," Hunter growled, "before your asses get fried."

I wanted to laugh at their antics, but two dragons held me in place with their sheer energy. Their beasts thundered in their chests, and when I was locked in their unwavering focus, there was no concentrating on anything else.

With their erections freed, I moved on to exploring the long lengths, pressing my nails into the thick vein that ran along the underside, before gentling my touch again.

Talon was the first to snap. He lifted me from the bed and hauled me against his chest. My legs enclosed around his stomach and he released a satisfied purr. "You fucking destroy me." His arms shook and it wasn't from a physical weakness. "I've never known a love like this, not even for my twin. Please, never break us again. It would be my end."

My heart splintered into what felt like dozens of pieces, and there was nothing I could do but make him a promise. "Never again. No matter what. We're stronger and safer together."

Talon's head tilted back to the ceiling, as if he prayed to the goddess. When he was done, he slid one hand into my hair, applying pressure to draw me into a kiss. "I love you, Honey," he whispered, and there was more green in his eyes today than I'd ever seen before.

"I love you too, Tal." I rocked against him, needing to ease the ache.

Talon turned me so that I was captured between him and Slade, and his twin took my weight, holding my legs open so Talon could press against my aching core. It took a minute for him to push through tight muscles to fully seat himself. My head fell back against Slade's chest, my hips tilting to change the angle slightly. Talon slid his thumb around my clit until I moaned and arched.

Using cum as lube once more, Slade coated my ass, and his fingers slid inside me first.

It felt so fucking good. When his cock parted my ass cheeks, my cunt clenched around Talon.

"Not going to last long today," he warned his twin, while staring right into my eyes. "You feel so fucking good, mate. All snug and warm, wrapped around my dick."

My chest heaved, and in the silence, all we could hear was Kellan's pained groan in the background. Finley laughed as he said, "That praise wasn't for you, moron."

Kellan groaned again, and I was so turned on to know they were enjoying watching me get fucked by their brothers. This was the first time we'd *all* been in a room together, and the proximity sent tingles through my throbbing clit.

Slade and Talon adjusted me until I was exactly how they wanted me between them. "Ready, Emmeline?" Slade asked, and I could only groan and nod.

"Words," Talon growled. "We need your words, sweetheart."

"Yes," I cried. "Holy shit. Please move or I might die. I need you both to fuck me. *Please.*"

Kellan wasn't the only one to groan—even Hunter's scent exploded. He certainly loved it when I begged.

Thankfully, for all of our sanities, the dragons were done proving their ability to restrain themselves. They started to move together, and while their experience with sex was minimal, their instinct was next-level. They knew the perfect force and rhythm to thrust into me, hitting all the right spots, until I couldn't breathe, think, or focus.

They were just so big. The sensation of being this full was almost too much to handle.

The build was slow, as I wrapped one hand around Slade's arm, and the other around Talon's shoulder. They held out longer than the other alphas, but not by much. When I clenched around them and cried out, the air turned electric as they shifted and bit into me, Slade first, and then Talon, who appeared to be positioned a little left of his original mark.

Slade palmed the back of my head and situated me so I could bite Talon, but when I was about to mark his throat, he tilted his head. "Different this time," he huffed. "Let's erase the bad memories."

I understood now why he had shifted his position—he didn't want us to be reminded of our first time. "Our new beginning," I whispered, while sinking my teeth in, my wolf right there with me.

Talon's dragon roared into the sky, and when he joined the quintet essence, I tore my teeth from him so I could bite Slade's throat.

As soon as the final dragon stepped into our bond, voices filled my head, and unlike last time, all I felt was joy.

*Mate!* Kellan cried, his beast howling with him.

*Mate,* I replied as tears slipped silently down my cheeks.

Yeah, I was crying again, but *fuck.*

The twins held me for a long time after we'd sealed our bond, giving me all the time I needed to move through the earthshattering feeling of having them back.

When I rested my head against Talon's chest, he leaned down and pressed a kiss to my temple.

*You okay, baby girl?* Hunter asked, always needing to check on me.

"It's hard to believe this is real," I whispered. "Our bond feels stronger than ever, our energy and essences are blending seamlessly once more, and the witch is dead."

Slade stole my attention from his twin by taking my weight off Talon so I was wrapped only in his arms. I'd told all my alphas I loved them during the bonding except him, and I was just opening my mouth to rectify that when he wrapped me up so tightly I couldn't breathe.

"I will protect you for the rest of my existence, Snow," he said, and the crack in his tone hit me right in my heart. "I will also kill and die for you without hesitation. You're the purest, most perfect thing I've ever claimed, and I will never hurt you." He sucked in a ragged breath, and I had to be mistaken, but he almost sounded nervous. "I've never said these words before, but I believe I finally understand their strength. I love you."

My heart stuttered and I tilted my head to an angle so I could see him, and the calm openness on his face. "I love you," he repeated with more force. "Now and always."

I wiggled until he released me, because I wanted to face him. "I love you so much," I told him fiercely, the tears still falling. "So damn much, Slade Riverson. But please don't *ever* die for me."

*None of you are allowed to die*, I reiterated through the bond, in case our beasts needed to hear it as well.

"We will never leave you," Hunter promised as he moved closer.

Kellan and Finley moved in as well, until I was surrounded by my alphas.

My five very naked alphas.

*Thank you, goddess.* Someone send her a gift basket and nicely worded letter, because she had delivered my perfect forever.

*Our* forever. In our bond, the beasts were snuggled as close as we were out here, and I knew I'd forever be grateful that when I'd run, they'd caught me.

And they would again.

Each and every time.

# EPILOGUE

## EMME

### THE AFTER...

In the days that followed Jewels' defeat, my alphas and I barely left the house. Constantine departed from Golden Claw to search for any remaining members of the magical community, and Florence and Gerry took some well-deserved vacation days, leaving us all alone.

With nothing to do but bask in the beauty of our bond.

We didn't talk to anyone. We didn't deal with the council. No one even worked.

Kellan and Finley had already missed their road games and therefore didn't need to be back on the team until next Friday, leaving us to spend our days eating, swimming, healing... and screwing through every bedroom of the house. Along with the pool, cinema, gym, kitchen... yeah, okay, you get the point. We christened every room and thoroughly enjoyed the experience.

This time together was a gift, and my hardest daily decision was which alphas to sleep beside. Usually, it was Hunter and Kellan together, and then Slade and Talon together. Finley occasionally joined Hunter and Kellan, but mostly he preferred to have me alone so he could sleep buried deep inside me. However I slept though, I was always surrounded by pack and love.

If Kassidy could experience even an iota of the happiness I was currently blissed out on, there was no way she'd still be refusing to see Henderson. *No way.*

Slade dragged my ass out of bed early the following week. *You need to keep training,* he said.

He was choosing to mind-speak a lot lately, and I could tell it calmed his beast when we were open in the bond. Along with me wearing my tracking necklace and staying in sight of his million cameras. *Jewels might be dead, but there could be more threats.*

He was right, and I wanted to grow stronger, so I only complained for half the drive to the training facility. Slade didn't even growl at me, just wore a damn smirk that told me he somewhat enjoyed my whine.

A ton of enforcers were already on the field, and I ran straight into a battle with Horton, where I beat him two times in a row before he figured out my new strategy and kicked my ass the next three times. I also managed to hold my own with Slade for about two minutes.

On the drive home, we discussed the plans for Kellan's birthday tomorrow. "Track day again," I chanted, pumping my fist in excitement. "Is his gift ready?"

Slade nodded, his Lambo picking up speed. *Yeah, they were delivered yesterday, along with paper if you want to wrap them.*

We kept Kellan from hearing this conversation for obvious reasons, and I was thrilled at how easy it was now to choose who I shared information with. At least with everyone other than Slade, who insisted on knowing everything.

The dragon refused to be excluded from any part of my life, and arguing with him was futile.

*Stubborn lizard.*

*Not a lizard, Snow.*

Yeah, yeah. Luckily, there was one part of my life I had managed to keep from him, simply by ensuring all communication about *Prank Wars* was done via text. It had been harder than expected, but if everything went to plan, I believed we could pull it off.

*After* Kellan's birthday.

On our street, the house came into view, along with a familiar Range Rover parked out front. I stared at it as we passed to enter the garage, trying to figure out how I felt about seeing it there.

"What are they doing here?" I finally muttered when we were parked in the garage. "I'm not sure I'm ready to speak to them yet."

Slade took a second to respond. "You've cried a few times in your sleep," he said softly, meeting my gaze. His expression was neutral, but his eyes burned. "I know you think about them a lot. It's time for some closure—in whatever way works for you. If you want me to kill them, it's done. If you never want to see them again, I'll kick them out of Golden Claw. And if you want to forgive them, we'll stand by your side. It's all in your hands, Snow."

My wolf howled, and magic surged in our bond as every beast responded. There was nothing foreign about my magic now, and when it combined with the strength of our quintet, there was a scary level of power available to us. Cora and Warrick were no physical threat, that was for sure, but emotional was a whole other story.

"Yeah, I think you're right," I admitted, while still making no move to open my door and leave the safety of the car. He let me sit for many minutes, until eventually he got out and opened my door. Still, all he did after was hold a hand out for me, just waiting there for when I was ready.

Eventually I found the fortitude to grasp on to his lifeline and exit the car. "I do miss Cora and Warrick," I admitted. "But I'm not sure my trust in them will ever be the same. Even knowing they were victims too."

"Just talk to them," Slade advised, remaining strong and steady at my side.

When we entered the living room, the rest of our pack were there on the long couch. I hadn't used this room as much since the Christmas tree came down in February. I wished for its cheery glow more than ever today.

Cora and Warrick were awkwardly perched on the small couch. The tension was thick as everyone silently stared into the middle of the room. In the bond, my alphas were exuding annoyance, since anything or anyone who hurt me was on their shit list.

*Sorry we didn't tell you, little mate,* Hunter said. *They ambushed us, and you were almost home anyway. Figured you could bail if you saw their car.*

*I almost did,* I replied, barely suppressing a laugh.

Hunter grinned, but it wasn't with happiness. All dark and predatory.

When I moved through the doorway, Cora's head popped up. "Emme," she breathed, pushing to her feet.

Warrick stood as well, his eyes very dark and shiny as he looked me over. "I'm glad to see you're okay," he said, and there was genuine relief in his voice.

I had to press my bottom lip between my teeth to keep it from trembling, as the very sight of them triggered feelings of panic and fear. "Why are you here?" I asked, relieved that Slade remained solidly at my side, his hand wrapped around mine.

Cora swallowed roughly, looking briefly at Warrick before returning to me. "We're here to apologize. We don't expect you to forgive us, but we owe you a very large apology and explanation."

Like Warrick, there was nothing but sincerity in her tone, and a part of me appreciated that even not expecting forgiveness, they'd still come to deliver the apology.

"Okay, it is time that we talked," I said, stumbling over to the couch where the rest of my pack waited.

Slade released me so I could sit between Hunter and Kellan, who both reached out to touch me, offering their support. Slade joined Talon against the wall, fulfilling the role of dragon sentinels once again.

Cora and Warrick sat as well, turning to face me. "We never wanted to betray you," Warrick said first, the deeper rasp reminding me of the first day I'd met him.

It felt like a million years ago with everything that had happened between now and then.

"When I came to your street during the battle to save Cora, I had no idea that Jewels had returned to our house. It wasn't until all the enforcers left, and they took Marcus' body away, that she revealed herself and her plan."

"She wanted to hide away right under your noses," Cora said, sounding tired. "She wanted to create a nest at our house, where you'd never think to look. We tried to fight it at first."

Warrick nodded. "Yeah, I spent days in my wolf form attacking as she wove her shield. I fought as hard as I could, and tried to tear it all to pieces, but her magic was too strong. We ended up under her spell and under her control so fast it was terrifying."

Cora pressed a hand to her chest, which heaved as if the memories were choking the breath from her. "We couldn't even kill ourselves to stop her from moving forward with her plan... and trust me, Warrick tried."

As they described the true depravity of what they'd been through, a ragged sound escaped my constricted throat. To reach the point where taking your own life was the only option to escape...

"She hurt Richard and Sierra badly," Warrick continued. "They're still with the healers, but apparently there's a shortage of spells, and we're not sure how or *if* they'll fully recover."

Cora leaned forward until the tears streaking down her cheeks splattered on the floor. "We're so sorry that we almost cost you your life and pack. We're so sorry for the part we played, and as soon as we felt the wavering of her magic, we did what we could to save you. We would never have betrayed you of our own free will."

Warrick grasped his mate's hand, holding it so tightly that his knuckles were white. "I'm sorry I showed up at the hockey game. She controlled our actions. I tried to drive my car into a building, but I couldn't even manage that."

Hunter's hand flexed in mine. "It sounds as if there was no way for you to warn us about what she was doing."

They both shook their heads. "No way," Warrick said. "She controlled our actions and words outside of the house. Basically, when we were with you, it was Jewels speaking."

Cora batted at her tears, clearing her throat. "With all of that being said, we're still really fucking sorry. We should have found a way to help you."

"You did help me in the end," I said, remembering their wolves leaping through the doorway. They'd had no idea that I was all powered up and about to take the bitch down.

I stood, my alpha's hands slipping off me. "You risked your life to save me, even when you'd been suffering under her hold for weeks."

Cora stood as well and took two steps toward me before halting, as if she'd suddenly remembered that we weren't back to hugging. Only, it felt like a hug was exactly what we needed.

I closed the final distance and wrapped my arms around her, my chest aching as she froze in my hold for a beat, before her arms gripped me like I was the last anchor in her world.

As we stood there, Cora wasn't the only one sobbing. "I'm sorry. I'm so sorry, Emme," she whispered over and over.

"I forgive you," I finally managed to say. "Though there's really nothing to forgive. You were victims too, and for much longer than me. I have really missed you both, and I'm sorry about Richard and

Sierra. We will do everything in our power to make sure they're okay."

I didn't know shit about healing, but I'd learn if it saved them.

Warrick leapt to his feet and threw his arms around us both, and even with five alphas growling, none of them tore him away. At least not for the first ten seconds.

When we pulled apart, I was surprised by how quickly the healing had started between us. "Be at the racetrack tomorrow," I said on a whim. "Bring your best car and driving skills. It's Kellan's birthday and he's out for blood."

Golden whooped as he fist-pumped. "I'm going to kick all your asses tomorrow," he hollered. "I can already taste the birthday victory."

Warrick drew Cora against him with one hand, while the other wiped at the tears on his cheeks. "We'll be there," he said.

Cora nodded. "Thank you." There was a brief hesitation before she added, "I love you, Emme. I promise to make this up to you, and no matter what it takes, I will never betray your friendship again."

As far as I was concerned, they hadn't betrayed it in the first place.

There was nothing left to forgive.

# EPILOGUE PART TWO

EMME

I woke to the sensation of a warm tongue sliding along my clit. Kellan, who had requested me all to himself on his birthday, groaned and pulled me closer, lapping at my dripping core.

"Golden," I gasped, sleep and pleasure swirling in my head as I clutched the silky sheets.

A rumble spilled from his lips and sent vibrations from my clit to my damn toes. "Kellan Jackson," I rasped in a husky voice. "It's your birthday. I'm supposed to give you—"

He cut me off by sliding a finger inside me and curling it before he added a second. He timed each unhurried thrust with a maddening swirl of his tongue over my clit. The moment he stroked my g-spot, I exploded into an intense release, which had my vision flashing black and white, like my brain had fritzed out.

"That's it, baby," Kellan crooned, catching every drop of my cum, and when he finally lifted his face, his smile was wide and satisfied. "That's how you start a fucking birthday. With your favorite breakfast."

My breaths heaved in and out as I wiggled my fingers for him to come up to me. "Happy birthday, mate," I whispered as he crawled over me, our lips meeting in a kiss that was as slow and decadent as Kellan *eating his favorite breakfast*. "Holy shit, you did such a good job. I swear to the goddess, your tongue should be classified as a weapon against all females."

Kellan's pupils flared, and he sucked in a ragged breath. "Not all females, Shortcake. Just you. Always and only you."

He kissed me again, both of us tasting the sweet musk of my release. Without breaking away from me, he lifted his hips and I widened my legs. His first thrust was unhurried too, as if this morning was about savoring our time together.

My eyes nearly rolled back in my head at how good it felt.

"Best birthday ever," he whispered, violet gaze on my face. When I was with my alphas like this, they always felt like the gravity that kept me here.

"For the rest of your life, you get birthdays just like this," I promised, licking my way up his throat, needing more of his taste.

When we couldn't handle the edging any longer, his thrusts picked up momentum, and I loved that when my orgasm hit he tensed and called out my name too, spilling inside me.

Kellan stayed buried in me for the entire morning, even when we weren't actively fucking. Oftentimes, we were having perfectly normal conversation, as he channeled Finley's need to always be this close.

"Our contracts are up this year, but Coach said he wants us to stay on," he murmured, playing with my hair as I rested against his chest, a soothing heartbeat under my ear. "I think we're going to remain on the team. Fin was ready to quit on the spot, but I reminded him that not only is our enemy dead, you're cool with us still playing. We're young enough to beat people up and call it sport for many more years. Not to mention we'd both really miss the guys on our team."

I dragged my fingertips across the light stubble on his cheeks. "I'm more than cool with it. I want you to do whatever makes you happy, and I love watching you both on the ice. It's… like poetry in motion."

Kellan kissed me so suddenly that all thoughts of hockey vanished, and we lost another hour wrapped up in each other. Eventually, it was time to get dressed for our race day. Slade had left a new racing suit on my bed, this one a goldish pink to match my braided hair, with a black wolf on the back.

We found our pack in the kitchen, already dressed in their race suits, including Slade and Talon. The twins wore black and red and *fuck me* they looked incredible. Hunter's suit was a dark navy blue, Finley's olive green, and Kellan was wearing the hell out of a gold and black number.

Okay, I was *done for*.

"Guys, this is unfair," I said, waving my hand at them. "You were built to wear race suits, and I'm over here panting. I can't win under these conditions. It's cheating."

Through our mental bond they could feel the swells of my desire, despite the way I'd spent the morning. A morning which left me so sated I could barely feel my legs still.

"I don't need to cheat to beat you, Shortcake," Kellan said with a smirk as he bopped my nose. "I'm just that good."

"You're just that cocky," Hunter added with a nod. "One day, someone will knock you off that winning spot."

Kellan shrugged like he wasn't worried, and I truly loved his confidence. It was well-earned after all.

The alphas kissed me good morning—or good lunchtime, to be more accurate. Slade was last, and his nose lingered on my cheek as he breathed me in. "You look positively delicious," he said, kissing my lips. "I've got ten more suits arriving next week. You will model them for us."

"You got it," I said, excited that he'd bought me gifts.

Florence had prepared Kellan's *second* favorite breakfast, burritos, which we all wolfed down before heading to the garage. This time we'd get to drive our cars to the track, and I was excited to warm the Porsche up for the day.

Talon claimed my passenger seat, since he wasn't racing today.

As the engine roared to life, I let it settle, reaching over to grasp his hand. "It felt wrong being at the track without you last time. I'm glad you're here today."

He threaded our fingers together. "I might not be racing, but I want to be wherever you are, Honey." Aw, my corny sweetheart of a dragon. He was all tough and angry outside, with his gooey, soft center.

Following Hunter from the garage, I stayed close through the streets, the others behind us. Our speed remained sedate until we hit the back road out of town, where we got to open the engines up. This part wasn't about racing, but we certainly had fun testing our cars' limits.

By the time we pulled into the racetrack, I was amped up on adrenaline and ready for a real race. "That was more fun than I expected," Talon said, and I smirked at him.

I predicted that by next race we'd have him wanting to drive, though he might need a few more lessons first.

Hunter led us into the main track, and we parked our cars on the starting line. A few minutes later, Warrick's Mclaren pulled in with Cora riding shotgun, and I was surprised to see Kenzo as well. He had a Mitsubishi Lancer Evo, and while I'd never been a huge fan of JDM cars, his was in gorgeous condition. The final surprise of the day showed up a few minutes later in the form of a black-on-black BMW M3 CS, with none other than Kassidy behind the wheel.

I'd never heard her express much interest in cars or racing before, but you didn't buy that baby unless you enjoyed speed.

When Cora jumped out of the McLaren and hurried toward us, I was relieved to see a glow about her. The teal of her race suit set off her skin and hair nicely. I met her hug, thankful to feel our normal returning. Kassidy joined us a beat later, her race suit all black, which matched her wickedly cool car.

"Friends!" she cried. Hunter had told me that Cora and Warrick made their apologies to her too, and she had forgiven them.

"I'm so glad you could both be here," I said, feeling giddy at how amazing this day was shaping up to be, and it wasn't even my birthday. "I hope you give Kellan a run for his money, Kass."

Her smirk was filled with smug confidence. "Golden is going to have to work hard to hold on to his trophy. Even if it is his birthday."

Cora laughed, and she looked so carefree I had to ask, "Are Richard and Sierra doing better?"

"Yes," she nodded enthusiastically. "Oh, they're doing much better. The healers said you went over last night and sat with them."

I'd done more than sit, and I could tell Cora knew that. My magic might still be a secret in most circles, but my friends were aware of my hybrid nature. "Constantine gave me a few spells to try," I admitted softly.

Cora's lip trembled. "You're a better friend than we deserve. Thank you. Thank you so much."

Real friendships weren't about who showed up during the good times, but the shifters who stood by your side through the storms too. We'd experienced a lot of shitty weather lately, but we would be stronger moving forward. All of us.

"Come on," Kassidy said, dragging me over to Kellan.

"Ah, my competition has arrived," Golden said as he drooled a little over her car.

Kassidy just waggled her eyebrows, as if she was a shifter of mystery. Behind us a few bets were being placed between Finley and Warrick. "Is that everyone?" I asked, wondering if we were waiting on anyone else.

Kellan nodded, slinging his arm over my shoulders. "Yeah, Christian had to head back to his family for the week, but I'll catch up with him when he returns."

"Let's race, then," Hunter called, and we all put our game faces on as we headed for our cars, already positioned on the starting line.

When I was inside, I flexed my hands on the wheel, butterflies fluttering in my stomach. I turned to catch Talon's eye, who was sitting in an observation zone, only to find he wasn't alone. We had been waiting for one more, even if we didn't know it.

Constantine stood there, looking far less scruffy than usual, and when he waved in my direction, the butterflies were joined by a kick of warmth.

"Eyes on the prize, pretty mate," Kellan shouted, and I returned my gaze to the track in front of us.

*Always on the prize*, I shot back in our bond, watching the lights closely.

When the red switched to yellow, I planted my foot on the gas, keeping the other on the brake. Launch control was ready. *I was ready.*

"Let's race," I screamed as the green flashed.

My car lurched forward, the rush of speed like a shot of pure adrenaline in my veins. The initial lineup was similar to last time, with Slade out front, but the Evo shocked the hell out of me by keeping up with the Lambo off the initial launch. Warrick slipped in behind them both, with Kellan next, and Kassidy held the fifth spot in the M3 CS.

From the first launch, Kellan hit the track with more aggression than usual, swinging his car around corners like it was on rails. Hunter, Finley, and I remained at the back for the first and second lap, but by the third Hunter had passed Kenzo, falling in behind Warrick and Kassidy.

Slade and Kellan were out in front battling hard, and while the SVJ had more power, Kellan was on fire today, leaving them evenly matched. Warrick was solidly in third, but Kassidy could really freaking drive as she pushed him all the way. Hunter remained in fifth, Kenzo sixth, leaving Finley and me in the last two places.

Finley caught my eye, as we headed into the fourth lap, and I loved that we were side by side. *You and me, darlin'*, he drawled in my mind, and I cackled like a damn witch cliché.

*I'm going to beat you today, Grouchy. Hold on to your bear coat.*

Planting my foot, I took the next bend faster than I'd ever taken a turn out here and almost lost control. But this car's handling was near perfection, so with a lot of help from its traction control, I managed not to crash. *Thank you, Golden, for insisting I leave that on.*

His was dialed all the way off, of course.

*Careful, Emmeline,* Hunter ordered, his tone serious. *You're precious cargo, with nothing to prove here.*

Ignoring him, I took the next corner almost as fast, finding the perfect speed to half slide around the curve. By the fifth lap, Kellan was a car in front of Slade, with Hunter and Warrick side by side for third and fourth.

I closed in on Kenzo, who was sliding the track in true rally style, and while my Porsche couldn't drive like that without me possibly dying, I did catch him on the next straight by hitting my DRS button. This nifty little piece of tech adjusted the rear wing and front diffuser to reduce drag on straights. I'd never used it before, but fuck, Kellan was right, it really made a difference.

When I crossed the line beside Kenzo, I looked up to the flashing board to find I'd beaten my last race *combined lap time* by a good four seconds.

*Yes!*

This time Kellan caught me as I launched from the car, spinning me around in a circle. He'd also beaten his last combined time by three seconds, and in the bond his wolf was losing it.

"Best birthday ever!" he cried, his cheeks pink as he smiled so hard it had to be hurting his face.

It made me happy to see him happy, and I climbed him until our lips met in a breathless kiss. "Congratulations, baby," I murmured, pressing kisses all over his face. "Are you ready for your present?"

His eyes widened. "Didn't I get that all morning? 'Cause that was definitely a present."

With a snort, I smacked his shoulder. "That was a present for both of us. I got you something else of course."

I had to wiggle against him, and for a second he refused to release me. When he finally relented, he kept his eyes locked on me as I dashed over to the Lambo, where Slade was retrieving the wrapped gift. Taking the weighty box, I returned to Kellan, who'd been joined by Kenzo, Talon, and Constantine.

My father had not only tamed and cut his hair, but he was in new jeans and blue button-down, with runners on his feet. "You look amazing," I said, giving him a one-armed hug, since my other one was occupied by the heavy present. "Thanks for being here."

He pulled away wearing a slightly stunned expression, and I wondered how long it would take for this *family thing* not to take us by surprise. "I wouldn't have missed it," he said. "You drove amazing, by the way. I'm so proud of you."

And just like that I regressed all the way back to a child craving her father's approval. *Hello, childhood trauma.* Maybe it was time for me to book my own appointment with Dr. Karen, since I could no longer use the excuse that I was too busy saving shifter kind.

"Thank you. It means a lot to hear you say that," I said, sniffling to tamp down my emotions. "I hope you're around for more of these days."

Constantine nodded, the icy blue of his eyes lightening. "Hunter said there's a house available on your street if I want to claim it, and I might take him up on that offer."

My gaze snapped to my entitled alpha, who even in the midst of his conversation with Warrick, watched me closely. *Thank you.*

*Anything for you, baby girl. Absolutely anything.*

Kellan, who'd been as patient as he could manage, wrapped his arm around my shoulder and dragged me into his side. "I've been a very good boy waiting over here," he said in a rush, pressing his lips to the side of my head. "Can I have my present now? Please, pretty mate?"

This alpha… "I do love when you beg, Golden Boy."

*On my knees, baby?*

My thighs clenched and I shook my head. *I can still feel you between my thighs, Golden Boy. But yes. On your knees.*

He groaned. *Everyone here is about to see you get fucked. I hope you know that.*

*My dad is here.*

He shrugged, like he couldn't give less of a shit about that, but before he could haul me into his arms, I thrust the gift into his face. "Happy birthday, Golden!" My voice was higher than usual, but only my pack knew what was going on, as they drifted in the quintet essence.

The blue of Kellan's eyes was light as he gently removed the box from my grasp, hefting it up and down. "It's weighty," he mused, eyeing it closely as he turned it side to side. "I don't think I've ever been so excited to open a gift."

He tore through the shiny blue paper to reveal the ornate box below. It was similar to my *dagger box*, but his had its own unique spin, with sapphires and diamonds embedded in the carved wolf. Kellan's eyes were wide as he stared between me and the box. "Oh, Shortcake. You didn't!"

He lifted the lid slowly, and when the contents were revealed, he stared down like he couldn't believe his eyes. The pair of long blades were nestled inside the navy velvet lining, and when he brushed his fingers over the glinting steel, he released a small rasp. "Best birthday ever."

Making his day a little special was exactly what I'd hoped for.

"Plenty more where this came from," I informed him, and when Kellan looked at me, it was with even more reverence than the blades.

*Best birthday ever.*

# EPILOGUE PART THREE

SLADE

After the events of the last few weeks, it was hard for me to be away from Emmeline. Eventually, as life returned to normal, we all started to resume our regular life and duties, so I relied more on our bond, cameras, and her tracking necklace.

During training today, my phone remained open on the page with her location and the camera that was in her vicinity, watching her play in the pool with my twin.

*Safe at home.* Safely out of the hands of any who would think of harming or touching her.

Every night I relived the endless hours we spent flying toward Golden Claw, not knowing if Jewels had destroyed my reason for existence. It had been a day which fundamentally changed me, and it was only on the nights she slept in my arms that I was able to relax enough to even sleep.

The sole reason I was even at training today was that Talon was with her, throwing her across the pool as she shrieked in laughter. Emme was generally very good at not keeping me out of our bond, but she was holding it tighter today, and I couldn't bring myself to force my way in. Leaving me to rely on Talon and the video feed. The flashes of her in a red bikini had me really fucking distracted, and for the first time my enforcers almost kicked my obsessed ass.

When we were done for the day, my muscles burned in the way that let me know I'd pushed my limits. On the feed, Emme was lounging by the pool, so I did a quick flick through the cameras to scan the perimeter. My alarms hadn't triggered, but I no longer relied on just one source of detection.

The street looked fine, the guard hut functioning as per usual, the front and back of the house unremarkable. Then I checked room by room.

In the main living room, I paused as a flicker of a shadow in the corner caught my eye. When I adjusted my view, there was nothing there, and I shook my head, worried that my paranoia had finally reached its pinnacle. Moving through the various room feeds, I found those shadows in almost every single one.

*What the hell?*

When I dialed Hunter, his phone rang out, and I left a short voicemail to call me. Next, I tried the rest of my pack brothers, but with the same results. Tapping into the bond didn't help either, with my twin telling me there was nothing his dragon could sense, and Emme was still safe with him by the pool.

Unease settled in my gut as I raced through the training facility, ignoring alphas as they called out goodbyes. When I slid into my car, I flicked through the cameras again, pausing when a grotesque face briefly appeared in a shadow before disappearing just as quickly.

The SVJ took off in a squeal of tires, and I risked everyone's lives as I zoomed in on the cameras while flying along the street, only to find there was no longer a white-faced and red-lipped visage in the shadows.

*Emme!* I pushed against her wolf in the bond, and when her beast startled, I cursed my roughness. *Sorry, Snow. But I need you to stay out of the house. There's something weird happening inside. I'll be home in ten minutes. Don't leave Talon's side until then.*

Her beast shuddered. I wasn't the only one who held fresh memories of our last attack. *What's wrong, Scary? We're by the pool. Talon just did a quick sweep of the area, and there's nothing amiss here. My wolf can't sense anything either.*

Fucking hell!

*It might be magic again. I can't be sure. Just don't move from that spot. I'm only five away now.*

I pushed my car to its absolute limits, harder than even on the racetrack. When I screeched to a halt out front, I opened the cameras to find that every room in the house was filled with shadows now, though at least none of them had that fucked up face in them.

Crashing through the front door, I examined the front entrance, which looked normal and *shadowless*. Stalking farther inside, I expanded my senses, but couldn't pick up on any intruders either.

There was no sign of anything amiss as I headed for the pool area, finding Talon crouched protectively over Emme's lounger. "Brother," I called, and he took a step toward me. "We need to search the house."

Emme scrambled up to follow and my gaze slid over her curves. If this situation wasn't so dire, I'd be stripping the red bikini right off her perfect body. "Did you find someone inside?" she asked, her eyes widening as her scent flooded the area.

She tried to race by me, but I gently caught her around the center, lifting her off her feet. There was no struggle from her as she slumped against me, the damp swimsuit soaking into my clothes. "I'm scared, Slade," she whispered, and I wanted to just fucking kill them all.

It was my job to ensure she never felt fear, and I was failing her again. "If anyone is stupid enough to attack us at home, they will be destroyed."

My dragon rumbled his appreciation as she hugged around me. "What did you see in the cameras?"

Trying to explain it didn't work as expected. "The house is filled with shadows, but only on the cameras, and when I zoomed in..." A bead of sweat dripped from my temple. "I-I saw a clown."

Emme blinked, and parted her lips, before her brow furrowed. "Like... a circus clown? A *clown* clown? I don't understand."

*Yeah, burning the house down was an excellent option right now.* "I've never liked clowns," I reluctantly revealed a fear that no one knew about, except maybe Hunter. There'd been an incident with the television during a particularly fucked-up movie when we were young.

Talon looked so confused, like he couldn't understand the words coming out of my mouth. Emme pressed her lips together, her eyes flat-out laughing at me. "Did you perhaps watch a movie with a clown and red balloon when you were young?"

Muttering a curse, I glanced over my shoulder and returned her to her feet. "I'm going to check out the house. You wait here with Talon."

In typical omega fashion, she completely ignored me and stayed right on my ass as I re-entered the house. At least Talon was keeping *her* ass protected by bringing up the rear. As we stepped into the hallway, I caught a glimpse of red, but when I took off toward the theatre room, there was no sign of anyone.

The only scents in here were my pack's, and the only heartbeats were Emme's and Talon's.

Worry built in my chest as I explored the house room by room, finding nothing out of place and no shadows. "Are you sure you saw something?" Emme asked gently. "Show me the cameras."

Pulling out my phone, I flipped through the rooms again, only to find nothing on the screen now. "Let's check upstairs," I said, shaking my head. "My system is more thorough up there and I have recordings."

Emme remained closer as we ascended to the third floor, when I reached my room, I headed right for my *stalker wall* as Emme dubbed it. I hadn't really needed it recently, having my mate up close and personal instead. But when I pulled the curtains open, everything was exactly as I left it. I scanned the multiple screens, and a rage filled growl spilled from my lips as I caught sight of a shadowy clown standing right in the living room. As I stared, it lifted a long, shiny blade, and waved at the camera, like the *motherfucker* knew we watched.

Emme and Talon moved to stand on either side of me. "Do you see it?" I demanded, staring at the soon to be dead clown, who was taunting me with a wide, red smile.

Emme peered closely at every different frame of security, until I pointed toward the living room one. When I met her gaze, she looked more confused than ever. "I'm not sure what I'm supposed to be seeing."

I jabbed right at the footage, only to find there was no sign of the clown again. No shadows either. "Did your father find any witches left except for you two?" I asked her, trying to piece together what was happening. This was not a normal situation, so either I was being fucked with, or magic was involved.

She shook her head. "Nope. He's still searching, but from what he can tell, America is all but witch free these days. You think magic is involved with your little clown problem?"

She lifted her hands, and for the first time I could scent magic. "I can't sense anything," she said, and I caught the concerned expression she shot Talon's way.

My mate and brother thought I'd lost my dragon mind, and maybe they were right.

Turning from the security, I faced my *wall of Emme*, squinting at each picture to find a clown sticker across it. Tearing one down, I shoved it under their faces. "Surely you see the clowns on Emme's face? Someone is fucking with us."

They both stared at the image, and Emme reached out and grasped it, bringing it so close it almost touched her nose. She returned it to me with a frown. "It's just a picture of me when I was twelve."

Right then, in that moment, she tightened up the bond again... completely giving herself away. I *was* being fucked with, but it wasn't by an enemy. *My little brat was pranking me.*

Talon glanced over as well. "Where is the clown? Is this like that game Emme tried to play on Kellan's phone and lost?"

Ah, she had the whole pack in on it.

My dragon calmed right around the time our omega pouted. "Look, no one could find that weird little human in every image. His stripy shirt blended in perfectly to the background."

I glanced at the monitors to find the knife-wielding clown front and center, giving me the creepiest smile. Oh yeah. Whichever of my brothers was under that mask was getting his ass kicked.

Playing along, I snarled. "That's it. I'm burning this house down."

Emme gasped and called after me as I raced down to the living room, only to find it completely empty. The fucker was fast, which made me think it might be Kellan.

Scales rippled across my skin as I played their game. I'd barely hidden my smirk as the clown appeared, wrapping its arms around her. Excited for the beatdown about to happen, I launched myself at them, right as Emme spun in its arms and planted a kiss straight on red painted lips.

Halting, I raised one eyebrow and Emme examined my face before she sighed. "Ah, dammit. You knew."

Kellan cracked up, his outside finally reflecting the clown within. "Such a hard shifter to prank."

"You better shut up or I will kill you," I warned him, though my focus remained on the disappointed omega in front of me.

"You did have me for a while there," I admitted, and that got her perking right up.

"I did?"

Hunter and Finley spilled into the room, and I knew why there'd been no real sign of their involvement until now. Their scents were everywhere anyway, but more than that, they all wore devices around their necks that were designed to hide heartbeats when hunting.

In truth, I was impressed. "You gave it away by pretending not to see the clowns on the photos. Other than that, this was a solid prank."

Emme sighed. "Yeah, I thought I was a touch too clever, didn't I? But that was for your stupid list of names on your wall. Which I defaced and destroyed."

I already knew she'd scribbled all over it, but I had a copy stored on my computer for when I had a spare minute or two for a murder rampage. "I can't wait for your next attempt, Snow."

Hunter gave me a little shove, and I scowled at him for real while debating if I should break his pretty face. "Let me guess where she learned I had a tiny issue with clowns."

The entire room burst into laughter, and for once it didn't piss me off.

In truth, I'd missed these stupid prank wars.

Talon released a genuine laugh as he said, "This was fun. I never knew alphas were allowed to have fun."

Well, fuck, if a few clowns and me looking like an idiot amused them, I'd take this sort of prank any day. "You know you're in big trouble, Snow," I warned her, already calculating all the possible future pranks I could rain down on her. "You started Prank Wars 2.0. in a big way. It can only go bigger from here.

She showed no fear as she popped up on her toes, her boobs dangerously close to spilling from her bikini, which distracted me enough that I barely heard her reply.

"Bring it on, bestie," she trilled. "Nothing can top the look on your face when you saw those clown faces on my photos."

The part that had given her away was both disturbing and clever.

As another burst of laughter hit her, she overbalanced and fell into me. With my arms full of curves and soft skin, I had to acknowledge that while clowns might be my nemesis, this tiny slip of a female was the only one who could take me out. She was salvation and destruction in one omega package.

# EPILOGUE PART FOUR

EMME

**M**y leg bounced up and down, and I'd chewed all my nails off by the time we entered the third period of the game. Despite losing two and winning two of their road games, the Celtic Wolves had enough points to make it into the playoff rounds for the Shifter Cup. Just in time for Kellan and Finley to throw themselves full throttle into training and games.

Tonight was the game that would seal the cup winner, and the score was tied one apiece with the Red Pandas, who were playing like their lives depended on it.

But so were our boys.

Especially Henderson, who appeared to have something to prove. In related news, Kassidy sat in a nervous huddle beside Hunter on my right. Slade was on my left, and Talon beside him. Constantine rounded out the end of our row, and I loved that everyone had shown up to support the team.

Tyson and Julien had arrived with all of their pack, including little Lachlan. Danielle and Conrad even flew out to support their son, and we'd had the best time catching up without impending doom hanging over our heads. While they'd been momentarily pissed no one had called them for help when we were fighting for our lives, they understood there hadn't really been time.

Cora, Warrick, Richard, and Sierra finished off their row, and it was good to see them all out together. Their pack would never be the same again, but they were living for Marcus the best way they knew how.

As the final minutes of the third ticked away, I leaned forward, focused on the intense puck passing across the ice. There were plenty of attempts to score, but nothing made it past either goalie. When Henderson got it down to our end, he was checked hard into the boards, bouncing off to crash on the ice. I caught Kassidy's flinch and the way she ran a quick, worried glance over him before looking away. But she couldn't hide her clenched fists, which only eased when the big Viking shifter got to his feet and skated off.

The hard hits continued, and the crowd grew louder and more restless as both teams fought for their damn lives. With five minutes remaining, Finley pushed forward and joined Kellan, the two of them aggressively checking Pandas out of the way, while they passed back and forth to their teammates.

When they were triple-teamed, Kellan offloaded the puck to Henderson, and in the blink of an eye—so fast I literally almost missed it—he moved it on to Christian, who shot on goal. It slipped in the lower right corner, and when the red light flashed, half of the damn stadium jumped to their feet and screamed until we were all repairing some hearing damage.

The boys skated a few laps around the ice, and the lineup was switched up. I stared at the back of Kellan and Finley's heads as they dropped onto the bench.

"This is too fucking intense," I breathed, my heart racing.

Four minutes was an eternity in this game. Even being up one, I couldn't rest easy.

When the lines rotated again, the Pandas hadn't scored, and there was a mad scrimmage at one end, but no other shot made it past the goalie. At the final buzzer, the score remained two to one, and our boys were the cup winners again.

Kellan skated around the stadium with a giant golden trophy hoisted on his shoulder while the stadium shook from stomping feet, clapping, and screams.

The pride I felt as I watched them win had me jumping up and down and hugging Danielle like ten times. "They did so amazing," she wailed, her eyes filled with tears.

"They're talented our boys," I replied, equally as teary.

When she released me, Hunter drew me back between him and Slade, all of us standing and clapping still. "They played their asses off out there," he said, a note of pride in his voice.

"They really did."

Kellan and Finley slammed against the glass in front of us and waved me down. "Come on, Shortcake," Kellan shouted. I couldn't hear him over the crowd, but I read his lips.

Talon, Slade, and Hunter escorted me down to the ice, but before my feet made contact, Kellan scooped me into his arms. He hoisted me up on his shoulder and skated around like I was the prize he'd won.

"I'm so proud of you," I yelled, clutching his shoulder. "That was an intense game."

He laughed, shaking me in an unsettling way. "Wasn't my best game, but the boys pulled it together."

Brushing my hand through his hair, I said, "You played brilliantly, Golden. Your passes were outstanding all night, and Fin checked everyone who came close. Your goalie needs his own trophy, I swear to the goddess, and Henderson was on fire—"

Kellan swung me down into his arms and kissed the words out of me, right in front of everyone.

I got so caught up in his kiss, I barely realized he was still gliding us lazily around the now packed ice. When he handed me off to Finley, I got another victory lap in his arms. "I'm so happy you're here," he said, his eyes shiny as his voice cracked.

"I'm so proud of you," I told him; my Grouchy had never heard that enough growing up. "You were brilliant out there." He did his beary rumble, and I got another thorough kissing.

Eventually, they had to return me so they could shower and do their press obligations. "Where did all the others get to?" I asked when I was with Hunter, Talon, and Slade.

"Afterparty," Slade said shortly.

*Oh, right.* The team was throwing a huge party in one of the warehouses on the edge of Golden Claw. Whether it was to celebrate or commiserate, everyone had already planned to be there.

"Do you want to go?" Hunter asked, examining me closely.

I shook my head, but then turned it into a half-shrug. "I mean, if Kel and Finley want to celebrate their win, you know I'll be there. But I'd rather a quiet pack night at home."

Hunter wrapped his arm around me, his palm possessively draped over my stomach. "They just want to be where you are. We can decide later, but first… there's something we want to show you."

That piqued my interest, but no matter how much I badgered

them, no one would tell me what it was. And nothing slipped through the bond.

We ended up lingering in the stadium, waiting for the boys to finish up. Then all of us piled into the Benz, except for Slade, who had his bike. To fit, I perched on Finley's lap, with my legs over Kellan.

"The Pandas played their asses off today," Finley cheered, sounding elated but exhausted. "We were just slightly better."

"It was a close one," Hunter agreed, steering us through the city. The city lights flashed around us, lighting up the night, and for once the weather was perfect. The throes of winter had finally loosened its hold.

Kellan dropped his head back. "It's bittersweet when the season is over, but I'm looking forward to the break this year. Coach said training won't start for two months.

Finley's hand slid down the side of my throat, as his thumb gently stroked my skin. The calloused touch sending shivers down my spine. "Which will give us plenty of time to work on your car, Ice. We'll have it ready for summer."

That had me snuggling closer to him. "I can't wait. She's going to be perfect for summer driving with the top down."

Finley's lips pressed to the side of my throat, such a sweet, simple touch. "Oh yeah, we should head for the beach and make it a proper vacation."

The thought of vacations without having to run or hide left a deep ache in my chest. This time last year I'd been alone and in a dead-end life. Now the possibilities were endless, and I was loved endlessly.

When Hunter turned deeper into downtown Golden Claw, where the restaurants and food places were, I started trying to guess the surprise again.

"Did you make dinner reservations?" I asked, getting four smirks in return. "Did you buy a new apartment? Are we getting takeaway to eat naked off each other?"

Their scents exploded, and while trat clearly wasn't the surprise, judging by their groans, they were going to make it happen.

When Hunter parked, Talon opened the door and maneuvered me out without smashing my head. Once I was safely deposited on the sidewalk, I noticed the shop we stood in front of. It looked different to the last time I'd been here. The pretty pink and green signage was gone, leaving only huge windows and painted white brick.

Around the time Hunter gestured for me to follow him to the door, I started to put the pieces together. "Why are we at Chelsea's bakery?" I asked, though I already suspected.

Hunter unlocked and opened the door, stepping inside to hit the lights. I followed him to find the inside was also a blank space now. The previous styling had been stripped, leaving the bones of a bakery. "It's not Chelsea's bakery," Hunter said softly. "It's yours."

Even having suspected, it still took me by surprise. "I-I'm…I'm not a baker."

Kellan's heat pressed down my spine. "Baby, you're the best damn baker I've ever tasted."

Finley shook his head. "That's not how that saying goes. But true."

Slade walked through the door then and a snarl ripped from him. In his hand was a huge bunch of wild flowers, which he held out to me. "You didn't wait for me," he griped, and I forced myself not to laugh, taking the flowers from him.

"We literally just walked in, but thank you for the flowers," I said, wrapping one arm around him as I breathed in his smoky marshmallow scent. "Hunter said this shop is… *mine.*"

Finley reached over to run his fingers across my cheek, which was the moment I realized I was crying. "They're happy tears," I whispered, though they would already have felt that through the bond. "I can't believe you did this for me."

Slade brushed away a tear too, lifting the drop to press against his tongue. "This is barely a blip of what we're going to give you, Emmeline."

Hunter nodded. "You don't have to open a bakery if you don't want, but it's here, waiting for you."

I gasped, the flowers shaking as I pulled away from them. "Oh no, I want this. It's been a lifelong dream of mine to one day have my own café or business. Weirdly, I enjoyed working in them. And I love food —minus all the green monstrosities."

"You also hate carrots," Kellan reminded me.

"She's not a huge fan of corn, pumpkin, or sweet potato either," Finley added.

I waved them off. "Yeah, yeah. Greens and vegetables."

Hunter grunted. "Don't forget salad."

Ugh, I really hated salad.

Talon got us back on track as he strolled the shop, checking out every inch. "We're all going to help you run it," he said, and there was a glint of excitement on his face. "When I'm not training enforcers, I'll be here with you."

He'd recently started with his own squad, and his skills were turning out to be invaluable. Fletcher might have been a top-level evil asshole, but he'd trained his assassin well. Skills that would be passed on to keep Golden Claw safe for many future generations.

"We found our purpose," I whispered to him, and by his expression, it was clear he remembered that conversation we'd had long ago. When I'd reminded him that if we just survived our trials, we'd have the time to figure out our purpose.

"The lemon tarts are mine though," Kellan declared, a note of warning in his voice.

"Always yours first," I assured him, and then did a twirl to take in *my* bakery. I loved that it was stripped back so I could put my touch on it.

Images were already forming in my mind of how I wanted to decorate. I was determined to bring in a slice of every member of my pack: plants and books from Kellan, a roaring fire from Talon's and Slade's beasts, exposed brick and clean lines as Hunter enjoyed, and the warm cozy booths that would wrap around shifters like a Finley bear hug.

*Home.* This bakery would feel like home, and I hoped it would comfort shifters who weren't as blessed as me with such an amazing pack.

As my wolf howled in my mind, the other beasts pressed in closer, just as the alphas did in this bakery. The six of us let the essence flow between us, along with hope, love, and happiness.

"Thank you for catching me when I ran," I whispered as they wrapped me in their hold.

*My forever home.*

I couldn't wait to see what the future held.

# BONUS SCENE

I know that the text message threads are some of our favorites in this series, but unfortunately, with the mental link, it wasn't really needed for book 4.

Let's enjoy a bonus scene of this message thread which took place when they needed to coordinate the pranking of Slade:

Without him knowing about it.

## BONUS SCENE

### EMME

We took a break from swimming so I could coordinate the final steps. Keeping the phone hidden under the towel, Talon's broad shoulders also helped to block the camera view.

I rarely had my phone these days, but it was essential to plan the prank of all pranks. Hence why my wolf was firmly in place in the bond today.

When Hunter messaged, it took me an extra minute to decipher his words. I needed to practice my reading again, since I'd let that slip with everything happening.

Daddy of all Storms: Okay, I've got all the cameras
set up and will coordinate the integrated special
effects to work with our appearances.

Talon read over my shoulder. "That's why we shot some footage in advance," I whispered, keeping my head down so Slade couldn't lipread. No doubt it was one of his many thousands of skills. "Hunter will combine live and pre-shot images to really freak him out."

I wanted everything to feel eerie, like a haunted house.

When Hunter sent through a video of what he'd compiled so far, I was impressed with how freaky it all looked.

My phone buzzed again.

Golden: I swear, I missed my calling as an actor. I'm
going to be the scariest motherfucking clown that
ever clowned.

A snort escaped me, but you couldn't fault Kellan for his enthusiasm.

Grouchy: You've got half of it right. You are a clown.
I'm still not sure this is the smartest prank we could
pull on him. I'm sure the dragon is sensitive about
his little... uh, fear.

*GOLDEN CHANGED GROUCHY'S NAME*

Golden: Don't worry your pretty little head about it,
Fin Bear. Emme will protect us.

Scaredy Bear: Kellan, you won't have to paint on
fake blood if you keep that up. You'll be the most
authentically injured actor that ever existed.

With a laugh, I quickly typed a message, my heart aching at Kellan's name for me today.

Heart: You know I will protect you from Scary Shifter.

"You're the literal only one who could," Talon said with a shrug, like it was simple facts.

Maybe it was.

Daddy of all Storms: Emme is the only one who could.

Okay, we were all in agreement.

Heart: Cora will be in the guard hut in twenty minutes to do your makeup. Horton said that Slade will be finished working out in an hour, and that he's leaving his phone footage just on me and Talon in the pool. Do you need anything else from us?

Golden: Pool. Send nudes.

Scaredy Bear: Want me to drown him in front of you? I can do it. He still mostly swims doggy style in the shallow end.

Golden: Aw, Shortcake already knows that doggy style is my best fucking stroke.

Goddess have fucking mercy.

Daddy of all Storms: *eyeroll emoji* You walked into that one, Fin.

Heart: Protection withdrawn. You're both on your own.

Talon threw his head back and laughed. "Your mean streak is one of my favorite streaks. I get hard every time you raise your voice at one of us."

This alpha was the epitome of *if it looks like she's beating the crap out of me, just know, this is my happy place.*

"You're always hard," I reminded him, and case in point, when I looked down, there was an impressive outline on the front of his swim shorts.

"Can you blame me when I am mated to the sexiest fucking female in the world." His gaze burned as he ran it over all the bare skin my skimpy bikini left on display.

My scent spiked hard. Talon's hands were sliding down to cup my ass, as if he couldn't help himself.

When my phone buzzed again, I fumbled and almost dropped it.

> Daddy of all Storms: Ignore the idiots. This prank is
> going to work, baby girl. And then Slade is going to
> punish you while we all watch. It's a win-win all
> around.

My fingers trembled as I attempted to coherently reply.

> Heart: I think we're getting off track here. Everyone
> remember their role and get back to the house soon.
> Love you.

> Golden: I FUCKING LOVE YOU, PRETTY MATE.
> *heart emoji* *kissing face emoji*

> Scaredy Bear: I love you, darlin'. This is your best
> work, and I'm so happy to be part of it with you.

> Daddy of all Storms: We got you, baby girl. Let's do
> this together.

Talon slid my phone back under the towel, and then I was over his shoulder once more, heading for the pool.

"Okay, Honey," he said as he stroked a firm hand down my thigh. "Let's swim again. I really got the best end of this deal."

I was laughing all the way until he dumped us both in the pool. If we pulled this prank off, I'd get to call myself a true prank master.

For all of time.

# ACKNOWLEDGMENTS

I really didn't want to write this part today. I knew it meant this story was finished, and the pack that I fell so obsessively and heavily in love with had found their happily-ever-after.

I loved every part of writing this story, and I wish we could stay here forever. If you want to see more, let me know of course, as I left tendrils there for Kassidy. Girl is even more stubborn than our Emme, and I doubt she would crumble for her pack without a lot of persuasion.

Might be fun to see them try though.

As always, I need to thank my husband first and foremost. I've mentioned it before and I'll say it again, what this man doesn't know about cars isn't worth knowing. He helped me through so many of the details and scenes, and honestly, the only time I screwed up was when I went rogue. He now lives in fear of me randomly giving supercars back seats or abilities that would be impossible to pull off. Please know: any errors are mine. He's a car genius. He's also the most supportive, loving man, and I wouldn't be able to have this career without him. Thank you, hubby. I know how blessed I am.

Thanks to our gorgeous daughters as well, who graciously share me with fictional worlds. They're at the age where they really understand what I do now and want to read the stories. I love you both so much, but you have to wait until you're at least twenty-five. Or forty.

Thank you, Jane, for being the best assistant, keeping me in line, and cheering me on through the words and edits. Thank you also to my error-catching badass team, who are incredible at finding those final errors. I love you all!!

Thank you to Lee for the amazing edits, and Tamara for once again producing a stunning cover that captured my hopes and dreams for this final story. The entire series, really.

And lastly, I want to give a huge, incredibly heartfelt thanks to you all, the readers. We've been on this journey together for a long time now, and I am the luckiest author in the world to have you. I hope we have many more years together as a giant pack of book lovers.

Don't forget to come say hello on my social media (links).

Until next time, hugs and love.

Jaymin

my best life. But after my father tried to kill our leader, I'm labelled an outcast, traitor, less than dirt.

When I can't take pack life any longer, I run, but apparently they don't like losing their punching bag. Torin, the leader's son, drags me back before my first shift... a shift that will reveal my true mate. I never could have predicted who mine would be, but the moment my wolf looks upon him, I'm filled with hope for a brighter future.

Afterall, no one ever rejects their true mate, right?

Wrong. Very wrong.

When the wolves attack, my soul screams for vengeance, and somehow I touch the shadow world.

Somehow I bring him to our lands.

The Shadow Beast. Our shifter god. The devil himself.

Turns out being rejected by my mate was only the beginning.

*If you like sexy, dark paranormal romances, with humor, steam, action, a tough heroine and an antihero, this is for you. Rejected is full length (100k) words, is book one of three in Shadow Beast Shifters series, and ends on a cliffhanger. It's recommended for 18+ due to language and sexual situations.

# WHAT TO READ NEXT...

Try my new (MF) romantasy series, Weatherstone college Spellcaster
Book 1

Welcome to Weatherstone College...

Don't walk the halls late at night.

Don't disturb the ancient magic.

And don't, under any circumstances, ever trust a spellcaster.

When my magic bloomed at twenty-two, the last thing I expected was to receive an acceptance letter to the most prestigious witch college in the world. It's not that I don't have magic, it's just...unpredictable, but with Weatherstone a part of my family legacy, I'm determined to live up to their expectations.

A task that's almost derailed on my very first day when I come face-to-face with Logan Kingston. As the son of my father's enemy, I'm warned to avoid the powerful spellcaster at all costs, but apparently Logan did not receive the same memo. The more time I spend around him, the more I crave his unsettling attention, and as hate flirts with obsession, I'm left wondering if there's another side to the decades old feud between our fathers.

On top of that, Weatherstone is not at all like I expected. Built on the ancient blood of necromancers and battle, the magic here is as unpredictable as mine, and I sense a dark energy stalking my footsteps. When a monster attacks me, I have no choice but to turn to the strongest warlock in our school: Logan.

*Afterall, to fight a monster, I'll need a monster.*

# ALSO BY JAYMIN EVE

**Weatherstone College**

Book One: Spellcaster

Book Two: Night Witch (coming June 23rd)

**Fallen Fae Gods (Dark Romantasy dragon shifter/fae 18+) (complete)**

*Book One: Gilded Wings*

*Book Two: Crimson Skies*

**Shadow Beast Shifters (Dark and Sexy wolf shifter/ god Romantasy 18+) (complete)**

*Book One:* Rejected

*Book Two:* Reclaimed

*Book Three:* Reborn

*Book Four:* Deserted

*Book Five:* Compelled

*Book Six:* Glamoured

**Bluebell House Duet**

Book One: Forced Proximity

Book Two: Trauma Bonded (TBD)

**Boys of Bellerose (Dark, RH rock star romance 18+)(complete)**

*Book One:* Poison Roses

*Book Two:* Dirty Truths

*Book Three:* Shattered Dreams

*Book Four:* Beautiful Thorns

**Demon Pack (PNR/Urban Fantasy 18+) (Complete)**

*Book One:* Demon Pack

*Book Two:* Demon Pack Elimination

*Book Three:* Demon Pack Eternal

**Supernatural Prison Trilogy (Complete UF series 17+)**

*Book One*: Dragon Marked

*Book Two*: Dragon Mystics

*Book Three*: Dragon Mated

*Book Four:* Broken Compass

*Book Five:* Magical Compass

*Book Six:* Louis

*Book Seven:* Elemental Compass

**Supernatural Academy (Complete Urban Fantasy/PNR 18+)**

*Year One*

*Year Two*

*Year Three*

**Royals of Arbon Academy (Dark, complete Contemporary Romance 18+)**

*Book One:* Princess Ballot

*Book Two:* Playboy Princes

*Book Three:* Poison Throne

**Titan's Saga (PNR/UF. Sexy and humorous 18+)**

*Book One:* Releasing the Gods

*Book Two:* Wrath of the Gods

*Book Three:* Revenge of the Gods

**Dark Legacy (Complete Dark Contemporary high school romance 18+)**

*Book One:* Broken Wings

*Book Two:* Broken Trust

*Book Three:* Broken Legacy

**Secret Keepers Series (Complete PNR/Urban Fantasy )**

*Book One:* House of Darken

*Book Two:* House of Imperial

*Book Three:* House of Leights

*Book Four:* House of Royale

**Storm Princess Saga (Complete High Fantasy 18+)**

*Book One:* The Princess Must Die

*Book Two:* The Princess Must Strike

*Book Three:* The Princess Must Reign

**Curse of the Gods Series (Complete Reverse Harem Fantasy 18+)**

*Book One:* Trickery

*Book Two:* Persuasion

*Book Three:* Seduction

*Book Four:* Strength

*Novella:* Neutral

*Book Five:* Pain

**NYC Mecca Series (Complete - UF series)**

*Book One*: Queen Heir

*Book Two*: Queen Alpha

*Book Three*: Queen Fae

*Book Four*: Queen Mecca

**A Walker Saga (Complete - YA Fantasy)**

*Book One*: First World

*Book Two*: Spurn

*Book Three*: Crais

*Book Four*: Regali

*Book Five*: Nephilius

*Book Six*: Dronish

*Book Seven*: Earth

**Hive Trilogy (Complete UF/PNR series)**

*Book One*: Ash

*Book Two*: Anarchy

*Book Three*: Annihilate

**Sinclair Stories (Standalone Contemporary Romance 18+)**

Songbird